Praise for the novels of
***New York Times* bestselling author**
Diana Palmer

"Nobody does it better."
—*New York Times* bestselling author
Linda Howard

"Palmer knows how to make the sparks fly."
—*Publishers Weekly*

"Diana Palmer is a mesmerising storyteller
who captures the essence of what a
romance should be."
—*Affaire de Coeur*

"Nobody tops Diana Palmer when it comes to delivering
pure, undiluted romance.
I love her stories."
—*New York Times* bestselling author
Jayne Ann Krentz

D0610951

Also by **Diana Palmer**

NIGHT FEVER
ONE NIGHT IN NEW YORK
BEFORE SUNRISE
OUTSIDER
LAWMAN
HARD TO HANDLE
FEARLESS
DIAMOND SPUR
TRUE COLOURS
HEARTLESS
INNOCENCE PROTECTED

DIANA PALMER

Wed in Winter

M&B™

DID YOU PURCHASE THIS BOOK WITHOUT A COVER?
If you did, you should be aware it is stolen property as it was reported unsold and destroyed by a retailer. Neither the author nor the publisher has received any payment for this book.

All the characters in this book have no existence outside the imagination of the author, and have no relation whatsoever to anyone bearing the same name or names. They are not even distantly inspired by any individual known or unknown to the author, and all the incidents are pure invention.

All Rights Reserved including the right of reproduction in whole or in part in any form. This edition is published by arrangement with Harlequin Enterprises II B.V./S.à.r.l. The text of this publication or any part thereof may not be reproduced or transmitted in any form or by any means, electronic or mechanical, including photocopying, recording, storage in an information retrieval system, or otherwise, without the written permission of the publisher.

This book is sold subject to the condition that it shall not, by way of trade or otherwise, be lent, resold, hired out or otherwise circulated without the prior consent of the publisher in any form of binding or cover other than that in which it is published and without a similar condition including this condition being imposed on the subsequent purchaser.

M&B™ and M&B™ with the Rose Device
are trademarks of the publisher.
Harlequin Mills & Boon Limited, Eton House,
18-24 Paradise Road, Richmond, Surrey TW9 1SR

WED IN WINTER © Harlequin Books S.A. 2010

Sutton's Way © Diana Palmer 1989
Coltrain's Proposal © Diana Palmer 1995

ISBN: 978 0 263 88936 9

025-1210

Harlequin Mills & Boon policy is to use papers that are natural, renewable and recyclable products and made from wood grown in sustainable forests. The logging and manufacturing processes conform to the legal environmental regulations of the country of origin.

Printed in the UK
by CPI MacKays, Chatham, ME5 8TD

The prolific author of over one hundred books, **Diana Palmer** got her start as a newspaper reporter. One of the top ten romance writers in America, she has a gift for telling the most sensual tales with charm and humour. Diana lives with her family in Georgia.

Sutton's Way

Chapter One

The noise outside the cabin was there again, and Amanda shifted restlessly with the novel in her lap, curled up in a big armchair by the open fireplace in an Indian rug. Until now, the cabin had been paradise. There was three feet of new snow outside, she had all the supplies she needed to get her through the next few wintery weeks of Wyoming weather, and there wasn't a telephone in the place. Best of all, there wasn't a neighbor.

Well, there was, actually. But nobody in their right mind would refer to that man on the mountain as a neighbor. Amanda had only seen him once and once was enough.

She'd met him, if their head-on encounter could be referred to as a meeting, on a snowy Saturday last week. Quinn Sutton's majestic ranch house overlooked this cabin nestled against the mountainside. He'd been out in the snow on a horse-drawn sled that contained huge square bales of hay, and he was heaving them like feather pillows to a small herd of red-and-white cattle. The sight had touched Amanda, because it indicated concern. The tall, wiry rancher out in a blizzard feeding his starving cattle. She'd even smiled at the tender picture it made.

And then she'd stopped her four-wheel-drive vehicle and stuck her blond head out the window to ask directions to the Blalock Durning place, which was the cabin one of her aunt's friends was loaning her. And the tender picture dissolved into stark hostility.

The tall rancher turned toward her with the coldest black eyes and the hardest face she'd ever seen in her life. He had a day's growth of stubble, but the stubble didn't begin to cover up the frank homeliness of his lean face. He had amazingly high cheekbones, a broad forehead and a jutting chin, and he looked as if someone had taken a straight razor to one side of his face, which had a wide scratch. None of that bothered Amanda because Hank Shoeman and the other three men who made music with her group were even uglier than Quinn Sutton. But at least Hank and the boys could smile. This man looked as if he invented the black scowl.

"I said," she'd repeated with growing nervousness, "can you tell me how to get to Blalock Durning's cabin?"

Above the sheepskin coat, under the battered gray ranch hat, Quinn Sutton's tanned face didn't move a muscle. "Follow the road, turn left at the lodgepoles," he'd said tersely, his voice as deep as a rumble of thunder.

"Lodgepoles?" she'd faltered. "You mean Indian lodgepoles? What do they look like?"

"Lady," he said with exaggerated patience, "a lodgepole is a pine tree. It's tall and piney, and there are a stand of them at the next fork in the road."

"You don't need to be rude, Mr…?"

"Sutton," he said tersely. "Quinn Sutton."

"Nice to meet you," she murmured politely. "I'm Amanda." She wondered if anyone might accidentally recognize her here in the back of beyond, and on the off chance, she gave her mother's maiden name instead of her own last name. "Amanda Corrie," she added untruthfully. "I'm going to stay in the cabin for a few weeks."

"This isn't the tourist season," he'd said without the slightest pretense at friendliness. His black eyes cut her like swords.

"Good, because I'm not a tourist," she said.

"Don't look to me for help if you run out of wood or start hearing things in the dark," he added coldly. "Somebody will tell you eventually that I have no use whatsoever for women."

While she was thinking up a reply to that, a young boy of about twelve had come running up behind the sled.

"Dad!" he called, amazingly enough to Quinn Sutton. "There's a cow in calf down in the next pasture. I think it's a breech!"

"Okay, son, hop on," he told the boy, and his voice had become fleetingly soft, almost tender. He looked back at Amanda, though, and the softness left him. "Keep your door locked at night," he'd said. "Unless you're expecting Durning to join you," he added with a mocking smile.

She'd stared at him from eyes as black as his own and started to tell him that she didn't even know Mr. Durning, who was her aunt's friend, not hers. But she bit her tongue. It wouldn't do to give this man an opening. "I'll do that little thing," she agreed. She glanced at the boy, who was eyeing her curiously from his perch on the sled. "And it seems that you do have at least one use for women," she added with a vacant smile. "My condolences to your wife, Mr. Sutton."

She'd rolled up the window before he could speak and she'd whipped the four-wheel-drive down the road with little regard for safety, sliding all over the place on the slick and rutted country road.

She glared into the flames, consigning Quinn Sutton to them with all her angry heart. She hoped and prayed that there wouldn't ever be an accident or a reason she'd have to seek out his company. She'd rather have asked help from a passing timber wolf. His son hadn't seemed at all like him, she recalled. Sutton was as dangerous looking as a timber wolf, with a face like the side of a bombed mountain and eyes that were coal-black and cruel. In the sheepskin coat he'd been wearing with that raunchy Stetson that day, he'd looked like one of the old mountain men might have back in Wyoming's early days. He'd given Amanda some bad moments and she'd hated him after that uncomfortable confrontation. But the boy had been kind. He was redheaded and blue-eyed, nothing like his father, not a bit of resemblance.

She knew the rancher's name only because her aunt had mentioned him, and cautioned Amanda about going near the Sutton ranch. The ranch was called Ricochet, and Amanda had immediately thought of a bullet going awry. Probably one of Sutton's ancestors had thrown some lead now and again. Mr. Sutton looked a lot more like a bandit than he did a rancher, with his face unshaven, that wide, awful scrape on his cheek and his crooked nose. It was an unforgettable face all around, especially those eyes....

She pulled the Indian rug closer and gave the book in her slender hand a careless glance. She wasn't really in the mood to read. Memories kept tearing her heart. She leaned her blond head back against the chair and her dark eyes studied the flames with idle appreciation of their beauty.

The nightmare of the past few weeks had finally caught up with her. She'd stood onstage, with the lights beating down on her long blond hair and outlining the beige leather dress that was her trademark, and her voice had simply refused to cooperate. The shock of being unable to produce a single note had caused her to faint, to the shock and horror of the audience.

She came to in a hospital, where she'd been given what seemed to be every test known to medical science. But nothing would produce her singing voice, even though she could talk. It was, the doctor told her, purely a psychological problem, caused by the trauma of what had happened. She needed rest.

So Hank, who was the leader of the group, had called her aunt Bess and convinced her to arrange for Amanda to get away from it all. Her aunt's rich boyfriend had this holiday cabin in Wyoming's Grand Teton Mountains and was more than willing to let Amanda recuperate there. Amanda had protested, but Hank and the boys and her aunt had insisted. So here she was, in the middle of winter, in several feet of snow, with no television, no telephone and facilities that barely worked. Roughing it, the big, bearded bandleader had told her, would do her good.

She smiled when she remembered how caring and kind the guys had been. Her group was called Desperado, and her leather costume was its trademark. The four men who made up the rest of it were fine musicians, but they looked like the Hell's Angels on stage in denim and leather with thick black beards and mustaches and untrimmed hair. They were really pussycats under that rough exterior, but nobody had ever been game enough to try to find out if they were.

Hank and Deke and Jack and Johnson had been trying to get work at a Virginia night spot when they'd run into Amanda Corrie Callaway, who was also trying to get work there. The club needed a singer and a band, so it was a match made in heaven, although Amanda with her sheltered upbringing had been a little afraid of her new backup band. They, on the other hand, had been nervous around her because she was such a far cry from the usual singers they'd worked with. The shy, introverted young blonde made them self-conscious about their appearance. But their first performance together had been a phenomenal hit, and they'd been together four years now.

They were famous, now. Desperado had been on the music videos for two years, they'd done television shows and magazine interviews, and they were recognized everywhere they went. Especially Amanda, who went by the stage name of Mandy Callaway. It wasn't a bad life, and it was making them rich. But there wasn't much rest or time for a personal life. None of the group was married except Hank, and he was already getting a divorce. It was hard for a homebound spouse to accept the frequent absences that road tours required.

She still shivered from the look Quinn Sutton had given her, and now she was worried about her aunt Bess, though the woman was more liberal minded and should know the score. But Sutton had convinced Amanda that she wasn't the first woman to be at Blalock's cabin. She should have told that arrogant rancher what her real relationship with Blalock Durning was, but he probably wouldn't have believed her.

Of course, she could have put him in touch with Jerry and proved it. Jerry Allen, their road manager, was one of the best in the business. He'd kept them from starving during the beginning, and they had an expert crew of electricians and carpenters who made up the rest of the retinue. It took a huge bus to carry the people and equipment, appropriately called the "Outlaw Express."

Amanda had pleaded with Jerry to give them a few weeks' rest after the tragedy that had cost her her nerve, but he'd refused. Get back on the horse, he'd advised. And she'd tried. But the memories were just too horrible.

So finally he'd agreed to Hank's suggestion and she was officially on hiatus, as were the other members of the group, for a month. Maybe in that length of time she could come to grips with it, face it.

It had been a week and she felt better already. Or she would, if those strange noises outside the cabin would just stop! She had horrible visions of wolves breaking in and eating her.

"Hello?"

The small voice startled her. It sounded like a boy's. She got up, clutching the fire poker in her hand and went to the front door. "Who's there?" she called out tersely.

"It's just me. Elliot," he said. "Elliot Sutton."

She let out a breath between her teeth. Oh, no, she thought miserably, what was he doing here? His father would come looking for him, and she couldn't bear to have that…that savage anywhere around!

"What do you want?" she groaned.

"I brought you something."

It would be discourteous to refuse the gift, she guessed, especially since he'd apparently come through several feet of snow to bring it. Which brought to mind a really interesting question: where was his father?

She opened the door. He grinned at her from under a thick cap that covered his red hair.

"Hi," he said. "I thought you might like to have some

roasted peanuts. I did them myself. They're nice on a cold night."

Her eyes went past him to a sled hitched to a sturdy draft horse. "Did you come in that?" she asked, recognizing the sled he and his father had been riding the day she'd met them.

"Sure," he said. "That's how we get around in winter, what with the snow and all. We take hay out to the livestock on it. You remember, you saw us. Well, we usually take hay out on it, that is. When Dad's not laid up," he added pointedly, and his blue eyes said more than his voice did.

She knew she was going to regret asking the question before she opened her mouth. She didn't want to ask. But no young boy came to a stranger's house in the middle of a snowy night just to deliver a bag of roasted peanuts.

"What's wrong?" she asked with resigned perception.

He blinked. "What?"

"I said, what's wrong?" She made her tone gentler. He couldn't help it that his father was a savage, and he was worried under that false grin. "Come on, you might as well tell me."

He bit his lower lip and looked down at his snow-covered boots. "It's my dad," he said. "He's bad sick and he won't let me get the doctor."

So there it was. She knew she shouldn't have asked. "Can't your mother do something?" she asked hopefully.

"My mom ran off with Mr. Jackson from the livestock association when I was just a little feller," he replied, registering Amanda's shocked expression. "She and Dad got divorced and she died some years ago, but Dad doesn't talk about her. Will you come, miss?"

"I'm not a doctor," she said, hesitating.

"Oh, sure, I know that," he agreed eagerly, "but you're a girl. And girls know how to take care of sick folks, don't they?" The confidence slid away and he looked like what he was—a terrified little boy with nobody to turn to. "Please, lady," he added. "I'm scared. He's hot and shaking all over and—!"

"I'll get my boots on," she said. She gathered them from beside the fireplace and tugged them on, and then she went for a coat and stuffed her long blond hair under a stocking cap. "Do you have cough syrup, aspirins, throat lozenges—that sort of thing?"

"Yes, ma'am," he said eagerly, then sighed. "Dad won't take them, but we have them."

"Is he suicidal?" Amanda asked angrily as she went out the door behind him and locked the cabin before she climbed on the sled with the boy.

"Well sometimes things get to him," he ventured. "But he doesn't ever get sick, and he won't admit that he is. But he's out of his head and I'm scared. He's all I got."

"We'll take care of him," she promised, and hoped she could deliver on the promise. "Let's go."

"Do you know Mr. Durning well?" he asked as he called to the draft horse and started him back down the road and up the mountain toward the Sutton house.

"He's sort of a friend of a relative of mine," she said evasively. The sled ride was fun, and she was enjoying the cold wind and snow in her face, the delicious mountain air. "I'm only staying at the cabin for a few weeks. Just time to...get over something."

"Have you been sick, too?" he asked curiously.

"In a way," she said noncommittally.

The sled went jerkily up the road, around the steep hill. She held on tight and hoped the big draft horse had steady feet. It was a harrowing ride at the last, and then they were up, and the huge redwood ranch house came into sight, blazing with light from its long, wide front porch to the gabled roof.

"It's a beautiful house," Amanda said.

"My dad added on to it for my mom, before they married," he told her. He shrugged. "I don't remember much about her, except she was redheaded. Dad sure hates women." He glanced at her apologetically. "He's not going to like me bringing you...."

"I can take care of myself," she returned, and smiled reassuringly. "Let's go see how bad it is."

"I'll get Harry to put up the horse and sled," he said, yelling toward the lighted barn until a grizzled old man appeared. After a brief introduction to Amanda, Harry left and took the horse away.

"Harry's been here since Dad was a boy," Elliot told her as he led her down a bare-wood hall and up a steep staircase to the second storey of the house. "He does most everything, even cooks for the men." He paused outside a closed door, and gave Amanda a worried look. "He'll yell for sure."

"Let's get it over with, then."

She let Elliot open the door and look in first, to make sure his father had something on.

"He's still in his jeans," he told her, smiling as she blushed. "It's okay."

She cleared her throat. So much for pretended sophistication, she thought, and here she was twenty-four years old. She avoided Elliot's grin and walked into the room.

Quinn Sutton was sprawled on his stomach, his bare muscular arms stretched toward the headboard. His back gleamed with sweat, and his thick, black hair was damp with moisture. Since it wasn't hot in the room, Amanda decided that he must have a high fever. He was moaning and talking unintelligibly.

"Elliot, can you get me a basin and some hot water?" she asked. She took off her coat and rolled up the sleeves of her cotton blouse.

"Sure thing," Elliot told her, and rushed out of the room.

"Mr. Sutton, can you hear me?" Amanda asked softly. She sat down beside him on the bed, and lightly touched his bare shoulder. He was hot, all right—burning up. "Mr. Sutton," she called again.

"No," he moaned. "No, you can't do it…!"

"Mr. Sutton…"

He rolled over and his black eyes opened, glazed with fever, but Amanda barely noticed. Her eyes were on the rest of him, male perfection from shoulder to narrow hips. He was darkly tanned, too, and thick, black hair wedged from his chest down his flat stomach to the wide belt at his hips. Amanda, who was remarkably innocent not only for her age, but for her profession as well, stared like a star-struck girl. He was beautiful, she thought, amazed at the elegant lines of his body, at the ripple of muscle and the smooth, glistening skin.

"What the hell do you want?" he rasped.

So much for hero worship, she thought dryly. She lifted her eyes back to his. "Elliot was worried," she said quietly. "He came and got me. Please don't fuss at him. You're raging with fever."

"Damn the fever, get out," he said in a tone that might have stopped a charging wolf.

"I can't do that," she said. She turned her head toward the door where Elliot appeared with a basin full of hot water and a towel and washcloth over one arm.

"Here you are, lady," he said. "Hi, Dad," he added with a wan smile at his furious father. "You can beat me when you're able again."

"Don't think I won't," Quinn growled.

"There, there, you're just feverish and sick, Mr. Sutton," Amanda soothed.

"Get Harry and have him throw her off my land," Quinn told Elliot in a furious voice.

"How about some aspirin, Elliot, and something for him to drink? A small whiskey and something hot—"

"I don't drink whiskey," Quinn said harshly.

"He has a glass of wine now and then," Elliot ventured.

"Wine, then." She soaked the cloth in the basin. "And you might turn up the heat. We don't want him to catch a chill when I sponge him down."

"You damned well aren't sponging me down!" Quinn raged.

She ignored him. "Go and get those things, please, Elliot, and the cough syrup, too."

"You bet, lady!" he said grinning.

"My name is Amanda," she said absently.

"Amanda," the boy repeated, and went back downstairs.

"God help you when I get back on my feet," Quinn said with fury. He laid back on the pillow, shivering when she touched him with the cloth. "Don't…!"

"I could fry an egg on you. I have to get the fever down. Elliot said you were delirious."

"Elliot's delirious to let you in here," he shuddered. Her fingers accidentally brushed his flat stomach and he arched, shivering. "For God's sake, don't," he groaned.

"Does your stomach hurt?" she asked, concerned. "I'm sorry." She soaked the cloth again and rubbed it against his shoulders, his arms, his face.

His black eyes opened. He was breathing roughly, and his face was taut. The fever, she imagined. She brushed back her long hair, and wished she'd tied it up. It kept flowing down onto his damp chest.

"Damn you," he growled.

"Damn you, too, Mr. Sutton." She smiled sweetly. She

finished bathing his face and put the cloth and basin aside. "Do you have a long-sleeved shirt?"

"Get out!"

Elliot came back with the medicine and a small glass of wine. "Harry's making hot chocolate," he said with a smile. "He'll bring it up. Here's the other stuff."

"Good," she said. "Does your father have a pajama jacket or something long-sleeved?"

"Sure!"

"Traitor," Quinn groaned at his son.

"Here you go." Elliot handed her a flannel top, which she proceeded to put on the protesting and very angry Mr. Sutton.

"I hate you," Quinn snapped at her with his last ounce of venom.

"I hate you, too," she agreed. She had to reach around him to get the jacket on, and it brought her into much too close proximity to him. She could feel the hair on his chest rubbing against her soft cheek, she could feel her own hair smoothing over his bare shoulder and chest. Odd, that shivery feeling she got from contact with him. She ignored it forcibly and got his other arm into the pajama jacket. She fastened it, trying to keep her fingers from touching his chest any more than necessary because the feel of that pelt of hair disturbed her. He shivered violently at the touch of her hands and her long, silky hair, and she assumed it was because of his fever.

"Are you finished?" Quinn asked harshly.

"Almost." She pulled the covers over him, found the

electric-blanket control and turned it on. Then she ladled cough syrup into him, gave him aspirin and had him take a sip of wine, hoping that she wasn't overdosing him in the process. But the caffeine in the hot chocolate would probably counteract the wine and keep it from doing any damage in combination with the medicine. A sip of wine wasn't likely to be that dangerous anyway, and it might help the sore throat she was sure he had.

"Here's the cocoa," Harry said, joining them with a tray of mugs filled with hot chocolate and topped with whipped cream.

"That looks delicious. Thank you so much," Amanda said, and smiled shyly at the old man.

He grinned back. "Nice to be appreciated." He glared at Quinn. "Nobody else ever says so much as a thank-you!"

"It's hard to thank a man for food poisoning," Quinn rejoined weakly.

"He ain't going to die," Harry said as he left. "He's too damned mean."

"That's a fact," Quinn said and closed his eyes.

He was asleep almost instantly. Amanda drew up a chair and sat down beside him. He'd still need looking after, and presumably the boy went to school. It was past the Christmas holidays.

"You go to school, don't you?" she asked Elliot.

He nodded. "I ride the horse out to catch the bus and then turn him loose. He comes to the barn by himself. You're staying?"

"I'd better, I guess," she said. "I'll sit with him. He may get worse in the night. He's got to see a doctor tomorrow. Is there one around here?"

"There's Dr. James in town, in Holman that is," he said. "He'll come out if Dad's bad enough. He has a cancer patient down the road and he comes to check on her every few days. He could stop by then."

"We'll see how your father is feeling. You'd better get to bed," she said and smiled at him.

"Thank you for coming, Miss…Amanda," Elliot said. He sighed. "I don't think I've ever been so scared."

"It's okay," she said. "I didn't mind. Good night, Elliot."

He smiled at her. "Good night."

He went out and closed the door. Amanda sat back in her chair and looked at the sleeping face of the wild man. He seemed vulnerable like this, with his black eyes closed. He had the thickest lashes she'd ever seen, and his eyebrows were thick and well shaped above his deep-set eyes. His mouth was rather thin, but it was perfectly shaped, and the full lower lip was sensuous. She liked that jutting chin, with its hint of stubbornness. His nose was formidable and straight, and he wasn't that bad looking…asleep. Perhaps it was the coldness of his eyes that made him seem so much rougher when he was awake. Not that he looked that unintimidating even now. He had so many coarse edges….

She waited a few minutes and touched his forehead. It was a little cooler, thank God, so maybe he was going to be better by morning. She went into the bathroom and washed her face and went back to sit by him. Somewhere in the night, she fell asleep with her blond head pillowed on the big arm of the chair. Voices woke her.

"Has she been there all night, Harry?" Quinn was asking.

"Looks like. Poor little critter, she's worn out."

"I'll shoot Elliot!"

"Now, boss, that's no way to treat the kid. He got scared, and I didn't know what to do. Women know things about illness. Why, my mama could doctor people and she never had no medical training. She used herbs and things."

Amanda blinked, feeling eyes on her. She found Quinn Sutton gazing steadily at her from a sitting position on the bed.

"How do you feel?" she asked without lifting her sleepy head.

"Like hell," he replied. "But I'm a bit better."

"Would you like some breakfast, ma'am?" Harry asked with a smile. "And some coffee?"

"Coffee. Heavenly. But no breakfast, thanks, I won't impose," she said drowsily, yawning and stretching uninhibitedly as she sat up, her full breasts beautifully outlined against the cotton blouse in the process.

Quinn felt his body tautening again, as it had the night before so unexpectedly and painfully when her hands had touched him. He could still feel them, and the brush of her long, silky soft hair against his skin. She smelled of gardenias and the whole outdoors, and he hated her more than ever because he'd been briefly vulnerable.

"Why did you come with Elliot?" Quinn asked her when Harry had gone.

She pushed back her disheveled hair and tried not to think how bad she must look without makeup and with her hair uncombed. She usually kept it in a tight braid on top of her head when she wasn't performing. It made her feel vulnerable to have its unusual length on display for a man like Quinn Sutton.

"Your son is only twelve," she answered him belatedly. "That's too much responsibility for a kid," she added. "I know. I had my dad to look after at that age, and no mother. My dad drank," she added with a bitter smile. "Excessively. When he drank he got into trouble. I can remember knowing how to call a bail bondsman at the age of thirteen. I never dated, I never took friends home with me. When I was eighteen, I ran away from home. I don't even know if he's still alive, and I don't care."

"That's one problem Elliot won't ever have," he replied quietly. "Tough girl, aren't you?" he added, and his black eyes were frankly curious.

She hadn't meant to tell him so much. It embarrassed her, so she gave him her most belligerent glare. "Tough enough, thanks," she said. She got out of the chair. "If you're well enough to argue, you ought to be able to take care of yourself. But if that fever goes up again, you'll need to see the doctor."

"I'll decide that," he said tersely. "Go home."

"Thanks, I'll do that little thing." She got her coat and put it on without taking time to button it. She pushed her hair up under the stocking cap, aware of his eyes on her the whole time.

"You don't fit the image of a typical hanger-on," he said unexpectedly.

She glanced at him, blinking with surprise. "I beg your pardon?"

"A hanger-on," he repeated. He lifted his chin and studied her with mocking thoroughness. "You're Durning's latest lover, I gather. Well, if it's money you're after, he's the perfect choice. A pretty little tramp could go far with him... Damn!"

She stood over him with the remains of his cup of hot chocolate all over his chest, shivering with rage.

"I'm sorry," she said curtly. "That was a despicable thing to do to a sick man, but what you said to me was inexcusable."

She turned and went to the door, ignoring his muffled curses as he threw off the cover and sat up.

"I'd cuss, too," she said agreeably as she glanced back at him one last time, her eyes running helplessly over the broad expanse of hair-roughened skin. "All that sticky hot chocolate in that thicket on your chest," she mused. "It will probably take steam cleaning to remove it. Too bad you can't attract a 'hanger-on' to help you bathe it out. But, then, you aren't as rich as Mr. Durning, are you?" And she walked out, her nose in the air. As she went toward the stairs, she imagined that she heard laughter. But of course, that couldn't have been possible.

Chapter Two

Amanda regretted the hot-chocolate incident once she was back in the cabin, even though Quinn Sutton had deserved every drop of it. How dare he call her such a name!

Amanda was old-fashioned in her ideas. A real country girl from Mississippi who'd had no example to follow except a liberated aunt and an alcoholic parent, and she was like neither of them. She hardly even dated these days. Her working gear wasn't the kind of clothing that told men how conventional her ideals were. They saw the glitter and sexy outfit and figured that Amanda, or just "Mandy" as she was known onstage, lived like her alter ego looked. There were times when she rued the day she'd ever signed on with Desperado, but she was too famous and making too much money to quit now.

She put her hair in its usual braid and kept it there for the rest of the week, wondering from time to time about

Quinn Sutton and whether or not he'd survived his illness. Not that she cared, she kept telling herself. It didn't matter to her if he turned up his toes.

There was no phone in the cabin, and no piano. She couldn't play solitaire, she didn't have a television. There was only the radio and the cassette player for company, and Mr. Durning's taste in music was really extreme. He liked opera and nothing else. She'd have died for some soft rock, or just an instrument to practice on. She could play drums as well as the synthesizer and piano, and she wound up in the kitchen banging on the counter with two stainless-steel knives out of sheer boredom.

When the electricity went haywire in the wake of two inches of freezing rain on Sunday night, it was almost a relief. She sat in the darkness laughing. She was trapped in a house without heat, without light, and the only thing she knew about fireplaces was that they required wood. The logs that were cut outside were frozen solid under the sleet and there were none in the house. There wasn't even a pack of matches.

She wrapped up in her coat and shivered, hating the solitude and the weather and feeling the nightmares coming back in the icy night. She didn't want to think about the reason her voice had quit on her, but if she spent enough time alone, she was surely going to go crazy reliving that night onstage.

Lost in thought, in nightmarish memories of screams and her own loss of consciousness, she didn't hear the first knock on the door until it came again.

"Miss Corrie!" a familiar angry voice shouted above the wind.

She got up, feeling her way to the door. "Keep your shirt on," she muttered as she threw it open.

Quinn Sutton glared down at her. "Get whatever you'll need for a couple of days and come on. The power's out. If you stay here you'll freeze to death. It's going below zero tonight. My ranch has an extra generator, so we've still got the power going."

She glared back. "I'd rather freeze to death than go anywhere with you, thanks just the same."

He took a slow breath. "Look, your morals are your own business. I just thought—"

She slammed the door in his face and turned, just in time to have him kick in the door and come after her.

"I said you're coming with me, lady," he said shortly. He bent and picked her up bodily and started out the door. "And to hell with what you'll need for a couple of days."

"Mr.…Sutton!" she gasped, stunned by the unexpected contact with his hard, fit body as he carried her easily out the door and closed it behind them.

"Hold on," he said tautly and without looking at her. "The snow's pretty heavy right through this drift."

In fact, it was almost waist-deep. She hadn't been outside in two days, so she hadn't noticed how high it had gotten. Her hands clung to the old sheepskin coat he was wearing. It smelled of leather and tobacco and whatever soap he used, and the furry collar was warm against her cold cheek. He made her feel small and helpless, and she wasn't sure she liked it.

"I don't like your tactics," she said through her teeth as the wind howled around them and sleet bit into her face like tiny nails.

"They get results. Hop on." He put her up on the sled, climbed beside her, grasped the reins and turned the horse back toward the mountain.

She wanted to protest, to tell him to take his offer and go to hell. But it was bitterly cold and she was shivering too badly to argue. He was right, and that was the hell of it. She could freeze to death in that cabin easily enough, and nobody would have found her until spring came or until her aunt persuaded Mr. Durning to come and see about her.

"I don't want to impose," she said curtly.

"We're past that now," he replied. "It's either this or bury you."

"I'm sure I know which you'd prefer," she muttered, huddling in her heavy coat.

"Do you?" he asked, turning his head. In the daylight glare of snow and sleet, she saw an odd twinkle in his black eyes. "Try digging a hole out there."

She gave him a speaking glance and resigned herself to going with him.

He drove the sled right into the barn and left her to wander through the aisle, looking at the horses and the two new calves in the various stalls while he dealt with unhitching and stalling the horse.

"What's wrong with these little things?" she asked, her hands in her pockets and her ears freezing as she nodded toward the two calves.

"Their mamas starved out in the pasture," he said quietly. "I couldn't get to them in time."

He sounded as if that mattered to him. She looked up at his dark face, seeing new character in it. "I didn't think a cow or two would matter," she said absently.

"I lost everything I had a few months back," he said matter-of-factly. "I'm trying to pull out of bankruptcy, and right now it's a toss-up as to whether I'll even come close. Every cow counts." He looked down at her. "But it isn't just the money. It disturbs me to see anything die from lack of attention. Even a cow."

"Or a mere woman?" she said with a faint smile. "Don't worry, I know you don't want me here. I'm...grateful to you for coming to my rescue. Most of the firewood was frozen and Mr. Durning apparently doesn't smoke, because there weren't a lot of matches around."

He scowled faintly. "No, Durning doesn't smoke. Didn't you know?"

She shrugged. "I never had reason to ask," she said, without telling him that it was her aunt, not herself, who would know about Mr. Durning's habits. Let him enjoy his disgusting opinion of her.

"Elliot said you'd been sick."

She lifted a face carefully kept blank. "Sort of," she replied.

"Didn't Durning care enough to come with you?"

"Mr. Sutton, my personal life is none of your business," she said firmly. "You can think whatever you want to about me. I don't care. But for what it's worth, I hate men probably as much as you hate women, so you won't have to hold me off with a stick."

His face went hard at the remark, but he didn't say anything. He searched her eyes for one long moment and then turned toward the house, gesturing her to follow.

Elliot was overjoyed with their new houseguest. Quinn Sutton had a television and all sorts of tapes, and there was, surprisingly enough, a brand-new keyboard on a living-room table.

She touched it lovingly, and Elliot grinned at her. "Like it?" he asked proudly. "Dad gave it to me for Christmas. It's not an expensive one, you know, but it's nice to practice on. Listen."

He turned it on and flipped switches, and gave a pretty decent rendition of a tune by Genesis.

Amanda, who was formally taught in piano, smiled at his efforts. "Very good," she praised. "But try a B-flat instead of a B at the end of that last measure and see if it doesn't give you a better sound."

Elliot cocked his head. "I play by ear," he faltered.

"Sorry." She reached over and touched the key she wanted. "That one." She fingered the whole chord. "You have a very good ear."

"But I can't read music," he sighed. His blue eyes searched her face. "You can, can't you?"

She nodded, smiling wistfully. "I used to long for piano

lessons. I took them in spurts and then begged a…friend to let me use her piano to practice on. It took me a long time to learn just the basics, but I do all right."

"All right" meant that she and the boys had won a Grammy award for their last album and it had been one of her own songs that had headlined it. But she couldn't tell Elliot that. She was convinced that Quinn Sutton would have thrown her out the front door if he'd known what she did for a living. He didn't seem like a rock fan, and once he got a look at her stage costume and her group, he'd probably accuse her of a lot worse than being his neighbor's live-in lover. She shivered. Well, at least she didn't like Quinn Sutton, and that was a good thing. She might get out of here without having him find out who she really was, but just in case, it wouldn't do to let herself become interested in him.

"I don't suppose you'd consider teaching me how to read music?" Elliot asked. "For something to do, you know, since we're going to be snowed in for a while, the way it looks."

"Sure, I'll teach you," she murmured, smiling at him. "If your dad doesn't mind," she added with a quick glance at the doorway.

Quinn Sutton was standing there, in jeans and a red-checked flannel shirt with a cup of black coffee in one hand, watching them.

"None of that rock stuff," he said shortly. "That's a bad influence on kids."

"Bad influence?" Amanda was almost shocked, despite the fact that she'd gauged his tastes very well.

"Those raucous lyrics and suggestive costumes, and satanism," he muttered. "I confiscated his tapes and put them away. It's indecent."

"Some of it is, yes," she agreed quietly. "But you can't lump it all into one category, Mr. Sutton. And these days, a lot of the groups are even encouraging chastity and going to war on drug use…"

"You don't really believe that bull, do you?" he asked coldly.

"It's true, Dad," Elliot piped up.

"You can shut up," he told his son. He turned. "I've got a lot of paperwork to get through. Don't turn that thing on high, will you? Harry will show you to your room when you're ready to bed down, Miss Corrie," he added, and looked as if he'd like to have shown her to a room underwater. "Or Elliot can."

"Thanks again," she said, but she didn't look up. He made her feel totally inadequate and guilty. In a small way, it was like going back to that night…

"Don't stay up past nine, Elliot," Quinn told his son.

"Okay, Dad."

Amanda looked after the tall man with her jaw hanging loose. "What did he say?" she asked.

"He said not to stay up past nine," Elliot replied. "We all go to bed at nine," he added with a grin at her expression. "There, there, you'll get used to it. Ranch life, you know. Here, now, what was that about a B-flat? What's a B-flat?"

She was obviously expected to go to bed with the chickens and probably get up with them, too. Absently she picked up the keyboard and began to explain the basics of music to Elliot.

"Did he really hide all your tapes?" she asked curiously.

"Yes, he did," Elliot chuckled, glancing toward the stairs. "But I know where he hid them." He studied her with pursed lips. "You know, you look awfully familiar somehow."

Amanda managed to keep a calm expression on her face, despite her twinge of fear. Her picture, along with that of the men in the group, was on all their albums and tapes. God forbid that Elliot should be a fan and have one of them, but they were popular with young people his age. "They say we all have a counterpart, don't they?" she asked and smiled. "Maybe you saw somebody who looked like me. Here, this is how you run a C scale…."

She successfully changed the subject and Elliot didn't bring it up again. They went upstairs a half hour later, and she breathed a sigh of relief. Since the autocratic Mr. Sutton hadn't given her time to pack, she wound up sleeping in her clothes under the spotless white sheets. She only hoped that she wasn't going to have the nightmares here. She couldn't bear the thought of having Quinn Sutton ask her about them. He'd probably say that she'd gotten just what she deserved.

But the nightmares didn't come. She slept with delicious abandon and didn't dream at all. She woke up the next morning oddly refreshed just as the sun was coming up, even before Elliot knocked on her door to tell her that Harry had breakfast ready downstairs.

She combed out her hair and rebraided it, wrapping it around the crown of her head and pinning it there as she'd had it last night. She tidied herself after she'd washed up, and went downstairs with a lively step.

Quinn Sutton and Elliot were already making great inroads into huge, fluffy pancakes smothered in syrup when she joined them.

Harry brought in a fresh pot of coffee and grinned at her. "How about some hotcakes and sausage?" he asked.

"Just a hotcake and a sausage, please," she said and grinned back. "I'm not much of a breakfast person."

"You'll learn if you stay in these mountains long," Quinn said, sparing her a speaking glance. "You need more meat on those bones. Fix her three, Harry."

"Now, listen…" she began.

"No, you listen," Quinn said imperturbably, sipping black coffee. "My house, my rules."

She sighed. It was just like old times at the orphanage, during one of her father's binges when she'd had to live with Mrs. Brim's rules. "Yes, sir," she said absently.

He glared at her. "I'm thirty-four, and you aren't young enough to call me 'sir.'"

She lifted startled dark eyes to his. "I'm twenty-four," she said. "Are you really just thirty-four?" She flushed even as she said it. He did look so much older, but she hadn't meant to say anything. "I'm sorry. That sounded terrible."

"I look older than I am," he said easily. "I've got a friend down in Texas who thought I was in my late thirties, and he's known me for years. No need to apologize." He didn't add that he had a lot of mileage on him, thanks to his ex-wife. "You look younger than twenty-four," he did add.

He pushed away his empty plate and sipped coffee, staring at her through the steam rising from it. He was wearing a blue-checked flannel shirt this morning, buttoned up to his throat, with jeans that were well fitting but not overly tight. He didn't dress like the men in Amanda's world, but then, the men she knew weren't the same breed as this Teton man.

"Amanda taught me all about scales last night," Elliot said excitedly. "She really knows music."

"How did you manage to learn?" Quinn asked her, and she saw in his eyes that he was remembering what she'd told him about her alcoholic father.

She lifted her eyes from her plate. "During my dad's binges, I stayed at the local orphanage. There was a lady there who played for her church. She taught me."

"No sisters or brothers?" he asked quietly.

She shook her head. "Nobody in the world, except an aunt." She lifted her coffee cup. "She's an artist, and she's been living with her latest lover—"

"You'd better get to school, son," Quinn interrupted tersely, nodding at Elliot.

"I sure had, or I'll be late. See you!"

He grabbed his books and his coat and was gone in a flash, and Harry gathered the plates with a smile and vanished into the kitchen.

"Don't talk about things like that around Elliot," Quinn said shortly. "He understands more than you think. I don't want him corrupted."

"Don't you realize that most twelve-year-old boys know more about life than grown-ups these days?" she asked with a faint smile.

"In your world, maybe. Not in mine."

She could have told him that she was discussing the way things were, not the way she preferred them, but she knew it would be useless. He was so certain that she was wildly liberated. She sighed. "Maybe so," she murmured.

"I'm old-fashioned," he added. His dark eyes narrowed on her face. "I don't want Elliot exposed to the liberated outlook of the so-called modern world until he's old enough to understand that he has a choice. I don't like a society that ridicules honor and fidelity and innocence. So I fight back in the only way I can. I go to church on Sunday, Miss Corrie," he mused, smiling at her curious expression. "Elliot goes, too. You might not know it from watching television or going to movies, but there are still a few people in America who also go to church on Sunday, who work hard all week and find their relaxation in ways that don't involve drugs, booze or casual sex. How's that for a shocking revelation?"

"Nobody ever accused Hollywood of portraying real life," she replied with a smile. "But if you want my honest opinion, I'm pretty sick of gratuitous sex, filthy language and graphic violence in the newer movies. In fact, I'm so sick of it that I've gone back to watching the old-time movies from the 1940s." She laughed at his expression. "Let me tell you, these old movies had real handicaps—the actors all had to keep their clothes on and they couldn't swear. The writers were equally limited, so they created some of the most gripping dramas ever produced. I love them. And best of all, you can even watch them with kids."

He pursed his lips, his dark eyes holding hers. "I like George Brent, George Sanders, Humphrey Bogart, Bette Davis and Cary Grant best," he confessed. "Yes, I watch them, too."

"I'm not really all that modern myself," she confessed, toying with the tablecloth. "I live in the city, but not in the fast lane." She put down her coffee cup. "I can understand why you feel the way you do, about taking Elliot to church and all. Elliot told me a little about his mother..."

He closed up like a plant. "I don't talk to outsiders about my personal life," he said without apology and got up, towering over her. "If you'd like to watch television or listen to music, you're welcome. I've got work to do."

"Can I help?" she asked.

His heavy eyebrows lifted. "This isn't the city."

"I know how to cut open a bale of hay," she said. "The orphanage was on a big farm. I grew up doing chores. I can even milk a cow."

"You won't milk the kind of cows I keep," he returned. His dark eyes narrowed. "You can feed those calves in the barn, if you like. Harry can show you where the bottle is."

Which meant that he wasn't going to waste his time on her. She nodded, trying not to feel like an unwanted guest. Just for a few minutes she'd managed to get under that hard reserve. Maybe that was good enough for a start. "Okay."

His black eyes glanced over her hair. "You haven't worn it down since the night Elliot brought you here," he said absently.

"I don't ever wear it down at home, as a rule," she said quietly. "It…gets in my way." It got recognized, too, she thought, which was why she didn't dare let it loose around Elliot too often.

His eyes narrowed for an instant before he turned and shouldered into his jacket.

"Don't leave the perimeter of the yard," he said as he stuck his weather-beaten Stetson on his dark, thick hair. "This is wild country. We have bears and wolves, and a neighbor who still sets traps."

"I know my limitations, thanks," she said. "Do you have help, besides yourself?"

He turned, thrusting his big, lean hands into work gloves. "Yes, I have four cowboys who work around the place. They're all married."

She blushed. "Thank you for your sterling assessment of my character."

"You may like old movies," he said with a penetrating stare. "But no woman with your kind of looks is a virgin at twenty-four," he said quietly, mindful of Harry's sharp ears. "And I'm a backcountry man, but I've been married and I'm not stupid about women. You won't play me for a fool."

She wondered what he'd say if he knew the whole truth about her. But it didn't make her smile to reflect on that. She lowered her eyes to the thick white mug. "Think what you like, Mr. Sutton. You will anyway."

"Damned straight."

He walked out without looking back, and Amanda felt a vicious chill even before he opened the door and went out into the cold white yard.

She waited for Harry to finish his chores and then went with him to the barn, where the little calves were curled up in their stalls of hay.

"They're only days old," Harry said, smiling as he brought the enormous bottles they were fed from. In fact, the nipples were stretched across the top of buckets and filled with warm mash and milk. "But they'll grow. Sit down, now. You may get a bit dirty..."

"Clothes wash," Amanda said easily, smiling. But this outfit was all she had. She was going to have to get the elusive Mr. Sutton to take her back to the cabin to get more clothes, or she'd be washing out her things in the sink tonight.

She knelt down in a clean patch of hay and coaxed the calf to take the nipple into its mouth. Once it got a taste of the warm liquid, it wasn't difficult to get it to drink. Amanda loved the feel of its silky red-and-white coat under her fingers as she stroked it. The animal was a Hereford, and its big eyes were pink rimmed and soulful. The calf watched her while it nursed.

"Poor little thing," she murmured softly, rubbing between its eyes. "Poor little orphan."

"They're tough critters, for all that," Harry said as he fed the other calf. "Like the boss."

"How did he lose everything, if you don't mind me asking?"

He glanced at her and read the sincerity in her expression. "I don't guess he'd mind if I told you. He was accused of selling contaminated beef."

"Contaminated…how?"

"It's a long story. The herd came to us from down in the Southwest. They had measles. Not," he added when he saw her puzzled expression, "the kind humans get. Cattle don't break out in spots, but they do develop cysts in the muscle tissue and if it's bad enough, it means that the carcasses have to be destroyed." He shrugged. "You can't spot it, because there are no definite symptoms, and you can't treat it because there isn't a drug that cures it. These cattle had it and contaminated the rest of our herd. It was like the end of the world. Quinn had sold the beef cattle to the packing-plant operator. When the meat was ordered destroyed, he came back on Quinn to recover his money, but Quinn had already spent it to buy new cattle. We went to court… Anyway, to make a long story short, they cleared Quinn of any criminal charges and gave him the opportunity to make restitution. In turn, he sued the people who sold him the contaminated herd in the first place." He smiled ruefully. "We just about broke even, but it meant starting over from scratch. That was last year. Things are still rough, but Quinn's a tough customer and he's got a good business head. He'll get through it. I'd bet on him."

Amanda pondered that, thinking that Quinn's recent life had been as difficult as her own. At least he had Elliot. That must have been a comfort to him. She said as much to Harry.

He gave her a strange look. "Well, yes, Elliot's special to him," he said, as if there were things she didn't know. Probably there were.

"Will these little guys make it?" she asked when the calf had finished his bottle.

"I think so," Harry said. "Here, give me that bottle and I'll take care of it for you."

She sighed, petting the calf gently. She liked farms and ranches. They were so real, compared to the artificial life she'd known since she was old enough to leave home. She loved her work and she'd always enjoyed performing, but it seemed sometimes as if she lived in another world. Values were nebulous, if they even existed, in the world where she worked. Old-fashioned ideas like morality, honor, chastity were laughed at or ignored. Amanda kept hers to herself, just as she kept her privacy intact. She didn't discuss her inner feelings with anyone. Probably her friends and associates would have died laughing if they'd known just how many hang-ups she had, and how distant her outlook on life was from theirs.

"Here's another one," Quinn said from the front of the barn.

Amanda turned her head, surprised to see him because he'd ridden out minutes ago. He was carrying another small calf, but this one looked worse than the younger ones did.

"He's very thin," she commented.

"He's got scours." He laid the calf down next to her. "Harry, fix another bottle."

"Coming up, boss."

Amanda touched the wiry little head with its rough hide. "He's not in good shape," she murmured quietly.

Quinn saw the concern on her face and was surprised by it. He shouldn't have been, he reasoned. Why would she have come with Elliot in the middle of the night to nurse a man she didn't even like, if she wasn't a kind woman?

"He probably won't make it," he agreed, his dark eyes searching hers. "He'd been out there by himself for a long time. It's a big property, and he's a very small calf," he defended when she gave him a meaningful look. "It wouldn't be the first time we missed one, I'm sorry to say."

"I know." She looked up as Harry produced a third bottle, and her hand reached for it just as Quinn's did. She released it, feeling odd little tingles at the brief contact with his lean, sure hand.

"Here goes," he murmured curtly. He reached under the calf's chin and pulled its mouth up to slide the nipple in.

The calf could barely nurse, but after a minute it seemed to rally and then it fed hungrily.

"Thank goodness," Amanda murmured. She smiled at Quinn, and his eyes flashed as they met hers, searching, dark, full of secrets. They narrowed and then abruptly fell to her soft mouth, where they lingered with a kind of questioning irritation, as if he wanted very much to kiss her and hated himself for it. Her heart leaped at the knowledge. She seemed to have a new, built-in insight about this standoffish man, and she didn't understand either it or her attitude toward him. He was domineering and hardheaded and unpredictable and she should have disliked him. But she sensed a sensitivity in him that touched her heart. She wanted to get to know him.

"I can do this," he said curtly. "Why don't you go inside?"

She was getting to him, she thought with fascination. He was interested in her, but he didn't want to be. She watched the way he avoided looking directly at her again, the angry glance of his eyes.

Well, it certainly wouldn't do any good to make him furious at her, especially when she was going to be his unwanted houseguest for several more days, from the look of the weather.

"Okay," she said, giving in. She got to her feet slowly. "I'll see if I can find something to do."

"Harry might like some company while he works in the kitchen. Wouldn't you, Harry?" he added, giving the older man a look that said he'd damned sure better like some company.

"Of course I would, boss," Harry agreed instantly.

Amanda pushed her hands into her pockets with a last glance at the calves. She smiled down at them. "Can I help feed them while I'm here?" she asked gently.

"If you want to," Quinn said readily, but without looking up.

"Thanks." She hesitated, but he made her feel shy and tongue-tied. She turned away nervously and walked back to the house.

Since Harry had the kitchen well in hand, she volunteered to iron some of Quinn's cotton shirts. Harry had the ironing board set up, but not the iron, so she went into the closet and produced one. It looked old, but maybe it would do, except that it seemed to have a lot of something caked on it.

She'd just started to plug it in when Harry came into the room and gasped.

"Not that one!" he exclaimed, gently taking it away from her. "That's Quinn's!"

She opened her mouth to make a remark, when Harry started chuckling.

"It's for his skis," he explained patiently.

She nodded. "Right. He irons his skis. I can see that."

"He does. Don't you know anything about skiing?"

"Well, you get behind a speedboat with them on…"

"Not waterskiing. *Snow* skiing," he emphasized.

She shrugged. "I come from southern Mississippi." She

grinned at him. "We don't do much business in snow, you see."

"Sorry. Well, Quinn was an Olympic contender in giant slalom when he was in his late teens and early twenties. He would have made the team, but he got married and Elliot was on the way, so he gave it up. He still gets in plenty of practice," he added, shuddering. "On old Ironside peak, too. Nobody, but nobody, skis it except Quinn and a couple of other experts from Larry's Lodge over in Jackson Hole."

"I haven't seen that one on a map..." she began, because she'd done plenty of map reading before she came here.

"Oh, that isn't its official name, it's what Quinn calls it." He grinned. "Anyway, Quinn uses this iron to put wax on the bottom of his skis. Don't feel bad, I didn't know any better, either, at first, and I waxed a couple of shirts. Here's the right iron."

He handed it to her, and she plugged it in and got started. The elusive Mr. Sutton had hidden qualities, it seemed. She'd watched the winter Olympics every four years on television, and downhill skiing fascinated her. But it seemed to Amanda that giant slalom called for a kind of reckless skill and speed that would require ruthlessness and single-minded determination. Considering that, it wasn't at all surprising to her that Quinn Sutton had been good at it.

Chapter Three

Amanda helped Harry do dishes and start a load of clothes in the washer. But when she took them out of the dryer, she discovered that several of Quinn's shirts were missing buttons and had loose seams.

Harry produced a needle and some thread, and Amanda set to work mending them. It gave her something to do while she watched a years-old police drama on television.

Quinn came in with Elliot a few hours later.

"Boy, the snow's bad," Elliot remarked as he rubbed his hands in front of the fire Harry had lit in the big stone fireplace. "Dad had to bring the sled out to get me, because the bus couldn't get off the main highway."

"Speaking of the sled," Amanda said, glancing at Quinn, "I've got to have a few things from the cabin. I'm really sorry, but I'm limited to what I'm wearing…"

"I'll run you down right now, before I go out again."

She put the mending aside. "I'll get my coat."

"Elliot, you can come, too. Put your coat back on," Quinn said unexpectedly, ignoring his son's surprised glance.

Amanda didn't look at him, but she understood why he wanted Elliot along. She made Quinn nervous. He was attracted to her and he was going to fight it to the bitter end. She wondered why he considered her such a threat.

He paused to pick up the shirt she'd been working on, and his expression got even harder as he glared at her. "You don't need to do that kind of thing," he said curtly.

"I've got to earn my keep somehow." She sighed. "I can feed the calves and help with the housework, at least. I'm not used to sitting around doing nothing," she added. "It makes me nervous."

He hesitated. An odd look rippled over his face as he studied the neat stitches in his shirtsleeve where the rip had been. He held it for a minute before he laid it gently back on the sofa. He didn't look at Amanda as he led the way out the door.

It didn't take her long to get her things together. Elliot wandered around the cabin. "There are knives all over the counter," he remarked. "Want me to put them in the sink?"

"Go ahead. I was using them for drumsticks," she called as she closed her suitcase.

"They don't look like they'd taste very good." Elliot chuckled.

She came out of the bedroom and gave him an amused

glance. "Not that kind of drumsticks, you turkey. Here." She put down the suitcase and took the blunt stainless-steel knives from him. She glanced around to make sure Quinn hadn't come into the house and then she broke into an impromptu drum routine that made Elliot grin even more.

"Say, you're pretty good," he said.

She bowed. "Just one of my minor talents," she said. "But I'm better with a keyboard. Ready to go?"

"Whenever you are."

She started to pick up her suitcase, but Elliot reached down and got it before she could, a big grin on his freckled face. She wondered again why he looked so little like his father. She knew that his mother had been a redhead, too, but it was odd that he didn't resemble Quinn in any way at all.

Quinn was waiting on the sled, his expression unreadable, impatiently smoking his cigarette. He let them get on and turned the draft horse back toward his own house. It was snowing lightly and the wind was blowing, not fiercely but with a nip in it. Amanda sighed, lifting her face to the snow, not caring that her hood had fallen back to reveal the coiled softness of her blond hair. She felt alive out here as she never had in the city, or even back East. There was something about the wilderness that made her feel at peace with herself for the first time since the tragedy that had sent her retreating here.

"Enjoying yourself?" Quinn asked unexpectedly.

"More than I can tell you," she replied. "It's like no other place on earth."

He nodded. His dark eyes slid over her face, her cheeks flushed with cold and excitement, and they lingered there for one long moment before he forced his gaze back to the trail. Amanda saw that look and it brought a sense of foreboding. He seemed almost angry.

In fact, he was. Before the day was out, it was pretty apparent that he'd withdrawn somewhere inside himself and had no intention of coming out again. He barely said two words to Amanda before bedtime.

"He's gone broody," Elliot mused before he and Amanda called it a night. "He doesn't do it often, and not for a long time, but when he's got something on his mind, it's best not to get on his nerves."

"Oh, I'll do my best," Amanda promised, and crossed her heart.

But that apparently didn't do much good, in her case, because he glared at her over breakfast the next morning and over lunch, and by the time she finished mending a window curtain in the kitchen and helped Harry bake a cake for dessert, she was feeling like a very unwelcome guest.

She went out to feed the calves, the nicest of her daily chores, just before Quinn was due home for supper. Elliot had lessons and he was holed up in his room trying to get them done in time for a science-fiction movie he wanted to watch after supper. Quinn insisted that homework came first.

She fed two of the three calves and Harry volunteered to feed the third, the little one that Quinn had brought home with scours, while she cut the cake and laid the table.

She was just finishing the place settings when she heard the sled draw up outside the door.

Her heart quickened at the sound of Quinn's firm, measured stride on the porch. The door opened and he came in, along with a few snowflakes.

He stopped short at the sight of her in an old white apron with wisps of blond hair hanging around her flushed face, a bowl of whipped potatoes in her hands.

"Don't you look domestic?" he asked with sudden, bitter sarcasm.

The attack was unexpected, although it shouldn't have been. He'd been irritable ever since the day before, when he'd noticed her mending his shirt.

"I'm just helping Harry," she said. "He's feeding the calves while I do this."

"So I noticed."

She put down the potatoes, watching him hang up his hat and coat with eyes that approved his tall, fit physique, the way the red-checked flannel shirt clung to his muscular torso and long back. He was such a lonely man, she thought, watching him. So alone, even with Elliot and Harry here. He turned unexpectedly, catching her staring and his dark eyes glittered.

He went to the sink to wash his hands, almost vibrating with pent-up anger. She sensed it, but it only piqued her curiosity. He was reacting to her. She felt it, knew it, as she picked up a dish towel and went close to him to wrap it gently over his wet hands. Her big black eyes searched his, and she let her fingers linger on his while time seemed to end in the warm kitchen.

His dark eyes narrowed, and he seemed to have stopped breathing. He was aware of so many sensations. Hunger. Anger. Loneliness. Lust. His head spun with them, and the scent of her was pure, soft woman, drifting up into his nostrils, cocooning him in the smell of cologne and shampoo. His gaze fell helplessly to her soft bow of a mouth and he wondered how it would feel to bend those few inches and take it roughly under his own. It had been so long since he'd kissed a woman, held a woman. Amanda was particularly feminine, and she appealed to everything that was masculine in him. He almost vibrated with the need to reach out to her.

But that way lay disaster, he told himself firmly. She was just another treacherous woman, probably bored with confinement, just keeping her hand in with attracting men. He probably seemed like a pushover, and she was going to use her charms to make a fool of him. He took a deep, slow breath and the glitter in his eyes became even more pronounced as he jerked the towel out of her hands and moved away.

"Sorry," she mumbled. She felt her cheeks go hot, because there had been a cold kind of violence in the action that warned her his emotions weren't quite under control. She moved away from him. Violence was the one thing she did expect from men. She'd lived with it for most of her life until she'd run away from home.

She went back to the stove, stirring the sauce she'd made to go with the boiled dumpling.

"Don't get too comfortable in the kitchen," he warned her. "This is Harry's private domain and he doesn't like trespassers. You're just passing through."

"I haven't forgotten that, Mr. Sutton," she replied, and her eyes kindled with dark fire as she looked at him. There was no reason to make her feel so unwelcome. "Just as soon as the thaw comes, I'll be out of your way for good."

"I can hardly wait," he said, biting off the words.

Amanda sighed wearily. It wasn't her idea of the perfect rest spot. She'd come away from the concert stage needing healing, and all she'd found was another battle to fight.

"You make me feel so at home, Mr. Sutton," she said wistfully. "Like part of the family. Thanks so much for your gracious hospitality, and do you happen to have a jar of rat poison…?"

Quinn had to bite hard to keep from laughing. He turned and went out of the kitchen as if he were being chased.

After supper, Amanda volunteered to wash dishes, but Harry shooed her off. Quinn apparently did book work every night, because he went into his study and closed the door, leaving Elliot with Amanda for company. They'd watched the science-fiction movie Elliot had been so eager to see and now they were working on the keyboard.

"I think I've got the hang of C major," Elliot announced, and ran the scale, complete with turned under thumb on the key of F.

"Very good," she enthused. "Okay, let's go on to G major."

She taught him the scale and watched him play it, her mind on Quinn Sutton's antagonism.

"Something bothering you?" Elliot asked suspiciously.

She shrugged. "Your dad doesn't want me here."

"He hates women," he said. "You knew that, didn't you?"

"Yes. But why?"

He shook his head. "It's because of my mother. She did something really terrible to him, and he never talks about her. He never has. I've got one picture of her, in my room."

"I guess you look like her," she said speculatively.

He handed her the keyboard. "I've got red hair and freckles like she had," he confessed. "I'm just sorry that I… well, that I don't look anything like Dad. I'm glad he cares about me, though, in spite of everything. Isn't it great that he likes me?"

What an odd way to talk about his father, Amanda thought as she studied him. She wanted to say something else, to ask about that wording, but it was too soon. She hid her curiosity in humor.

"'There are more things in heaven and earth, Horatio, than are dreamt of in your philosophy,'" she intoned deeply.

He chuckled. "Hamlet," he said. "Shakespeare. We did that in English class last month."

"Culture in the high country." She applauded. "Very good, Elliot."

"I like rock culture best," he said in a stage whisper. "Play something."

She glanced toward Quinn's closed study door with a grimace. "Something soft."

"No!" he protested, and grinned. "Come on, give him hell."

"Elliot!" she chided.

"He needs shaking up, I tell you, he's going to die an old maid. He gets all funny and red when unmarried ladies talk to him at church, and just look at how grumpy he's been since you've been around. We've got to save him, Amanda," he said solemnly.

She sighed. "Okay. It's your funeral." She flicked switches, turning on the auto rhythm, the auto chords, and moved the volume to maximum. With a mischievous glance at Elliot, she swung into one of the newest rock songs, by a rival group, instantly recognizable by the reggae rhythm and sweet harmony.

"Good God!" came a muffled roar from the study.

Amanda cut off the keyboard and handed it to Elliot.

"No!" Elliot gasped.

But it was too late. His father came out of the study and saw Elliot holding the keyboard and started smoldering.

"It was her!" Elliot accused, pointing his finger at her.

She peered at Quinn over her drawn-up knees. "Would

I play a keyboard that loud in your house, after you warned me not to?" she asked in her best meek voice.

Quinn's eyes narrowed. They went back to Elliot.

"She's lying," Elliot said. "Just like the guy in those truck commercials on TV…!"

"Keep it down," Quinn said without cracking a smile. "Or I'll give that thing the decent burial it really needs. And no more damned rock music in my house! That thing has earphones. Use them!"

"Yes, sir," Elliot groaned.

Amanda saluted him. "We hear and obey, excellency!" she said with a deplorable Spanish accent. "Your wish is our command. We live only to serve…!"

The slamming of the study door cut her off. She burst into laughter while Elliot hit her with a sofa cushion.

"You animal," he accused mirthfully. "Lying to Dad, accusing me of doing something I never did! How could you?"

"Temporary insanity," she gasped for breath. "I couldn't help myself."

"We're both going to die," he assured her. "He'll lie awake all night thinking of ways to get even and when we least expect it, pow!"

"He's welcome. Here. Run that G major scale again."

He let her turn the keyboard back on, but he was careful to move the volume switch down as far as it would go.

It was almost nine when Quinn came out of the study and turned out the light.

"Time for bed," he said.

Amanda had wanted to watch a movie that was coming on, but she knew better than to ask. Presumably they did occasionally watch television at night. She'd have to ask one of these days.

"Good night, Dad. Amanda," Elliot said, grinning as he went upstairs with a bound.

"Did you do your homework?" Quinn called up after him.

"Almost."

"What the hell does that mean?" he demanded.

"It means I'll do it first thing in the morning! 'Night, Dad!"

A door closed.

Quinn glared at Amanda. "That won't do," he said tersely. "His homework comes first. Music is a nice hobby, but it's not going to make a living for him."

Why not, she almost retorted, it makes a six-figure annual income for me, but she kept her mouth shut.

"I'll make sure he's done his homework before I offer to show him anything else on the keyboard. Okay?"

He sighed angrily. "All right. Come on. Let's go to bed."

She put her hands over her chest and gasped, her eyes wide and astonished. "Together? Mr. Sutton, really!"

His dark eyes narrowed in a veiled threat. "Hell will freeze over before I wind up in bed with you," he said icily. "I told you, I don't want used goods."

"Your loss," she sighed, ignoring the impulse to lay a lamp across his thick skull. "Experience is a valuable commodity in my world." She deliberately smoothed her hands down her waist and over her hips, her eyes faintly coquettish as she watched him watching her movements. "And I'm very experienced," she drawled. In music, she was.

His jaw tautened. "Yes, it does show," he said. "Kindly keep your attitudes to yourself. I don't want my son corrupted."

"If you really meant that, you'd let him watch movies and listen to rock music and trust him to make up his own mind about things."

"He's only twelve."

"You aren't preparing him to live in the real world," she protested.

"This," he said, "is the real world for him. Not some fancy apartment in a city where women like you lounge around in bars picking up men."

"Now you wait just a minute," she said. "I don't lounge around in bars to pick up men." She shifted her stance. "I hang out in zoos and flash elderly men in my trench coat."

He threw up his hands. "I give up."

"Good! Your room or mine?"

He whirled, his dark eyes flashing. Her smile was purely provocative and she was deliberately baiting him, he could sense it. His jaw tautened and he wanted to pick her up and shake her for the effect her teasing was having on him.

"Okay, I quit," Amanda said, because she could see that he'd reached the limits of his control and she wasn't quite brave enough to test the other side of it. "Good night. Sweet dreams."

He didn't answer her. He followed her up the stairs and watched her go into her room and close the door. After a minute, he went into his own room and locked the door. He laughed mirthlessly at his own rash action, but he hoped she could hear the bolt being thrown.

She could. It shocked her, until she realized that he'd done it deliberately, probably trying to hurt her. She laid back on her bed with a long sigh. She didn't know what to do about Mr. Sutton. He was beginning to get to her in a very real way. She had to keep her perspective. This was only temporary. It would help to keep it in mind.

Quinn was thinking the same thing. But when he turned out the light and closed his eyes, he kept feeling Amanda's loosened hair brushing down his chest, over his flat stomach, his loins. He shuddered and woke up sweating in the middle of the night. It was the worst and longest night of his life.

The next morning, Quinn glared at Amanda across the breakfast table after Elliot had left for school.

"Leave my shirts alone," he said curtly. "If you find any more tears, Harry can mend them."

Her eyebrows lifted. "I don't have germs," she pointed out. "I couldn't contaminate them just by stitching them up."

"Leave them alone," he said harshly.

"Okay. Suit yourself." She sighed. "I'll just busy myself making lacy pillows for your bed."

He said something expressive and obscene; her lips fell open and she gaped at him. She'd never heard him use language like that.

It seemed to bother him that he had. He put down his fork, left his eggs and went out the door as if leopards were stalking him.

Amanda stirred her eggs around on the plate, feeling vaguely guilty that she'd given him such a hard time that he'd gone without half his breakfast. She didn't know why she needled him. It seemed to be a new habit, maybe to keep him at bay, to keep him from noticing how attracted she was to him.

"I'm going out to feed the calves, Harry," she said after a minute.

"Dress warm. It's snowing again," he called from upstairs.

"Okay."

She put on her coat and hat and wandered out to the barn through the path Quinn had made in the deep snow. She'd never again grumble at little two- and three-foot drifts in the city, she promised herself. Now that she knew what real snow was, she felt guilty for all her past complaints.

The barn was warmer than the great outdoors. She pushed snowflakes out of her eyes and face and went to fix the bottles as Harry had shown her, but Quinn was already there and had it done.

"No need to follow me around trying to get my attention," Amanda murmured with a wicked smile. "I've already noticed how sexy and handsome you are."

He drew in a furious breath, but just as he was about to speak she moved closer and put her fingers against his cold mouth.

"You'll break my heart if you use ungentlemanly language, Mr. Sutton," she told him firmly. "I'll just feed the calves and admire you from afar, if you don't mind. It seems safer than trying to throw myself at you."

He looked torn between shaking her and kissing her. She stood very still where he towered above her, even bigger than usual in that thick shepherd's coat and his tall, gray Stetson. He looked down at her quietly, his narrowed eyes lingering on her flushed cheeks and her soft, parted mouth.

Her hands were resting against the coat, and his were on her arms, pulling. She could hardly breathe as she realized that he'd actually touched her voluntarily. He jerked her face up under his, and she could see anger and something like bitterness in the dark eyes that held hers until she blushed.

"Just what are you after, city girl?" he asked coldly.

"A smile, a kind word and, dare I say it, a round of hearty laughter?" she essayed with wide eyes, trying not to let him see how powerfully he affected her.

His dark eyes fell to her mouth. "Is that right? And nothing more?"

Her breath came jerkily through her lips. "I…have to feed the calves."

His eyes narrowed. "Yes, you do." His fingers on her arms contracted, so that she could feel them even through the sleeves of her coat. "Be careful what you offer me," he said in a voice as light and cold as the snow outside the barn. "I've been without a woman for one hell of a long time, and I'm alone up here. If you're not what you're making yourself out to be, you could be letting yourself in for some trouble."

She stared up at him only half comprehending what he was saying. As his meaning began to filter into her consciousness, her cheeks heated and her breath caught in her throat.

"You...make it sound like a threat," she breathed.

"It is a threat, Amanda," he replied, using her name for the first time. "You could start something you might not want to finish with me, even with Elliot and Harry around."

She bit her lower lip nervously. She hadn't considered that. He looked more mature and formidable than he ever had before, and she could feel the banked-down fires in him kindling even as he held her.

"Okay," she said after a minute.

He let her go and moved away from her to get the bottles. He handed them to her with a long, speculative look.

"It's all right," she muttered, embarrassed. "I won't attack you while your back is turned. I almost never rape men."

He lifted an eyebrow, but he didn't smile. "You crazed female sex maniac," he murmured.

"Goody Two-Shoes," she shot back.

A corner of his mouth actually turned up. "You've got

that one right," he agreed. "Stay close to the house while it's snowing like this. We wouldn't want to lose you."

"I'll just bet we wouldn't," she muttered and stuck her tongue out at his retreating back.

She knelt down to feed the calves, still shaken by her confrontation with Quinn. He was an enigma. She was almost certain that he'd been joking with her at the end of the exchange, but it was hard to tell from his poker face. He didn't look like a man who'd laughed often or enough.

The littlest calf wasn't responding as well as he had earlier. She cuddled him and coaxed him to drink, but he did it without any spirit. She laid him back down with a sigh. He didn't look good at all. She worried about him for the rest of the evening, and she didn't argue when the television was cut off at nine o'clock. She went straight to bed, with Quinn and Elliot giving her odd looks.

Chapter Four

Amanda was subdued at the breakfast table, more so when Quinn started watching her with dark, accusing eyes. She knew she'd deliberately needled him for the past two days, and now she was sorry. He'd hinted that her behavior was about to start something, and she was anxious not to make things any worse than they already were.

The problem was that she was attracted to him. The more she saw of him, the more she liked him. He was different from the superficial, materialistic men in her own world. He was hardheaded and stubborn. He had values, and he spoke out for them. He lived by a rigid code of ethics, and honor was a word that had great meaning for him. Under all that, he was sensitive and caring. Amanda couldn't help the way she was beginning to feel about him. She only wished that she hadn't started off on the wrong foot with him.

She set out to win him over, acting more like her real self. She was polite and courteous and caring, but without the rough edges she'd had in the beginning. She still did the mending, despite his grumbling, and she made cushions for the sofa out of some cloth Harry had put away. But all her domestic actions only made things worse. Quinn glared at her openly now, and his lack of politeness raised even Harry's eyebrows.

Amanda had a sneaking hunch that it was attraction to her that was making him so ill humored. He didn't act at all like an experienced man, despite his marriage, and the way he looked at her was intense. If she could bring him out into the open, she thought, it might ease the tension a little.

She did her chores, including feeding the calves, worrying even more about the littlest one because he wasn't responding as well today as he had the day before. When Elliot came home, she refused to help him with the keyboard until he did his homework. With a rueful smile and a knowing glance at his dad, he went up to his room to get it over with.

Meanwhile, Harry went out to get more firewood and Amanda was left in the living room with Quinn watching an early newscast.

The news was, as usual, all bad. Quinn put out his cigarette half angrily, his dark eyes lingering on Amanda's soft face.

"Don't you miss the city?" he asked.

She smiled. "Sure. I miss the excitement and my friends.

But it's nice here, too." She moved toward the big armchair he was sitting in, nervously contemplating her next move. "You don't mind all that much, do you? Having me around, I mean?"

He glared up at her. He was wearing a blue-checked flannel shirt, buttoned up to the throat, and the hard muscles of his chest strained against it. He looked twice as big as usual, his dark hair unruly on his broad forehead as he stared up into her eyes.

"I'm getting used to you, I guess," he said stiffly. "Just don't get too comfortable."

"You really don't want me here, do you?" she asked quietly.

He sighed angrily. "I don't like women," he muttered.

"I know." She sat down on the arm of his chair, facing him. "Why not?" she asked gently.

His body went taut at the proximity. She was too close. Too female. The scent of her got into his nostrils and made him shift restlessly in the chair. "It's none of your damned business why not," he said evasively. "Will you get up from there?"

She warmed at the tone of his voice. So she did disturb him! Amanda smiled gently as she leaned forward. "Are you sure you want me to?" she asked and suddenly threw caution to the wind and slid down into his lap, putting her soft mouth hungrily on his.

He stiffened. He jerked. His big hands bit into her arms so hard they bruised. But for just one long, sweet moment, his hard mouth gave in to hers and he gave her back the kiss, his lips rough and warm, the pressure bruising, and he groaned as if all his dreams had come true at once.

He tasted of smoke for the brief second that he allowed the kiss. Then he was all bristling indignation and cold fury. He slammed to his feet, taking her with him, and literally threw her away, so hard that she fell against and onto the sofa.

"Damn you," he ground out. His fists clenched at his sides. His big body vibrated with outrage. "You cheap little tart!"

She lay trembling, frightened of the violence in his now white face and blazing dark eyes. "I'm not," she defended feebly.

"Can't you live without it for a few days, or are you desperate enough to try to seduce me?" he hissed. His eyes slid over her with icy contempt. "It won't work. I've told you already, I don't want something that any man can have! I don't want any part of you, least of all your overused body!"

She got to her feet on legs that threatened to give way under her, backing away from his anger. She couldn't even speak. Her father had been like that when he drank too much, white-faced, icy hot, totally out of control. And when he got that way, he hit. She cringed away from Quinn as he moved toward her and suddenly, she whirled and ran out of the room.

He checked his instinctive move to go after her. So she was scared, was she? He frowned, trying to understand why. He'd only spoken the truth; did she not like hearing what she was? The possibility that he'd been wrong, that she wasn't a cheap little tart, he wouldn't admit even to himself.

He sat back down and concentrated on the television without any real interest. When Elliot came downstairs, Quinn barely looked up.

"Where's Amanda going?" he asked his father.

Quinn raised an eyebrow. "What?"

"Where's Amanda going in such a rush?" Elliot asked again. "I saw her out the window, tramping through waist-deep snow. Doesn't she remember what you told her about old McNaber's traps? She's headed straight for them if she keeps on the way she's headed… Where are you going?"

Quinn was already on his feet and headed for the back door. He got into his shepherd's coat and hat without speaking, his face pale, his eyes blazing with mingled fear and anger.

"She was crying," Harry muttered, sparing him a glance. "I don't know what you said to her, but—"

"Shut up," Quinn said coldly. He stared the older man down and went out the back door and around the house, following in the wake Amanda's body had made. She was already out of sight, and those traps would be buried under several feet of snow. Bear traps, and she wouldn't see them until she felt them. The thought of that merciless metal biting her soft flesh didn't bear thinking about, and it would be his fault because he'd hurt her.

Several meters ahead, into the woods now, Amanda

was cursing silently as she plowed through the snowdrifts, her black eyes fierce even through the tears. Damn Quinn Sutton, she panted. She hoped he got eaten by moths during the winter, she hoped his horse stood on his foot, she hoped the sled ran over him and packed him into the snow and nobody found him until spring. It was only a kiss, after all, and he'd kissed her back just for a few seconds.

She felt the tears burning coldly down her cheeks as they started again. Damn him. He hadn't had to make her feel like such an animal, just because she'd kissed him. She cared about him. She'd only wanted to get on a friendlier footing with him. But now she'd done it. He hated her for sure, she'd seen it in his eyes, in his face, when he'd called her those names. Cheap little tart, indeed! Well, Goody Two-Shoes Sutton could just hold his breath until she kissed him again, so there!

She stopped to catch her breath and then plowed on. The cabin was somewhere down here. She'd stay in it even if she did freeze to death. She'd shack up with a grizzly bear before she'd spend one more night under Quinn Sutton's roof. She frowned. Were there grizzly bears in this part of the country?

"Amanda, stop!"

She paused, wondering if she'd heard someone call her name, or if it had just been the wind. She was in a break of lodgepole pines now, and a cabin was just below in the valley. But it wasn't Mr. Durning's cabin. Could that be McNaber's…?

"Amanda!"

That was definitely her name. She glanced over her shoulder and saw the familiar shepherd's coat and dark worn Stetson atop that arrogant head.

"Eat snow, Goody Two-Shoes!" she yelled back. "I'm going home!"

She started ahead, pushing hard now. But he had the edge, because he was walking in the path she'd made. He was bigger and faster, and he had twice her stamina. Before she got five more feet, he had her by the waist.

She fought him, kicking and hitting, but he simply wrapped both arms around her and held on until she finally ran out of strength.

"I hate you," she panted, shivering as the cold and the exertion got to her. "I hate you!"

"You'd hate me more if I hadn't stopped you," he said, breathing hard. "McNaber lives down there. He's got bear traps all over the place. Just a few more steps, and you'd have been up to your knees in them, you little fool! You can't even see them in snow this deep!"

"What would you care?" she groaned. "You don't want me around. I don't want to stay with you anymore. I'll take my chances at the cabin!"

"No, you won't, Amanda," he said. His embrace didn't even loosen. He whipped her around, his big hands rough on her sleeves as he shook her. "You're coming back with me, if I have to carry you!"

She flinched, the violence in him frightening her. She swallowed, her lower lip trembling and pulled feebly against his hands.

"Let go of me," she whispered. Her voice shook, and she hated her own cowardice.

He scowled. She was paper-white. Belatedly he realized what was wrong and his hands released her. She backed away as far as the snow would allow and stood like a young doe at bay, her eyes dark and frightened.

"Did he hit you?" he asked quietly.

She didn't have to ask who. She shivered. "Only when he drank," she said, her voice faltering. "But he always drank." She laughed bitterly. "Just…don't come any closer until you cool down, if you please."

He took a slow, steadying breath. "I'm sorry," he said, shocking her. "No, I mean it. I'm really sorry. I wouldn't have hit you, if that's what you're thinking. Only a coward would raise his hand to a woman," he said with cold conviction.

She wrapped her arms around herself and stood, just breathing, shivering in the cold.

"We'd better get back before you freeze," he said tautly. Her very defensiveness disarmed him. He felt guilty and protective all at once. He wanted to take her to his heart and comfort her, but even as he stepped toward her, she backed away. He hadn't imagined how much that would hurt until it happened. He stopped and stood where he was, raising his hands in an odd gesture of helplessness. "I won't touch you," he promised. "Come on, honey. You can go first."

Tears filmed her dark eyes. It was the first endearment she'd ever heard from him and it touched her deeply. But she knew it was only casual. Her behavior had shocked him and he didn't know what to do. She let out a long breath.

Without a quip or comeback, she eased past him warily and started back the way they'd come. He followed her, giving thanks that he'd been in time, that she hadn't run afoul of old McNaber's traps. But now he'd really done it. He'd managed to make her afraid of him.

She went ahead of him into the house. Elliot and Harry took one look at her face and Quinn's and didn't ask a single question.

She sat at the supper table like a statue. She didn't speak, even when Elliot tried to bring her into the conversation. And afterward, she curled up in a chair in the living room and sat like a mouse watching television.

Quinn couldn't know the memories he'd brought back, the searing fear of her childhood. Her father had been a big man, and he was always violent when he drank. He was sorry afterward, sometimes he even cried when he saw the bruises he'd put on her. But it never stopped him. She'd run away because it was more than she could bear, and fortunately there'd been a place for runaways that took her in. She'd learned volumes about human kindness from those people. But the memories were bitter and Quinn's bridled violence had brought them sweeping in like storm clouds.

Elliot didn't ask her about music lessons. He excused himself a half hour early and went up to bed. Harry had long since gone to his own room.

Quinn sat in his big chair, smoking his cigarette, but he started when Amanda put her feet on the floor and glanced warily at him.

"Don't go yet," he said quietly. "I want to talk to you."

"We don't have anything to say to each other," she said quietly. "I'm very sorry for what I did this afternoon. It was impulsive and stupid, and I promise I'll never do it again. If you can just put up with me until it thaws a little, you'll never have to see me again."

He sighed wearily. "Is that what you think I want?" he asked, searching her face.

"Of course it is," she replied simply. "You've hated having me here ever since I came."

"Maybe I have. I've got more reason to hate and distrust women than you'll ever know. But that isn't what I want to talk about," he said, averting his gaze from her wan face. He didn't like thinking about that kiss and how disturbing it had been. "I want to know why you thought I might hit you."

She dropped her eyes to her lap. "You're big, like my father," she said. "When he lost his temper, he always hit."

"I'm not your father," Quinn pointed out, his dark eyes narrowing. "And I've never hit anyone in a temper, except maybe another man from time to time when it was called for. I never raised my hand to Elliot's mother, although I felt like it a time or two, in all honesty. I never lifted a hand to her even when she told me she was pregnant with Elliot."

"Why should you have?" she asked absently. "He's your son."

He laughed coldly. "No, he isn't."

She stared at him openly. "Elliot isn't yours?" she asked softly.

He shook his head. "His mother was having an affair with a married man and she got caught out." He shrugged. "I was twenty-two and grass green and she mounted a campaign to marry me. I guess I was pretty much a sitting duck. She was beautiful and stacked and she had me eating out of her hand in no time. We got married and right after the ceremony, she told me what she'd done. She laughed at how clumsy I'd been during the courtship, how she'd had to steel herself not to be sick when I'd kissed her. She told me about Elliot's father and how much she loved him, then she dared me to tell people the truth about how easy it had been to make me marry her." He blew out a cloud of smoke, his eyes cold with memory. "She had me over a barrel. I was twice as proud back then as I am now. I couldn't bear to have the whole community laughing at me. So I stuck it out. Until Elliot was born, and she and his father took off for parts unknown for a weekend of love. Unfortunately for them, he wrecked the car in his haste to get to a motel and killed both of them outright."

"Does Elliot know?" she asked, her voice quiet as she glanced toward the staircase.

"Sure," he said. "I couldn't lie to him about it. But I

took care of him from the time he was a baby, and I raised him. That makes me his father just as surely as if I'd put the seed he grew from into his mother's body. He's my son, and I'm his father. I love him."

She studied his hard face, seeing behind it to the pain he must have suffered. "You loved her, didn't you?"

"Calf love," he said. "She came up on my blind side and I needed somebody to love. I'd always been shy and clumsy around girls. I couldn't even get a date when I was in school because I was so rough-edged. She paid me a lot of attention. I was lonely." His big shoulders shrugged. "Like I said, a sitting duck. She taught me some hard lessons about your sex," he added, his narrowed eyes on her face. "I've never forgotten them. And nobody's had a second chance at me."

Her breath came out as a sigh. "That's what you thought this afternoon, when I kissed you," she murmured, reddening at her own forwardness. "I'm sorry. I didn't realize you might think I was playing you for a sucker."

He frowned. "Why did you kiss me, Amanda?"

"Would you believe, because I wanted to?" she asked with a quiet smile. "You're a very attractive man, and something about you makes me weak in the knees. But you don't have to worry about me coming on to you again," she added, getting to her feet. "You teach a pretty tough lesson yourself. Good night, Mr. Sutton. I appreciate your telling me about Elliot. You needn't worry that I'll say anything to him or to anybody else. I don't carry tales, and I don't gossip."

She turned toward the staircase, and Quinn's dark eyes followed her. She had an elegance of carriage that touched him, full of pride and grace. He was sorry now that he'd slapped her down so hard with cruel words. He really hadn't meant to. He'd been afraid that she was going to let him down, that she was playing. It hadn't occurred to him that she found him attractive or that she'd kissed him because she'd really wanted to.

He'd made a bad mistake with Amanda. He'd hurt her and sent her running, and now he wished he could take back the things he'd said. She wasn't like any woman he'd ever been exposed to. She actually seemed unaware of her beauty, as if she didn't think much of it. Maybe he'd gotten it all wrong and she wasn't much more experienced than he was. He wished he could ask her. She disturbed him very much, and now he wondered if it wasn't mutual.

Amanda was lying in bed, crying. The day had been horrible, and she hated Quinn for the way he'd treated her. It wasn't until she remembered what he'd told her that she stopped crying and started thinking. He'd said that he'd never slept with Elliot's mother, and that he hadn't been able to get dates in high school. Presumably that meant that his only experience with women had been after Elliot's mother died. She frowned. There hadn't been many women, she was willing to bet. He seemed to know relatively nothing about her sex. She frowned. If he still hated women, how had he gotten any experience? Finally her mind grew tired of trying to work it out and she went to sleep.

* * *

Amanda was up helping Harry in the kitchen the next morning when Quinn came downstairs after a wild, erotic dream that left him sweating and swearing when he woke up. Amanda had figured largely in it, with her blond hair loose and down to her lower spine, his hands twined in it while he made love to her in the stillness of his own bedroom. The dream had been so vivid that he could almost see the pink perfection of her breasts through the bulky, white knit sweater she was wearing, and he almost groaned as his eyes fell to the rise and fall of her chest under it.

She glanced at Quinn and actually flushed before she dragged her eyes back down to the pan of biscuits she was putting into the oven.

"I didn't know you could make biscuits," Quinn murmured.

"Harry taught me," she said evasively. Her eyes went back to him again and flitted away.

He frowned at that shy look until he realized why he was getting it. He usually kept his shirts buttoned up to his throat, but this morning he'd left it open halfway down his chest because he was still sweating from that dream. He pursed his lips and gave her a speculative stare. He wondered if it were possible that he disturbed her as much as she disturbed him. He was going to make it his business to find out before she left here. If for no other reason than to salve his bruised ego.

He went out behind Elliot, pausing in the doorway. "How's the calf?" he asked Amanda.

"He wasn't doing very well yesterday," she said with a sigh. "Maybe he's better this morning."

"I'll have a look at him before I go out." He glanced out at the snow. "Don't try to get back to the cabin again, will you? You can't get through McNaber's traps without knowing where they are."

He actually sounded worried. She studied his hard face quietly. That was nice. Unless, of course, he was only worried that she might get laid up and he'd have to put up with her for even longer.

"Is the snow ever going to stop?" she asked.

"Hard to say," he told her. "I've seen it worse than this even earlier in the year. But we'll manage, I suppose."

"I suppose." She glared at him.

He pulled on his coat and buttoned it, propping his hat over one eye. "In a temper this morning, are we?" he mused.

His eyes were actually twinkling. She shifted back against the counter, grateful that Harry had gone off to clean the bedrooms. "I'm not in a temper. Cheap little tarts don't have tempers."

One eyebrow went up. "I called you that, didn't I?" He let his eyes run slowly down her body. "You shouldn't have kissed me like that. I'm not used to aggressive women."

"Rest assured that I'll never attack you again, Goody Two-Shoes."

He chuckled softly. "Won't you? Well, disappointment is a man's lot, I suppose."

Her eyes widened. She wasn't sure she'd even heard him. "You were horrible to me!"

"I guess I was." His dark eyes held hers, making little chills up and down her spine at the intensity of the gaze. "I thought you were playing games. You know, a little harmless fun at the hick's expense."

"I don't know how to play games with men," she said stiffly, "and nobody, anywhere, could call you a hick with a straight face. You're a very masculine man with a keen mind and an overworked sense of responsibility. I wouldn't make fun of you even if I could."

His dark eyes smiled into hers. "In that case, we might call a truce for the time being."

"Do you think you could stand being nice to me?" she asked sourly. "I mean, it would be a strain, I'm sure."

"I'm not a bad man," he pointed out. "I just don't know much about women, or hadn't that thought occurred?"

She searched his eyes. "No."

"We'll have to have a long talk about it one of these days." He pulled the hat down over his eyes. "I'll check on the calves for you."

"Thanks." She watched him go, her heart racing at the look in his eyes just before he closed the door. She was more nervous of him now than ever, but she didn't know what to do about it. She was hoping that the chinook would come before she had to start worrying too much. She was too confused to know what to do anymore.

Chapter Five

Amanda finished the breakfast dishes before she went out to the barn. Quinn was still there, his dark eyes quiet on the smallest of the three calves. It didn't take a fortune-teller to see that something was badly wrong. The small animal lay on its side, its dull, lackluster red-and-white coat showing its ribs, its eyes glazed and unseeing while it fought to breathe.

She knelt beside Quinn and he glanced at her with concern.

"You'd better go back in the house, honey," he said.

Her eyes slid over the small calf. She'd seen pets die over the years, and now she knew the signs. The calf was dying. Quinn knew it, too, and was trying to shield her.

That touched her, oddly, more than anything he'd said or done since she'd been on Ricochet. She looked up at him. "You're a nice man, Quinn Sutton," she said softly.

He drew in a slow breath. "When I'm not taking bites out of you, you mean?" he replied. "It hurts like hell when you back away from me. You'll never know how sorry I am for what happened yesterday."

One shock after another. At least it took her mind off the poor, laboring creature beside them. "I'm sorry, too," she said. "I shouldn't have been so…" She stopped, averting her eyes. "I don't know much about men, Quinn," she said finally. "I've spent my whole adult life backing away from involvement, emotional or physical. I know how to flirt, but not much more." She risked a glance at him, and relaxed when she saw his face. "My aunt is Mr. Durning's lover, you know. She's an artist. A little flighty, but nice. I've…never had a lover."

He nodded quietly. "I've been getting that idea since we wound up near McNaber's cabin yesterday. You reacted pretty violently for an experienced woman." He looked away from her. That vulnerability in her pretty face was working on him again. "Go inside now. I can deal with this."

"I'm not afraid of death," she returned. "I saw my mother die. It wasn't scary at all. She just closed her eyes."

His dark eyes met hers and locked. "My father went the same way." He looked back down at the calf. "It won't be long now."

She sat down in the hay beside him and slid her small hand into his big one. He held it for a long moment. Finally his voice broke the silence. "It's over. Go have a cup of coffee. I'll take care of him."

She hadn't meant to cry, but the calf had been so little and helpless. Quinn pulled her close, holding her with quiet comfort, while she cried. Then he wiped the tears away with his thumbs and smiled gently. "You'll do," he murmured, thinking that sensitivity and courage was a nice combination in a woman.

She was thinking the exact same thing about him. She managed a watery smile and with one last, pitying look at the calf, she went into the house.

Elliot would miss it, as would she, she thought. Even Quinn had seemed to care about it, because she saw him occasionally sitting by it, petting it, talking to it. He loved little things. It was evident in all the kittens and puppies around the place, and in the tender care he took of all his cattle and calves. And although Quinn cursed old man McNaber's traps, Elliot had told her that he stopped by every week to check on the dour old man and make sure he had enough chopped wood and supplies. For a taciturn iceman, he had a surprisingly warm center.

She told Harry what had happened and sniffed a little while she drank black coffee. "Is there anything I can do?" she asked.

He smiled. "You do enough," he murmured. "Nice to have some help around the place."

"Quinn hasn't exactly thought so," she said dryly.

"Oh, yes he has," he said firmly as he cleared away the dishes they'd eaten his homemade soup and corn bread in. "Quinn could have taken you to Mrs. Pearson down the mountain if he'd had a mind to. He doesn't have to let you stay here. Mrs. Pearson would be glad of the company." He glanced at her and grinned at her perplexed expression. "He's been watching you lately. Sees the way you sew up his shirts and make curtains and patch pillows. It's new to him, having a woman about. He has a hard time with change."

"Don't we all?" Amanda said softly, remembering how clear her own life had been until that tragic night. But it was nice to know that Quinn had been watching her. Certainly she'd been watching him. And this morning, everything seemed to have changed between them. "When will it thaw?" she asked, and now she was dreading it, not anticipating it. She didn't want to leave Ricochet. Or Quinn.

Harry shrugged. "Hard to tell. Days. Weeks. This is raw mountain country. Can't predict a chinook. Plenty think they can, though," he added, and proceeded to tell her about a Blackfoot who predicted the weather with jars of bear grease.

She was much calmer but still sad when Quinn finally came back inside.

He spared her a glance before he shucked his coat, washed his hands and brawny forearms and dried them on a towel.

He didn't say anything to her, and Harry, sensing the atmosphere, made himself scarce after he'd poured two cups of coffee for them.

"Are you all right?" he asked her after a minute, staring down at her bent head.

"Sure." She forced a smile. "He was so little, Quinn." She stopped when her voice broke and lowered her eyes to the table. "I guess you think I'm a wimp."

"Not really." Without taking time to think about the consequences, his lean hands pulled her up by the arms, holding her in front of him so that her eyes were on a level with his deep blue, plaid flannel shirt. The sleeves were rolled up, and it was open at the throat, where thick, dark hair curled out of it. He looked and smelled fiercely masculine and Amanda's knees weakened at the unexpected proximity. His big hands bit into her soft flesh, and she wondered absently if he realized just how strong he was.

The feel of him so close was new and terribly exciting, especially since he'd reached for her for the first time. She didn't know what to expect, and her heart was going wild. She raised her eyes to his throat. His pulse was jumping and she stared at it curiously, only half aware of his hold and the sudden increase of his breathing.

He was having hell just getting a breath. The scent of her was in his nostrils, drowning him. Woman smell. Sweet and warm. His teeth clenched. It was bad enough having to look at her, but this close, she made his blood run hot and wild as it hadn't since he was a young man. He didn't know what he was doing, but the need for her had haunted him for days. He wanted so badly to kiss her, the way she'd kissed him the day before, but in a different way. He wasn't quite sure how to go about it.

"You smell of flowers," he said roughly.

That was an interesting comment from a nonpoetic

man. She smiled a little to herself. "It's my shampoo," she murmured.

He drew in a steadying breath. "You don't wear your hair down at all, do you?"

"Just at night," she replied, aware that his face was closer than it had been, because she could feel his breath on her forehead. He was so tall and overwhelming this close. He made her feel tiny and very feminine.

"I'm sorry about the calf, Amanda," he said. "We lose a few every winter. It's part of ranching."

The shock of her name on his lips made her lift her head. She stared up at him curiously, searching his dark, quiet eyes. "I suppose so. I shouldn't have gotten so upset, though. I guess men don't react to things the way women do."

"You don't know what kind of man I am," he replied. His hands felt vaguely tremulous. He wondered if she knew the effect she had on him. "As it happens, I get attached to the damned things, too." He sighed heavily. "Little things don't have much choice in this world. They're at the mercy of everything and everybody."

Her eyes softened as they searched his. He sounded different when he spoke that way. Vulnerable. Almost tender. And so alone.

"You aren't really afraid of me, are you?" he asked, as if the thought was actually painful.

She grimaced. "No. Of course not. I was ashamed of what I'd done, and a little nervous of the way you reacted to it, that's all. I know you wouldn't hurt me." She drew in a soft breath. "I know you resent having me here," she confessed. "I resented having to depend on you for shelter. But the snow will melt soon, and I'll leave."

"I thought you'd had lovers," he confessed quietly. "The way you acted...well, it just made all those suspicions worse. I took you at face value."

Amanda smiled. "It was all put-on. I don't even know why I did it. I guess I was trying to live up to your image of me."

He loved the sensation her sultry black eyes aroused in him. Unconsciously his hands tightened on her arms. "You haven't had a man, ever?" he asked huskily.

The odd shadow of dusky color along his cheekbones fascinated her. She wondered about the embarrassment asking the question had caused. "No. Not ever," she stammered.

"The way you look?" he asked, his eyes eloquent.

"What do you mean, the way I look?" she said, bristling.

"You know you're beautiful," he returned. His eyes darkened. "A woman who looks like you do could have her pick of men."

"Maybe," she agreed without conceit. "But I've never wanted a man in my life, to be dominated by a man. I've made my own way in the world. I'm a musician," she told him, because that didn't give away very much. "I support myself by playing a keyboard."

"Yes, Elliot told me. I've heard you play for him. You're good." He felt his heartbeat increasing as he looked at her.

She smelled so good. He looked down at her mouth and remembered how it had felt for those few seconds when he'd given in to her playful kiss. Would she let him do it? He knew so little about those subtle messages women were supposed to send out when they wanted a man's lovemaking. He couldn't read Amanda's eyes. But her lips were parted and her breath was coming rather fast from between them. Her face was flushed, but that could have been from the cold.

She gazed up into his eyes and couldn't look away. He wasn't handsome. His face really seemed as if it had been chipped away from the side of the Rockies, all craggy angles and hard lines. His mouth was thin and faintly cruel looking. She wondered if it would feel as hard as it looked if he was in control, dominating her lips. It had been different when she'd kissed him….

"What are you thinking?" he asked huskily, because her eyes were quite frankly on his mouth.

"I…was wondering," she whispered hesitantly, "how hard your mouth would be if you kissed me."

His heart stopped and then began to slam against his chest. "Don't you know already?" he asked, his voice deeper, harsher. "You kissed me."

"Not…properly."

He wondered what she meant by properly. His wife had only kissed him when she had to, and only in the very beginning of their courtship. She always pushed him away and murmured something about mussing her makeup. He couldn't remember one time when he'd kissed anyone with passion, or when he'd ever been kissed by anyone else like that.

His warm, rough hands let go of her arms and came up to frame her soft oval face. His breath shuddered out of his chest when she didn't protest as he bent his dark head.

"Show me what you mean…by properly," he whispered.

He had to know, she thought dizzily. But his lips touched hers and she tasted the wind and the sun on them. Her hands clenched the thick flannel shirt and she resisted searching for buttons, but she wanted very much to touch that thicket of black, curling hair that covered his broad chest. She went on her tiptoes and pushed her mouth against his, the force of the action parting his lips as well as her own, and she felt him stiffen and heard him groan as their open mouths met.

She dropped back onto her feet, her wide, curious eyes meeting his stormy ones.

"Like that?" he whispered gruffly, bending to repeat the action with his own mouth. "I've never done it…with my mouth open," he said, biting off the words against her open lips.

She couldn't believe he'd said that. She couldn't believe, either, the sensations rippling down to her toes when she gave in to the force of his ardor and let him kiss her that way, his mouth rough and demanding as one big hand slid to the back of her head to press her even closer.

A soft sound passed her lips, a faint moan, because she couldn't get close enough to him. Her breasts were flattened against his hard chest, and she felt his heartbeat against them. But she wanted to be closer than that, enveloped, crushed to him.

"Did I hurt you?" he asked in a shaky whisper that touched her lips.

"What?" she whispered back dizzily.

"You made a sound."

Her eyes searched his, her own misty and half closed and rapt. "I moaned," she whispered. Her nails stroked him through the shirt and she liked the faint tautness of his body as he reacted to it. "I like being kissed like that." She rubbed her forehead against him, smelling soap and detergent and pure man. "Could we take your shirt off?" she whispered.

Her hands were driving him nuts, and he was wondering the same thing himself. But somewhere in the back of his mind he remembered that Harry was around, and that it might look compromising if he let her touch him that way. In fact, it might get compromising, because he felt his body harden in a way it hadn't since his marriage. And because it made him vulnerable and he didn't want her to feel it, he took her gently by the arms and moved her away from him with a muffled curse.

"Harry," he said, his breath coming deep and rough.

She colored. "Oh, yes." She moved back, her eyes a little wild.

"You don't have to look so threatened. I won't do it again," he said, misunderstanding her retreat. Had he frightened her again?

"Oh, it's not that. You didn't frighten me." She lowered her eyes to the floor. "I'm just wondering if you'll think I'm easy...."

He scowled. "Easy?"

"I don't usually come on to men," she said softly. "And I've never asked anybody to take his shirt off before." She glanced up at him, fascinated by the expression on his face. "Well, I haven't," she said belligerently. "And you don't have to worry; I won't throw myself at you anymore, either. I just got carried away in the heat of the moment...."

His eyebrows arched. None of what she was saying made sense. "Like you did yesterday?" he mused, liking the color that came and went in her face. "I did accuse you of throwing yourself at me," he said on a long sigh.

"Yes. You seem to think I'm some sort of liberated sex maniac."

His lips curled involuntarily. "Are you?" he asked, and sounded interested.

She stamped her foot. "Stop that. I don't want to stay here anymore!"

"I'm not sure it's a good idea myself," he mused, watching her eyes glitter with rage. God, she was pretty! "I mean, if you tried to seduce me, things could get sticky."

The red in her cheeks got darker. "I don't have any plans to seduce you."

"Well, if you get any, you'd better tell me in advance," he said, pulling a cigarette from his shirt pocket. "Just so I can be prepared to fight you off."

That dry drawl confused her. Suddenly he was a different man, full of male arrogance and amusement. Things had shifted between them during that long, hard kiss. The distance had shortened, and he was looking at her with an expression she couldn't quite understand.

"How did you get to the age you are without winding up in someone's bed?" Quinn asked then. He'd wondered at her shyness with him and then at the way she blushed all the time. He didn't know much about women, but he wanted to know everything about her.

Amanda wrapped her arms around herself and shrugged. When he lit his cigarette and still stood there waiting for an answer, she gave in and replied. "I couldn't give up control," she said simply. "All my life I'd been dominated and pushed around by my father. Giving in to a man seemed like throwing away my rights as a person. Especially giving in to a man in bed," she stammered, averting her gaze. "I don't think there's anyplace in the world where a man is more the master than in a bedroom, despite all the liberation and freedom of modern life."

"And you think that women should dominate there."

She looked up. "Well, not dominate." She hesitated. "But a woman shouldn't be used just because she's a woman."

His thin mouth curled slightly. "Neither should a man."

"I wasn't using you," she shot back.

"Did I accuse you?" he returned innocently.

She swallowed. "No, I guess not." She folded her arms over her breasts, wincing because the tips were hard and unexpectedly tender.

"That hardness means you feel desire," he said, grinning when she gaped and then glared at him. She made him feel about ten feet tall. "I read this book about sex," he continued. "It didn't make much sense to me at the time, but it's beginning to."

"I am not available as a living model for sex education!"

He shrugged. "Suit yourself. But it's a hell of a loss to my education."

"You don't need educating," she muttered. "You were married."

He nodded. "Sure I was." He pursed his lips and let his eyes run lazily over her body. "Except that she never wanted me, before or after I married her."

Amanda's lips parted. "Oh, Quinn," she said softly. "I'm sorry."

"So was I, at the time." He shook his head. "I used to wonder at first why she pulled back every time I kissed her. I guess she was suffering it until she could get me to put the ring on her finger. Up until then, I thought it was her scruples that kept me at arm's length. But she never had many morals." He stared at Amanda curiously, surprised at how easy it was to tell her things he'd never shared with another human being. "After I found out what she really was, I couldn't have cared less about sharing her bed."

"No, I don't suppose so," she agreed.

He lifted the cigarette to his lips and his eyes narrowed as he studied her. "Elliot's almost thirteen," he said. "He's been my whole life. I've taken care of him and done for him. He knows there's no blood tie between us, but I love him and he loves me. In all the important ways, I'm his father and he's my son."

"He loves you very much," she said with a smile. "He talks about you all the time."

"He's a good boy." He moved a little closer, noticing how she tensed when he came close. He liked that reaction a lot. It told him that she was aware of him, but shy and reticent. "You don't have men," he said softly. "Well, I don't have women."

"Not for…a few months?" she stammered, because she couldn't imagine that he was telling the truth.

He shrugged his powerful shoulders. "Well, not for a bit longer than that. Not much opportunity up here. And I can't go off and leave Elliot while I tomcat around town. It's been a bit longer than thirteen years."

"A bit?"

He looked down at her with a curious, mocking smile. "When I was a boy, I didn't know how to get girls. I was big and clumsy and shy, so it was the other boys who scored." He took another draw, a slightly jerky one, from his cigarette. "I still have the same problem around most women. It's not so much hatred as a lack of ability, and shyness. I don't know how to come on to a woman," he confessed with a faint smile.

Amanda felt as if the sun had just come out. She smiled back. "Don't you, really?" she asked softly. "I thought it was just that you found me lacking, or that I wasn't woman enough to interest you."

He could have laughed out loud at that assumption. "Is that why you called me Goody Two-Shoes?" he asked pleasantly.

She laughed softly. "Well, that was sort of sour grapes." She lowered her eyes to his chest. "It hurt my feelings that you thought I didn't have any morals, when I'd never made one single move toward any other man in my whole life."

He felt warm all over from that shy confession. It took down the final brick in his wall of reserve. She wasn't like any woman he'd ever known. "I'm glad to know that. But you and I have more in common than a lack of technique," he said, hesitating.

"We do?" she asked. Her soft eyes held his. "What do you mean?"

He turned and deliberately put out his cigarette in the ashtray on the table beside them. He straightened and looked down at her speculatively for a few seconds before he went for broke. "Well, what I mean, Amanda," he replied finally, "is that you aren't the only virgin on the place."

Chapter Six

"I didn't hear that," Amanda said, because she knew she hadn't. Quinn Sutton couldn't have told her that he was a virgin.

"Yes, you did," he replied. "And it's not all that far-fetched. Old McNaber down the hill's never had a woman, and he's in his seventies. There are all sorts of reasons why men don't get experience. Morals, scruples, isolation, or even plain shyness. Just like women," he added with a meaningful look at Amanda. "I couldn't go to bed with somebody just to say I'd had sex. I'd have to care about her, want her, and I'd want her to care about me. There are idealistic people all over the world who never find that particular combination, so they stay celibate. And really, I think that people who sleep around indiscriminately are in the minority even in these liberated times. Only a fool takes that sort of risk with the health dangers what they are."

"Yes, I know." She watched him with fascinated eyes. "Haven't you ever…wanted to?" she asked.

"Well, that's the problem, you see," he replied, his dark eyes steady on her face.

"What is?"

"I have…wanted to. With you."

She leaned back against the counter, just to make sure she didn't fall down. "With me?"

"That first night you came here, when I was so sick, and your hair drifted down over my naked chest. I shivered, and you thought it was with fever," he mused. "It was a fever, all right, but it didn't have anything to do with the virus."

Her fingers clenched the counter. She'd wondered about his violent reaction at the time, but it seemed so unlikely that a cold man like Quinn Sutton would feel that way about a woman. He was human, she thought absently, watching him.

"That's why I've given you such a hard time," he confessed with narrowed, quiet eyes. "I don't know how to handle desire. I can't throw you over my shoulder and carry you upstairs, not with Elliot and Harry around, even if you were the kind of woman I thought at first you were. The fact that you're as innocent as I am only makes it more complicated."

She looked at him with new understanding, as fascinated by him as he seemed to be by her. He wasn't that bad looking, she mused. And he was terribly strong, and sexy in an earthy kind of way. She especially liked his eyes. They were much more expressive than that poker face.

"Fortunately for you, I'm kind of shy, too," she murmured.

"Except when you're asking men to take their clothes off," Quinn said, nodding.

Harry froze in the doorway with one foot lifted while Amanda gaped at him and turned red.

"Put your foot down and get busy," Quinn muttered irritably. "Why were you standing there?"

"I was getting educated." Harry chuckled. "I didn't know Amanda asked people to take their clothes off!"

"Only me," Quinn said, defending her. "And just my shirt. She's not a bad girl."

"Will you stop!" Amanda buried her face in her hands. "Go away!"

"I can't. I live here," Quinn pointed out. "Did I smell brandy on your breath?" he asked suddenly.

Harry grimaced even as Amanda's eyes widened. "Well, yes you do," he confessed. "She was upset and crying and all…"

"How much did you give her?" Quinn persisted.

"Only a few drops," Harry promised. "In her coffee, to calm her."

"Harry, how could you!" Amanda laughed. The coffee had tasted funny, but she'd been too upset to wonder why.

"Sorry," Harry murmured dryly. "But it seemed the thing to do."

"It backfired," Quinn murmured and actually smiled.

"You stop that!" Amanda told him. She sat down at the table. "I'm not tipsy. Harry, I'll peel those apples for the pie if I can have a knife."

"Let me get out of the room first, if you please," Quinn said, glancing at her dryly. "I saw her measuring my back for a place to put it."

"I almost never stab men with knives," she promised impishly.

He chuckled. He reached for his hat and slanted it over his brow, buttoning his old shepherd's coat because it was snowing outside again.

Amanda looked past him, the reason for all the upset coming back now as she calmed down. Her expression became sad.

"If you stay busy, you won't think about it so much," Quinn said quietly. "It's part of life, you know."

"I know." She managed a smile. "I'm fine. Despite Harry," she added with a chuckle, watching Harry squirm before he grinned back.

Quinn's dark eyes met hers warmly for longer than he meant, so that she blushed. He tore his eyes away finally, and went outside.

Harry didn't say anything, but his smile was speculative.

Elliot came home from school and persuaded Amanda to get out the keyboard and give him some more pointers. He admitted that he'd been bragging about her to his classmates and that she was a professional musician.

"Where do you play, Amanda?" Elliot asked curiously, and he stared at her with open puzzlement. "You look so familiar somehow."

She sat very still on the sofa and tried to stay calm. Elliot had already told her that he liked rock music and she knew Quinn had hidden his tapes. If there was a tape in his collection by Desperado, it would have her picture on the cover along with that of her group.

"Do I really look familiar?" she asked with a smile. "Maybe I just have that kind of face."

"Have you played with orchestras?" he persisted.

"No. Just by myself, sort of. In nightclubs," she improvised. Well, she had once sung in a nightclub, to fill in for a friend. "Mostly I do backup. You know, I play with groups for people who make tapes and records."

"Wow!" he exclaimed. "I guess you know a lot of famous singers and musicians?"

"A few," she agreed.

"Where do you work?"

"In New York City, in Nashville," she told him. "All over. Wherever I can find work."

He ran his fingers up and down the keyboard. "How did you ever wind up here?"

"I needed a rest," she said. "My aunt is…a friend of Mr. Durning. She asked him if I could borrow the cabin, and he said it was all right. I had to get away from work for a while."

"This doesn't bother you, does it? Teaching me to play, I mean?" he asked and looked concerned.

"No, Elliot, it doesn't bother me. I'm enjoying it." She ran a scale and taught it to him, then showed him the cadences of the chords that went with it.

"It's so complicated," he moaned.

"Of course it is. Music is an art form, and it's complex. But once you learn these basics, you can do anything with a chord. For instance…"

She played a tonic chord, then made an impromptu song from its subdominant and seventh chords and the second inversion of them. Elliot watched, fascinated.

"I guess you've studied for years," he said with a sigh.

"Yes, I have, and I'm still learning," she said. "But I love it more than anything. Music has been my whole life."

"No wonder you're so good at it."

She smiled. "Thanks, Elliot."

"Well, I'd better get my chores done before supper," he said, sighing. He handed Amanda the keyboard. "See you later."

She nodded. He went out. Harry was feeding the two calves that were still alive, so presumably he'd tell Elliot about the one that had died. Amanda hadn't had the heart to talk about it.

Her fingers ran over the keyboard lovingly and she began to play a song that her group had recorded two years back, a sad, dreamy ballad about hopeless love that had won them a Grammy. She sang it softly, her pure, sweet voice haunting in the silence of the room as she tried to sing for the first time in weeks.

"Elliot, for Pete's sake, turn that radio down, I'm on

the telephone!" came a pleading voice from the back of the house.

She stopped immediately, flushing. She hadn't realized that Harry had come back inside. Thank God he hadn't seen her, or he might have asked some pertinent questions. She put the keyboard down and went to the kitchen, relieved that her singing voice was back to normal again.

Elliot was morose at the supper table. He'd heard about the calf and he'd been as depressed as Amanda had. Quinn didn't look all that happy himself. They all picked at the delicious chili Harry had whipped up; nobody had much of an appetite.

After they finished, Elliot did his homework while Amanda put the last stitches into a chair cover she was making for the living room. Quinn had gone off to do his paperwork and Harry was making bread for the next day.

It was a long, lazy night. Elliot went to bed at eight-thirty and not much later Harry went to his room.

Amanda wanted to wait for Quinn to come back, but something in her was afraid of the new way he looked at her. He was much more a threat now than he had been before, because she was looking at him with new and interested eyes. She was drawn to him more than ever. But he didn't know who she really was, and she couldn't tell him. If she were persuaded into any kind of close relationship with him, it could lead to disaster.

So when Elliot went to bed, so did Amanda. She sat at

the dresser and let down her long hair, brushing it with slow, lazy strokes, when there was a knock at the door.

She was afraid that it might be Quinn, and she hesitated. But surely he wouldn't make any advances toward her unless she showed that she wanted them. Of course he wouldn't.

She opened the door, but it wasn't Quinn. It was Elliot. And as he stared at her, wheels moved and gears clicked in his young mind. She was wearing a long granny gown in a deep beige, a shade that was too much like the color of the leather dress she wore onstage. With her hair loose and the color of the gown, Elliot made the connection he hadn't made the first time he saw her hair down.

"Yes?" she prompted, puzzled by the way he was looking at her. "Is something wrong, Elliot?"

"Uh, no," he stammered. "Uh, I forgot to say good-night. Good night!" He grinned.

He turned, red-faced, and beat a hasty retreat, but not to his own room. He went to his father's and searched quickly through the hidden tapes until he found the one he wanted. He held it up, staring blankly at the cover. There were four men who looked like vicious bikers surrounding a beautiful woman in buckskin with long, elegant, blond hair. The group was one of his favorites—Desperado. And the woman was Mandy. Amanda. His Amanda. He caught his breath. Boy, would she be in for it if his dad found out who she was! He put the tape into his pocket, feeling guilty for taking it when Quinn had told him not to. But these were desperate circumstances. He had to protect Amanda until he could figure out how to tell her that he knew the truth. Meanwhile, having her in the same house with him was sheer undiluted heaven! Imagine, a singing star that famous in his house. If only he could tell the guys! But that was too risky, because it might get back to Dad. He sighed. Just his luck, to find a rare jewel and have to hide it to keep someone from stealing it. He closed the door to Quinn's bedroom and went quickly back to his own.

Amanda slept soundly, almost missing breakfast. Outside, the sky looked blue for the first time in days, and she noticed that the snow had stopped.

"Chinook's coming," Harry said with a grin. "I knew it would."

Quinn's dark eyes studied Amanda's face. "Well, it will be a few days before they get the power lines back up again," he muttered. "So don't get in an uproar about it."

"I'm not in an uproar," Harry returned with a frown. "I just thought it was nice that we'll be able to get off the mountain and lay in some more supplies. I'm getting tired of beef. I want a chicken."

"So do I!" Elliot said fervently. "Or bear, or beaver or moose, anything but beef!"

Quinn glared at both of them. "Beef pays the bills around here," he reminded them.

They looked so guilty that Amanda almost laughed out loud.

"I'm sorry, Dad," Elliot sighed. "I'll tell my stomach to shut up about it."

Quinn's hard face relaxed. "It's all right. I wouldn't mind a chicken stew, myself."

"That's the spirit," Elliot said. "What are we going to do today? It's Saturday," he pointed out. "No school."

"You could go out with me and help me feed cattle," Quinn said.

"I'll stay here and help Harry," Amanda said, too quickly.

Quinn's dark eyes searched hers. "Harry can manage by himself. You can come with me and Elliot."

"You'll enjoy it," Elliot assured her. "It's a lot of fun. The cattle see us and come running. Well, as well as they can run in several feet of snow," he amended.

It was fun, too. Amanda sat on the back of the sled with Elliot and helped push the bales of hay off. Quinn cut the strings so the cattle could get to the hay. They did come running, reminding Amanda so vividly of women at a sale that she laughed helplessly until the others had to be told why she was laughing.

They came back from the outing in a new kind of harmony, and for the first time, Amanda understood what it felt like to be part of a family. She looked at Quinn and wondered how it would be if she never had to leave here, if she could stay with him and Elliot and Harry forever.

But she couldn't, she told herself firmly. She had to remember that this was a vacation, with the real world just outside the door.

Elliot was allowed to stay up later on Saturday night, so they watched a science-fiction movie together while

Quinn grumbled over paperwork. The next morning they went to church on the sled, Amanda in the one skirt and blouse she'd packed, trying not to look too conspicuous as Quinn's few neighbors carefully scrutinized her.

When they got back home, she was all but shaking. She felt uncomfortable living with him, as if she really was a fallen woman now. He cornered her in the kitchen while she was washing dishes to find out why she was so quiet.

"I didn't think about the way people would react if you went with us this morning," he said quietly. "I wouldn't have subjected you to that if I'd just thought."

"It's okay," she said, touched by his concern. "Really. It was just a little uncomfortable."

He sighed, searching her face with narrowed eyes. "Most people around here know how I feel about women," he said bluntly. "That was why you attracted so much attention. People get funny ideas about woman haters who take in beautiful blondes."

"I'm not beautiful," she stammered shyly.

He stepped toward her, towering over her in his dress slacks and good white shirt and sedate gray tie. He looked handsome and strong and very masculine. She liked the spicy cologne he wore. "You're beautiful, all right," he murmured. His big hand touched her cheek, sliding down it slowly, his thumb brushing with soft abrasion over her full mouth.

Her breath caught as she looked up into his dark, soft eyes. "Quinn?" she whispered.

He drew her hands out of the warm, soapy water, still holding her gaze, and dried them on a dishcloth. Then he guided them, first one, then the other, up to his shoulders.

"Hold me," he whispered as his hands smoothed over her waist and brought her gently to him. "I want to kiss you."

She shivered from the sensuality in that soft whisper, lifting her face willingly.

He bent, brushing his mouth lazily over hers. "Isn't this how we did it before?" he breathed, parting his lips as they touched hers. "I like the way it feels to kiss you like this. My spine tingles."

"So…does mine." She slid her hands hesitantly into the thick, cool strands of hair at his nape and she went on tiptoe to give him better access to her mouth.

He accepted the invitation with quiet satisfaction, his mouth growing slowly rougher and hungrier as it fed on hers. He made a sound under his breath and all at once he bent, lifting her clear off the floor in a bearish embrace. His mouth bit hers, parting her lips, and she clung to him, moaning as the fever burned in her, too.

He let her go at once when Elliot called, "What?" from the living room. "Amanda, did you say something?"

"No… No, Elliot," she managed in a tone pitched a little higher than normal. Her answer appeared to satisfy him, because he didn't ask again. Harry was outside, but he probably wouldn't stay there long.

She looked up at Quinn, surprised by the intent stare

he was giving her. He liked the way she looked, her face flushed, her mouth swollen from his kisses, her eyes wide and soft and faintly misty with emotion.

"I'd better get out of here," he said hesitantly.

"Yes." She touched her lips with her fingers and he watched the movement closely.

"Did I hurt your mouth?" he asked quietly.

She shook her head. "No. Oh, no, not at all," she said huskily.

Quinn nodded and sighed heavily. He smiled faintly and then turned and went back into the living room without another word.

It was a long afternoon, made longer by the strain Amanda felt being close to him. She found her eyes meeting his across the room and every time she flushed from the intensity of the look. Her body was hungry for him, and she imagined the reverse was equally true. He watched her openly now, with smoldering hunger in his eyes. They had a light supper and watched a little more television. But when Harry went to his room and Elliot called good-night and went up to bed, Amanda weakly stayed behind.

Quinn finished his cigarette with the air of a man who had all night, and then got up and reached for Amanda, lifting her into his arms.

"There's nothing to be afraid of," he said quietly, searching her wide, apprehensive eyes as he turned and carried her into his study and closed the door behind them.

It was a fiercely masculine room. The furniture was dark wood with leather seats, the remnants of more prosperous times. He sat down in a big leather armchair with Amanda in his lap.

"It's private here," he explained. His hand moved one of hers to his shirt and pressed it there, over the tie. "Even Elliot doesn't come in when the door's shut. Do you still want to take my shirt off?" he asked with a warm smile.

Amanda sighed. "Well, yes," she stammered. "I haven't done this sort of thing before…."

"Neither have I, honey," he murmured dryly. "I guess we'll learn it together, won't we?"

She smiled into his dark eyes. "That sounds nice." She lowered her eyes to the tie and frowned when she saw how it was knotted.

"Here, I'll do it." He whipped it off with the ease of long practice and unlooped the collar button. "Now. You do the rest," he said deeply, and looked like a man anticipating heaven.

Her fingers, so adept on a keyboard, fumbled like two left feet while she worried buttons out of buttonholes. He was heavily muscled, tanned skin under a mass of thick, curling black hair. She remembered how it had looked that first night she'd been here, and how her hands had longed to touch it. Odd, because she'd never cared what was under a man's shirt before.

She pressed her hands flat against him, fascinated by the quick thunder of his heartbeat under them. She looked up into dark, quiet eyes.

"Shy?" he murmured dryly.

"A little. I always used to run a mile when men got this close."

The smile faded. His big hand covered hers, pressing them closer against him. "Wasn't there ever anyone you wanted?"

She shook her head. "The men I'm used to aren't like you. They're mostly rounders with a line a mile long. Everything is just casual to them, like eating mints." She flushed a little. "Intimacy isn't a casual thing to me."

"Or to me." His chest rose and fell heavily. He touched her bright head. "Now will you take your hair down, Amanda?" he asked gently. "I've dreamed about it for days."

Amanda smiled softly. "Have you, really? It's something of a nuisance to wash and dry, but I've gotten sort of used to it." She unbraided it and let it down, enchanted by Quinn's rapt fascination with it. His big hands tangled in it, as if he loved the feel of it. He brought his face down and kissed her neck through it, drawing her against his bare chest.

"It smells like flowers," he whispered.

"I washed it before church this morning," she replied. "Elliot loaned me his blow-dryer but it still took all of thirty minutes to get the dampness out." She relaxed with a sigh, nuzzling against his shoulder while her fingers tugged at the thick hair on his chest. "You feel furry. Like a bear," she murmured.

"You feel silky," he said against her hair. With his hand, Quinn tilted her face up to his and slid his mouth onto hers in the silent room. He groaned softly as her lips parted under his. His arms lifted and turned her, wrapped her up, so that her breasts were lying on his chest and her cheek was pressed against his shoulder by the force of the kiss.

He tasted of smoke and coffee, and if his mouth wasn't expert, it was certainly ardent. She loved kissing him. She curled her arms around his neck and turned a little more, hesitating when she felt the sudden stark arousal of his body.

Her eyes opened, looking straight into his, and she colored.

"I'm sorry," he murmured, starting to shift her, as if his physical reaction to her embarrassed him.

"No, Quinn," she said, resisting gently, holding his gaze as she relaxed into him, shivering a little. "There's nothing to apologize for. I…like knowing you want me," she whispered, lowering her eyes to his mouth. "It just takes a little getting used to. I've never let anyone hold me like this."

His chest swelled with that confession. His cheek rested on her hair as he settled into the chair and relaxed himself, taking her weight easily. "I'm glad about that," he said. "But it isn't just physical with me. I wanted you to know."

She smiled against his shoulder. "It isn't just physical with me, either." She touched his hard face, her fingers moving over his mouth, loving the feel of it, the smell of his body, the warmth and strength of it. "Isn't it incredible?" She laughed softly. "I mean, at our ages, to be so green…"

He laughed, too. It would have stung to have heard that

from any other woman, but Amanda was different. "I've never minded less being inexperienced," he murmured.

"Oh, neither have I." She sighed contentedly.

His big hand smoothed over her shoulder and down her back to her waist and onto her rib cage. He wanted very much to run it over her soft breast, but that might be too much too soon, so he hesitated.

Amanda smiled to herself. She caught his fingers and, lifting her face to his eyes, deliberately pulled them onto her breast, her lips parting at the sensation that steely warmth imparted. The nipple hardened and she caught her breath as Quinn's thumb rubbed against it.

"Have you ever seen a woman…without her top on?" she whispered, her long hair gloriously tangled around her face and shoulders.

"No," he replied softly. "Only in pictures." His dark eyes watched the softness his fingers were tracing. "I want to see you that way. I want to touch your skin…like this."

She drew his hand to the buttons of her blouse and lay quietly against him, watching his hard face as he loosened the buttons and pulled the fabric aside. The bra seemed to fascinate him. He frowned, trying to decide how it opened.

"It's a front catch," she whispered. She shifted a little, and found the catch. Her fingers trembled as she loosened it. Then, watching him, she carefully peeled it away from the high, taut throb of her breasts and watched him catch his breath.

"My God," he breathed reverently. He touched her

with trembling fingers, his eyes on the deep mauve of her nipples against the soft pink thrust of flesh, his body taut with sudden aching longing. "My God, I've never seen anything so beautiful."

He made her feel incredibly feminine. She closed her eyes and arched back against his encircling arm, moaning softly.

"Kiss me…there," she whispered huskily, aching for his mouth.

"Amanda…" He bent, delighting in her femininity, the obvious rapt fascination of the first time in her actions so that even if he hadn't suspected her innocence he would have now. His lips brushed over the silky flesh, and his hands lifted her to him, arched her even more. She tasted of flower petals, softly trembling under his warm, ardent mouth, her breath jerking past her parted lips as she lay with her eyes closed, lost in him.

"It's so sweet, Quinn," she whispered brokenly.

His lips brushed up her body to her throat, her chin, and then they locked against her mouth. He turned her slowly, so that her soft breasts lay against the muted thunder of his hair-roughened chest. He felt her shiver before her arms slid around his neck and she deliberately pressed closer, drawing herself against him and moaning.

"Am I hurting you?" he asked huskily, his mouth poised just above hers, a faint tremor in his arms. "Amanda, am I hurting you?"

"No." She opened her eyes and they were like black pools, soft and deep and quiet. With her blond hair waving at her temples, her cheeks, her shoulders, she was so beautiful that Quinn's breath caught.

He sat just looking at her, indulging his hunger for the sight of her soft breasts, her lovely face. She lay quietly in his arms without a protest, barely breathing as the spell worked on them.

"I'll live on this the rest of my life," he said roughly, his voice deep and soft in the room, with only an occasional crackle from the burning fire in the potbellied stove to break the silence.

"So will I," she whispered. She reached up to his face, touching it in silence, adoring its strength. "We shouldn't have done this," she said miserably. "It will make it…so much more difficult, when I have to leave. The thaw…!"

His fingers pressed against her lips. "One day at a time," he said. "Even if you leave, you aren't getting away from me completely. I won't let go. Not ever."

Tears stung her eyes. The surplus of emotion sent them streaming down her cheeks and Quinn caught his breath, brushing them away with his long fingers.

"Why?" he whispered.

"Nobody ever wanted to keep me before," she explained with a watery smile. "I've always felt like an extra person in the world."

He found that hard to imagine, as beautiful as she was. Perhaps her reticence made her of less value to sophisticated men, but not to him. He found her a pearl beyond price.

"You're not an extra person in my world," he replied. "You fit."

She sighed and nuzzled against him, closing her eyes as she drank in the exquisite pleasure of skin against skin, feeling his heart beat against her breasts. She shivered.

"Are you cold?" he asked.

"No. It's…so wonderful, feeling you like this," she whispered. "Quinn?"

He eased her back in his arm and watched her, understanding as she didn't seem to understand what was wrong.

His big, warm hand covered her breast, gently caressing it. "It's desire," he whispered softly. "You want me."

"Yes," she whispered.

"You can't have me. Not like this. Not in any honorable way." He sighed heavily and lifted her against him to hold her, very hard. "Now hold on, real tight. It will pass."

She shivered helplessly, drowning in the warmth of his body, in its heat against her breasts. But he was right. Slowly the ache began to ease away and her body stilled with a huge sigh.

"How do you know so much when you've…when you've never…?"

"I told you, I read a book. Several books." He chuckled, the laughter rippling over her sensitive breasts. "But, my God, reading was never like this!"

She laughed, too, and impishly bit his shoulder right through the cloth.

Then he shivered. "Don't," he said huskily.

She lifted her head, fascinated by the expression on his face. "Do you like it?" she asked hesitantly.

"Yes, I like it," he said with a rueful smile. "All too

much." He gazed down at her bareness and his eyes darkened. "I like looking at your breasts, too, but I think we'd better stop this while we can."

He tugged the bra back around her with a grimace and hooked the complicated catch. He deftly buttoned her blouse up to her throat, his eyes twinkling as they met hers.

"Disappointed?" he murmured. "So am I. I have these dreams every night of pillowing you on your delicious hair while we make love until you cry out."

She could picture that, too, and her breath lodged in her throat as she searched his dark eyes. His body, bare and moving softly over hers on white sheets, his face above her…

She moaned.

"Oh, I want it, too," he whispered, touching his mouth with exquisite tenderness to hers. "You in my bed, your arms around me, the mattress moving under us." He lifted his head, breathing unsteadily. "I might have to hurt you a little at first," he said gruffly. "You understand?"

"Yes." She smoothed his shirt, absently drawing it back together and fastening the buttons with a sense of possession. "But only a little, and I could bear it for what would come afterward," she said, looking up. "Because you'd pleasure me then."

"My God, would I," he whispered. "Pleasure you until you were exhausted." He framed her face in his hands and kissed her gently. "Please go to bed, Amanda, before I double over and start screaming."

She smiled against his mouth and let him put her on

her feet. She laughed when she swayed and he had to catch her.

"See what you do to me?" she mused. "Make me dizzy."

"Not half as dizzy as you make me." He smoothed down her long hair, his eyes adoring it. "Pretty little thing," he murmured.

"I'm glad you like me," she replied. "I'll do my best to stay this way for the next fifty years or so, with a few minor wrinkles."

"You'll be beautiful to me when you're an old lady. Good night."

She moved away from him with flattering reluctance, her dark eyes teasing his. "Are you sure you haven't done this before?" she asked with a narrow gaze. "You're awfully good at it for a beginner."

"That makes two of us," he returned dryly.

She liked the way he looked, with his hair mussed and his thin mouth swollen from her kisses, and his shirt disheveled. It made her feel a new kind of pride that she could disarrange him so nicely. After one long glance, she opened the door and went out.

"Lock your door," he whispered.

She laughed delightedly. "No, you lock yours the way you did the other night."

He shifted uncomfortably. "That was a low blow. I'm sorry."

"Oh, I was flattered," she corrected. "I've never felt so

dangerous in all my life. I wish I had one of those long, black silk negligees…"

"Will you get out of here?" he asked pleasantly. "I think I did mention the urge to throw you on the floor and ravish you?"

"With Elliot right upstairs? Fie, sir, think of my reputation."

"I'm trying to, if you'll just go to bed!"

"Very well, if I must." She started up the staircase, her black eyes dancing as they met his. She tossed her hair back and smiled at him. "Good night, Quinn."

"Good night, Amanda. Sweet dreams."

"They'll be sweet from now on," she agreed. She turned reluctantly and went up the staircase. He watched her until she went into her room and closed the door.

It wasn't until she was in her own room that she realized just what she'd done.

She wasn't some nice domestic little thing who could fit into Quinn's world without any effort. She was Amanda Corrie Callaway, who belonged to a rock group with a worldwide reputation. On most streets in most cities, her face was instantly recognizable. How was Quinn going to take the knowledge of who she really was—and the fact that she'd deceived him by leading him to think she was just a vacationing keyboard player? She groaned as she put on her gown. It didn't bear thinking about. From sweet heaven to nightmare in one hour was too much.

Chapter Seven

Amanda hardly slept from the combined shock of Quinn's ardor and her own guilt. How could she tell him the truth now? What could she say that would take away the sting of her deceit?

She dressed in jeans and the same button-up pink blouse she'd worn the night before and went down to breakfast.

Quinn looked up as she entered the room, his eyes warm and quiet.

"Good morning," she said brightly.

"Good morning yourself," Quinn murmured with a smile. "Sleep well?"

"Barely a wink," she said, sighing, her own eyes holding his.

He chuckled, averting his gaze before Elliot became suspicious. "Harry's out feeding your calves," he said, "and I'm on my way over to Eagle Pass to help one of my neighbors feed some stranded cattle. You'll have to stay with Elliot—it's teacher workday."

"I forgot," Elliot wailed, head in hands. "Can you imagine that I actually forgot? I could have slept until noon!"

"There, there," Amanda said, patting his shoulder. "Don't you want to learn some more chords?"

"Is that what you do?" Quinn asked curiously, because now every scrap of information he learned about her was precious. "You said you played a keyboard for a living. Do you teach music?"

"Not really," she said gently. "I play backup for various groups," she explained. "That rock music you hate…" she began uneasily.

"That's all right," Quinn replied, his face open and kind. "I was just trying to get a rise out of you. I don't mind it all that much, I guess. And playing backup isn't the same thing as putting on those god-awful costumes and singing suggestive lyrics. Well, I'm gone. Stay out of trouble, you two," he said as he got to his feet in the middle of Amanda's instinctive move to speak, to correct his assumption that all she did was play backup. She wanted to tell him the truth, but he winked at her and Elliot and got into his outdoor clothes before she could find a way to break the news. By the time her mind was working again, he was gone.

She sat back down, sighing. "Oh, Elliot, what a mess," she murmured, her chin in her hands.

"Is that what you call it?" he asked with a wicked smile. "Dad's actually grinning, and when he looked at you, you blushed. I'm not blind, you know. Do you like him, even if he isn't Mr. America?"

"Yes, I like him," she said with a shy smile, lowering her eyes. "He's a pretty special guy."

"I think so, myself. Eat your breakfast. I want to ask you about some new chords."

"Okay."

They were working on the keyboard when the sound of an approaching vehicle caught Amanda's attention. Quinn hadn't driven anything motorized since the snow had gotten so high.

"That's odd," Elliot said, peering out the window curtain. "It's a four-wheel drive… Oh, boy." He glanced at Amanda. "You aren't gonna like this."

She lifted her eyebrows. "I'm not?" she asked, puzzled.

The knock at the back door had Harry moving toward it before Amanda and Elliot could. Harry opened it and looked up and up and up. He stood there staring while Elliot gaped at the grizzly-looking man who loomed over him in a black Western costume, complete with hat.

"I'm looking for Mandy Callaway," he boomed.

"Hank!"

Amanda ran to the big man without thinking, to be lifted high in the air while he chuckled and kissed her warmly on one cheek, his whiskers scratching.

"Hello, peanut!" he grinned. "What are you doing up here? The old trapper down the hill said you hadn't been in Durning's cabin since the heavy snow came."

"Mr. Sutton took me in and gave me a roof over my head. Put me down," she fussed, wiggling.

He put her back on her feet while Harry and Elliot still gaped.

"This is Hank," she said, holding his enormous hand as she turned to face the others. "He's a good friend, and a terrific musician, and I'd really appreciate it if you wouldn't tell Quinn he was here just yet. I'll tell him myself. Okay?"

"Sure," Harry murmured. He shook his head. "You for real, or do you have stilts in them boots?"

"I used to be a linebacker for the Dallas Cowboys." Hank grinned.

"That would explain it," Harry chuckled. "Your secret's safe with me, Amanda." He excused himself and went to do the washing.

"Me, too," Elliot said, grinning, "as long as I get Mr. Shoeman's autograph before he leaves."

Amanda let out a long breath, her eyes frightened as they met Elliot's.

"That's right," Elliot said. "I already knew you were Mandy Callaway. I've got a Desperado tape. I took it out of Dad's drawer and hid it as soon as I recognized you. You'll tell him when the time's right. Won't you?"

"Yes, I will, Elliot," she agreed. "I'd have done it already except that...well, things have gotten a little complicated."

"You can say that again." Elliot led the way into the living room, watching Hank sit gingerly on a sofa that he dwarfed. "I'll just go make sure that tape's hidden," he said, leaving them alone.

"Complicated, huh?" Hank said. "I hear this Sutton man's a real woman hater."

"He was until just recently." She folded her hands in her lap. "And he doesn't approve of rock music." She sighed and changed the subject. "What's up, Hank?"

"We've got a gig at Larry's Lodge," he said. "I know, you don't want to. Listen for a minute. It's to benefit cystic fibrosis, and a lot of other stars are going to be in town for it, including a few pretty well-known singers." He named some of them and Amanda whistled. "See what I mean? It's strictly charity, or I wouldn't have come up here bothering you. The boys and I want to do it." His dark eyes narrowed. "Are you up to it?"

"I don't know. I tried to sing here a couple of times, and my voice seems to be good enough. No more lapses. But in front of a crowd..." She spread her hands. "I don't know, Hank."

"Here." He handed her three tickets to the benefit. "You think about it. If you can, come on up. Sutton might like the singers even if he doesn't care for our kind of music." He studied her. "You haven't told him, have you?"

She shook her head, smiling wistfully. "Haven't found the right way yet. If I leave it much longer, it may be too late."

"The girl's family sent you a letter," he said. "Thanking you for what you tried to do. They said you were her heroine...aw, now, Mandy, stop it!"

She collapsed in tears. He held her, rocking her, his face red with mingled embarrassment and guilt.

"Mandy, come on, stop that," he muttered. "It's all over and done with. You've got to get yourself together. You can't hide out here in the Tetons for the rest of your life."

"Can't I?" she wailed.

"No, you can't. Hiding isn't your style. You have to face the stage again, or you'll never get over it." He tilted her wet face. "Look, would you want somebody eating her guts out over you if you'd been Wendy that night? It wasn't your fault, damn it! It wasn't anybody's fault; it was an accident, pure and simple."

"If she hadn't been at the concert…"

"If, if, if," he said curtly. "You can't go back and change things to suit you. It was her time. At the concert, on a plane, in a car, however, it would still have been her time. Are you listening to me, Mandy?"

She dabbed her eyes with the hem of her blouse. "Yes, I'm listening."

"Come on, girl. Buck up. You can get over this if you set your mind to it. Me and the guys miss you, Mandy. It's not the same with just the four of us. People are scared of us when you aren't around."

That made her smile. "I guess they are. You do look scruffy, Hank," she murmured.

"You ought to see Johnson." He sighed. "He's let his beard go and he looks like a scrub brush. And Deke says he won't change clothes until you come back."

"Oh, my God," Amanda said, shuddering, "tell him I'll think hard about this concert, okay? You poor guys. Stay upwind of him."

"We're trying." He got up, smiling down at her. "Everything's okay. You can see the letter when you come to the lodge. It's real nice. Now stop beating yourself. Nobody else blames you. After all, babe, you risked your life trying to save her. Nobody's forgotten that, either."

She leaned against him for a minute, drawing on his strength. "Thanks, Hank."

"Anytime. Hey, kid, you still want that autograph?" he asked.

Elliot came back into the room with a pad and pen. "Do I!" he said, chuckling.

Hank scribbled his name and Desperado's curlicue logo underneath. "There you go."

"He's a budding musician," Amanda said, putting an arm around Elliot. "I'm teaching him the keyboard. One of these days, if we can get around Quinn, we'll have him playing backup for me."

"You bet." Hank chuckled, and ruffled Elliot's red hair. "Keep at it. Mandy's the very best. If she teaches you, you're taught."

"Thanks, Mr. Shoeman."

"Just Hank. See you at the concert. So long, Mandy."

"So long, pal."

"What concert?" Elliot asked excitedly when Hank had driven away.

Amanda handed him the three tickets. "To a benefit in

Jackson Hole. The group's going to play there. Maybe. If I can get up enough nerve to get back onstage again."

"What happened, Amanda?" he asked gently.

She searched his face, seeing compassion along with the curiosity, so she told him, fighting tears all the way.

"Gosh, no wonder you came up here to get away," Elliot said with more than his twelve years worth of wisdom. He shrugged. "But like he said, you have to go back someday. The longer you wait, the harder it's going to be."

"I know that," she groaned. "But Elliot, I…" She took a deep breath and looked down at the floor. "I love your father," she said, admitting it at last. "I love him very much, and the minute he finds out who I am, my life is over."

"Maybe not," he said. "You've got another week until the concert. Surely in all that time you can manage to tell him the truth. Can't you?"

"I hope so," she said with a sad smile. "You don't mind who I am, do you?" she asked worriedly.

"Don't be silly." He hugged her warmly. "I think you're super, keyboard or not."

She laughed and hugged him back. "Well, that's half the battle."

"Just out of curiosity," Harry asked from the doorway, "who was the bearded giant?"

"That was Hank Shoeman," Elliot told him. "He's the drummer for Desperado. It's a rock group. And Amanda—"

"—plays backup for him," she volunteered, afraid to give too much away to Harry.

"Well, I'll be. He's a musician?" Harry shook his head. "Would have took him for a bank robber," he mumbled.

"Most people do, and you should see the rest of the group." She grinned. "Don't give me away, Harry, okay? I promise I'll tell Quinn, but I've got to do it the right way."

"I can see that," he agreed easily. "Be something of a shock to him to meet your friend after dark, I imagine."

"I imagine so," she said, chuckling. "Thanks, Harry."

"My pleasure. Desperado, huh? Suits it, if the rest of the group looks like he does."

"Worse," she said, and shuddered.

"Strains the mind, don't it?" Harry went off into the kitchen and Amanda got up after a minute to help him get lunch.

Quinn wasn't back until late that afternoon. Nobody mentioned Hank's visit, but Amanda was nervous and her manner was strained as she tried not to show her fears.

"What's wrong with you?" he asked gently during a lull in the evening while Elliot did homework and Harry washed up. "You don't seem like yourself tonight."

She moved close to him, her fingers idly touching the sleeve of his red flannel shirt. "It's thawing outside," she said, watching her fingers move on the fabric. "It won't be long before I'll be gone."

He sighed heavily. His fingers captured hers and held them. "I've been thinking about that. Do you really have to get back?"

She felt her heart jump. Whatever he was offering, she

wanted to say yes and let the future take care of itself. But she couldn't. She grimaced. "Yes, I have to get back," she said miserably. "I have commitments to people. Things I promised to do." Her fingers clenched his. "Quinn, I have to meet some people at Larry's Lodge in Jackson Hole next Friday night." She looked up. "It's at a concert and I have tickets. I know you don't like rock, but there's going to be all kinds of music." Her eyes searched his. "Would you go with me? Elliot can come, too. I…want you to see what I do for a living."

"You and your keyboard?" he mused gently.

"Sort of," she agreed, hoping she could find the nerve to tell him everything before next Friday night.

"Okay," he replied. "A friend of mine works there—I used to be with the Ski Patrol there, too. Sure, I'll go with you." The smile vanished, and his eyes glittered down at her. "I'll go damned near anywhere with you."

Amanda slid her arms around him and pressed close, shutting her eyes as she held on for dear life. "That goes double for me, mountain man," she said half under her breath.

He bent his head, searching for her soft mouth. She gave it to him without a protest, without a thought for the future, gave it to him with interest, with devotion, with ardor. Her lips opened invitingly, and she felt his hands on her hips with a sense of sweet inevitability, lifting her into intimate contact with the aroused contours of his body.

"Frightened?" he whispered unsteadily just over her mouth when he felt her stiffen involuntarily.

"Of you?" she whispered back. "Don't be absurd. Hold me any way you want. I adore you…!"

He actually groaned as his mouth pressed down hard on hers. His arms contracted hungrily and he gave in to the pleasure of possession for one long moment.

Her eyes opened and she watched him, feeding on the slight contortion of his features, his heavy brows drawn over his crooked nose, his long, thick lashes on his cheek as he kissed her. She did adore him, she thought dizzily. Adored him, loved him, worshiped him. If only she could stay with him forever like this.

Quinn lifted his head and paused as he saw her watching him. He frowned slightly, then bent again. This time his eyes stayed open, too, and she went under as he deepened the kiss. Her eyes closed in self-defense and she moaned, letting him see the same vulnerability she'd seen in him. It was breathlessly sweet.

"This is an education," he said, laughing huskily, when he drew slightly away from her.

"Isn't it, though?" she murmured, moving his hands from her hips up to her waist and moving back a step from the blatant urgency of his body. "Elliot and Harry might come in," she whispered.

"I wouldn't mind," he said unexpectedly, searching her flushed face. "I'm not ashamed of what I feel for you, or embarrassed by it."

"This from a confirmed woman hater?" she asked with twinkling eyes.

"Well, not exactly confirmed anymore," he confessed. He

lifted her by the waist and searched her eyes at point-blank range until she trembled from the intensity of the look. "I couldn't hate you if I tried, Amanda," he said quietly.

"Oh, I hope not," she said fervently, thinking ahead to when she would have to tell him the truth about herself.

He brushed a lazy kiss across her lips. "I think I'm getting the hang of this," he murmured.

"I think you are, too," she whispered. She slid her arms around his neck and put her warm mouth hungrily against his, sighing when he caught fire and answered the kiss with feverish abandon.

A slight, deliberate cough brought them apart, both staring blankly at the small redheaded intruder.

"Not that I mind," Elliot said, grinning, "but you're blocking the pan of brownies Harry made."

"You can think of brownies at a time like this?" Amanda groaned. "Elliot!"

"Listen, he can think of brownies with a fever of a hundred and two," Quinn told her, still holding her on a level with his eyes. "I've seen him get out of a sickbed to pinch a brownie from the kitchen."

"I like brownies, too," Amanda confessed with a warm smile, delighted that Quinn didn't seem to mind at all that Elliot had seen them in a compromising position. That made her feel lighter than air.

"Do you?" Quinn smiled and brushed his mouth gently against hers, mindless of Elliot's blatant interest, before he put her back on her feet. "Harry makes his from scratch, with real baker's chocolate. They're something special."

"I'll bet they are. Here. I'll get the saucers," she volunteered, still catching her breath.

Elliot looked like the cat with the canary as she dished up brownies. It very obviously didn't bother him that Amanda and his dad were beginning to notice each other.

"Isn't this cozy?" he remarked as they went back into the living room and Amanda curled up on the sofa beside his dad, who never sat there.

"Cozy, indeed," Quinn murmured with a warm smile for Amanda.

She smiled back and laid her cheek against Quinn's broad chest while they watched television and ate brownies. She didn't move even when Harry joined them. And she knew she'd never been closer to heaven.

That night they were left discreetly alone, and she lay in Quinn's strong arms on the long leather couch in his office while wood burned with occasional hisses and sparks in the potbellied stove.

"I've had a raw deal with this place," he said eventually between kisses. "But it's good land, and I'm building a respectable herd of cattle. I can't offer you wealth or position, and we've got a ready-made family. But I can take care of you," he said solemnly, looking down into her soft eyes. "And you won't want for any of the essentials."

Her fingers touched his lean cheek hesitantly. "You don't know anything about me," she said. "When you know my background, you may not want me as much as you think you do." She put her fingers against his mouth. "You have to be sure."

"Damn it, I'm already sure," he muttered.

But was he? She was the first woman he'd ever been intimate with. Couldn't that blind him to her real suitability? What if it was just infatuation or desire? She was afraid to take a chance on his feelings, when she didn't really know what they were.

"Let's wait just a little while longer before we make any plans, Quinn. Okay?" she asked softly, turning in his hard arms so that her body was lying against his. "Make love to me," she whispered, moving her mouth up to his. "Please…"

He gave in with a rough groan, gathering her to him, crushing her against his aroused body. He wanted her beyond rational thought. Maybe she had cold feet, but he didn't. He knew what he wanted, and Amanda was it.

His hands smoothed the blouse and bra away with growing expertise and he fought out of his shirt so that he could feel her soft skin against his. But it wasn't enough. He felt her tremble and knew that it was reflected in his own arms and legs. He moved against her with a new kind of sensuousness, lifting his head to hold her eyes while he levered her onto her back and eased over her, his legs between both of hers in their first real intimacy.

She caught her breath, but she didn't push him to try to get away.

"It's just that new for you, isn't it?" he whispered huskily as his hips moved lazily over hers and he groaned. "God, it burns me to…feel you like this."

"I know." She arched her back, loving his weight, loving

the fierce maleness of his body. Her arms slid closer around him and she felt his mouth open on hers, his tongue softly searching as it slid inside, into an intimacy that made her moan. She began to tremble.

His lean hand slid under her, getting a firm grip, and he brought her suddenly into a shocking, shattering position that made her mindless with sudden need. She clutched him desperately, shuddering, her nails digging into him as the contact racked her like a jolt of raw electricity.

He pulled away from her without a word, shuddering as he lay on his back, trying to get hold of himself.

"I'm sorry," he whispered. "I didn't mean to let it go so far with us."

She was trembling, too, trying to breathe while great hot tears rolled down her cheeks. "Gosh, I wanted you," she whispered tearfully. "Wanted you so badly, Quinn!"

"As badly as I wanted you, honey," he said heavily. "We can't let things get that hot again. It was a close call. Closer than you realize."

"Oh, Quinn, couldn't we make love?" she asked softly, rolling over to look down into his tormented face. "Just once...?"

He framed his face in his hands and brought her closed eyes to his lips. "No. I won't compromise you."

She hit his big, hair-roughened chest. "Goody Two-Shoes...!"

"Thank your lucky stars that I am," he chuckled. His eyes dropped to her bare breasts and lingered there before he caught the edges of her blouse and tugged them together.

"You sex-crazed female, haven't you ever heard about pregnancy?"

"That condition where I get to have little Quinns?"

"Stop it, you're making it impossible for me," he said huskily. "Here, get up before I lose my mind."

She sat up with a grimace. "Spoilsport."

"Listen to you," he muttered, putting her back into her clothes with a wry grin. "I'll give you ten to one that you'd be yelling your head off if I started taking off your jeans."

She went red. "My jeans…!"

His eyebrows arched. "Amanda, would you like me to explain that book I read to you? The part about how men and women…"

She cleared her throat. "No, thanks, I think I've got the hang of it now," she murmured evasively.

"We might as well add a word about birth control," he added with a chuckle when he was buttoning up his own shirt. "You don't take the Pill, I assume?"

She shook her head. The whole thing was getting to be really embarrassing!

"Well, that leaves prevention up to me," he explained. "And that would mean a trip into town to the drugstore, since I never indulged, I never needed to worry about prevention. *Now* do you get the picture?"

"Boy, do I get the picture." She grimaced, avoiding his knowing gaze.

"Good girl. That's why we aren't lying down anymore."

She sighed loudly. "I guess you don't want children."

"Sure I do. Elliot would love brothers and sisters, and I'm crazy about kids." He took her slender hands in his and smoothed them over with his thumbs. "But kids should be born inside marriage, not outside it. Don't you think so?"

She took a deep breath, and her dark eyes met his. "Yes."

"Then we'll spend a lot of time together until you have to meet your friends at this concert," he said softly. "And afterward, you and I will come in here again and I'll ask you a question."

"Oh, Quinn," she whispered with aching softness.

"Oh, Amanda," he murmured, smiling as his lips softly touched hers. "But right now, we go to bed. Separately. Quick!"

"Yes, sir, Mr. Sutton." She got up and let him lead her to the staircase.

"I'll get the lights," he said. "You go on up. In the morning after we get Elliot off to school you can come out with me, if you want to."

"I want to," she said simply. She could hardly bear to be parted from him even overnight. It was like an addiction, she thought as she went up the staircase. Now if only she could make it last until she had the nerve to tell Quinn the truth….

The next few days went by in a haze. The snow began to melt and the skies cleared as the long-awaited chinook blew in. In no time at all it was Friday night and Amanda was getting into what Elliot would recognize as her stage costume. She'd brought it, with her other things, from the Durning cabin. She put it on, staring at herself in the mirror. Her hair hung long and loose, in soft waves below her waist, in the beige leather dress with the buckskin boots that matched, she was the very picture of a sensuous woman. She left off the headband. There would be time for that if she could summon enough courage to get onstage. She still hadn't told Quinn. She hadn't had the heart to destroy the dream she'd been living. But tonight he'd know. And she'd know if they had a future. She took a deep breath and went downstairs.

Chapter Eight

Amanda sat in the audience with Quinn and Elliot at a far table while the crowded hall rang with excited whispers. Elliot was tense, like Amanda, his eyes darting around nervously. Quinn was frowning. He hadn't been quite himself since Amanda came down the staircase in her leather dress and boots, looking expensive and faintly alien. He hadn't asked any questions, but he seemed as uptight as she felt.

Her eyes slid over him lovingly, taking in his dark suit. He looked out of place in fancy clothes. She missed the sight of him in denim and his old shepherd's coat, and wondered fleetingly if she'd ever get to see him that way again after tonight—if she'd ever lie in his arms on the big sofa and warm to his kisses while the fire burned in the stove. She almost groaned. Oh, Quinn, she thought, I love you.

Elliot looked uncomfortable in his blue suit. He was watching for the rest of Desperado while a well-known

Las Vegas entertainer warmed up the crowd and sang his own famous theme song.

"What are you looking for, son?" Quinn asked.

Elliot shifted. "Nothing. I'm just seeing who I know."

Quinn's eyebrows arched. "How would you know anybody in this crowd?" he muttered, glancing around. "My God, these are show people. Entertainers. Not people from our world."

That was a fact. But hearing it made Amanda heartsick. She reached out and put her hand over Quinn's.

"Your fingers are like ice," he said softly. He searched her worried eyes. "Are you okay, honey?"

The endearment made her warm all over. She smiled sadly and slid her fingers into his, looking down at the contrast between his callused, work-hardened hand and her soft, pale one. His was a strong hand, hers was artistic. But despite the differences, they fit together perfectly. She squeezed her fingers. "I'm fine," she said. "Quinn…"

"And now I want to introduce a familiar face," the Las Vegas performer's voice boomed. "Most of you know the genius of Desperado. The group has won countless awards for its topical, hard-hitting songs. Last year, Desperado was given a Grammy for 'Changes in the Wind,' and Hank Shoeman's song 'Outlaw Love' won him a country music award and a gold record. But their fame isn't the reason we're honoring them tonight."

To Amanda's surprise, he produced a gold plaque. "As some of you may remember, a little over a month ago, a teenage girl died at a Desperado concert. The group's lead singer leaped into the crowd, disregarding her own safety, and was very nearly trampled trying to protect the fan. Because of that tragedy, Desperado went into seclusion. We're proud to tell you tonight that they're back and they're in better form than ever. This plaque is a token of respect from the rest of us in the performing arts to a very special young woman whose compassion and selflessness have won the respect of all."

He looked out toward the audience where Amanda sat frozen. "This is for you—Amanda Corrie Callaway. Will you come up and join the group, please? Come on, Mandy!"

She bit her lower lip. The plaque was a shock. The boys seemed to know about it, too, because they went to their instruments grinning and began to play the downbeat that Desperado was known for, the deep throbbing counter rhythm that was their trademark.

"Come on, babe!" Hank called out in his booming voice, he and Johnson and Deke and Jack looking much more like backwoods robbers than musicians with their huge bulk and outlaw gear.

Amanda glanced at Elliot's rapt, adoring face, and then looked at Quinn. He was frowning, his dark eyes searching the crowd. She said a silent goodbye as she got to her feet. She reached into her pocket for her headband and put it on her head. She couldn't look at him, but she felt his shocked stare as she walked down the room toward the stage, her steps bouncing as the rhythm got into her feet and her blood.

"Thank you," she said huskily, kissing the entertainer's

cheek as she accepted the plaque. She moved in between Johnson and Deke, taking the microphone. She looked past Elliot's proud, adoring face to Quinn's. He seemed to be in a state of dark shock. "Thank you all. I've had a hard few weeks. But I'm okay now, and I'm looking forward to better times. God bless, people. This one is for a special man and a special boy, with all my love." She turned to Hank, nodded, and he began the throbbing drumbeat of "Love Singer."

It was a song that touched the heart, for all its mad beat. The words, in her soft, sultry, clear voice caught every ear in the room. She sang from the heart, with the heart, the words fierce with meaning as she sang them to Quinn. "Love you, never loved anybody but you, never leave me lonely, love…singer."

But Quinn didn't seem to be listening to the words. He got to his feet and jerked Elliot to his. He walked out in the middle of the song and never looked back once.

Amanda managed to finish, with every ounce of willpower she had keeping her onstage. She let the last few notes hang in the air and then she bowed to a standing ovation. By the time she and the band did an encore and she got out of the hall, the truck they'd come in was long gone. There was no note, no message. Quinn had said it all with his eloquent back when he walked out of the hall. He knew who she was now, and he wanted no part of her. He couldn't have said it more clearly if he'd written it in blood.

She kept hoping that he might reconsider. Even after she

went backstage with the boys, she kept hoping for a phone call or a glimpse of Quinn. But nothing happened.

"I guess I'm going to need a place to stay," Amanda said with a rueful smile, her expression telling her group all they needed to know.

"He couldn't handle it, huh?" Hank asked quietly. "I'm sorry, babe. We've got a suite, there's plenty of room for one more. I'll go up and get your gear tomorrow."

"Thanks, Hank." She took a deep breath and clutched the plaque to her chest. "Where's the next gig?"

"That's my girl," he said gently, sliding a protective arm around her. "San Francisco's our next stop. The boys and I are taking a late bus tomorrow." He grimaced at her knowing smile. "Well, you know how I feel about airplanes."

"Chicken Little," she accused. "Well, I'm not going to sit on a bus all day. I'll take the first charter out and meet you guys at the hotel."

"Whatever turns you on," Hank chuckled. "Come on. Let's get out of here and get some rest."

"You did good, Amanda," Johnson said from behind her. "We were proud."

"You bet," Deke and Jack seconded.

She smiled at them all. "Thanks, group. I shocked myself, but at least I didn't go dry the way I did last time." Her heart was breaking in two, but she managed to hide it. Quinn, she moaned inwardly. Oh, Quinn, was I just an interlude, an infatuation?

She didn't sleep very much. The next morning Amanda watched Hank start out for Ricochet then went down to a breakfast that she didn't even eat while she waited for him to return.

He came back three hours later, looking ruffled.

"Did you get my things?" she asked when he came into the suite.

"I got them." He put her suitcase down on the floor. "Part at Sutton's place, part at the Durning cabin. Elliot sent you a note." He produced it.

"And…Quinn?"

"I never saw him," he replied tersely. "The boy and the old man were there. They didn't mention Sutton and I didn't ask. I wasn't feeling too keen on him at the time."

"Thanks, Hank."

He shrugged. "That's the breaks, kid. It would have been a rough combination at best. You're a bright-lights girl."

"Am I?" she asked, thinking how easily she'd fit into Quinn's world. But she didn't push it. She sat down on the couch and opened Elliot's scribbled note.

Amanda,

I thought you were great. Dad didn't say anything all the way home and last night he went into his study and didn't come out until this morning. He went hunting, he said, but he didn't take any bullets. I hope you are okay. Write me when you can. I love you.

Your friend, Elliot.

She bit her lip to keep from crying. Dear Elliot. At least he still cared about her. But her fall from grace in Quinn's eyes had been final, she thought bitterly. He'd never forgive her for deceiving him. Or maybe it was just that he'd gotten over his brief infatuation with her when he found out who she really was. She didn't know what to do. She couldn't remember ever feeling so miserable. To have discovered something that precious, only to lose it forever. She folded Elliot's letter and put it into her purse. At least it would be something to remember from her brief taste of heaven.

For the rest of the day, the band and Jerry, the road manager, got the arrangements made for the San Francisco concert, and final travel plans were laid. The boys were to board the San Francisco bus the next morning. Amanda was to fly out on a special air charter that specialized in flights for business executives. They'd managed to fit her in at the last minute when a computer-company executive had canceled his flight.

"I wish you'd come with us," Hank said hesitantly. "I guess I'm overreacting and all, but I hate airplanes."

"I'll be fine," she told him firmly. "You and the boys have a nice trip and stop worrying about me. I'll be fine."

"If you say so," Hank mumbled.

"I do say so." She patted him on the shoulder. "Trust me."

He shrugged and left, but he didn't look any less worried. Amanda, who'd gotten used to his morose predictions, didn't pay them any mind.

She went to the suite and into her bedroom early that night. Her fingers dialed the number at Ricochet. She had to try one last time, she told herself. There was at least the hope that Quinn might care enough to listen to her explanation. She had to try.

The phone rang once, twice, and she held her breath, but on the third ring the receiver was lifted.

"Sutton," came a deep weary-sounding voice.

Her heart lifted. "Oh, Quinn," she burst out. "Quinn, please let me try to explain—"

"You don't have to explain anything to me, Amanda," he said stiffly. "I saw it all on the stage."

"I know it looks bad," she began.

"You lied to me," he said. "You let me think you were just a shy little innocent who played a keyboard, when you were some fancy big-time entertainer with a countrywide following."

"I knew you wouldn't want me if you knew who I was," she said miserably.

"You knew I'd see right through you if I knew," he corrected, his voice growing angrier. "You played me for a fool."

"I didn't!"

"All of it was a lie. Nothing but a lie! Well, you can go back to your public, Miss Callaway, and your outlaw buddies, and make some more records or tapes or whatever the hell they are. I never wanted you in the first place except in bed, so it's no great loss to me." He was grimacing, and she couldn't see the agony in his eyes as he forced the words out. Now that he knew who and what she was, he didn't dare let himself weaken. He had to make her go back to her own life, and stay out of his. He had nothing to give her, nothing that could take the place of fame and fortune and the world at her feet. He'd never been more aware of his own inadequacies as he had been when he'd seen Amanda on that stage and heard the applause of the audience. It ranked as the worst waking nightmare of his life, putting her forever out of his reach.

"Quinn!" she moaned. "Quinn, you don't mean that!"

"I mean it," he said through his teeth. He closed his eyes. "Every word. Don't call here again, don't come by, don't write. You're a bad influence on Elliot now that he knows who you are. I don't want you. You've worn out your welcome at Ricochet." He hung up without another word.

Amanda stared at the telephone receiver as if it had sprouted wings. Slowly she put it back in the cradle just as the room splintered into wet crystal around her.

She put on her gown mechanically and got into bed, turning out the bedside light. She lay in the dark and Quinn's words echoed in her head with merciless coolness. *Bad influence. Don't want you. Worn out your welcome. Never wanted you anyway except in bed.*

She moaned and buried her face in her pillow. She didn't know how she was going to go on, with Quinn's cold contempt dogging her footsteps. He hated her now. He thought she'd been playing a game, enjoying herself while she made a fool out of him. The tears burned her eyes. How quickly it had all ended, how finally. She'd hoped to keep in touch with Elliot, but that wouldn't be possible anymore. She was a bad influence on Elliot, so he wouldn't be allowed to contact her. She sobbed her hurt into the cool linen. Somehow, being denied contact with Elliot was the last straw. She'd grown so fond of the boy during those days she'd spent at Ricochet, and he cared about her, too. Quinn was being unnecessarily harsh. But perhaps he was right, and it was for the best. Maybe she could learn to think that way eventually. Right now she had a concert to get to, a sold-out one from what the boys and Jerry had said. She couldn't let the fans down.

Amanda got up the next morning, looking and feeling as if it were the end of the world. The boys took her suitcase downstairs, not looking too closely at her face without makeup, her long hair arranged in a thick, haphazard bun. She was wearing a dark pantsuit with a cream-colored blouse, and she looked miserable.

"We'll see you in San Francisco," Jerry told her with a smile. "I have to go nursemaid these big, tough guys, so you make sure the pilot of your plane has all his marbles, okay?"

"I'll check him out myself," she promised. "Take care of yourselves, guys. I'll see you in California."

"Okay. Be good, babe," Hank called. He and the others filed into the bus Jerry had chartered and Jerry hugged her impulsively and went in behind them.

She watched the bus pull away, feeling lost and alone, not for the first time. It was cold and snowy, but she hadn't wanted her coat. It was packed in her suitcase, and had already been put on the light aircraft. With a long sigh, she went back to the cab and sat disinterestedly in it as it wound over the snowy roads to the airport.

Fortunately the chinook had thawed the runways so that the planes were coming and going easily. She got out at the air charter service hangar and shook hands with the pilot.

"Don't worry, we're in great shape," he promised Amanda with a grin. "In fact, the mechanics just gave us another once-over to be sure. Nothing to worry about."

"Oh, I wasn't worried," she said absently and allowed herself to be shepherded inside. She slid into an empty aisle seat on the right side and buckled up. Usually she preferred to sit by the window, but today she wasn't in the mood for sightseeing. One snow-covered mountain looked pretty much like another to her, and her heart wasn't in this flight or the gig that would follow it. She leaned back and closed her eyes.

It seemed to take forever for all the businessmen to get aboard. Fortunately there had been one more cancellation, so she had her seat and the window seat as well. She didn't feel like talking to anyone, and was hoping she wouldn't have to sit by some chatterbox all the way to California.

She listened to the engines rev up and made sure that her seat belt was properly fastened. They would be off as soon as the tower cleared them, the pilot announced. Amanda sighed. She called a silent goodbye to Quinn Sutton, and Elliot and Harry, knowing that once this plane lifted off, she'd never see any of them again. She winced at the thought. Oh, Quinn, she moaned inwardly, why wouldn't you *listen?*

The plane got clearance and a minute later, it shot down the runway and lifted off. But it seemed oddly sluggish. Amanda was used to air travel, even to charter flights, and she opened her eyes and peered forward worriedly as she listened to the whine become a roar.

She was strapped in, but a groan from behind took her mind off the engine. The elderly man behind her was clutching his chest and groaning.

"What's wrong?" she asked the worried businessman in the seat beside the older man.

"Heart attack, I think." He grimaced. "What can we do?"

"I know a little CPR," she said. She unfastened her seat belt; so did the groaning man's seat companion. But just as they started to lay him on the floor, someone shouted something. Smoke began to pour out of the cockpit, and the pilot called for everyone to assume crash positions. Amanda turned, almost in slow motion. She could feel the force of gravity increase as the plane started down. The floor went out from under her and her last conscious thought was that she'd never see Quinn again....

Elliot was watching television without much interest, wishing that his father had listened when Amanda had phoned the night before. He couldn't believe that he was going to be forbidden to even speak to her again, but Quinn had insisted, his cold voice giving nothing away as he'd made Elliot promise to make no attempt to contact her.

It seemed so unfair, he thought. Amanda was no wild party girl, surely his father knew that? He sighed heavily and munched on another potato chip.

The movie he was watching was suddenly interrupted as the local station broke in with a news bulletin. Elliot listened for a minute, gasped and jumped up to get his father.

Quinn was in the office, not really concentrating on what he was doing, when Elliot burst in. The boy looked odd, his freckles standing out in an unnaturally pale face.

"Dad, you'd better come here," he said uneasily. "Quick!"

Quinn's first thought was that something had happened to Harry, but Elliot stopped in front of the television. Quinn frowned as his dark eyes watched the screen. They were showing the airport.

"What's this all—" he began, then stopped to listen.

"…plane went down about ten minutes ago, according to our best information," the man, probably the airport manager, was saying. "We've got helicopters flying in to look for the wreckage, but the wind is up, and the area the plane went down in is almost inaccessible by road."

"What plane?" Quinn asked absently.

"To repeat our earlier bulletin—" the man on television seemed to oblige "—a private charter plane has been reported lost somewhere in the Grand Teton Mountains just out of Jackson Hole. One eyewitness interviewed by KWJC-TV newsman Bill Donovan stated that he saw flames shooting out of the cockpit of the twin-engine aircraft and that he watched it plummet into the mountains and vanish. Aboard the craft were prominent San Francisco businessmen Bob Doyle and Harry Brown, and the lead singer of the rock group Desperado, Mandy Callaway."

Quinn sat down in his chair hard enough to shake it. He knew his face was as white as Elliot's. In his mind, he could hear his own voice telling Mandy he didn't want her anymore, daring her to ever contact him again. Now she was dead, and he felt her loss as surely as if one of his arms had been severed from his body.

That was when he realized how desperately he loved her. When it was too late to take back the harsh words, to go after her and bring her home where she belonged. He thought of her soft body lying in the cold snow, and a sound broke from his throat. He'd sent her away because he loved her, not because he'd wanted to hurt her, but she wouldn't have known that. Her last memory of him would have been a painful, hateful one. She'd have died thinking he didn't care.

"I don't believe it," Elliot said huskily. He was shaking his head. "I just don't believe it. She was onstage Friday night, singing again—" His voice broke and he put his face in his hands.

Quinn couldn't bear it. He got up and went past a startled Harry and out the back door in his shirtsleeves, so upset that he didn't even feel the cold. His eyes went to the barn, where he'd watched Amanda feed the calves, and around the back where she'd run from him that snowy afternoon and he'd had to save her from McNaber's bear traps. His big fists clenched by his sides and he shuddered with the force of the grief he felt, his face contorting.

"Amanda!" He bit off the name.

A long time later, he was aware of someone standing nearby. He didn't turn because his face would have said too much.

"Elliot told me," Harry said hesitantly. He stuck his hands into his pockets. "They say where she is, they may not be able to get her out."

Quinn's teeth clenched. "I'll get her out," he said huskily. "I won't leave her out there in the cold." He swallowed. "Get my skis and my boots out of the storeroom, and my insulated ski suit out of the closet. I'm going to call the lodge and talk to Terry Meade."

"He manages Larry's Lodge, doesn't he?" Harry recalled.

"Yes. He can get a chopper to take me up."

"Good thing you've kept up your practice," Harry muttered. "Never thought you'd need the skis for something this awful, though."

"Neither did I." He turned and went back inside. He might have to give up Amanda forever, but he wasn't giving her up to that damned mountain. He'd get her out somehow.

He grabbed the phone, ignoring Elliot's questions, and called the lodge, asking for Terry Meade in a tone that got instant action.

"Quinn!" Terry exclaimed. "Just the man I need. Look, we've got a crash—"

"I know," Quinn said tightly. "I know the singer. Can you get me a topo map of the area and a chopper? I'll need a first-aid kit, too, and some flares—"

"No sooner said than done," Terry replied tersely. "Although I don't think that first-aid kit will be needed, Quinn, I'm sorry."

"Well, pack it anyway, will you?" He fought down nausea. "I'll be up there in less than thirty minutes."

"We'll be waiting."

Quinn got into the ski suit under Elliot's fascinated gaze.

"You don't usually wear that suit when we ski together," he told his father.

"We don't stay out that long," Quinn explained. "This suit is a relatively new innovation. It's such a tight weave that it keeps out moisture, but it's made in such a way that it allows sweat to get out. It's like having your own heater along."

"I like the boots, too," Elliot remarked. They were blue, and they had a knob on the heel that allowed them to be tightened to fit the skier's foot exactly. Boots had to fit tight to work properly. And the skis themselves were equally fascinating. They had special brakes that unlocked when the skier fell, which stopped the ski from sliding down the hill.

"Those sure are long skis," Elliot remarked as his father took precious time to apply hot wax to them.

"Longer than yours, for sure. They fit my height," Quinn said tersely. "And they're short compared to jumping skis."

"Did you ever jump, Dad, or did you just do downhill?"

"Giant slalom," he replied. "Strictly Alpine skiing. That's going to come in handy today."

Elliot sighed. "I don't guess you'll let me come along?"

"No chance. This is no place for you." His eyes darkened. "God knows what I'll find when I get to the plane."

Elliot bit his lower lip. "She's dead, isn't she, Dad?" he asked in a choked tone.

Quinn's expression closed. "You stay here with Harry, and don't tie up the telephone. I'll call home as soon as I know anything."

"Take care of yourself up there, okay?" Elliot murmured as Quinn picked up the skis and the rest of his equipment, including gloves and ski cap. "I don't say it a lot, but I love you, Dad."

"I love you, too, son." Quinn pulled him close and gave him a quick, rough hug. "I know what I'm doing. I'll be okay."

"Good luck," Harry said as Quinn went out the back door to get into his pickup truck.

"I'll need it," Quinn muttered. He waved, started the truck, and pulled out into the driveway.

Terry Meade was waiting with the Ski Patrol, the helicopter pilot, assorted law enforcement officials and the civil defense director and trying to field the news media gathered at Larry's Lodge.

"This is the area where we think they are," Terry said grimly, showing Quinn the map. "What you call Ironside peak, right? It's not in our patrol area, so we don't have anything to do with it officially. The helicopter tried and failed to get into the valley below it because of the wind. The trees are dense down there and visibility is limited by blowing snow. Our teams are going to start here," he pointed at various places on the map. "But this hill is a killer." He grinned at Quinn. "You cut your teeth on it when you were practicing for the Olympics all those years ago, and you've kept up your practice there. If anyone can ski it, you can."

"I'll get in. What then?"

"Send up a flare. I'm packing a cellular phone in with the other stuff you asked for. It's got a better range than our walkie-talkies. Everybody know what to do? Right. Let's go."

He led them out of the lodge. Quinn put on his goggles, tugged his ski cap over his head and thrust his hands into his gloves. He didn't even want to think about what he might have to look at if he was lucky enough to find the downed plane. He was having enough trouble living with what he'd said to Amanda the last time he'd talked to her.

He could still hear her voice, hear the hurt in it when he'd told her he didn't want her. Remembering that was like cutting open his heart. For her sake, he'd sent her away. He was a poor man. He had so little to offer such a famous, beautiful woman. At first, at the lodge, his pride had been cut to ribbons when he discovered who she was, and how she'd fooled him, how she'd deceived him. But her adoration had been real, and when his mind was functioning again, he realized that. He'd almost phoned her back, he'd even dialed the number. But her world was so different from his. He couldn't let her give up everything she'd worked all her life for, just to live in the middle of nowhere. She deserved so much more. He sighed wearily. If she died, the last conversation would haunt him until the day he died. He didn't think he could live with it. He didn't want to have to try. She had to be alive. Oh, dear God, she had to be!

Chapter Nine

The sun was bright, and Quinn felt its warmth on his face as the helicopter set him down at the top of the mountain peak where the plane had last been sighted.

He was alone in the world when the chopper lifted off again. He checked his bindings one last time, adjusted the lightweight backpack and stared down the long mountainside with his ski poles restless in his hands. This particular slope wasn't skied as a rule. It wasn't even connected with the resort, which meant that the Ski Patrol didn't come here, and that the usual rescue toboggan posted on most slopes wouldn't be in evidence. He was totally on his own until he could find the downed plane. And he knew that while he was searching this untamed area, the Ski Patrol would be out in force on the regular slopes looking for the aircraft.

He sighed heavily as he stared down at the rugged,

untouched terrain, which would be a beginning skier's nightmare. Well, it was now or never. Amanda was down there somewhere. He had to find her. He couldn't leave her there in the cold snow for all eternity.

He pulled down his goggles, suppressed his feelings and shoved the ski poles deep as he propelled himself down the slope. The first couple of minutes were tricky as he had to allow for the slight added weight of the backpack. But it took scant time to adjust, to balance his weight on the skis to compensate.

The wind bit his face, the snow flew over his dark ski suit as he wound down the slopes, his skis throwing up powdered snow in his wake. It brought back memories of the days when he'd maneuvered through the giant slalom in Alpine skiing competition. He'd been in the top one percent of his class, a daredevil skier with cold nerve and expert control on the slopes. This mountain was a killer, but it was one he knew like the back of his hand. He'd trained on this peak back in his early days of competition, loving the danger of skiing a slope where no one else came. Even for the past ten years or so, he'd honed his skill here every chance he got.

Quinn smiled to himself, his body leaning into the turns, not too far, the cutting edge of his skis breaking his speed as he maneuvered over boulders, down the fall line, around trees and broken branches or over them, whichever seemed more expedient.

His dark eyes narrowed as he defeated the obstacles. At least, thank God, he was able to do something instead of going through hell sitting at home waiting for word. That in itself was a blessing, even if it ended in the tragedy everyone seemed to think it would. He couldn't bear to imagine Amanda dead. He had to think positively. There were people who walked away from airplane crashes. He had to believe that she could be one of them. He had to keep thinking that or go mad.

He'd hoped against hope that when he got near the bottom of the hill, under those tall pines and the deadly updrafts and downdrafts that had defeated the helicopter's reconnoitering, that he'd find the airplane. But it wasn't there. He turned his skis sideways and skidded to a stop, looking around him. Maybe the observer had gotten his sighting wrong. Maybe it was another peak, maybe it was miles away. He bit his lower lip raw, tasting the lip balm he'd applied before he came onto the slope. If anyone on that plane was alive, time was going to make the difference. He had to find it quickly, or Amanda wouldn't have a prayer if she'd managed to survive the initial impact.

He started downhill again, his heartbeat increasing as the worry began to eat at him. On an impulse, he shot across the fall line, parallel to it for a little while before he maneuvered back and went down again in lazy S patterns. Something caught his attention. A sound. Voices!

He stopped to listen, turning his head. There was wind, and the sound of pines touching. But beyond it was a voice, carrying in the silence of nature. Snow blanketed most sound, making graveyard peace out of the mountain's spring noises.

Quinn adjusted his weight on the skis and lifted his hands to his mouth, the ski poles dangling from his wrists. "Hello! Where are you?" he shouted, taking a chance that the vibration of his voice wouldn't dislodge snow above him and bring a sheet of it down on him.

"Help!" voices called back. "We're here! We're here!"

He followed the sound, praying that he wasn't following an echo. But no, there, below the trees, he saw a glint of metal in the lowering sun. The plane! Thank God, there were survivors! Now if only Amanda was one of them…

He went the rest of the way down. As he drew closer, he saw men standing near the almost intact wreckage of the aircraft. One had a bandage around his head, another was nursing what looked like a broken arm. He saw one woman, but she wasn't blond. On the ground were two still forms, covered with coats. Covered up.

Please, God, no, he thought blindly. He drew to a stop.

"I'm Sutton. How many dead?" he asked the man who'd called to him, a burly man in a gray suit and white shirt and tie.

"Two," the man replied. "I'm Jeff Coleman, and I sure am glad to see you." He shook hands with Quinn. "I'm the pilot. We had a fire in the cockpit and it was all I could do to set her down at all. God, I feel bad! For some reason, three of the passengers had their seat belts off when we hit." He shook his head. "No hope for two of them. The third's concussed and looks comatose."

Quinn felt himself shaking inside as he asked the

question he had to ask. "There was a singer aboard," he said. "Amanda Callaway."

"Yeah." The pilot shook his head and Quinn wanted to die, he wanted to stop breathing right there… "She's the concussion."

Quinn knew his hand shook as he pushed his goggles up over the black ski cap. "Where is she?" he asked huskily.

The pilot didn't ask questions or argue. He led Quinn past the two bodies and the dazed businessmen who were standing or sitting on fabric they'd taken from the plane, trying to keep warm.

"She's here," the pilot told him, indicating a makeshift stretcher constructed of branches and pillows from the cabin, and coats that covered the still body.

"Amanda," Quinn managed unsteadily. He knelt beside her. Her hair was in a coiled bun on her head. Her face was alabaster white, her eyes closed, long black lashes lying still on her cheekbones. Her mouth was as pale as the rest of her face, and there was a bruise high on her forehead at the right temple. He stripped off his glove and felt the artery at her neck. Her heart was still beating, but slowly and not very firmly. Unconscious. Dying, perhaps. "Oh, God," he breathed.

He got to his feet and unloaded the backpack as the pilot and two of the other men gathered around him.

"I've got a modular phone," Quinn said, "which I hope to God will work." He punched buttons and waited, his dark eyes narrowed, holding his breath.

It seemed to take forever. Then a voice, a recognizable voice, came over the wire. "Hello."

"Terry!" Quinn called. "It's Sutton. I've found them."

"Thank God!" Terry replied. "Okay, give me your position."

Quinn did, spreading out his laminated map to verify it, and then gave the report on casualties.

"Only one unconscious?" Terry asked again.

"Only one," Quinn replied heavily.

"We'll have to airlift you out, but we can't do it until the wind dies down. You understand, Quinn, the same downdrafts and updrafts that kept the chopper out this morning are going to keep it out now."

"Yes, I know, damn it," Quinn yelled. "But I've got to get her to a hospital. She's failing already."

Terry sighed. "And there you are without a rescue toboggan. Listen, what if I get Larry Hale down there?" he asked excitedly. "You know Larry; he was national champ in downhill a few years back, and he's a senior member of the Ski Patrol now. We could airdrop you the toboggan and some supplies for the rest of the survivors by plane. The two of you could tow her to a point accessible by chopper. Do you want to risk it, Quinn?"

"I don't know if she'll be alive in the morning, Terry," Quinn said somberly. "I'm more afraid to risk doing nothing than I am of towing her out. It's fairly level, if I remember right, all the way to the pass that leads from Caraway Ridge into Jackson Hole. The chopper might be able to fly down

Jackson Hole and come in that way, without having to navigate the peaks. What do you think?"

"I think it's a good idea," Terry said. "If I remember right, they cleared that pass from the Ridge into Jackson Hole in the fall. It should still be accessible."

"No problem," Quinn said, his jaw grim. "If it isn't cleared, I'll clear it, by hand if necessary."

Terry chuckled softly. "Hale says he's already on the way. We'll get the plane up—hell of a pity he can't land where you are, but it's just too tricky. How about the other survivors?"

Quinn told him their conditions, along with the two bodies that would have to be airlifted out.

"Too bad," he replied. He paused for a minute to talk to somebody. "Listen, Quinn, if you can get the woman to Caraway Ridge, the chopper pilot thinks he can safely put down there. About the others, can they manage until morning if we drop the supplies?"

Quinn looked at the pilot. "Can you?"

"I ate snakes in Nam and Bill over there served in Antarctica." He grinned. "Between us, we can keep these pilgrims warm and even feed them. Sure, we'll be okay. Get that little lady out if you can."

"Amen," the man named Bill added, glancing at Amanda's still form. "I've heard her sing. It would be a crime against art to let her die."

Quinn lifted the cellular phone to his ear. "They say they can manage, Terry. Are you sure you can get them out in the morning?"

"If we have to send the snowplow in through the valley or send in a squad of snowmobiles and a horse-drawn sled, you'd better believe we'll get them out. The Ski Patrol is already working out the details."

"Okay."

Quinn unloaded his backpack. He had flares and matches, packets of high protein dehydrated food, the first-aid kit and some cans of sterno.

"Paradise," the pilot said, looking at the stores. "With that, I can prepare a seven-course meal, build a bonfire and make a house. But those supplies they're going to drop will come in handy, just the same."

Quinn smiled in spite of himself. "Okay."

"We can sure use this first-aid kit, but I've already set a broken arm and patched a few cuts. Before I became a pilot, I worked in the medical corps."

"I had rescue training when I was in the Ski Patrol," Quinn replied. He grinned at the pilot. "But if I ever come down in a plane, I hope you're on it."

"Thanks. I hope none of us ever come down again." He glanced at the two bodies. "God, I'm sorry about them." He glanced at Amanda. "I hope she makes it."

Quinn's jaw hardened. "She's a fighter," he said. "Let's hope she cares enough to try." He alone knew how defeated she'd probably felt when she left the lodge. He'd inflicted some terrible damage with his coldness. Pride had forced him to send her away, to deny his own happiness. Once he knew how famous and wealthy she was in her own right, he hadn't felt that he had the right to ask her to give it all up to live with him and Elliot in the wilds of Wyoming. He'd been doing what he thought was best for her. Now he only wanted her to live.

He took a deep breath. "Watch for the plane and Hale, will you? I'm going to sit with her."

"Sure." The pilot gave him a long look that he didn't see before he went back to talk to the other survivors.

Quinn sat down beside Amanda, reaching for one cold little hand under the coats that covered her. It was going to be a rough ride for her, and she didn't need any more jarring. But if they waited until morning, without medical help, she could die. It was much riskier to do nothing than it was to risk moving her. And down here in the valley, the snow was deep and fairly level. It would be like Nordic skiing; cross-country skiing. With luck, it would feel like a nice lazy sleigh ride to her.

"Listen to me, honey," he said softly. "We've got a long way to go before we get you out of here and to a hospital. You're going to have to hold on for a long time." His hand tightened around hers, warming it. "I'll be right with you every step of the way. I won't leave you for a second. But you have to do your part, Amanda. You have to fight to stay alive. I hope that you still want to live. If you don't, there's something I need to tell you. I sent you away not because I hated you, Amanda, but because I loved you so much. I loved you enough to let you go back to the life you needed. You've got to stay alive so that I can tell you that," he added, stopping because his voice broke.

He looked away, getting control back breath by breath.

He thought he felt her fingers move, but he couldn't be sure. "I'm going to get you out of here, honey, one way or the other, even if I have to walk out with you in my arms. Try to hold on, for me." He brought her hand to his mouth and kissed the palm hungrily. "Try to hold on, because if you die, so do I. I can't keep going unless you're somewhere in the world, even if I never see you again. Even if you hate me forever."

He swallowed hard and put down her hand. The sound of an airplane in the distance indicated that supplies were on the way. Quinn put Amanda's hand back under the cover and bent to brush his mouth against her cold, still one.

"I love you," he whispered roughly. "You've got to hold on until I can get you out of here."

He stood, his face like the stony crags above them, his eyes glittering as he joined the others.

The plane circled and seconds later, a white parachute appeared. Quinn held his breath as it descended, hoping against hope that the chute wouldn't hang up in the tall trees and that the toboggan would soft-land so that it was usable. A drop in this kind of wind was risky at best.

But luck was with them. The supplies and the sled made it in one piece. Quinn and the pilot and a couple of the sturdier survivors unfastened the chute and brought the contents back to the wreckage of the commuter plane. The sled was even equipped with blankets and a pillow and straps to keep Amanda secured.

Minutes later, the drone of a helicopter whispered on

the wind, and not long after that, Hale started down the mountainside.

It took several minutes. Quinn saw the flash of rust that denoted the distinctive jacket and white waist pack of the Ski Patrol above, and when Hale came closer, he could see the gold cross on the right pocket of the jacket—a duplicate of the big one stenciled on the jacket's back. He smiled, remembering when he'd worn that same type of jacket during a brief stint as a ski patrolman. It was a special kind of occupation, and countless skiers owed their lives to those brave men and women. The National Ski Patrol had only existed since 1938. It was created by Charles Dole of Connecticut, after a skiing accident that took the life of one of his friends. Today, the Ski Patrol had over 10,000 members nationally, of whom ninety-eight percent were volunteers. They were the first on the slopes and the last off, patrolling for dangerous areas and rescuing injured people. Quinn had once been part of that elite group and he still had the greatest respect for them.

Hale was the only color against the whiteness of the snow. The sun was out, and thank God it hadn't snowed all day. It had done enough of that last night.

Quinn's nerves were stretched. He hadn't had a cigarette since he'd arrived at the lodge, and he didn't dare have one now. Nicotine and caffeine tended to constrict blood vessels, and the cold was dangerous enough without giving it any help. Experienced skiers knew better than to stack the odds against themselves.

"Well, I made it." Hale grinned, getting his breath.

"How are you, Quinn?" He extended a hand and Quinn shook it.

The man in the Ski Patrol jacket nodded to the others, accepted their thanks for the supplies he'd brought with him, which included a makeshift shelter and plenty of food and water and even a bottle of cognac. But he didn't waste time. "We'd better get moving if we hope to get Miss Callaway out of here by dark."

"She's over here," Quinn said. "God, I hate doing this," he added heavily when he and Hale were standing over the unconscious woman. "If there was any hope, any at all, that the chopper could get in here..."

"You can feel the wind for yourself," Hale replied, his eyes solemn. "We're the only chance she has. We'll get her to the chopper. Piece of cake," he added with a reassuring smile.

"I hope so," Quinn said somberly. He bent and nodded to Hale. They lifted her very gently onto the long sled containing the litter. It had handles on both ends, because it was designed to be towed. They attached the towlines, covered Amanda carefully and set out, with reassurances from the stranded survivors.

There was no time to talk. The track was fairly straightforward, but it worried Quinn, all the same, because there were crusts that jarred the woman on the litter. He towed, Hale guided, their rhythms matching perfectly as they made their way down the snow-covered valley. Around them, the wind sang through the tall firs and lodgepole pines, and Quinn thought about the old trappers and mountain men who must have come through this valley a hundred, two hundred years before. In those days of poor sanitation and even poorer medicine, Amanda wouldn't have stood a chance.

He forced himself not to look back. He had to concentrate on getting her to the Ridge. All that was important now, was that she get medical help while it could still do her some good. He hadn't come all this way to find her alive, only to lose her.

It seemed to take forever. Once, Quinn was certain that they'd lost their way as they navigated through the narrow pass that led to the fifty-mile valley between the Grand Tetons and the Wind River Range, an area known as Jackson Hole. But he recognized landmarks as they went along, and eventually they wound their way around the trees and along the sparkling river until they reached the flats below Caraway Ridge.

Quinn and Hale were both breathing hard by now. They'd changed places several times, so that neither got too tired of towing the toboggan, and they were both in peak condition. But it was still a difficult thing to do.

They rested, and Quinn reached down to check Amanda's pulse. It was still there, and even seemed to be, incredibly, a little stronger than it had been. But she was pale and still and Quinn felt his spirits sink as he looked down at her.

"There it is," Hale called, sweeping his arm over the ridge. "The chopper."

"Now if only it can land," Quinn said quietly, and he began to pray.

The chopper came lower and lower, then it seemed to shoot up again and Quinn bit off a hard word. But the pilot corrected for the wind, which was dying down, and eased the helicopter toward the ground. It seemed to settle inch by inch until it landed safe. The pilot was out of it before the blades stopped.

"Let's get out of here," he called to the men. "If that wind catches up again, I wouldn't give us a chance in hell of getting out. It was a miracle that I even got in!"

Quinn released his bindings in a flash, leaving his skis and poles for Hale to carry, along with his own. He got one side of the stretcher while the pilot, fortunately no lightweight himself, got the other. They put the stretcher in the back of the broad helicopter, on the floor, and Quinn and Hale piled in—Hale in the passenger seat up front, Quinn behind with Amanda, carefully laying ski equipment beside her.

"Let's go!" the pilot called as he revved up the engine.

It was touch and go. The wind decided to play tag with them, and they almost went into a lodgepole pine on the way up. But the pilot was a tenacious man with good nerves. He eased down and then up, down and up until he caught the wind off guard and shot up out of the valley and over the mountain.

Quinn reached down and clasped Amanda's cold hand in his. Only a little longer, honey, he thought, watching her with his heart in his eyes. Only a little longer, for God's sake, hold on!

It was the longest ride of his entire life. He spared one thought for the people who'd stayed behind to give Amanda her chance and he prayed that they'd be rescued without any further injuries. Then his eyes settled on her pale face and stayed there until the helicopter landed on the hospital lawn.

The reporters, local, state and national, had gotten word of the rescue mission. They were waiting. Police kept them back just long enough for Amanda to be carried into the hospital, but Quinn and Hale were caught. Quinn volunteered Hale to give an account of the rescue and then he ducked out, leaving the other man to field the enthusiastic audience while he trailed quickly behind the men who'd taken Amanda into the emergency room.

He drank coffee and smoked cigarettes and glared at walls for over an hour until someone came out to talk to him. Hale had to go back to the lodge, to help plan the rescue of the rest of the survivors, but he promised to keep in touch. After he'd gone, Quinn felt even more alone. But at last a doctor came into the waiting room, and approached him.

"Are you related to Miss Callaway?" the doctor asked with narrowed eyes.

Quinn knew that if he said no, he'd have to wait for news of her condition until he could find somebody who was related to her, and he had no idea how to find her aunt.

"I'm her fiancé," he said without moving a muscle in his face. "How is she?"

"Not good," the doctor, a small wiry man, said bluntly. "But I believe in miracles. We have her in intensive care, where she'll stay until she regains consciousness. She's badly concussed. I gather she hasn't regained consciousness since the crash?" Quinn shook his head. "That sleigh ride and helicopter lift didn't do any good, either," he added firmly, adding when he saw the expression on Quinn's tormented face, "but I can understand the necessity for it. Go get some sleep. Come back in the morning. We won't know anything until then. Maybe not until much later. Concussion is tricky. We can't predict the outcome, as much as we'd like to."

"I can't rest," Quinn said quietly. "I'll sit out here and drink coffee, if you don't mind. If this is as close to her as I can get, it'll have to do."

The doctor took a slow breath. "We keep spare beds in cases like this," he said. "I'll have one made up for you when you can't stay awake any longer." He smiled faintly. "Try to think positively. It isn't medical, exactly, but sometimes it works wonders. Prayer doesn't hurt, either."

"Thank you," Quinn said.

The doctor shrugged. "Wait until she wakes up. Good night."

Quinn watched him go and sighed. He didn't know what to do next. He phoned Terry at the lodge to see if Amanda's band had called. Someone named Jerry and a man called Hank had been phoning every few minutes, he was told. Quinn asked for a phone number and Terry gave it to him.

He dialed the area code. California, he figured as he waited for it to ring.

"Hello?"

"This is Quinn Sutton," he began.

"Yes, I recognize your voice. It's Hank here. How is she?"

"Concussion. Coma, I guess. She's in intensive care and she's still alive. That's about all I know."

There was a long pause. "I'd hoped for a little more than that."

"So had I," Quinn replied. He hesitated. "I'll phone you in the morning. The minute I know anything. Is there anybody we should notify…her aunt?"

"Her aunt is a scatterbrain and no help at all. Anyway, she's off with Blalock Durning in the Bahamas on one of those incommunicado islands. We couldn't reach her if we tried."

"Is there anybody else?" Quinn asked.

"Not that I know of." There was a brief pause. "I feel bad about the way things happened. I hate planes, you know. That's why the rest of us went by bus. We stopped here in some hick town to make sure Amanda got her plane, and Terry told us what happened. We got a motel room and we're waiting for a bus back to Jackson. It will probably be late tomorrow before we get there. We've already canceled the gig. We can't do it without Amanda."

"I'll book a room for you," Quinn said.

"Make it a suite," Hank replied, "and if you need anything, you know, anything, you just tell us."

"I've got plenty of cigarettes and the coffee machine's working. I'm fine."

"We'll see you when we get there. And Sutton—thanks. She really cares about you, you know?"

"I care about her," he said stiffly. "That's why I sent her away. My God, how could she give all that up to live on a mountain in Wyoming?"

"Amanda's not a city girl, though," Hank said slowly. "And she changed after those days she spent with you. Her heart wasn't with us anymore. She cried all last night..."

"Oh, God, don't," Quinn said.

"Sorry, man," Hank said quietly. "I'm really sorry, that's the last thing I should have said. Look, go smoke a cigarette. I think I'll tie one on royally and have the boys put me to bed. Tomorrow we'll talk. Take care."

"You, too."

Quinn hung up. He couldn't bear to think of Amanda crying because of what he'd done to her. He might lose her even yet, and he didn't know how he was going to go on living. He felt so alone.

He was out of change after he called the lodge and booked the suite for Hank and the others, but he still had to talk to Elliot and Harry. He dialed the operator and called collect. Elliot answered the phone immediately.

"How is she?" he asked quickly.

Quinn went over it again, feeling numb. "I wish I knew more," he concluded. "But that's all there is."

"She can't die," Elliot said miserably. "Dad, she just can't!"

"Say a prayer, son," he replied. "And don't let Harry teach you any bad habits while I'm gone."

"No, sir, I won't," Elliot said with a feeble attempt at humor. "You're going to stay, I guess?"

"I have to," Quinn said huskily. He hesitated. "I love her."

"So do I," Elliot said softly. "Bring her back when you come."

"If I can. If she'll even speak to me when she wakes up," Quinn said with a total lack of confidence.

"She will," Elliot told him. "You should have listened to some of those songs you thought were so horrible. One of hers won a Grammy. It was all about having to give up things we love to keep from hurting them. She always seemed to feel it when somebody was sad or hurt, you know. And she risked her own life trying to save that girl at the concert. She's not someone who thinks about getting even with people. She's got too much heart."

Quinn drew deeply from his cigarette. "I hope so, son," he said. "You get to bed. I'll call you tomorrow."

"Okay. Take care of yourself. Love you, Dad."

"Me, too, son," Quinn replied. He hung up. The waiting area was deserted now, and the hospital seemed to have gone to sleep. He sat down with his foam cup of black coffee and finished his cigarette. The room looked like he felt—empty.

Chapter Ten

It was late morning when the nurse came to shake Quinn gently awake. Apparently around dawn he'd gone to sleep sitting up, with an empty coffee cup in his hand. He thought he'd never sleep at all.

He sat up, drowsy and disheveled. "How is Amanda?" he asked immediately.

The nurse, a young blonde, smiled at him. "She's awake and asking for you."

"Oh, thank God," he said heavily. He got quickly to his feet, still a little groggy, and followed her down to the intensive-care unit, where patients in tiny rooms were monitored from a central nurses' station and the hum and click and whir of life-supporting machinery filled the air. If she was asking for him, she must not hate him too much. That thought sustained him as he followed the nurse into one of the small cubicles where Amanda lay.

Amanda looked thinner than ever in the light, her face pinched, her eyes hollow, her lips chapped. They'd taken her hair down somewhere along the way and tied it back with a pink ribbon. She was propped up in bed, still with the IV in position, but she'd been taken off all the other machines.

She looked up and saw Quinn and all the weariness and pain went out of her face. She brightened, became beautiful despite her injuries, her eyes sparkling. Her last thought when she'd realized in the plane what was going to happen had been of Quinn. Her first thought when she'd regained consciousness had been of him. The pain, the grief of having him turn away from her was forgotten. He was here, now, and that meant he had to care about her.

"Oh, Quinn!" she whispered tearfully, and held out her arms.

He went to her without hesitation, ignoring the nurses, the aides, the whole world. His arms folded gently around her, careful of the tubes attached to her hand, and his head bent over hers, his cheek on her soft hair, his eyes closed as he shivered with reaction. She was alive. She was going to live. He felt as if he were going to choke to death on his own rush of feeling.

"My God," he whispered shakily. "I thought I'd lost you."

That was worth it all, she thought, dazed from the emotion in his voice, at the tremor in his powerful body as he held her. She clung to him, her slender arms around his neck, drowning in pleasure. She'd wondered if he hadn't sent her away in a misguided belief that it was for her own good. Now she was sure of it. He couldn't have looked that haggard, that terrible, unless she mattered very much to him. Her aching heart soared. "They said you brought me out."

"Hale and I did," he said huskily. He lifted his head, searching her bright eyes slowly. "It's been the longest night of my life. They said you might die."

"Oh, we Callaways are tough birds," she said, wiping away a tear. She was still weak and sore and her headache hadn't completely gone away. "You look terrible, my darling," she whispered on a choked laugh.

The endearment fired his blood. He had to take a deep breath before he could even speak. His fingers linked with hers. "I felt pretty terrible when we listened to the news report, especially when I remembered the things I said to you." He took a deep breath. "I didn't know if you'd hate me for the rest of your life, but even if you did, I couldn't just sit on my mountain and let other people look for you." His thumb gently stroked the back of her pale hand. "How do you feel, honey?"

"Pretty bad. But considering it all, I'll do. I'm sorry about the men who died. One of them was having a heart attack," she explained. "The other gentleman who was sitting with him alerted me. We both unfastened our seat belts to try and give CPR. Just after I got up, the plane started down," she said. "Quinn, do you believe in predestination?"

"You mean, that things happen the way they're meant

to in spite of us?" He smiled. "I guess I do." His dark eyes slid over her face hungrily. "I'm so glad it wasn't your time, Amanda."

"So am I." She reached up and touched his thin mouth with just the tips of her fingers. "Where is it?" she asked with an impish smile as a sudden delicious thought occurred to her.

He frowned. "Where's what?"

"My engagement ring," she said. "And don't try to back out of it," she added firmly when he stood there looking shocked. "You told the doctor and the whole medical staff that I was your fiancée, and you're not ducking out of it now. You're going to marry me."

His eyebrows shot up. "I'm what?" he said blankly.

"You're going to marry me. Where's Hank? Has anybody phoned him?"

"I did. I was supposed to call him back." He checked his watch and grimaced. "I guess it's too late now. He and the band are on the way back here."

"Good. They're twice your size and at least as mean." Her eyes narrowed. "I'll tell them you seduced me. I could be pregnant." She nodded, thinking up lies fast while Quinn's face mirrored his stark astonishment. "That's right, I could."

"You could not," he said shortly. "I never…!"

"But you're going to," she said with a husky laugh. "Just wait until I get out of here and get you alone. I'll wrestle you down and start kissing you, and you'll never get away in time."

"Oh, God," he groaned, because he knew she was right. He couldn't resist her that way, it was part of the problem.

"So you'll have to marry me first," she continued. "Because I'm not that kind of girl. Not to mention that you aren't that kind of guy. Harry likes me and Elliot and I are already friends, and I could even get used to McNaber if he'll move those traps." She pursed her lips, thinking. "The concert tour is going to be a real drag, but once it's over, I'll retire from the stage and just make records and tapes and CDs with the guys. Maybe a video now and again. They'll like that, too. We're all basically shy and we don't like live shows. I'll compose songs. I can do that at the house, in between helping Harry with the cooking and looking after sick calves, and having babies," she added with a shy smile.

He wanted to sit down. He hadn't counted on this. All that had mattered at the time was getting her away from the wreckage and into a hospital where she could be cared for. He hadn't let himself think ahead. But she obviously had. His head spun with her plans.

"Listen, you're an entertainer," he began. His fingers curled around hers and he looked down at them with a hard, grim sigh. "Amanda, I'm a poor man. All I've got is a broken-down ranch in the middle of nowhere. You'd have a lot of hardships, because I won't live on your money. I've got a son, even if he isn't mine, and..."

She brought his hand to her cheek and held it there,

nuzzling her cheek against it as she looked up at him with dark, soft, adoring eyes. "I love you," she whispered.

He faltered. His cheeks went ruddy as the words penetrated, touched him, excited him. Except for his mother and Elliot, nobody had ever said that to him before Amanda had. "Do you?" he asked huskily. "Still? Even after the way I walked off and left you there at the lodge that night? After what I said to you on the phone?" he added, because he'd had too much time to agonize over his behavior, even if it had been for what he thought was her own good.

"Even after that," she said gently. "With all my heart. I just want to live with you, Quinn. In the wilds of Wyoming, in a grass shack on some island, in a mansion in Beverly Hills—it would all be the same to me—as long as you loved me back and we could be together for the rest of our lives."

He felt a ripple of pure delight go through him. "Is that what you really want?" he asked, searching her dark eyes with his own.

"More than anything else in the world," she confessed. "That's why I couldn't tell you who and what I really was. I loved you so much, and I knew you wouldn't want me…" Her voice trailed off.

"I want you, all right," he said curtly. "I never stopped. Damn it, woman, I was trying to do what was best for you!"

"By turning me out in the cold and leaving me to starve to death for love?" she asked icily. "Thanks a bunch!"

He looked away uncomfortably. "It wasn't that way

and you know it. I thought maybe it was the novelty. You know, a lonely man in the backwoods," he began.

"You thought I was having the time of my life playing you for a fool," she said. Her head was beginning to hurt, but she had to wrap it all up before she gave in and asked for some more medication. "Well, you listen to me, Quinn Sutton, I'm not the type to go around deliberately trying to hurt people. All I ever wanted was somebody to care about me—just me, not the pretty girl on the stage."

"Yes, I know that now," he replied. He brought her hand to his mouth and softly kissed the palm. The look on his face weakened her. "So you want a ring, do you? It will have to be something sensible. No flashy diamonds, even if I could give you something you'd need sunglasses to look at."

"I'll settle for the paper band on a King Edward cigar if you'll just marry me," she replied.

"I think I can do a little better than that," he murmured dryly. He bent over her, his lips hovering just above hers. "And no long engagement," he whispered.

"It takes three days, doesn't it?" she whispered back. "That *is* a long engagement. Get busy!"

He stifled a laugh as he brushed his hard mouth gently over her dry one. "Get well," he whispered. "I'll read some books real fast."

She colored when she realized what kind of books he was referring to, and then smiled under his tender kiss. "You do that," she breathed. "Oh, Quinn, get me out of here!"

"At the earliest possible minute," he promised.

The band showed up later in the day while Quinn was out buying an engagement ring for Amanda. He'd already called and laughingly told Elliot and Harry what she'd done to him, and was delighted with Elliot's pleasure in the news and Harry's teasing. He did buy her a diamond, even if it was a moderate one, and a gold band for each of them. It gave him the greatest kind of thrill to know that he was finally marrying for all the right reasons.

When he got back to the hospital, the rest of the survivors had been airlifted out and all but one of them had been treated and released. The news media had tried to get to Amanda, but the band arrived shortly after Quinn left and ran interference. Hank gave out a statement and stopped them. The road manager, as Quinn found out, had gone on to San Francisco to make arrangements for canceling the concert.

The boys were gathered around Amanda, who'd been moved into a nice private room. She was sitting up in bed, looking much better, and her laughing dark eyes met Quinn's the minute he came in the door.

"Hank brought a shotgun," she informed him. "And Deke and Johnson and Jack are going to help you down the aisle. Jerry's found a minister, and Hank's already arranged a blood test for you right down the hall. The license—"

"Is already applied for," Quinn said with a chuckle. "I did that myself. Hello, boys," he greeted them, shaking hands as he was introduced to the rest of the band. "And you can unload the shotgun. I'd planned to hold it on Amanda, if she tried to back out."

"Me, back out? Heaven forbid!" she exclaimed, smiling as Quinn bent to kiss her. "Where's my ring?" she whispered against his hard mouth. "I want it on, so these nurses won't make eyes at you. There's this gorgeous redhead..."

"I can't see past you, pretty thing," he murmured, his eyes soft and quiet in a still-gaunt face. "Here it is." Quinn produced it and slid it on her finger. He'd measured the size with a small piece of paper he'd wrapped around her finger, and he hoped that the method worked. He needn't have worried, because the ring was a perfect fit, and she acted as if it were the three-carat monster he'd wanted to get her. Her face lit up, like her pretty eyes, and she beamed as she showed it to the band.

"Did you sleep at all?" Hank asked him while the others gathered around Amanda.

"About an hour, I think," Quinn murmured dryly. "You?"

"I couldn't even get properly drunk," Hank said, sighing, "so the boys and I played cards until we caught the bus. We slept most of the way in. It was a long ride. From what I hear," he added with a level look, "you and that Hale fellow had an even longer one, bringing Amanda out of the mountains."

"You'll never know." Quinn looked past him to Amanda, his dark eyes full of remembered pain. "I had to decide whether or not to move her. I thought it was riskier to leave her there until the next morning. If we'd waited, we had no guarantee that the helicopter would have been able to land even then. She could have died. It's a miracle she didn't."

"Miracles come in all shapes and sizes," Hank mused, staring at her. "She's been ours. Without her, we'd never have gotten anywhere. But being on the road has worn her out. The boys and I were talking on the way back about cutting out personal appearances and concentrating on videos and albums. I think Amanda might like that. She'll have enough to do from now on, I imagine, taking care of you and your boy," he added with a grin. "Not to mention all those new brothers and sisters you'll be adding. I grew up on a ranch," he said surprisingly. "I have five brothers."

Quinn's eyebrows lifted. "Are they all runts like you?" he asked with a smile.

"I'm the runt," Hank corrected.

Quinn just shook his head.

Amanda was released from the hospital two days later. Every conceivable test had been done, and fortunately there were no complications. The doctor had been cautiously optimistic at first, but her recovery was rapid—probably due, the doctor said with a smile, to her incentive. He gave Amanda away at the brief ceremony, held in the hospital's chapel just before she was discharged, and one of the nurses was her matron of honor. There were a record four best men; the band. But for all its brevity and informality, it was a ceremony that Amanda would never forget. The Methodist minister who performed it had a way with words, and Amanda and Quinn felt just as married as if they'd had the service performed in a huge church with a large crowd present.

The only mishap was that the press found out about the wedding, and Amanda and Quinn and the band were mobbed as they made their way out of the hospital afterward. The size of the band members made them keep well back. Hank gave them his best wildman glare while Jack whispered something about the bandleader becoming homicidal if he was pushed too far. They escaped in two separate cars. The driver of the one taking Quinn and Amanda to the lodge managed to get them there over back roads, so that nobody knew where they were.

Terry had given them the bridal suite, on the top floor of the lodge, and the view of the snowcapped mountains was exquisite. Amanda, still a little shaky and very nervous, stared out at them with mixed feelings.

"I don't know if I'll ever think of them as postcards again," she remarked to Quinn, who was trying to find places to put everything from their suitcase. He'd had to go to Ricochet for his suit and a change of clothing.

"What, the mountains?" he asked, smiling at her. "Well, it's not a bad thing to respect them. But airplanes don't crash that often, and when you're well enough, I'm going to teach you to ski."

She turned and looked at him for a long time. Her wedding outfit was an off-white, a very simple shirtwaist dress with a soft collar and no frills. But with her long hair around her shoulders and down to her waist, framed in the light coming through the window, she looked the picture of a bride. Quinn watched her back and sighed, his eyes lingering on the small sprig of lily of the valley she was wearing in her hair—a present from a member of the hospital staff.

"One of the nurses brought me a newspaper," Amanda said. "It told all about how you and Mr. Hale got me out." She hesitated. "They said that only a few men could ski that particular mountain without killing themselves."

"I've been skiing it for years," he said simply. He took off the dark jacket of his suit and loosened his tie with a long sigh. "I knew that the Ski Patrol would get you out, but they usually only work the lodge slopes—you know, the ones with normal ski runs. The peak the plane landed on was off the lodge property and out-of-the-way. It hadn't even been inspected. There are all sorts of dangers on slopes like that—fallen trees, boulders, stumps, debris, not to mention the threat of avalanche. The Ski Patrol marks dangerous runs where they work. They're the first out in the morning and the last off the slopes in the afternoon."

"You seem to know a lot about it," Amanda said.

"I used to be one of them," he replied with a grin. "In my younger days. It's pretty rewarding."

"There was a jacket Harry showed me," she frowned. "A rust-colored one with a big gold cross on the back…"

"My old patrol jacket." He chuckled. "I wouldn't part with it for the world. If I'd thought of it, I'd have worn it that day." His eyes darkened as he looked at her. "Thank

God I knew that slope," he said huskily. "Because I'd bet money that you wouldn't have lasted on that mountain overnight."

"I was thinking about you when the plane went down," she confessed. "I wasn't sure that I'd ever see you again."

"Neither was I when I finally got to you." He took off his tie and threw it aside. His hand absently unfastened the top buttons of his white shirt as he moved toward her. "I was trying so hard to do the right thing," he murmured. "I didn't think I could give you what you needed, what you were used to."

"I'm used to you, Mr. Sutton," she murmured with a smile. Amanda slid her arms under his and around him, looking up at him with her whole heart in her dark eyes. "Bad temper, irritable scowl and all. Anything you can't give me, I don't want. Will that do?"

His broad chest rose and fell slowly. "I can't give you much. I've lost damned near everything."

"You have Elliot and Harry and me," she pointed out. "And some fat, healthy calves, and in a few years, Elliot will have a lot of little brothers and sisters to help him on the ranch."

A faint dusky color stained his high cheekbones. "Yes."

"Why, Mr. Sutton, honey, you aren't shy, are you?" she whispered dryly as she moved her hands back around to his shirt and finished unbuttoning it down his tanned, hair-roughened chest.

"Of course I'm shy," he muttered, heating up at the feel

of her slender hands on his skin. He caught his breath and shuddered when she kissed him there. His big hands slid into her long, silky hair and brought her even closer. "I like that," he breathed roughly. "Oh, God, I love it!"

She drew back after a minute, her eyes sultry, drowsy. "Wouldn't you like to do that to me?" she whispered. "I like it, too."

He fumbled with buttons until he had the dress out of the way and she was standing in nothing except a satin teddy. He'd never seen one before, except in movies, and he stared at her with his breath stuck somewhere in his chest. It was such a sexy garment low on her lace-covered breasts, nipped at her slender waist, hugging her full hips. Below it were her elegant silk-clad legs, although he didn't see anything holding up her hose.

"It's a teddy," she whispered. "If you want to slide it down," she added shyly, lowering her eyes to his pulsating chest, "I could step out of it."

He didn't know if he could do that and stay on his feet. The thought of Amanda unclothed made his knees weak. But he slid the straps down her arms and slowly, slowly, peeled it away from her firm, hard-tipped breasts, over her flat stomach, and then over the panty hose she was wearing. He caught them as well and eased the whole silky mass down to the floor.

She stepped out of it, so much in love with him that all her earlier shyness was evaporating. It was as new for him as it was for her, and that made it beautiful. A true act of love.

She let him look at her, fascinated by the awe in his hard face, in the eyes that went over her like an artist's brush, capturing every line, every soft curve before he even touched her.

"Amanda, you're the most beautiful creature I've ever seen," he said finally. "You look like a drawing of a fairy I saw in an old-time storybook…all gold and ivory."

She reached up and leaned close against him, shivering a little when her breasts touched his bare chest. The hair was faintly abrasive and very arousing. She moved involuntarily and gasped at the sensation.

"Do you want to help me?" he whispered as he stripped off his shirt and his hands went to his belt.

"I…" She hesitated, her nerve retreating suddenly at the intimacy of it. She grimaced. "Oh, Quinn, I'm such a coward!" She hid her face against his chest and felt his laughter.

"Well, you're not alone," he murmured. "I'm not exactly an exhibitionist myself. Look, why don't you get under the covers and close your eyes, and we'll pretend it's dark."

She looked up at him and laughed. "This is silly."

"Yes, I know." He sighed. "Well, honey, we're married. I guess it's time to face all the implications of sharing a bed."

He sat down, took off his boots and socks, stood to unbuckle his belt, holding her eyes, and slid the zip down. Everything came off, and seconds later, she saw for herself all the differences between men and women.

"You've gone scarlet, Mrs. Sutton," he observed.

"You aren't much whiter yourself, Mr. Sutton," she replied.

He laughed and reached for her and she felt him press against her. It was incredible, the feel of skin against skin, hair-rough flesh against silky softness. He bent and found her mouth and began to kiss her lazily, while his big, rough hands slid down her back and around to her hips. His mouth opened at the same time that his fingers pulled her thighs against his, and she felt for the first time the stark reality of arousal.

He felt her gasp and lifted his head, searching her flushed face. "That has to happen before anything else can," he whispered. "Don't be afraid. I think I know enough to make it easy for you."

"I love you, Quinn," she whispered back, forcing her taut muscles to relax, to give in to him. She leaned her body into his with a tiny shiver and lifted her mouth. "However it happens between us, it will be all right."

He searched her eyes and nodded. His mouth lowered to hers. He kissed her with exquisite tenderness while his hands found the softness of her breasts. Minutes later, his mouth traced them, covered the hard tips in a warm, moist suction that drew new sounds from her. He liked that, so he lifted her and put her on the big bed, and found other places to kiss her that made the sounds louder and more tormented.

The book had been very thorough and quite explicit, so he knew what to do in theory. Practice was very different. He hadn't known that women could lose control, too.

That their bodies were so soft, or so strong. That their eyes grew wild and their faces contorted as the pleasure built in them, that they wept with it. Her pleasure became his only goal in the long, exquisite oblivion that followed.

By the time he moved over her, she was more than ready for him, she was desperate for him. He whispered to her, gently guided her body to his as he fought for control of his own raging need so that he could satisfy hers first.

There was one instant when she stiffened and tried to pull away, but he stopped then and looked down into her frightened eyes.

"It will only hurt for a few seconds," he whispered huskily. "Link your hands in mine and hold on. I'll do it quickly."

"All…all right." She felt the strength in his hands and her eyes met his. She swallowed.

He pushed, hard. She moaned a little, but her body accepted him instantly and without any further difficulty.

Her eyes brightened. Her lips parted and she breathed quickly and began to smile. "It's gone," she whispered. "Quinn, I'm a woman now…."

"My woman," he whispered back. The darkness grew in his eyes. He bent to her mouth and captured it, held it as he began to move, his body dancing above hers, teaching it the rhythm. She followed where he led, gasping as the cadence increased, as the music began to grow in her mind and filtered through her arms and legs. She held on to him with the last of her strength, proud of his stamina, of the power in his body that was taking hers from reality and into a place she'd never dreamed existed.

She felt the first tremors begin, and work into her like fiery pins, holding her body in a painful arch as she felt the tension build. It grew to unbearable levels. Her head thrashed on the pillow and she wanted to push him away, to make him stop, because she didn't think she could live through what was happening to her. But just as she began to push him the tension broke and she fell, crying out, into a hot, wild satisfaction that convulsed her. Above her, Quinn saw it happen and finally gave in to the desperate fever of his own need. He drove for his own satisfaction and felt it take him, his voice breaking on Amanda's name as he went into the fiery depths with her.

Afterward, he started to draw away, but her arms went around him and refused to let go. He felt her tears against his hot throat.

"Are you all right?" he asked huskily.

"I died," she whispered brokenly. Her arms contracted. "Don't go away, please don't. I don't want to let you go," she moaned.

He let his body relax, giving her his full weight. "I'll crush you, honey," he whispered in her ear.

"No, you won't." She sighed, feeling his body pulse with every heartbeat, feeling the dampness of his skin on her own, the glory of his flesh touching hers. "This is nice."

He laughed despite his exhaustion. "There's a new word for it," he murmured. He growled and bit her shoulder gently. "Wildcat," he whispered proudly. "You bit me. Do you remember? You bit me and dug your nails into my hips and screamed."

"So did you," she accused, flushing. "I'll have bruises on my thighs…"

"Little ones," he agreed. He lifted his head and searched her dark, quiet eyes. "I couldn't help that, at the last. I lost it. Really lost it. Are you as sated as I am?" he mused. "I feel like I've been walking around like half a person all my life, and I've just become whole."

"So do I." Her eyes searched his, and she lifted a lazy hand to trace his hard, thin lips. After a few seconds, she lifted her hips where they were still joined to his and watched his eyes kindle. She drew in a shaky breath and did it again, delighting in the sudden helpless response of his body.

"That's impossible," he joked. "The book said so."

Amanda pulled his mouth down to hers. "Damn the book," she said and held on as he answered her hunger with his own.

They slept and finally woke just in time to go down to dinner. But since neither of them wanted to face having to get dressed, they had room service send up a tray. They drank champagne and ate thick steaks and went back to bed. Eventually they even slept.

The next morning, they set out for Ricochet, holding hands all the way home.

Chapter Eleven

Elliot and Harry were waiting at the door when Quinn brought Amanda home. There was a big wedding cake on the table that Harry had made, and a special present that Elliot had made Harry drive him to town in the sleigh to get—a new Desperado album with a picture of Amanda on the cover.

"What a present," Quinn murmured, smiling at Amanda over the beautiful photograph. "I guess I'll have to listen to it now, won't I?"

"I even got Hank Shoeman's autograph," Elliot enthused. "Finally I can tell the guys at school! I've been going nuts ever since I realized who Amanda was…."

"You knew?" Quinn burst out. "And you didn't tell me? So that's why that tape disappeared."

"You were looking for it?" Elliot echoed.

"Sure, just after we got home from the lodge that night

I deserted Amanda," Quinn said with a rueful glance at her. "I was feeling pretty low. I just wanted to hear her voice, but the tape was missing."

"Sorry, Dad," Elliot said gently. "I'll never do it again, but I was afraid you'd toss her out if you knew she was a rock singer. She's really terrific, you know, and that song that won a Grammy was one of hers."

"Stop, you'll make me blush," Amanda groaned.

"I can do that," Quinn murmured dryly and the look he gave Amanda brought scarlet color into her hot cheeks.

"You were in the paper, Dad," Elliot continued excitedly. "And on the six-o'clock news, too! They told all about your skiing days and the Olympic team. Dad, why didn't you keep going? They said you were one of the best giant slalom skiers this country ever produced, but that you quit with a place on the Olympic team in your pocket."

"It's a long story, Elliot," he replied.

"It was because of my mother, wasn't it?" the boy asked gravely.

"Well, you were on the way and I didn't feel right about deserting her at such a time."

"Even though she'd been so terrible to you?" he probed.

Quinn put his hands on his son's shoulders. "I'll tell you for a fact, Elliot, you were mine from the day I knew about your existence. I waited for you like a kid waiting for a Christmas present. I bought stuff and read books about babies and learned all the things I'd need to know to help your mother raise you. I'd figured, you see, that she might eventually decide that having you was pretty special. I'm sorry that she didn't."

"That's okay," Elliot said with a smile. "You did."

"You bet I did. And do."

"Since you like kids so much, you and Amanda might have a few of your own," Elliot decided. "I can help. Me and Harry can wash diapers and make formula..."

Amanda laughed delightedly. "Oh, you doll, you!" She hugged Elliot. "Would you really not mind other kids around?"

"Heck, no," Elliot said with genuine feeling. "All the other guys have little brothers and sisters. It gets sort of lonely, being the only one." He looked up at her admiringly. "And they'd be awful pretty, if some of them were girls."

She grinned. "Maybe we'll get lucky and have another redhead, too. My mother was redheaded. So was my grandmother. It runs in the family."

Elliot liked that, and said so.

"Hank Shoeman has a present for you, by the way," she told Elliot. "No, there's no use looking in the truck, he ordered it."

Elliot's eyes lit up. "What is it? An autographed photo of the group?"

"It's a keyboard," Amanda corrected gently, smiling at his awe. "A real one, a Moog like I play when we do instrumentals."

"Oh, my gosh!" Elliot sat down. "I've died and gone to heaven. First I get a great new mother and now I get a Moog. Maybe I'm real sick and have a high fever," he frowned, feeling his forehead.

"No, you're perfectly well," Quinn told him. "And I guess it's all right if you play some rock songs," he added with a grimace. "I got used to turnips, after all, that time when Harry refused to cook any more greens. I guess I can get used to loud music."

"I refused to cook greens because we had a blizzard and canned turnips was all I had," Harry reminded him, glowering. "Now that Amanda's here, we won't run out of beans and peas and such, because she'll remember to tell me we're out so I can get some more."

"I didn't forget to remind you," Quinn muttered.

"You did so," Elliot began. "I remember—"

"That's it, gang up on me," Quinn glowered at them.

"Don't you worry, sweet man, I'll protect you from ghastly turnips and peas and beans," she said with a quick glance at Harry and Elliot. "I like asparagus, so I'll make sure that's all we keep here. Don't you guys like asparagus?"

"Yes!" they chorused, having been the culprits who told Amanda once that Quinn hated asparagus above all food in the world.

Quinn groaned.

"And I'll make liver and onions every night," Amanda added. "We love that, don't we, gang?"

"We sure do!" they chorused again, because they knew it was the only meat Quinn wouldn't eat.

"I'll go live with McNaber," he threatened.

Amanda laughed and slid her arms around him. "Only if we get to come, too." She looked up at him. "It's all right. We all really hate asparagus and liver and onions."

"That's a fact, we do," Elliot replied. "Amanda, are you going to go on tour with the band?"

"No," she said quietly. "We'd all gotten tired of the pace. We're going to take a well-earned rest and concentrate on videos and albums."

"I've got this great idea for a video," Elliot volunteered.

She grinned. "Okay, tiger, you can share it with us when Hank and the others come for a visit."

His eyes lit up. "They're all coming? The whole group?"

"My aunt is marrying Mr. Durning," she told him, having found out that tidbit from Hank. "They're going to live in Hawaii, and the band has permission to use the cabin whenever they like. They've decided that if I like the mountains so much, there must be something special about them. Our next album is going to be built around a mountain theme."

"Wow." Elliot sighed. "Wait'll I tell the guys."

"You and the guys can be in the video," Amanda promised. "We'll find some way to fit you into a scene or two." She studied Harry. "We'll put Harry in, too."

"Oh, no, you won't!" he said. "I'll run away from home first."

"If you do, we'll starve to death." Amanda sighed. "I can't do cakes and roasts. We'll have to live on potatoes and fried eggs."

"Then you just make a movie star out of old Elliot and I'll stick around," he promised.

"Okay," Amanda said, "but what a loss to women everywhere. You'd have been super, Harry."

He grinned and went back to the kitchen to cook. Elliot eventually wandered off, too, and Quinn took Amanda into the study and closed the door.

They sat together in his big leather armchair, listening to the crackling of the fire in the potbellied stove.

"Remember the last time we were in here together?" he asked lazily between kisses.

"Indeed, I do," she murmured with a smile against his throat. "We almost didn't stop in time."

"I'm glad we did." He linked her fingers with his. "We had a very special first time. A real wedding night. That's marriage the way it was meant to be; a feast of first times."

She touched his cheek lightly and searched his dark eyes. "I'm glad we waited, too. I wanted so much to go to my husband untouched. I just want you to know that it was worth the wait. I love you, really love you, you know?" She sighed shakily. "That made it much more than my first intimate experience."

He brought his mouth down gently on hers. "I felt just that way about it," he breathed against her lips. "I never asked if you wanted me to use anything…?"

"So I wouldn't get pregnant?" She smiled gently. "I love kids."

"So do I." He eased back and pulled her cheek onto his chest, smoothing her long, soft hair as he smiled down into her eyes. "I never dreamed I'd find anyone like you. I'd given up on women. On life, too, I guess. I've been bitter and alone for such a long time, Amanda. I feel like I was just feverish and dreaming it all."

"You aren't dreaming." She pulled him closer to her and kissed him with warm, slow passion. "We're married and I'm going to love you for the rest of my life, body and soul. So don't get any ideas about trying to get away. I've caught you fair and square and you're all mine."

He chuckled. "Really? If you've caught me, what are you going to do with me?"

"Have I got an answer for that," she whispered with a sultry smile. "You did lock the door, didn't you?" she murmured, her voice husky as she lifted and turned so that she was facing him, her knees beside him on the chair. His heart began to race violently.

"Yes, I locked the door. What are you…Amanda!"

She smiled against his mouth while her hands worked at fastenings. "That's my name, all right," she whispered. She nipped his lower lip gently and laughed delightedly when she felt him helping her. "Life is short. We'd better start living it right now."

"I couldn't possibly agree more," he whispered back, and his husky laugh mingled with hers in the tense silence of the room.

Beside them, the burning wood crackled and popped in the stove while the snow began to fall again outside the window. Amanda had started it, but almost immediately Quinn took control and she gave in with a warm laugh. She knew already that things were done Sutton's way around Ricochet. And this time, she didn't really mind at all.

★ ★ ★ ★ ★

Coltrain's Proposal

Chapter One

The little boy's leg was bleeding profusely. Dr. Louise Blakely knew exactly what to do, but it was difficult to get the right pressure on the cut so that the nicked artery would stop emptying onto the brown, dead December grass.

"It hurts!" the little boy, Matt, cried. "Ow!"

"We have to stop the bleeding," she said reasonably. She smiled at him, her dark eyes twinkling in a face framed by thick, medium blond hair. "Maybe your mom could get you an ice cream after we've patched you up." She glanced at the white-faced lady beside them, who nodded enthusiastically. "Okay?"

"Well…" He grimaced, holding his leg above where Lou was putting pressure to bear.

"Only a minute more," she promised, looking around for the ambulance she'd asked a bystander to call. It was on the way. She could hear the siren. Even in a small town like Jacobsville, there was an efficient ambulance service. "You're going to get to ride in a real ambulance," she told the child. "You can tell your friends all about it on Monday at school!"

"Will I have to go back?" he asked, enthusiastic now. "Maybe I could stay in the hospital for a whole week?"

"I really think the emergency room is as far as you're going to get this time." Lou chuckled. "Now pay attention while they're loading you up, so that you can remember everything!"

"I sure will!" he said.

She stood up as the ambulance pulled alongside the police car and two attendants jumped out. They started loading the boy onto a stretcher. Lou had a brief word with the female EMT and described the boy's injuries and gave instructions. She was on staff at the local hospital where he would be taken, and she planned to follow the ambulance in her own car.

The police officer who'd been citing the reckless driver for hitting the small boy on the bicycle came over to talk to Lou. "Good thing you were having lunch in the café," he remarked with a grin. "That was a bad cut."

"He'll be okay," Lou said as she closed her medical bag. She always had it in the car when she left the office, and this time it had paid off.

"You're Dr. Coltrain's partner, aren't you?" he asked suddenly.

"Yes." She didn't add anything to that. The expression

on the officer's face said enough. Most people around Jacobsville knew that Dr. Coltrain had as little use for his partner as he had for alcohol. He'd made it all too evident in the months she'd been sharing his practice.

"He's a good man," the officer added. "Saved my wife when her lung collapsed." He smiled at the memory. "Nothing shakes him up. Nor you, either, judging by what I just saw. You're a good hand in an emergency."

"Thanks." She gave him a brief smile and went to her small gray Ford to follow the ambulance to the hospital.

The emergency room was full, as usual. It was Saturday and accidents always doubled on weekends. She nodded to a couple of her patients that she recognized, and she kept walking, right behind the trolley that was taking young Matt to a treatment room.

Dr. Coltrain was on his way back from surgery. They met in the hall. The green surgical uniform looked sloppy on some of the surgeons, but not on Coltrain. Despite the cap that hid most of his thick red hair, he looked elegant and formidable.

"Why are you here on Saturday? I'm supposed to be doing rounds today for both of us," he asked sharply.

Here he goes again, practicing Coltrain's First Law…jump to conclusions, she thought. She didn't grin, but she felt like it.

"I wound up at a car accident scene," she began.

"The hospital pays EMTs to work wrecks," he continued, glaring at her while hospital personnel came and went around them.

"I did not go out to—" she began hotly.

"Don't let this happen again, or I'll have a word with Wright, and you'll be taken off staff here. Is that clear?" he added coldly. Wright was the hospital administrator and Coltrain was medical chief of staff. He had the authority to carry out the threat.

"Will you listen?" she asked irritably. "I didn't go out with the ambulance…!"

"Doctor, are you coming?" one of the EMTs called to her.

Coltrain glanced toward the EMT and then back at Louise, irritably jerking off his cap and mask. His pale blue eyes were as intimidating as his stance. "If your social life is this stale, Doctor, perhaps you need to consider a move," he added with biting sarcasm.

She opened her mouth to reply, but he was already walking away. She threw up her hands furiously. She couldn't ever get a word in, because he kept talking, or interrupted her, and then stormed off without giving her a chance to reply. It was useless to argue with him, anyway. No matter what she said or did, she was always in the wrong.

"One day you'll break something," she told his retreating back. "And I'll put you in a body cast, so help me God!"

A passing nurse patted her on the shoulder. "There, there, Doctor, you're doing it again."

She ground her teeth together. It was a standing joke in the hospital staff that Louise Blakely ended up talking to herself every time she argued with Dr. Coltrain. That meant that she talked to herself almost constantly. Presumably he heard her from time to time, but he never gave a single indication that he had.

With a furious groan deep in her throat, she turned down the hall to join the EMT.

It took an hour to see to the boy, who had more than one cut that needed stitches. His mother was going to have to buy him a lot of ice cream to make up for the pain, Lou thought, and she'd been wrong about another thing, too—he did have to stay overnight in the hospital. But that would only give him status among his peers, she thought, and left him smiling with a cautionary word about the proper way to ride a bicycle in town.

"No need to worry about that," his mother said firmly. "He won't be riding his bike across city streets anymore!"

She nodded and left the emergency room, her bag in hand. She looked more like a teenager on holiday than a doctor, she mused, in her blue jeans and T-shirt and sneakers. She'd pulled her long blond hair up into its habitual bun and she wore no makeup to enhance her full mouth or her deep brown eyes. She had no man to impress, except the one she loved, and he wouldn't notice if she wore tar and feathers to the office they shared. "Copper" Coltrain had no interest in Lou Blakely, except as an efficient co-worker. Not that he ever acknowledged her efficiency; instead he found fault with her constantly. She wondered often why he ever agreed to work with her in the first place, when he couldn't seem to stand the sight of her. She wondered, too, why she kept hanging on where she wasn't wanted. The hunger her poor heart felt for him was her only excuse. And one day, even that wouldn't be enough.

Dr. Drew Morris, the only friend she had on staff, came down the hall toward her. Like Coltrain, he'd been operating, because he was wearing the same familiar green surgical clothing. But where Coltrain did chest surgery, Drew's talents were limited to tonsils, adenoids, appendices and other minor surgeries. His speciality was pediatrics. Coltrain's was chest and lungs, and many of his patients were elderly.

"What are you doing here? It's too early or too late for rounds, depending on your schedule," he added with a grin. "Besides, I thought Copper was doing them today."

Copper, indeed. Only a handful of people were privileged to call Dr. Coltrain by that nickname, and she wasn't numbered among them.

She grimaced at him. He was about her height, although she was tall, and he had dark hair and eyes and was a little overweight. He was the one who'd phoned her at the Austin hospital where she was working just after her parents' deaths, and he'd told her about the interviews Coltrain was holding for a partner. She'd jumped at the chance for a new start, in the hometown where her mother and father had both been born. And amazingly, in light of his ongoing animosity toward her, Coltrain had asked her to join him after a ten-minute interview.

"There was an accident in front of the café," she said.

"I was having lunch there. I haven't been to the grocery store yet," she added with a grimace. "I hate shopping."

"Who doesn't?" He smiled. "Doing okay?"

She shrugged. "As usual."

He stuck his hands on his hips and shook his head. "It's my fault. I thought it would get better, but it hasn't, has it? It's been almost a year, and he still suffers you."

She winced. She didn't quite avert her face fast enough to hide it.

"You poor kid," he said gently. "I'm sorry. I suppose I was too enthusiastic about getting you here. I thought you needed a change, after…well, after your parents' deaths. This looked like a good opportunity. Copper's one of the best surgeons I've ever known, and you're a skilled family practitioner. It seemed a good match of talent, and you've taken a load off him in his regular practice so that he could specialize in the surgery he's so skilled at." He sighed. "How wrong can a man be?"

"I signed a contract for one year," she reminded him. "It's almost up."

"Then what?"

"Then I'll go back to Austin."

"You could work the ER," he teased. It was a standing joke between them. The hospital had to contract out the emergency room staff, because none of the local doctors wanted to do it. The job was so demanding that one young resident had walked out in the middle of the unnecessary examination of a known hypochondriac at two in the morning and never came back.

Lou smiled, remembering that. "No, thanks. I like private practice, but I can't afford to set up and equip an office of my own just yet. I'll go back to the drawing board. There's bound to be a practice somewhere in Texas."

"You're fit for this one," he said shortly.

"Not to hear my partner tell it," she said curtly. "I'm never right, didn't you know?" She let out a long breath. "Anyway, I'm in a rut, Drew. I need a change."

"Maybe you do, at that." He pursed his lips and smiled. "What you really need is a good social life. I'll be in touch."

She watched him walk away with grave misgivings. She hoped that he didn't mean what it sounded like he meant. She wanted nothing to do with Drew in a romantic way, although she did like him. He was a kind man, a widower who'd been in love with his wife and was still, after five years, getting over her. Drew was a native of Jacobsville, and knew Lou's parents. He'd been very fond of her late mother. He'd met up with them again in Austin—that's where Lou had met him.

Lou decided not to take Drew's teasing seriously because she knew about his devotion to his wife's memory. But he'd looked very solemn when he'd remarked that her social life needed uplifting.

She was probably imagining things, she told herself. She started out to the parking lot and met Dr. Coltrain, dressed in an expensive gray vested suit, bent on the same destination. She ground her teeth together and slowed her pace, but she still reached the doors at the same time he did.

He spared her a cold glance. "You look unprofessional," he said curtly. "At least have the grace to dress decently if you're going to cruise around with the ambulance service."

She stopped and looked up at him without expression. "I wasn't cruising anywhere. I don't have a boat, so how could I cruise?"

He just looked at her. "They don't need any new EMTs…"

"You shut up!" she snapped, surprising him speechless. "Now you listen to me for a change, and don't interrupt!" she added, holding up her hand when his thin lips parted. "There was an accident in town. I was in the café, so I gave assistance. I don't need to hang out with the ambulance crew for kicks, Doctor! And how I dress on my days off is none of your—" she almost turned blue biting back the curse *"—business,* Doctor!"

He was over his shock. His hand shot out and caught the wrist of her free hand, the one that wasn't holding her black medical bag, and jerked. She caught her breath at the shock of his touch and squirmed, wrestling out of his grip. The muted violence of it brought back protective instincts that she'd almost forgotten. She stood very still, holding her breath, her eyes the size of saucers as she looked at him and waited for that hand to tighten and twist…

But it didn't. He, unlike her late father, never seemed to lose control. He released her abruptly. His blue eyes narrowed. “Cold as ice, aren’t you?” he drawled mockingly. “You’d freeze any normal man to death. Is that why you never married, Doctor?”

It was the most personal thing he’d ever said to her, and one of the most insulting.

“You just think what you like,” she said.

“You might be surprised at what I think,” he replied. He looked at the hand he’d touched her with and laughed deep in his throat. “Frostbitten,” he pronounced. “No wonder Drew Morris doesn’t take you out. He’d need a blowtorch, wouldn’t he?” he added with a meaningful, unblinking blue stare.

“Maybe so, but you’d need a grenade launcher,” she retorted without thinking.

He lifted an eyebrow and gave her a look that held mingled contempt and distaste. “You’d be lucky.”

The remark was painful, but she didn’t let him see that. Her own eyebrows lifted. “Really?” She laughed and walked off to her car, happy to have seen him stiffen. She walked past his Mercedes without even a glance. Take that, she thought furiously. She didn’t care what he thought about her, she told herself. She spent most of her free time telling herself that. But she did care about him, far too much. That was the whole problem.

He thought she was cold, but she wasn’t. It was quite the reverse where he was concerned. She always jerked away when he came too close, when he touched her infrequently. It wasn’t because she found him repulsive but because his touch excited her so much. She trembled when he was too close, her breathing changed. She couldn't control her shaky legs or her shaky voice. The only solution had been to distance herself physically from him, and that was what she'd done.

There were other reasons, too, why she avoided physical involvement. They were none of his business, or anyone else's. She did her job and avoided trouble as much as possible. But just lately, her job was becoming an ordeal.

She drove home to the small dilapidated white house on the outskirts of town. It was in a quiet neighborhood that was just beginning to go downhill. The rent was cheap. She'd spent weekends painting the walls and adding bits and pieces to the house's drab interior. She had it all but furnished now, and it reflected her own quiet personality. But there were other dimensions to the room, like the crazy cat sculpture on the mantel and the colorful serapes on the chairs, and the Indian pottery and exotic musical instruments on the bookshelf. The paintings were her own, disturbingly violent ones with reds and blacks and whites in dramatic chaos. A visitor would have found the combinations of flowers amid those paintings confusing. But, then, she'd never had a visitor. She kept to herself.

Coltrain did, too, as a rule. He had visitors to his ranch from time to time, but his invitations even when they included the medical staff invariably excluded Louise. The omission had caused gossip, which no one had been brave enough to question to his face. Louise didn't care if he never invited her to his home. After all, she never invited him to hers.

Secretly she suspected that he was grieving for Jane Parker, his old flame who'd just recently married Todd Burke. Jane was blond and blue-eyed and beautiful, a former rodeo star with a warm heart and a gentle personality.

Lou often wondered why he'd ever agreed to work with someone he disliked so much, and on such short acquaintance. He and Dr. Drew Morris were friends, and she'd tried to question Drew about her sudden acceptance, but Drew was a clam. He always changed the subject.

Drew had known her parents in Jacobsville and he had been a student of her father's at the Austin teaching hospital where he'd interned. He'd become an ally of her mother during some really tough times, but he didn't like Lou's father. He knew too much about his home life, and how Lou and her mother were treated.

There had been one whisper of gossip at the Jacobsville hospital when she'd first gone there on cases. She'd heard one of the senior nurses remark that it must disturb "him" to have Dr. Blakely's daughter practicing at this hospital and thank God she didn't do surgery. Lou had wanted to question the nurse, but she'd made herself scarce after that and eventually had retired.

Louise had never found out who "he" was or what was disturbing about having another Blakely practice at the Jacobsville hospital. But she did begin to realize that her father had a past here.

"What did my father do at this hospital, Drew?" she'd asked him one day suddenly, while they were doing rounds at the hospital.

He'd seemed taken aback. "He was a surgeon on staff, just as I am," he said after a hesitation.

"He left here under a cloud, didn't he?" she persisted.

He shook his head. "There was no scandal, no cloud on his reputation. He was a good surgeon and well respected, right until the end. You know that. Even if he was less than admirable as a husband and father, he was an exceptional surgeon."

"Then why the whispers about him when I first came here?"

"It was nothing to do with his skill as a surgeon," he replied quietly. "It's nothing that really even concerns you, except in a roundabout way."

"But what…?"

They'd been interrupted and he'd looked relieved. She hadn't asked again. But she wondered more and more. Perhaps it had affected Dr. Coltrain in some way and that was why he disliked Lou. But wouldn't he have mentioned it in a whole year?

She didn't ever expect to understand the so-controlled Dr. Coltrain or his venomous attitude toward her. He'd been much more cordial when she first became his partner. But about the time she realized that she was in love with him, he became icy cold and antagonistic. He'd been that way ever since, raising eyebrows everywhere.

The remark he'd made this morning about her coldness was an old one. She'd jerked back from him at a Christmas party, soon after she'd come to work in his office in Jacobsville, to avoid a kiss under the mistletoe.

She could hardly have admitted that even then the thought of his hard, thin mouth on hers made her knees threaten to buckle. Her attraction to him had been explosive and immediate, a frightening experience to a woman whose whole life had been wrapped around academic excellence and night upon night of exhaustive studying. She had no social life at all—even in high school. It had been the one thing that kept her father's vicious sarcasm and brutality at bay, as long as she made good grades and stayed on the dean's list.

Outside achievements had been the magic key that kept the balance in her dysfunctional family. She studied and won awards and scholarships and praise, and her father basked in it. She thought that he'd never felt much for her, except pride in her ability to excel. He was a cruel man and grew crueler as his addiction climbed year after year to new heights. Drugs had caused the plane crash. Her mother had died with him. God knew, that was fitting, because she'd loved him to the point of blindness, overlooking his brutality, his addiction, his cruelty in the name of fidelity.

Lou wrapped her arms around herself, feeling the chill of fear. She'd never marry. Any woman could wake up in a relationship that damaging. All she had to do was fall in love, lose control, give in to a man's dominance. Even the best man could become a predator if he sensed vulnerability in a woman. So she would never be vulnerable, she assured herself. She would never be at a man's mercy as her mother had been.

But Copper Coltrain made her vulnerable, and that was why she avoided any physical contact with him. She couldn't give in to the feelings he roused in her, for fear of becoming a victim. Loneliness might be a disease, but it was certainly a more manageable one than love.

The ringing of the telephone caught her attention.

"Dr. Blakely?" Brenda, her office nurse, queried. "Sorry to bother you at home, but Dr. Coltrain said there's been a wreck on the north end of town and they'll be bringing the victims to the emergency room. Since he's on call, you'll have to cover the two-hour Saturday clinic at the office."

"I'll be right over," she promised, wasting no more time in conversation.

The clinic was almost deserted. There was a football game at the local high school that night, and it was sunny and unseasonably warm outside for early December. It didn't really surprise Lou that she only needed to see a handful of patients.

"Poor Dr. Coltrain," Brenda said with a sigh as they finished the last case and closed up the office. "I'll bet he won't be in until midnight."

"It's a good thing he isn't married," Lou remarked. "He'd have no home life at all, as hard as he works."

Brenda glanced at her, but with a kind smile. "That is true. But he should be thinking about it. He's in his thirties now, and time is passing him by." She turned the key in the lock. "Pity about Miss Parker marrying that Burke man, isn't it? Dr. Coltrain was sweet on her for so many years. I always thought—I guess most people here did—that they were made for each other. But she was never more than friendly. If you saw them together, it was obvious that she didn't feel what he did."

In other words, Dr. Coltrain had felt a long and unrequited love for the lovely blond former rodeo cowgirl, Jane Parker. That much, Lou had learned from gossip. It must have hurt him very badly when she married someone else.

"What a pity that we can't love to order," Lou remarked quietly, thinking how much she'd give to be unscarred and find Dr. Coltrain as helplessly drawn to her as she was to him. That was the stuff of fantasy, however.

"Wasn't it surprising about Ted Regan and Coreen Tarleton, though?" Brenda added with a chuckle.

"Indeed it was," Lou agreed, smiling as she remembered having Ted for a patient. "She was shaking all over when she got him to me with that gored arm. He was cool. Nothing shakes Ted. But Coreen was as white as milk."

"I thought they were already married," Brenda groaned. "Well, I was new to the area and I didn't know them. I do now," she added, laughing. "I pass them at least once a week on their way to the obstetrician's office. She's due any day."

"She'll be a good mother, and Ted will certainly be a good father. Their children will have a happy life."

Brenda caught the faint bitterness in the words and

glanced at Lou, but the other woman was already calling her goodbyes and walking away.

She went home and spent the rest of the weekend buried in medical journals and the latest research on the new strain of bacteria that had, researchers surmised, mutated from a deadly scarlet fever bacterium that had caused many deaths at the turn of the century.

Chapter Two

Monday morning brought a variety of new cases, and Louise found herself stuck with the most routine of them, as usual. She and Coltrain were supposed to be partners, but when he wasn't operating, he got the interesting, challenging illnesses. Louise got fractured ribs and colds.

He'd been stiff with her this morning, probably because he was still fuming over the argument they'd had about his mistaken idea of her weekend activities. Accusing her of lollygagging with the EMTs for excitement; really!

She watched his white-coated back disappear into an examination room down the hall in their small building and sighed half-angrily as she went back to check an X ray in the files. The very worst thing about unrequited love, she thought miserably, was that it fed on itself. The more her partner in the medical practice ignored and antagonized her, the harder she had to fight her dreams about him. She didn't want to get married; she didn't even want to get involved. But he made her hungry.

He'd spent a lot of time with Jane Parker until she married that Burke man, and Lou had long ago given up hope that he would ever notice her in the same way he always noticed Jane. The two of them had grown up together, though, whereas Lou had only been in partnership with him for a year. She was a native of Austin, not Jacobsville. Small towns were like extended families. Everybody knew each other, and some families had been friends for more than one generation. Lou was a true outsider here, even though she *was* a native Texan. Perhaps that was one of many reasons that Dr. Coltrain found her so forgettable.

She wasn't bad looking. She had long, thick blond hair and big brown eyes and a creamy, blemish-free complexion. She was tall and willowy, but still shorter than her colleague. She lacked his fiery temper and his authoritarian demeanor. He was tall and whipcord lean, with flaming red hair and blue eyes and a dark tan from working on his small ranch when he wasn't treating patients. That tan was odd in a redhead, although he did have a smattering of freckles over his nose and the backs of his big hands. She'd often wondered if the freckles went any farther, but she had yet to see him without his professional white coat over his very formal suit. He wasn't much on casual dressing at work. At home, she was sure that he dressed less formally.

That was something Lou would probably never know. She'd never been invited to his home, despite the fact that most of the medical staff at the local hospital had. Lou was automatically excluded from any social gathering that he coordinated.

Other people had commented on his less than friendly behavior toward her. It puzzled them, and it puzzled her, because she hadn't become his partner in any underhanded way. He had known from the day of her application that she was female, so it couldn't be that. Perhaps, she thought wistfully, he was one of those old-line dominating sort of men who thought women had no place in medicine. But he'd been instrumental in getting women into positions of authority at the hospital, so that theory wasn't applicable, either. The bottom line was that he simply did not like Louise Blakely, medical degree or no medical degree, and she'd never known why.

She really should ask Drew Morris why, she told herself with determination. It had been Drew, a surgeon and friend of her family, who'd sent word about the opening in Coltrain's practice. He'd wanted to help Lou get a job near him, so that he could give her some moral support in the terrible days following the deaths of her parents. She, in turn, had liked the idea of being in practice in a small town, one where she knew at least one doctor on the staff of the hospital. Despite growing up in Austin, it was still a big city and she was lonely. She was twenty-eight, a loner whose whole life had been medicine. She'd made sure that her infrequent dates never touched her heart, and she was innocent in an age when innocence was automatically looked on with disdain or suspicion.

Her nurse stuck her head in the doorway. "There's a call for you. Dr. Morris is on line two."

"Thanks, Brenda."

She picked up the receiver absently, her finger poised over the designated line. But when she pressed it, before she could say a word, the sentence she'd intercepted accidentally blared in her ear in a familiar deep voice.

"…told you I wouldn't have hired her in the first place, if I had known who she was related to. I did you a favor, never realizing she was Blakely's daughter. You can't imagine that I'll ever forgive her father for what he did to the girl I loved, do you? She's been a constant reminder, a constant torment!"

"That's harsh, Copper," Drew began.

"It's how I feel. She's nothing but a burden here. But to answer your question, hell no, you're not stepping on my toes if you ask her out on a date! I find Louise Blakely repulsive and repugnant, and an automaton with no attractions whatsoever. Take her with my blessing. I'd give real money if she'd get out of my practice and out of my life, and the sooner the better!" There was a click and the line, obviously open, was waiting for her.

She clicked the receiver to announce her presence and said, as calmly as she could, "Dr. Lou Blakely."

"Lou! It's Drew Morris," came the reply. "I hope I'm not catching you at a bad moment?"

"No." She cleared her throat and fought to control her scattered emotions. "No, not at all. What can I do for you?"

"There's a dinner at the Rotary Club Thursday. How about going with me?"

She and Drew occasionally went out together, in a friendly but not romantic way. She would have refused, but what Coltrain had said made her mad. "Yes, I would like to, thanks," she said.

Drew laughed softly. "Great! I'll pick you up at six on Thursday, then."

"See you then."

She hung up, checked the X ray again meticulously, and put it away in its file. Brenda ordinarily pulled the X rays for her, but it was Monday and, as usual, they were overflowing with patients who'd saved their weekend complaints for office hours.

She went back to her patient, her color a little high, but no disturbance visible in her expression.

She finished her quota of patients and then went into her small office. Mechanically she picked up a sheet of letterhead paper, with Dr. Coltrain's name on one side and hers on the other. Irrelevantly, she thought that the stationery would have to be replaced now.

She typed out a neat resignation letter, put it in an envelope and went to place it on Dr. Coltrain's desk. It was lunchtime and he'd already left the building. He made sure he always did, probably to insure that he didn't risk having Lou invite herself to eat with him.

Brenda scowled as her boss started absently toward the back door. "Shouldn't you take off your coat first?" she asked hesitantly.

Lou did, without a word, replaced it in her office, whipped her leather fanny pack around her waist and left the building.

It would have been nice if she'd had someone to talk to, she thought wistfully, about this latest crisis. She sat alone in the local café, drinking black coffee and picking at a small salad. She didn't mingle well with people. When she wasn't working, she was quiet and shy, and she kept to herself. It was difficult for strangers to approach her, but she didn't realize that. She stared into her coffee and remembered every word Coltrain had said to Drew Morris about her. He hated her. He couldn't possibly have made it clearer. She was repugnant, he'd said.

Well, perhaps she was. Her father had told her so, often enough, when he was alive. He and her mother were from Jacobsville but hadn't lived in the area for years. He had never spoken of his past. Not that he spoke to Lou often, anyway, except to berate her grades and tell her that she'd never measure up.

"Excuse me?"

She looked up. The waitress was staring at her. "Yes?" she asked coolly.

"I don't mean to pry, but are you all right?"

The question surprised Lou, and touched her. She managed a faint smile through her misery. "Yes. It's been a… long morning. I'm not really hungry."

"Okay." The waitress smiled again, reassuringly, and went away.

Just as Lou was finishing her coffee, Coltrain came in the front door. He was wearing the elegant gray suit that looked so good on him, and carrying a silver belly Stetson by the brim. He looked furiously angry as his pale eyes scanned the room and finally spotted Lou, sitting all alone.

He never hesitated, she thought, watching him walk purposefully toward her. There must be an emergency…

He slammed the opened envelope down on the table in front of her. "What the hell do you mean by that?" he demanded in a dangerously quiet tone.

She raised her dark, cold eyes to his. "I'm leaving," she explained and averted her gaze.

"I know that! I want to know why!"

She looked around. The café was almost empty, but the waitress and a local cowboy at the counter were glancing at them curiously.

Her chin came up. "I'd rather not discuss my private business in public, if you don't mind," she said stiffly.

His jaw clenched, and his eyes grew glittery. He stood back to allow her to get up. He waited while she paid for her salad and coffee and then followed her out to where her small gray Ford was parked.

Her heart raced when he caught her by the arm before she could get her key out of her jeans pocket. He jerked her around, not roughly, and walked her over to Jacobsville's small town square, to a secluded bench in a grove of live oak and willow trees. Because it was barely December, there were no leaves on the trees and it was cool, despite her nervous perspiration. She tried to throw off his hand, to no avail.

He only loosened his grip on her when she sat down on a park bench. He remained standing, propping his boot on the bench beside her, leaning one long arm over his knee to study her. "This is private enough," he said shortly. "Why are you leaving?"

"I signed a contract to work with you for one year. It's almost up, anyway," she said icily. "I want out. I want to go home."

"You don't have anyone left in Austin," he said, surprising her.

"I have friends," she began.

"You don't have those, either. You don't have friends at all, unless you count Drew Morris," he said flatly.

Her fingers clenched around her car keys. She looked at them, biting into the flesh even though not a speck of emotion showed on her placid features.

His eyes followed hers to her lap and something moved in his face. There was an expression there that puzzled her. He reached down and opened her rigid hand, frowning when he saw the red marks the keys had made in her palm.

She jerked her fingers away from him.

He seemed disconcerted for a few seconds. He stared at her without speaking and she felt her heart beating wildly against her ribs. She hated being helpless.

He moved back, watching her relax. He took another step and saw her release the breath she'd been holding. Every trace of anger left him.

"It takes time for a partnership to work," he said abruptly. "You've only given this one a year."

"That's right," she said tonelessly. "*I've* given it a year."

The emphasis she placed on the first word caught his attention. His blue eyes narrowed. "You sound as if you don't think I've given it any time at all."

She nodded. Her eyes met his. "You didn't want me in the practice. I suspected it from the beginning, but it wasn't until I heard what you told Drew on the phone this morning that—"

His eyes flashed oddly. "You heard what I said?" he asked huskily. "You heard…all of it!" he exclaimed.

Her lips trembled just faintly. "Yes," she said.

He was remembering what he'd told Drew Morris in a characteristic outburst of bad temper. He often said things in heat that he regretted later, but this he regretted most of all. He'd never credited his cool, unflappable partner with any emotions at all. She'd backed away from him figuratively and physically since the first day she'd worked at the clinic. Her physical withdrawal had maddened him, although he'd always assumed she was frigid.

But in the past five minutes, he'd learned disturbing things about her without a word being spoken. He'd hurt her. He didn't realize she'd cared that much about his opinion. Hell, he'd been furious because he'd just had to diagnose leukemia in a sweet little boy of four. It had hurt him to do that, and he'd lashed out at Morris over Lou in frustration at his own helplessness. But he'd had no idea that she'd overheard his vicious remarks. She was going to leave and it was no less than he deserved. He was genuinely sorry. She wasn't going to believe that, though. He could tell by her mutinous expression, in her clenched hands, in the tight set of her mouth.

"You did Drew a favor and asked me to join you, probably over some other doctor you really wanted," she said with a forced smile. "Well, no harm done. Perhaps you can get him back when I leave."

"Wait a minute," he began shortly.

She held up a hand. "Let's not argue about it," she said, sick at knowing his opinion of her, his real opinion. "I'm tired of fighting you to practice medicine here. I haven't done the first thing right, according to you. I'm a burden. Well, I just want out. I'll go on working until you can replace me." She stood up.

His hand tightened on the brim of his hat. He was losing this battle. He didn't know how to pull his irons out of the fire.

"I had to tell the Dawes that their son has leukemia," he said, hating the need to explain his bad temper. "I say things I don't mean sometimes."

"We both know that you meant what you said about me," she said flatly. Her eyes met his levelly. "You've hated me from almost the first day we worked together. Most of the time, you can't even be bothered to be civil to me. I didn't know that you had a grudge against me from the outset…"

She hadn't thought about that until she said it, but there

was a subtle change in his expression, a faint distaste that her mind locked on.

"So you heard that, too." His jaw clenched on words he didn't want to say. But maybe it was as well to say them. He'd lived a lie for the past year.

"Yes." She gripped the wrought-iron frame of the park bench hard. "What happened? Did my father cause someone to die?"

His jaw tautened. He didn't like saying this. "The girl I wanted to marry got pregnant by him. He performed a secret abortion and she was going to marry me anyway." He laughed icily. "A fling, he called it. But the medical authority had other ideas, and they invited him to resign."

Lou's fingers went white on the cold wrought iron. Had her mother known? What had happened to the girl afterward?

"Only a handful of people knew," Coltrain said, as if he'd read her thoughts. "I doubt that your mother did. She seemed very nice—hardly a fit match for a man like that."

"And the girl?" she asked levelly.

"She left town. Eventually she married." He rammed his hands into his pockets and glared at her. "If you want the whole truth, Drew felt sorry for you when your parents died so tragically. He knew I was looking for a partner, and he recommended you so highly that I asked you. I didn't connect the name at first," he added on a mocking note. "Ironic, isn't it, that I'd choose as a partner the daughter of a man I hated until the day he died."

"Why didn't you tell me?" she asked irritably. "I would have resigned!"

"You were in no fit state to be told anything," he replied with reluctant memories of her tragic face when she'd arrived. His hands clenched in his pockets. "Besides, you'd signed a one-year contract. The only way out was if you resigned."

It all made sense immediately. She was too intelligent not to understand why he'd been so antagonistic. "I see," she breathed. "But I didn't resign."

"You were made of stronger stuff than I imagined," he agreed. "You wouldn't back down an inch. No matter how rough it got, you threw my own bad temper back at me." He rubbed his fingers absently over the car keys in his pocket while he studied her. "It's been a long time since anyone around here stood up to me like that," he added reluctantly.

She knew that without being told. He was a holy terror. Even grown men around Jacobsville gave him a wide berth when he lost his legendary temper. But Lou never had. She stood right up to him. She wasn't fiery by nature, but her father had been viciously cruel to her. She'd learned early not to show fear or back down, because it only made him worse. The same rule seemed to apply to Coltrain. A weaker personality wouldn't have lasted in his office one week, much less one year, male or female.

She knew now that Drew Morris had been doing what he thought was a good deed. Perhaps he'd thought it wouldn't matter to Coltrain after such a long time to have a Blakely working for him. But he'd obviously underestimated the man. Lou would have realized at once, on the shortest acquaintance, that Coltrain didn't forgive people.

He stared at her unblinkingly. "A year. A whole year, being reminded every day I took a breath what your father cost me. There were times when I'd have done anything to make you leave. Just the sight of you was painful." He smiled wearily. "I think I hated you, at first."

That was the last straw. She'd loved him, against her will and all her judgment, and he was telling her that all he saw when he looked at her was an ice woman whose father had betrayed him with the woman he loved. He hated her.

It was too much all at once. Lou had always had impeccable control over her emotions. It had been dangerous to let her father know that he was hurting her, because he enjoyed hurting her. And now here was the one man she'd ever loved telling her that he hated her because of her father.

What a surprise it would be for him to learn that her father, at the last, had been little more than a high-class drug addict, stealing narcotics from the hospital where he worked in Austin to support his growing habit. He'd been as high as a kite on narcotics, in fact, when the plane he was piloting went down, killing himself and his wife.

Tears swelled her eyelids. Not a sound passed her lips as they overflowed in two hot streaks down her pale cheeks.

He caught his breath. He'd seen her tired, impassive,

worn-out, fighting mad, and even frustrated. But he'd never seen her cry. His lean hand shot out and touched the track of tears down one cheek, as if he had to touch them to make sure they were real.

She jerked back from him, laughing tearfully. "So that was why you were so horrible to me." She choked out the words. "Drew never said a word…no wonder you suffered me! And I was silly enough to dream…!" The laughter was harsher now as she dashed away the tears, staring at him with eyes full of pain and loss. "What a fool I've been," she whispered poignantly. "What a silly fool!"

She turned and walked away from him, gripping the car keys in her hand. The sight of her back was as eloquently telling as the words that haunted him. She'd dreamed… what?

For the next few days, Lou was polite and remote and as courteous as any stranger toward her partner. But something had altered in their relationship. He was aware of a subtle difference in her attitude toward him, in a distancing of herself that was new. Her eyes had always followed him, and he'd been aware of it at some subconscious level. Perhaps he'd been aware of more than covert glances, too. But Lou no longer watched him or went out of her way to seek him out. If she had questions, she wrote them down and left them for him on his desk. If there were messages to be passed on, she left them with Brenda.

The one time she did seek him out was Thursday afternoon as they closed up.

"Have you worked out an advertisement for someone to replace me?" she asked him politely.

He watched her calm dark eyes curiously. "Are you in such a hurry to leave?" he asked.

"Yes," she said bluntly. "I'd like to leave after the Christmas holidays." She turned and would have gone out the door, but his hand caught the sleeve of her white jacket. She slung it off and backed away. "At the first of the year."

He glared at her, hating the instinctive withdrawal that came whenever he touched her. "You're a good doctor," he said flatly. "You've earned your place here."

High praise for a man with his grudges. She looked over her shoulder at him, her eyes wounded. "But you hate me, don't you? I heard what you said to Drew, that every time you looked at me you remembered what my father had done and hated me all over again."

He let go of her sleeve, frowning. He couldn't find an answer.

"Well, don't sweat it, Doctor," she told him. "I'll be gone in a month and you can find someone you like to work with you."

She laughed curtly and walked out of the office.

She dressed sedately that evening for the Rotary Club dinner, in a neat off-white suit with a pink blouse. But she left her blond hair long around her shoulders for once, and used a light dusting of makeup. She didn't spend much time looking in the mirror. Her appearance had long ago ceased to matter to her.

Drew was surprised by it, though, and curious. She looked strangely vulnerable. But when he tried to hold her hand, she drew away from him. He'd wanted to ask her for a long time if there were things in her past that she might like to share with someone. But Louise was an unknown quantity, and she could easily shy away. He couldn't risk losing her altogether.

Drew held her arm as they entered the hall, and Lou was disconcerted to find Dr. Coltrain there. He almost never attended social functions unless Jane Parker was in attendance. But a quick glance around the room ascertained that Jane wasn't around. She wondered if the doctor had brought a date. It didn't take long to have that question answered, as a pretty young brunette came up beside him and clung to his arm as if it was the ticket to heaven.

Coltrain wasn't looking at her, though. His pale, narrow eyes had lanced over Lou and he was watching her closely. He hadn't seen her hair down in the year they'd worked together. She seemed more approachable tonight than he'd ever noticed, but she was Drew's date. Probably Drew's woman, too, he thought bitterly, despite her protests and reserve.

But trying to picture Lou in Drew's bed was more difficult than he'd thought. It wasn't at all in character. She was rigid in her views, just as she was in her mode of dress and her hairstyle. Just because she'd loosened that glorious hair tonight didn't mean that she'd suddenly become uninhibited. Nonetheless, the change disturbed him, because it was unexpected.

"Copper's got a new girl, I see," Drew said with a grin. "That's Nickie Bolton," he added. "She works as a nurse's aide at the hospital."

"I didn't recognize her out of uniform," Lou murmured.

"I did," he said. "She's lovely, isn't she?"

She nodded amiably. "Very young, too," she added with an indulgent smile.

He took her hand gently and smiled down at her. "You aren't exactly over the hill yourself," he teased.

She smiled up at him with warm eyes. "You're a nice man, Drew."

Across the room, a redheaded man's grip tightened ominously on a glass of punch. For over a year, Louise had avoided even his lightest touch. A few days ago, she'd thrown off his hand violently. But there she stood not only allowing Drew to hold her hand, but actually smiling at him. She'd never smiled at Coltrain that way; she'd never smiled at him any way at all.

His companion tapped him on the shoulder.

"You're with me, remember?" she asked with a pert smile. "Stop staring daggers at your partner. You're off duty. You don't have to fight all the time, do you?"

He frowned slightly. "What do you mean?"

"Everyone knows you hate her," Nickie said pleasantly. "It's common gossip at the hospital. You rake her over the coals and she walks around the corridors, red in the face and talking to herself. Well, most of the time, anyway. Once, Dr. Simpson found her crying in the nursery. But she doesn't usually cry, no matter how bad she hurts. She's pretty tough, in her way. I guess she's had to be, huh? Even if there are more women in medical school these days, you don't see that many women doctors yet. I'll bet she had to fight a lot of prejudice when she was in medical school."

That came as a shock. He'd never seen Lou cry until today, and he couldn't imagine her being upset at any temperamental display of his. Or was it, he pondered uneasily, just that she'd learned how not to show her wounds to him?

Chapter Three

At dinner, Lou sat with Drew, as far away from Coltrain and his date as she could get. She listened attentively to the speakers and whispered to Drew in the spaces between speakers. But it was torture to watch Nickie's small hand smooth over Coltrain's, to see her flirt with him. Lou didn't know how to flirt. There were a lot of things she didn't know. But she'd learned to keep a poker face, and she did it very well this evening. The one time Coltrain glanced down the table toward her, he saw nothing on her face or in her eyes that could tell him anything. She was unreadable.

After the meeting, she let Drew hold her hand as they walked out of the restaurant. Behind them, Coltrain was glaring at her with subdued fury.

When they made it to the parking lot, she found that the other couple had caught up with them.

"Nice bit of surgery this morning, Copper," Drew remarked. "You do memorable stitches. I doubt if Mrs. Blake will even have a scar to show around."

He managed a smile and held Nickie's hand all the tighter. "She was adamant about that," he remarked. "It seems that her husband likes perfection."

"He'll have a good time searching for it in this imperfect world," Drew replied. "I'll see you in the morning. And I'd like your opinion on my little strep-throat patient. His mother wants the whole works taken out, tonsils and adenoids, but he doesn't have strep often and I don't like unnecessary surgery. Perhaps she'd listen to you."

"Don't count on it," Copper said dryly. "I'll have a look if you like, though."

"Thanks."

"My pleasure." He glanced toward Lou, who hadn't said a word. "You were ten minutes late this morning," he added coldly.

"Oh, I overslept," she replied pleasantly. "It wears me out to follow the EMTs around looking for work."

She gave him a cool smile and got into the car before he realized that she'd made a joke, and at his expense.

"Be on time in the morning," he admonished before he walked away with Nickie on his arm.

"On time," Lou muttered beside Drew in the comfortable Ford he drove. Her hands crushed her purse. "I'll give him on time! I'll be sitting in *his* parking spot at eight-thirty on the dot!"

"He does it on purpose," he told her as he started the car. "I think he likes to make you spark at him."

"He's overjoyed that I'm leaving," she muttered. "And so am I!"

He gave her a quick glance and hid his smile. "If you say so."

She twisted her small purse in her lap, fuming, all the way back to her small house.

"I haven't been good company, Drew," she said as he walked her to the door. "I'm sorry."

He patted her shoulder absently. "Nothing wrong with the company," he said, correcting her. He smiled down at her. "But you really do rub Copper the wrong way, don't you?" he added thoughtfully. "I've noticed that antagonism from a distance, but tonight is the first time I've seen it at close range. Is he always like that?"

She nodded. "Always, from the beginning. Well, not quite," she confessed, remembering. "From last Christmas."

"What happened last Christmas?"

She studied him warily.

"I won't tell him," he promised. "What happened?"

"He tried to kiss me under the mistletoe and I, well, I sort of ducked and pulled away." She flushed. "He rattled me. He does, mostly. I get shaky when he comes too close. He's so forceful, and so physical. Even when he wants to talk to me, he's forever trying to grab me by the wrist or a sleeve. It's as if he knows how much it disturbs me, so he does it on purpose, just to make me uncomfortable."

He reached down and caught her wrist very gently, watching her face distort and feeling the instinctive, helpless jerk of her hand.

He let go at once. "Tell me about it, Lou."

With a wan smile, she rubbed her wrist. "No. It's history."

"It isn't, you know. Not if it makes you shaky to have people touch you…"

"Not everyone, just him," she muttered absently.

His eyebrows lifted, but she didn't seem to be aware of what she'd just confessed.

She sighed heavily. "I'm so tired," she said, rubbing the back of her neck. "I don't usually get so tired from even the longest days."

He touched her forehead professionally and frowned. "You're a bit warm. How do you feel?"

"Achy. Listless." She grimaced. "It's probably that virus that's going around. I usually get at least one every winter."

"Go to bed and if you aren't better tomorrow, don't go in," he advised. "Want me to prescribe something?"

She shook her head. "I'll be okay. Nothing does any good for a virus, you know that."

He chuckled. "Not even a sugarcoated pill?"

"I can do without a placebo. I'll get some rest. Thanks for tonight. I enjoyed it."

"So did I. I haven't done much socializing since Eve died. It's been five long years and I still miss her. I don't think I'll ever get over her enough to start a new relationship with anyone. I only wish we'd had a child. It might have made it easier."

She was studying him, puzzled. "It's said that many people marry within months of losing a mate," she began.

"I don't fit that pattern," he said quietly. "I only loved once. I'd rather have my memories of those twelve years with Eve than a hundred years with someone else. I suppose that sounds old-fashioned."

She shook her head. "It sounds beautiful," she said softly. "Lucky Eve, to have been loved so much."

He actually flushed. "It was mutual."

"I'm sure it was, Drew. I'm glad to have a friend like you."

"That works both ways." He smiled ruefully. "I'd like to take you out occasionally, so that people will stop thinking of me as a mental case. The gossip is beginning to get bad."

"I'd love to go out with you," she replied. She smiled. "I'm not very worldly, you know. It was books and exams and medicine for eight long years, and then internship. I was an honor student. I never had much time for men." Her eyes darkened. "I never wanted to have much time for them. My parents' marriage soured me. I never knew it could be happy or that people could love each other enough to be faithful—" She stopped, embarrassed.

"I knew about your father," he said. "Most of the hospital staff did. He liked young girls."

"Dr. Coltrain told me," she said miserably.

"He what?"

She drew in a long breath. "I overheard what he said to you on the telephone the other day. I'm leaving. My year is up after New Year's, anyway," she reminded him. "He told me what my father had done. No wonder he didn't want me here. You shouldn't have done it, Drew. You shouldn't have forced him to take me on."

"I know. But it's too late, isn't it? I thought I was helping, if that's any excuse." He searched her face. "Maybe I hoped it would help Copper, too. He was infatuated with Jane Parker. She's a lovely, sweet woman, and she has a temper, but she was never a match for Copper. He's the sort who'd cow a woman who couldn't stand up to him."

"Just like my father," she said shortly.

"I've never mentioned it, but one of your wrists looks as if it's suffered a break."

She flushed scarlet and drew back. "I have to go in now. Thanks again, Drew."

"If you can't talk to me, you need to talk to someone," he said. "Did you really think you could go through life without having the past affect the future?"

She smiled sweetly. "Drive carefully going home."

He shrugged. "Okay. I'll drop it."

"Good night."

"Good night."

She watched him drive away, absently rubbing the wrist he'd mentioned. She wouldn't think about it, she told herself. She'd go to bed and put it out of her mind.

Only it didn't work that way. She woke up in the middle of the night in tears, frightened until she remembered where she was. She was safe. It was over. But she felt sick and her throat was dry. She got up and found a pitcher, filling it with ice and water. She took a glass along with her and went back to bed. Except for frequent trips to the bathroom, she finally slept soundly.

There was a loud, furious knock at the front door. It kept on and on, followed by an equally loud voice. What a blessing that she didn't have close neighbors, she thought drowsily, or the police would be screaming up the driveway.

She tried to get up, but surprisingly, her feet wouldn't support her. She was dizzy and weak and sick at her stomach. Her head throbbed. She lay back down with a soft groan.

A minute later, the front door opened and a furious redheaded man in a lab coat came in the bedroom door.

"So this is where you are," he muttered, taking in her condition with a glance. "You couldn't have called?"

She barely focused on him. "I was up most of the night…"

"With Drew?"

She couldn't even manage a glare. "Being sick," she corrected. "Have you got anything on you to calm my stomach? I can't keep down anything to stop the nausea."

"I'll get something."

He went back out, grateful that she kept a key under the welcome mat. He didn't relish having to break down doors, although he had in the past to get to a patient.

He got his medical bag and went back into the bedroom. She was pale and she had a fever. He turned off the electronic thermometer and checked her lungs. Clear, thank God.

Her pulse was a little fast, but she seemed healthy enough. "A virus," he pronounced.

"No!" she exclaimed with weak sarcasm.

"You'll live."

"Give me the medicine, please," she asked, holding out a hand.

"Can you manage?"

"If you'll get me to the bathroom, sure."

He helped her up, noticing the frailty of her body. She didn't seem that thin in her clothing, but she was wearing silky pajamas that didn't conceal the slender lines of her body. He supported her to the door, and watched the door close behind her.

Minutes later, she opened the door again and let him help her back into bed.

He watched her for a minute and then, with resolution, he picked up the telephone. He punched in a number. "This is Dr. Coltrain. Send an ambulance out to Dr. Blakely's home, 23 Brazos Lane. That's right. Yes. Thank you."

She glared at him. "I will not…!"

"Hell, yes, you will," he said shortly. "I'm not leaving you out here alone to dehydrate. At the rate you're losing fluids, you'll die in three days."

"What do you care if I die?" she asked furiously.

He reached down to take her pulse again. This time, he caught the left wrist firmly, but she jerked it back. His blue eyes narrowed as he watched her color. Drew had been holding her right hand. At the table, it was her right hand he'd touched. But most of the time, Copper automatically reached for the left one…

He glanced down to where it lay on the coverlet and he noticed what Drew had; there was a definite break there, one which had been set but was visible.

She clenched her fist. "I don't want to go to the hospital."

"But you'll go, if I have to carry you."

She glared at him. It did no good at all. He went into the kitchen to turn off all the appliances except the refrigerator. On his way back, he paused to look around the living room. There were some very disturbing paintings on her walls, side by side with beautiful pastel drawings of flowers. He wondered who'd done them.

The ambulance arrived shortly. He watched the paramedics load her up and he laid the small bag she'd asked him to pack on the foot of the gurney.

"Thank you so much," she said with her last lucid breath. The medicine was beginning to take effect, and it had a narcotic in it to make her sleep.

"My pleasure, Dr. Blakely," he said. He smiled, but it didn't reach his eyes. They were watchful and thoughtful. "Do you paint?" he asked suddenly.

Her dark eyes blinked. "How did you know?" she murmured as she drifted off.

★ ★ ★

She awoke hours later in a private room, with a nurse checking her vital signs. "You're awake!" the nurse said with a smile. "Feeling any better?"

"A little." She touched her stomach. "I think I've lost weight."

"No wonder, with so much nausea. You'll be all right now. We'll take very good care of you. How about some soup and Jell-O and tea?"

"Coffee?" she asked hopefully.

The nurse chuckled. "Weak coffee, perhaps. We'll see." She charted her observations and went to see about supper.

It was modest fare, but delicious to a stomach that had hardly been able to hold anything. Imagine being sent to the hospital with a twenty-four-hour virus, Lou thought irritably, and wanted to find Dr. Coltrain and hit him.

Drew poked his head in the door while he was doing rounds. "I told you you felt feverish, didn't I?" he teased, smiling. "Better?"

She nodded. "But I would have been just fine at home."

"Not to hear your partner tell it. I expected to find your ribs sticking through your skin," he told her, chuckling. "I'll check on you later. Stay put."

She groaned and lay back. Patients were stacking up and she knew that Brenda had probably had to deal with angry ones all day, since Dr. Coltrain would have been operating in the morning. Everyone would be sitting in the waiting room until long after dark, muttering angrily.

It was after nine before he made rounds. He looked worn, and she felt guilty even if it couldn't be helped.

"I'm sorry," she said irritably when he came to the bedside.

He cocked an eyebrow. "For what?" He reached down and took her wrist—the right one—noticing that she didn't react while he felt her pulse.

"Leaving you to cope with my patients as well as your own," she said. The feel of his long fingers was disturbing. She began to fidget.

He leaned closer, to look into her eyes, and his hand remained curled around her wrist. He felt her pulse jump as his face neared hers and suddenly a new thought leapt into his shocked mind and refused to be banished.

She averted her gaze. "I'm all right," she said. She sounded breathless. Her pulse had gone wild under his searching fingers.

He stood up, letting go of her wrist. But he noticed the quick rise and fall of her chest with new interest. What an odd reaction for a woman who felt such antagonism toward him.

He picked up her chart, still frowning, and read what was written there. "You've improved. If you're doing this well in the morning, you can go home. Not to work," he added firmly. "Drew's going to come in and help me deal with the backlog in the morning while he has some free time."

"That's very kind of him."

"He's a kind man."

"Yes. *He* is."

He chuckled softly. "You don't like me, do you?" he asked through pursed lips. "I've never given you any reason to. I've been alternately hostile and sarcastic since the day you came here."

"Your normal self, Doctor," she replied.

His lips tugged up. "Not really. You don't know me."

"Lucky me."

His blue eyes narrowed thoughtfully. She'd reacted to him from the first as if he'd been contagious. Every approach he'd made had been met with instant withdrawal. He wondered why he'd never questioned her reactions. It wasn't revulsion. Oh, no. It was something much more disturbing on her part. She was vulnerable, and he'd only just realized it, when it was too late. She would leave before he had the opportunity to explore his own feelings.

He stuck his hands into his pockets and his eyes searched her pale, worn face. She wasn't wearing a trace of makeup. Her eyes held lingering traces of fever and her hair was dull, lackluster, disheveled by sleep. But even in that condition, she had a strange beauty.

"I know how I look, thanks," she muttered as she saw how he was looking at her. "You don't need to rub it in."

"Was I?" He studied her hostile eyes.

She dropped her gaze to her slender hands on the sheets. "You always do." Her eyes closed. "I don't need you to point out my lack of good looks, Doctor. My father never missed an opportunity to tell me what I was missing."

Her father. His expression hardened as the memories poured out. But even as they nagged at his mind, he began to remember bits and pieces of gossip he'd heard about the way Dr. Fielding Blakely treated his poor wife. He'd dismissed it at the time, but now he realized that Mrs. Blakely had to be aware of her husband's affairs. Had she not minded? Or was she afraid to mind…

He had more questions about Lou's family life than he had answers, and he was curious. Her reticence with him, her broken wrist, her lack of self-esteem—they began to add up.

His eyes narrowed. "Did your mother know that your father was unfaithful to her?" he asked.

She stared at him as if she didn't believe what she'd heard. "What?"

"You heard me. Did she know?"

She drew the sheet closer to her collarbone. "Yes." She bit off the word.

"Why didn't she leave him?"

She laughed bitterly. "You can't imagine."

"Maybe I can." He moved closer to the bed. "Maybe I can imagine a lot of things that never occurred to me before. I've looked at you for almost a year and I've never seen you until now."

She fidgeted under the cover. "Don't strain your imagination, Doctor," she said icily. "I haven't asked for your attention. I don't want it."

"Mine, or any other man's, right?" he asked gently.

She felt like an insect on a pin. "Will you stop?" she groaned. "I'm sick. I don't want to be interrogated."

"Is that what I'm doing? I thought I was showing a belated interest in my partner," he said lazily.

"I won't be your partner after Christmas."

"Why?"

"I've resigned. Have you forgotten? I even wrote it down and gave it to you."

"Oh. That. I tore it up."

Her eyes popped. "You what?"

"Tore it up," he said with a shrug. "I can't do without you. You have too many patients who won't come back if they have to see me."

"You had a fine practice…"

"Too fine. I never slept or took vacations. You've eased the load. You've made yourself indispensable. You have to stay."

"I do not." She shot her reply back instantly. "I hate you!"

He studied her, nodding slowly. "That's healthy. Much healthier than withdrawing like a frightened clam into a shell every time I come too close."

She all but gasped at such a blunt statement. "I do not…!"

"You do." He looked pointedly at her left wrist. "You've kept secrets. I'm going to worry you to death until you tell me every last one of them, beginning with why you can't bear to have anyone hold you by the wrist."

She couldn't get her breath. She felt her cheeks becoming hot as he stared down at her intently. "I'm not telling you any secrets," she assured him.

"Why not?" he replied. "I don't ever tell what I know."

She knew that. If a patient told him anything in confidence, he wouldn't share it.

She rubbed the wrist absently, wincing as she remembered how it had felt when it was broken, and how.

Coltrain, watching her, wondered how he could ever have thought her cold. She had a temper that was easily the equal of his own, and she never backed away from a fight. She'd avoided his touch, but he realized now that it was the past that made her afraid, not the present.

"You're mysterious, Lou," he said quietly. "You hold things in, keep things back. I've worked with you for a year, but I know nothing about you."

"That was your choice," she reminded him coolly. "You've treated me like a leper in your life."

He started to speak, took a breath and finally, nodded. "Yes. Through no fault of your own, I might add. I've held grudges."

She glanced at his hard, lean face. "You were entitled," she admitted. "I didn't know about my father's past. I probably should have realized there was a reason he never went back to Jacobsville, even to visit, while his brother was still alive here. Afterward, there wasn't even a cousin to write to. We all lost touch. My mother never seemed to mind that we didn't come back." She looked up at him. "She probably knew..." She flushed and dropped her eyes.

"But she stayed with him," he began.

"She had to!" The words burst out. "If she'd tried to leave, he'd have..." She swallowed and made a futile gesture with her hand.

"He'd have what? Killed her?"

She wouldn't look at him. She couldn't. The memories came flooding back, of his violence when he used narcotics, of the threats, her mother's fear, her own. The weeping, the cries of pain...

She sucked in a quick breath, and all the suffering was in the eyes she lifted to his when he took her hand.

His fingers curled hard around hers and held them, as if he could see the memories and was offering comfort.

"You'll tell me, one day," he said abruptly, his eyes steady on her own. "You'll tell me every bit of it."

She couldn't understand his interest. She searched his eyes curiously and suddenly felt a wave of feeling encompass her like a killing tide, knocking her breathless. Heat surged through her slender body, impaling her, and in his hard face she saw everything she knew of love, would ever know of it.

But he didn't want her that way. He never would. She was useful to the practice, but on a personal level, he was still clutching hard at the past; at the girl her father had taken from him, at Jane Parker. He was sorry for her, as he would be for anyone in pain, but it wasn't a personal concern.

She drew her hand away from his slowly and with a faint smile. "Thanks," she said huskily. "I…I think too hard sometimes. The past is long dead."

"I used to think so," he said, watching her. "Now, I'm not so sure."

She didn't understand what he was saying. It was just as well. The nurse came in to do her round and any personal conversation was banished at once.

Chapter Four

The next day, Lou was allowed to go home. Drew had eaten breakfast with her and made sure that she was well enough to leave before he agreed with Copper that she was fit. But when he offered to drive her home, Coltrain intervened. His partner, he said, was his responsibility. Drew didn't argue. In fact, when they weren't looking, he grinned.

Copper carried her bag into the house and helped her get settled on the couch. It was lunchtime and he hesitated, as if he felt guilty about not offering to take her out for a meal.

"I'm going to have some soup later," she murmured without looking at him. "I'm not hungry just yet. I expect you are."

"I could eat." He hesitated again, watching her with vague irritation. "Will you be all right?"

"It was only a virus," she said, making light of it. "I'm fine. Thank you for your concern."

"You might as well enjoy it, for novelty value if nothing else," he said without smiling. "It's been a long time since I've given a damn about a woman's comfort."

"I'm just a colleague," she replied, determined to show him that she realized there was nothing personal in their relationship. "It isn't the same thing."

"No, it isn't," he agreed. "I've been very careful to keep our association professional. I've never even asked you to my home, have I?"

He was making her uneasy with that unblinking stare. "So what? I've never asked you to mine," she replied. "I wouldn't presume to put you in such an embarrassing situation."

"Embarrassing? Why?"

"Well, because you'd have to find some logical excuse to refuse," she said.

He searched her quiet face and his eyes narrowed thoughtfully. "I don't know that I'd refuse. If you asked me."

Her heart leapt and she quickly averted her eyes. She wanted him to go, now, before she gave herself away. "Forgive me, but I'm very tired," she said.

She'd fended him off nicely, without giving offense. He wondered how many times over the years she'd done exactly that to other men.

He moved closer to her, noticing the way she tensed, the telltale quickening of her breath, the parting of her soft lips. She was affected by his nearness and trying valiantly to hide it. It touched him deeply that she was so vulnerable to him. He could have cursed himself for the way he'd treated her, for the antagonism that made her wary of any approach now.

He stopped when there was barely a foot of space between them, with his hands in his pockets so that he wouldn't make her any more nervous.

He looked down at her flushed oval face with curious pleasure. "Don't try to come in tomorrow if you don't feel like it. I'll cope."

"All right," she said in a hushed tone.

"Lou."

He hadn't called her by her first name before. It surprised her into lifting her eyes to his face.

"You aren't responsible for anything your father did," he said. "I'm sorry that I've made things hard for you. I hope you'll reconsider leaving."

She shifted uncomfortably. "Thank you. But I think I'd better go," she said softly. "You'll be happier with someone else."

"Do you think so? I don't agree." His hand lowered slowly to her face, touching her soft cheek, tracing it down to the corner of her mouth. It was the first intimate contact she'd ever had with him, and she actually trembled.

Her reaction had an explosive echo in his own body. His breath jerked into his throat and his teeth clenched as he looked at her mouth and thought he might die if he couldn't have it. But it was too soon. He couldn't…!

He drew back his hand as if she'd burned it. "I have

to go," he said tersely, turning on his heel. Her headlong response had prompted a reaction in him that he could barely contain at all. He had to distance himself before he reached for her and ruined everything.

Lou didn't realize why he was in such a hurry to leave. She assumed that he immediately regretted that unexpected caress and wanted to make sure that she didn't read anything into it.

"Thank you for bringing me home," she said formally.

He paused at the door and looked back at her, his eyes fiercely intent on her slender body in jeans and sweatshirt, on her loosened blond hair and exquisite complexion and dark eyes. "Thank your lucky stars that I'm leaving in time." He bit off the words.

He closed the door on her puzzled expression. He was acting very much out of character lately. She didn't know why, unless he was sorry he'd tried to talk her out of leaving the practice. Oh, well, she told herself, it was no longer her concern. She had to get used to the idea of being out of his life. He had nothing to offer her, and he had good reason to hate her, considering the part her father had played in his unhappy past.

She went into the kitchen and opened a can of tomato soup. She'd need to replenish her body before she could get back to work.

The can slipped in her left hand and she grimaced. Her dreams of becoming a surgeon had been lost overnight in one tragic act. A pity, her instructor had said, because she had a touch that few surgeons ever achieved, almost an instinctive knowledge of the best and most efficient way to sever tissue with minimum loss of blood. She would have been famous. But alas, the tendon had been severed with the compound fracture. And the best efforts of the best orthopedic surgeon hadn't been able to repair the damage. Her father hadn't even been sorry….

She shook her head to clear away the memories and went back to her soup. Some things were better forgotten.

She was back at work the day after her return home, a bit shaky, but game. She went through her patients efficiently, smiling at the grievance of one small boy whose stitches she'd just removed.

"Dr. Coltrain doesn't like little kids, does he?" he muttered. "I showed him my bad place and he said he'd seen worse!"

"He has," she told the small boy. She smiled at him. "But you've been very brave, Patrick my boy, and I'm giving you the award of honor." She handed him a stick of sugarless chewing gum and watched him grin. "Off with you, now, and mind you don't fall down banks into any more creeks!"

"Yes, ma'am!"

She handed his mother the charge sheet and was showing them out the door of the treatment cubicle just as Coltrain started to come into it. The boy glowered at him, smiled at Lou and went back to his waiting mother.

"Cheeky brat," he murmured, watching him turn the corner.

"He doesn't like you," she told him smugly. "You didn't sympathize with his bad place."

"Bad place." He harrumphed. "Two stitches. My God, what a fuss he made."

"It hurt," she informed him.

"He wouldn't let me take the damn stitches out, either. He said that I didn't know how to do it, but you did."

She grinned to herself at that retort while she dealt with the mess she'd made while working with Patrick.

"You don't like children, do you?" she asked.

He shrugged. "I don't know much about them, except what I see in the practice," he replied. "I deal mostly with adults since you came."

He leaned against the doorjamb and studied her with his hands in the pockets of his lab coat, a stethoscope draped around his neck. His eyes narrowed as he watched her work.

She became aware of the scrutiny and turned, her eyes meeting his and being captured there. She felt her heart race at the way he looked at her. Her hands stilled on her preparations for the next patient as she stood helplessly in thrall.

His lips compressed. He looked at her mouth and traced the full lower lip, the soft bow of the upper, with her teeth just visible where her lips parted. The look was intimate. He was wondering how it would feel to kiss her, and she knew it.

Muffled footsteps caught them unawares, and Brenda jerked open the sliding door of the cubicle. "Lou, I've got the wrong… Oh!" She bumped into Coltrain, whom she hadn't seen standing there.

"Sorry," he muttered. "I wanted to ask Lou if she'd seen the file on Henry Brady. It isn't where I left it."

Brenda grimaced as she handed it to him. "I picked it up mistakenly. I'm sorry."

"No harm done." He glanced back at Lou and went out without another word.

"Not another argument," Brenda groaned. "Honestly, partners should get along better than this."

Lou didn't bother to correct that assumption. It was much less embarrassing than what had really happened. Coltrain had never looked at her in that particular way before. She was glad that she'd resigned; she wasn't sure that she could survive any physical teasing from him. If he started making passes, she'd be a lot safer in Austin than she would be here.

After all he was a confirmed bachelor and there was no shortage of women on his arm at parties. Nickie was the latest in a string of them. And according to rumor, before Nickie, apparently he'd been infatuated with Jane Parker. He might be nursing a broken heart as well, since Jane's marriage.

Lou didn't want to be anybody's second-best girl. Besides, she never wanted to marry. It had been better when Coltrain treated her like the enemy. She wished he'd go back to his former behavior and stop looking at her mouth that way. She still tingled remembering the heat in his blue eyes. A man like that would be just plain hell to be loved by. He would be addictive. She had no taste for addictions and she knew already that Coltrain would break her heart if she let him. No, it was better that she leave. Then she wouldn't have the anguish of a hopeless relationship.

The annual hospital Christmas party was scheduled for Friday night, two weeks before Christmas so that the staff wouldn't be too involved with family celebrations to attend.

Lou hadn't planned to go, but Coltrain cornered her in his office as they prepared to leave that afternoon for the weekend.

"The Christmas party is tonight," he reminded her.

"I know. I'm not going."

"I'll pick you up in an hour," he said, refusing to listen when she tried to protest. "I know you still tire easily after the virus. We won't stay long."

"What about Nickie?" she asked irritably. "Won't she mind if you take your partner to a social event?"

Her antagonism surprised him. He lifted an indignant eyebrow. "Why should she?" he asked stiffly.

"You've been dating her."

"I escorted her to the Rotary Club meeting. I haven't proposed to her. And whatever you've heard to the contrary, she and I are not an item."

"You needn't bite my head off!" She shot the words at him.

His eyes dropped to her mouth and lingered there.

"I know something I'd like to bite," he said deep in his throat.

She actually gasped, so stunned by the remark that she couldn't even think of a reply.

His eyes flashed back up to catch hers. He was a bulldozer, she thought, and if she didn't stand up to him, he'd run right over her.

She stiffened her back. "I'm not going to any hospital dance with you," she said shortly. "You've given me hell for the past year. Do you think you can just walk in here and wipe all that out with an invitation? Not even an invitation, at that—a command!"

"Yes, I do," he returned curtly. "We both belong to the hospital staff, and nothing will start gossip quicker than having one of us stay away from an annual event. I do not plan to have any gossip going around here at my expense. I had enough of that in the past, thanks to your philandering father!"

She gripped her coat, furious at him. "You just got through saying that you didn't blame me for what he did."

"And I don't!" he said angrily. "But you're being blind and stupid."

"Thank you. Coming from you, those are compliments!"

He was all but vibrating with anger. He stared at her, glared at her, until her unsteady movement made him realize that she'd been ill.

He became less rigid. "Ben Maddox is going to be there tonight. He's a former colleague of ours from Canada.

He's just installed a massive computer system with linkups to medical networks around the world. I think it's too expensive for our purposes, but I agreed to hear him out about it. You're the high-tech expert," he added with faint sarcasm. "I'd like your opinion."

"My opinion? I'm honored. You've never asked for it before."

"I've never given a damn about it before," he retorted evenly. "But maybe there's something to this electronic revolution in medicine." He lifted his chin in a challenge. "Or so you keep telling me. Put your money where your mouth is, Doctor. Convince me."

She glared at him. "I'll drive my own car and see you there."

It was a concession, of sorts. He frowned slightly. "Why don't you want to ride with me? What are you afraid of?" he taunted softly.

She couldn't admit what frightened her. "It wouldn't look good to have us arrive together," she said. "It would give people something to talk about."

He was oddly disappointed, although he didn't quite know why. "All right, then."

She nodded, feeling that she'd won something. He nodded, too, and quietly left her. It felt like a sort of truce. God knew, they could use one.

Ben Maddox was tall, blond and drop-dead gorgeous. He was also married and the father of three. He had photographs, which he enjoyed showing to any of his old colleagues who were willing to look at them. But in addition to those photographs, he had information on a networking computer system that he used extensively in his own practice. It was an expensive piece of equipment, but it permitted the user instant access to medical experts in every field. As a diagnostic tool and a means of getting second opinions from recognized authorities, it was breathtaking. But so was the price.

Lou had worn a black silk dress with a lace overlay, a demure rounded neckline and see-through sleeves. Her hairstyle, a topknot with little tendrils of blond hair slipping down to her shoulders, looked sexy. So did her long, elegant legs in high heels, under the midknee fitted skirt. She wore no jewelry at all, except for a strand of pearls with matching earrings.

Watching her move, Coltrain was aware of old, unwanted sensations. At the party a year ago, she'd worn something a little more revealing, and he'd deliberately maneuvered her under the mistletoe out of mingled curiosity and desire. But she'd evaded him as if he had the plague, then and since. His ego had suffered a sharp blow. He hadn't felt confident enough to try again, so antagonism and anger had kept her at bay. Not that his memories of her father's betrayal hadn't added to his enmity.

She was animated tonight, talking to Ben about the computer setup as if she knew everything there was to know about the machines.

"Copper, you've got a savvy partner here," Ben remarked when he joined them. "She's computer literate!"

"She's the resident high-tech expert," Copper replied. "I like old-fashioned, hands-on medicine. She'd rather reach for a machine to make diagnoses."

"High tech is the way of the future," Ben said coaxingly.

"It's also the reason medical costs have gone through the roof," came the predictable reply. "The money we spend on these outrageously expensive machines has to be passed on to the patients. That raises our fees, the hospital's fees, the insurance companies' fees..."

"Pessimist!" Ben accused.

"I'm being realistic," Copper told him, lifting his highball glass in a mock toast. He drained it, feeling the liquor.

Ben frowned as his old colleague made his way past the dancers back to the buffet table. "That's odd," he remarked. "I don't remember ever seeing Copper take more than one drink."

Neither did Lou. She watched her colleague pour himself another drink and she frowned.

Ben produced a card from the computer company for her, and while he was explaining the setup procedure, she noticed Nickie going up to Coltrain. She was wearing an electric blue dress that could have started a riot. The woman was pretty anyway, but that dress certainly revealed most of her charms.

Nickie laughed and dragged Coltrain under the mistletoe, looking up to indicate it there, to the amusement of the others standing by. Coltrain laughed softly, whipped a lean arm around Nickie's trim waist and pulled her against his tall body. He bent his head, and the way he kissed her made Lou go hot all over. She'd never been in his arms, but she'd dreamed about it. The fever in that thin mouth, the way he twisted Nickie even closer, made her breath catch. She averted her eyes and flushed at the train of her own thoughts.

"Leave it to Coltrain to draw the prettiest girls." Ben chuckled. "The gossip mill will grind on that kiss for a month. He's not usually so uninhibited. He must be over his limit!"

She could have agreed. Her hand clenched around the piña colada she was nursing. "This computer system, is it reliable?" she asked through tight lips, forcing a smile.

"Yes, except in thunderstorms. Always unplug it, regardless of what they tell you about protective spikes. One good hit, and you could be down for days."

"I'll remember, if we get it."

"The system I have is expensive," Ben agreed, "but there are others available that would be just right for a small practice like yours and Copper's. In fact..."

His voice droned on and Lou tried valiantly to pay attention. She was aware at some level that Coltrain and Nickie were dancing and making the rounds of guests together. It was much later, and well into her second piña colada, when the lavish mistletoe began to get serious workouts.

Lou wasn't in the mood to dance. She refused Ben's offer, and several others. A couple of hours had passed and it felt safe to leave now, before her spirit was totally crushed by being consistently ignored by Coltrain. She put down her half-full glass. "I really do have to go," she told Ben. "I've been ill and I'm not quite back up to par yet." She shook his hand. "It was very nice to have met you."

"Same here. I wonder why Drew Morris didn't show up? I had hoped to see him again while I was here."

"I don't know," she said, realizing that she hadn't heard from Drew since she was released from the hospital. She had no idea where he was, and she hadn't asked.

"I'll check with Copper. He's certainly been elusive this evening. Not that I can blame him, considering his pretty companion over there." He raised his hand to catch the other man's eyes, to Lou's dismay.

Coltrain joined them with Nickie hanging on his arm. "Still here?" he asked Lou with a mocking smile. "I thought you'd be out the door and gone by now."

"I'm just about to leave. Do you know where Drew is?"

"He's in Florida at that pediatric seminar. Didn't Brenda tell you?"

"She was so busy she probably forgot," she said.

"So that's where the old devil has gone," Ben said ruefully. "I'm sorry I missed him."

"I'm sure he will be, too," Lou said. The sight of Nickie and Coltrain together was hurting her. "I'd better be off—"

"Oh, not yet," Copper said with glittery blue eyes. "Not before you've been kissed under the mistletoe, Doctor."

She flushed and laughed nervously. "I'll forgo that little ritual, I think."

"No, you won't." He sounded pleasant enough, but the expression on his face was dangerous. He moved away from Nickie and his lean arm shot around Lou's waist, maneuvering her under a low-hanging sprig of mistletoe tied with a red velvet bow. "You're not getting away this time," he said huskily.

Before she could think, react, protest, his head bent and his thin, cruel mouth fastened on hers with fierce intent. He didn't close his eyes when he kissed, she thought a bit wildly, he watched her all through it. His arm pressed her closer to the length of his muscular body, and his free hand came up so that his thumb could rub sensuously over her mouth while he kissed it, parting her lips, playing havoc with her nerves.

She gasped at the rough pleasure, and inadvertently gave him exactly what he wanted. His open mouth ground into hers, pressing her lips apart. She tasted him in an intimacy that she'd never shared with a man, in front of the amused hospital staff, while his cold eyes stared straight into hers.

She made a faint sound and he lifted his head, looking down at her swollen lips. His thumb traced over them with much greater tenderness than his mouth had given her, and he held her shocked eyes for a long moment before he reluctantly let her go.

"Merry Christmas, Dr. Blakely," he said in a mocking tone, although his voice was husky.

"And you, Dr. Coltrain," she said shakily, not quite meeting his eyes. "Good night, Ben…Nickie."

She slid away from them toward the door, on shaky legs, with a mouth that burned from his cold, fierce kiss. She barely remembered getting her coat and saying goodbye to the people she recognized on her way to the car park.

Coltrain watched her go with feelings he'd never encountered in his life. He was burning up with desire, and he'd had enough whiskey to threaten his control.

Nickie tugged on his sleeve. "You didn't kiss me like that," she protested, pouting prettily. "Why don't you take me home and we can…"

"I'll be back in a minute," he said, shaking her off.

She glared at him, coloring with embarrassment when she realized that two of the staff had overheard her. Rejection in private was one thing, but it hurt to have him make it so public. He hadn't called her since the night of the Rotary Club meeting. He'd just kissed her very nicely, but it looked different when he'd done it with his partner. She frowned. Something was going on. She followed at a distance. She was going to find out what.

Coltrain, unaware of her pursuit, headed after Lou with no real understanding of his own actions. He couldn't get the taste of her out of his head. He was pretty sure that she felt the same way. He couldn't let her leave until he knew…

Lou kept walking, but she heard footsteps behind her as she neared her car. She knew them, because she heard them every day on the slick tile of the office floor. She walked faster, but it did no good. Coltrain reached her car at the same time she reached it.

His hand came around her, grasping her car key and her fingers, pulling, turning her. She was pressed completely against the car by the warm weight of his body, and she looked up into a set, shadowy face while his mouth hovered just above her own in the starlit darkness.

"It wasn't enough," he said roughly. "Not nearly enough."

He bent and his mouth found hers expertly. His hands smoothed into hers and linked with her fingers. His hips slid sensuously over hers, seductive, refusing to entertain barriers or limits. His mouth began to open, brushing in soft strokes over her lips until they began to part, but she stiffened.

"Don't you know how to kiss?" he whispered, surprised. "Open your mouth, little one. Open it and fit it to mine… Yes, that's it."

She felt his tongue dance at the opening he'd made, felt it slowly ease into her mouth and penetrate, teasing, probing, tasting. Her fingers clutched helplessly at his and she shivered. It was so intimate, so…familiar! She moaned sharply as his hips began to caress hers. She felt him become aroused and her whole body vibrated.

His mouth grew more insistent then. He released one of her hands and his fingers played with her mouth, as they had inside, but now there was the heat and the magic they were generating, and it was no cold, clinical experiment. He groaned against her mouth and she felt his body go rigid all at once.

He bit her lower lip, hard, when her teeth clenched at

the soft probing of his tongue. Suddenly she came to her senses and realized what was happening. He tasted blatantly of whiskey. He'd had too much to drink and he'd forgotten which woman he was with. Did he think she was Nickie? she wondered dizzily. Was that why he was making love to her? And that was what it was, she realized with a shock. Only a lover would take such intimacy for granted, be so blind to surroundings and restraint.

Chapter Five

Despite the pleasure she felt, the whiskey on his breath brought back unbearable memories of another man who drank; memories not of kisses, but of pain and fear. Her hands pressed against his warm shirtfront under the open dinner jacket and she pushed, only vaguely aware of thick hair under the silkiness of the fabric.

"No," she whispered into his insistent mouth.

He didn't seem to hear her. His mouth hardened and a sound rumbled out of the back of his throat. "For God's sake, stop fighting me," he whispered fiercely. "Open your mouth!"

The intimacy he was asking for frightened her. She twisted her face, breathing like a runner. "Jebediah…no!" she whispered frantically.

The fear in her voice got through the intoxication. His mouth stilled against her cheek, but his body didn't withdraw. She could feel it against every inch of her like a warm, steely brand. His breathing wasn't steady, and over her breasts, his heart was beating like a frenzied bass drum.

It suddenly dawned on him what he was doing, and with whom.

"My God!" he whispered fiercely. His hands tightened for an instant before they fell away from her. A faint shudder went through his powerful body as he slowly, so slowly, pushed himself away from her, balancing his weight on his hands against the car doorframe.

She felt his breath on her swollen mouth as he fought for control. He was still too close.

"You haven't used my given name before," he said as he levered farther away from her. "I didn't know you knew it."

"It's…on our contract," she said jerkily.

He removed his hands from the car and stood upright, dragging in air. "I've had two highballs," he said on an apologetic laugh. "I don't drink. It hit me harder than I realized."

He was apologizing, she thought dazedly. That was unexpected. He wasn't that kind of man. Or was he? She hadn't thought he was the type to get drunk and kiss women in that intimate, fierce way, either. Especially her.

She tried to catch her own breath. Her mouth hurt from the muted violence of his kisses and her legs felt weak. She leaned back against the car, only now noticing its coldness.

She hadn't felt it while he was kissing her. She touched her tongue to her lips and she tasted him on them.

She eased away from the car a little, shy now that he was standing back from her.

She was so shaky that she wondered how she was going to drive home. Then she wondered, with even more concern, how *he* was going to drive home.

"You shouldn't drive," she began hesitantly.

In the faint light from the hospital, she saw him smile sardonically. "Worried about me?" he chided.

She shouldn't have slipped like that. "I'd worry about anyone who'd had too much to drink," she began.

"All right, I won't embarrass you. Nickie can drive. She doesn't drink at all."

Nickie. Nickie would take him home and she'd probably stay to nurse him, too, in his condition. God only knew what might happen, but she couldn't afford to interfere. He'd had too much to drink and he'd kissed her, and she'd let him. Now she was ashamed and embarrassed.

"I have to go," she said stiffly.

"Drive carefully," he replied.

"Sure."

She found her keys where they'd fallen to the ground when he kissed her and unlocked the car door. She closed it once she was inside and started it after a bad fumble. He stood back from it, his hands in his pockets, looking dazed and not quite sober.

She hesitated, but Nickie came out the door, calling him. When he turned and raised a hand in Nickie's direction and answered her, laughing, Lou came to her senses. She lifted a hand toward both of them and drove away as quickly as she could. When she glanced back in the rearview mirror, it was to see Nickie holding Coltrain's hand as they went toward the building again.

So much for the interlude, she thought miserably. He'd probably only just realized who he'd kissed and was in shock.

That was close to the truth. Coltrain's head was spinning. He'd never dreamed that a kiss could be so explosive or addictive. There was something about Lou Blakely that made his knees buckle. He had no idea why he'd reacted so violently to her that he couldn't even let her leave. God knew what would have happened if she hadn't pushed him away when she did.

Nickie held on to him as they went back inside. "You've got her lipstick all over you," she accused.

He paused, shaken out of his brooding. Nickie was pretty, he thought, and uncomplicated. She already knew that he wasn't going to get serious however long they dated, because he'd told her so. It made him relax. He smiled down at her. "Wipe it off."

She pulled his handkerchief out of his pocket and did as he asked, smiling pertly. "Want to sample mine again?"

He tapped her on the nose. "Not tonight," he said. "We'd better leave. It's getting late."

"I'm driving," she told him.

"Yes, you are," he agreed.

She felt better. At least she was the one going home with him, not Lou. She wasn't going to give him up without a struggle, not when he was the best thing that had ever happened to her. Wealthy bachelor surgeons didn't come along every day of the week.

Lou drove home in a similar daze, overcome by the fervor of Coltrain's hard kisses. She couldn't understand why a man who'd always seemed to hate her had suddenly become addicted to her mouth; so addicted, in fact, that he'd followed her to her car. It had been the sweetest night of her life, but she had to keep her head and realize that it was an isolated incident. If Coltrain hadn't been drinking, it would never have happened. Maybe by Monday, she thought, he'd have convinced himself that it hadn't. She wished she could. She was more in love with him than ever, and he was as far out of her reach as he had ever been. Except that now he'd probably go even farther out of reach, because he'd lost his head and he wouldn't like remembering it.

She did her usual housework and answered emergency calls. She got more than her share because Dr. Coltrain had left word with their answering service that he was going to be out of town until Monday and Dr. Blakely would be covering for him.

Nice of him to ask her first, she thought bitterly, and tell her that he was going to be out of town. But perhaps he'd been reluctant to talk to her after what had happened. If the truth were known, he was more than likely as embarrassed as she was and just wanted to forget the whole thing.

She did his rounds and hers at the hospital, noticing absently that she was getting more attention than usual. Probably, she reasoned, because people were remembering the way Coltrain had kissed her. Maybe they thought something was going on between them.

"How's it going?" Drew asked on Sunday afternoon, grinning at her. "I hear I missed a humdinger of a kiss at the Christmas party," he added wickedly.

She blushed to her hairline. "Lots of people got kissed."

"Not like you did. Not so that he followed you out to the parking lot and damn near made love to you on the hood of your car." He chuckled.

"Who…?"

"Nickie," he said, confirming her worst nightmare. "She was watching, apparently, and she's sweet on Copper. I guess she thought it might turn him off you if there was a lot of gossip about what happened. Rumors fly, especially when they're about two doctors who seem to hate each other."

"He'll walk right into it when he comes back," she said uneasily. "What can I do?"

"Nothing, I'm afraid."

Her eyes narrowed. "That's what you think."

She turned on her heel and went in search of Nickie. She found her in a patient's room and waited calmly while the girl, nervous and very insecure once she saw Lou waiting for her, finished the chore she was performing.

She went out into the hall with Lou, and she looked apprehensive.

Lou clutched a clipboard to her lab jacket. She didn't smile. "I understand you've been feeding the rumor mill. I'll give you some good advice. Stop it while you can."

By now, Nickie's face had gone puce. "I never meant…I was kidding!" she burst out. "That's all, just kidding!"

Lou studied her without emotion. "I'm not laughing. Dr. Coltrain won't be laughing, either, when he hears about it. And I'll make sure he knows where it came from."

"That's spiteful!" Nickie cried. "I'm crazy about him!"

"No, you aren't," Lou said shortly. "You'd never subject him to the embarrassment you have with all this gossip if you really cared."

Nickie's hands locked together. "I'm sorry," she said on a long sigh. "I really am. I was just jealous," she confessed, avoiding Lou's eyes. "He wouldn't even kiss me good-night, but he'd kiss you that way, and he hates you."

"Try to remember that he'd had too much to drink," Lou said quietly. "Only a fool would read anything into a kiss under the mistletoe."

"I guess so," Nickie said, but she wasn't really convinced. "I'm sorry. You won't tell him it was me, will you?" she added worriedly. "He'll hate me. I care so much, Dr. Blakely!"

"I won't tell him," Lou said. "But no more gossip!"

"Yes, ma'am!" Nickie brightened, grinned and went

off down the hall, irrepressibly young and optimistic. Watching her, Lou felt ancient.

The next morning was Monday, and Lou went into the office to come face-to-face with a furious partner, who blocked her doorway and glared at her with blue eyes like arctic ice.

"Now what have I done?" she asked before he could speak, and slammed her bag down on her desk, ready to do battle.

"You don't know?" he taunted.

She folded her arms over her breasts and leaned back against the edge of the desk. "There's a terrible rumor going around the hospital," she guessed.

His eyebrow jerked, but the ice didn't leave his eyes. "Did you start it?"

"Of course," she agreed furiously. "I couldn't wait to tell everybody on staff that you bent me back over the hood of my car and ravished me in the parking lot!"

Brenda, who'd started in the door, stood there with her mouth open, intercepted a furious glare from two pairs of eyes, turned on her heel and got out.

"Could you keep your voice down?" Coltrain snapped.

"Gladly, when you stop making stupid accusations!"

He glared at her and she glared back.

"I was drinking!"

"That's it, announce it to everyone in the waiting room,

why don't you, and see how many patients run for their cars!" she raged.

He closed her office door, hard, and leaned back against it. "Who started the rumor?" he asked.

"That's more like it," she replied. "Don't accuse until you ask. I didn't start it. I have no wish to become the subject of gossip."

"Not even to force me to do something about the rumors?" he asked. "Such as announce our engagement?"

Her eyes went saucer-wide. "Please! I've just eaten!"

His jaw went taut. "I beg your pardon?"

"And so you should!" she said enthusiastically. "Marry you? I'd rather chain myself to a tree in an alligator swamp!"

He didn't answer immediately. He stared at her instead while all sorts of impractical ideas sifted through his mind.

A buzzer sounded on her desk. She reached over and pressed a button. "Yes?"

"What about the patients?" Brenda prompted.

"He doesn't *have* any patience," Lou said without thinking.

"Excuse me?" Brenda stammered.

"Oh. That sort of patients. Send my first one in, will you, Brenda? Dr. Coltrain was just leaving."

"No, he wasn't," he returned when her finger left the intercom button. "We'll finish this discussion after office hours."

"After office hours?" she asked blankly.

"Yes. But, don't get your hopes up about a repeat of Friday evening," he said with a mocking smile. "After all, I'm not drunk today."

Her eyes flashed murderously and her lips compressed. But he was already out the door.

Lou was never sure afterward how she'd managed to get through her patients without revealing her state of mind. She was furiously angry at Coltrain for his accusations and equally upset with Brenda for hearing what she'd said in retaliation. Now it would be all over the office as well as all over the hospital that she and Coltrain had something going. And they didn't! Despite Lou's helpless attraction to him, it didn't take much imagination to see that Coltrain didn't feel the same. Well, maybe physically he felt something for her, but emotionally he still hated her. A few kisses wouldn't change that!

She checked Mr. Bailey's firm, steady heartbeat, listened to his lungs and pronounced him over the pneumonia she'd been treating him for.

As she started to go, leaving Brenda to help him with his shirt, he called to her.

"What's this I hear about you and Doc Coltrain?" he teased. "Been kissing up a storm at the hospital Christmas party, they say. Any chance we'll be hearing wedding bells?"

He didn't understand, he told Brenda on his way out, why Dr. Blakely had suddenly screamed like that. Maybe she'd seen a mouse, Brenda replied helpfully.

When the office staff went home, Coltrain was waiting at the front entrance for Lou. He'd stationed himself there after checking with the hospital about a patient, and he hadn't moved, in case Lou decided to try to sneak out.

He was wearing the navy blue suit that looked so good on him, lounging against the front door with elegant carelessness, when she went out of her office. His red hair caught the reflection of the overhead light and seemed to burn like flames over his blue, blue eyes. They swept down over her neat gray pantsuit to her long legs encased in slacks with low-heeled shoes.

"That color looks good on you," he remarked.

"You don't need to flatter me. Just say what's on your mind, please, and let me go home."

"All right." His eyes fell to her soft mouth and lingered there. "Who started the rumors about us?"

She traced a pattern on her fanny pack. "I promised I wouldn't tell."

"Nickie," he guessed, nodding at her shocked expression.

"She's young and infatuated," she began.

"Not that young," he said with quiet insinuation.

Her eyes flashed before she could avert them. Her hand dug into the fanny pack for her car keys. "It's a nine-days wonder," she continued. "People will find something else to talk about."

"Nothing quite this spicy has happened since Ted Regan went chasing off to Victoria after Coreen Tarleton and she came home wearing his engagement ring."

"There's hardly any comparison," she said, "considering that everyone knows how we feel about each other!"

"How *do* we feel about each other, Lou?" he replied quietly, and watched her expression change.

"We're enemies," she returned instantly.

"Are we?" He searched her eyes in a silence that grew oppressive. His arms fell to his sides. "Come here, Lou."

She felt her breathing go wild. That could have been an invitation to bypass him and leave the building. But the look in his eyes told her it wasn't. Those eyes blazed like flames in his lean, tanned face, beckoning, promising pleasures beyond imagination.

He lifted a hand. "Come on, coward," he chided softly, and his lips curled at the edges. "I won't hurt you."

"You're sober," she reminded him.

"Cold sober," he agreed. "Let's see how it feels when I know what I'm doing."

Her heart stopped, started, raced. She hesitated, and he laughed softly and started toward her, with that slow, deliberate walk that spoke volumes about his intent.

"You mustn't," she spoke quickly, holding up a hand.

He caught the hand and jerked her against him, imprisoning her there with a steely arm. "I must." He corrected her, letting his eyes fall to her mouth. "I *have* to know." He bit off the words against her lips.

She never found out what he had to know, because the instant she felt his lips probing her mouth, she went under in a blaze of desire unlike anything she'd felt before. She gasped, opened her lips, yielded to his enveloping arms without a single protest. If anything, she pushed closer into his arms, against that steely body that was instantly aroused by the feel of her.

She tried to speak, to protest, but he pushed his tongue into her mouth with a harsh groan, and his arms lifted her so that she fit perfectly against him from breast to thigh. She fought, frightened by the intimacy and the sensations kindled in her untried body.

Her frantic protest registered at once. He remembered she'd had the same reaction the night of the Christmas party. His mouth lifted, and his searching eyes met hers.

"You couldn't be a virgin," he said, making it sound more like an accusation than a statement of fact.

She bit her lip and dropped her eyes, shamed and embarrassed. "Rub it in," she growled.

"My God." He eased her back onto her feet and held her by the upper arms so that she wouldn't fall. "My God! How old are you, thirty?"

"Twenty-eight," she said unsteadily, gasping for breath. Her whole body felt swollen. Her dark eyes glowered up at him as she pushed back her disheveled hair. "And you needn't look so shocked, you of all people should know that some people still have a few principles! You're a doctor, after all!"

"I thought virgins were a fairy tale," he said flatly. "Damn it!"

Her chin lifted. "What's wrong, Doctor, did you see me as a pleasant interlude between patients?"

His lips compressed. He rammed his hands into his

trouser pockets, all too aware of a throbbing arousal that wouldn't go away. He turned to the door and jerked it open. All weekend he'd dreamed of taking Louise Blakely home with him after work and seducing her in his big king-size bed. She was leaving anyway, and the hunger he felt for her was one he had to satisfy or go mad. It had seemed so simple. She wanted him; he knew she did. People were already talking about them, so what would a little more gossip matter? She'd be gone at the first of the year, anyway.

But now he had a new complication, one he'd never dreamed of having. She was no young girl, but it didn't take an expert to know why she backed away from intimacy like a repressed adolescent. He'd been baiting her with that accusation of virginity, but she hadn't realized it. She'd taken it at face value and she'd given him a truth he didn't even want. She was innocent. How could he seduce her now? On the other hand, how was he going to get rid of this very inconvenient and noticeable desire for her?

Watching him, Lou was cursing her own headlong response. She hated having him know how much she wanted him.

"Any man could have made me react that way!" she flared defensively, red-faced. "Any experienced man!"

His head turned and he stared at her, seeing through the flustering words to the embarrassment.

"It's all right," he said gently. "We're both human. Don't beat your conscience to death over a kiss, Lou."

She went even redder and her hands clenched at her sides. "I'm still leaving!"

"I know."

"And I won't let you seduce me!"

He turned. "I won't try," he said solemnly. "I don't seduce virgins."

She bit her lip and tasted him on it. She winced.

"Why?" he asked quietly.

She glared at him.

"Why?" he persisted.

Her eyes fell under that piercing blue stare. "Because I don't want to end up like my mother," she said huskily.

Of all the answers he might have expected, that was the last. "Your mother? I don't understand."

She shook her head. "You don't need to. It's personal. You and I are business partners until the end of the month, and then nothing that happened to me will be any concern of yours."

He didn't move. She looked vulnerable, hurt. "Counseling might be of some benefit," he said gently.

"I don't need counseling."

"Tell me how your wrist got broken, Lou," he said matter-of-factly.

She stiffened.

"Oh, a layman wouldn't notice, it's healed nicely. But surgery is my business. I know a break when I see one. There are scars, too, despite the neat stitching job. How did it happen?"

She felt weak. She didn't want to talk to him, of all

people, about her past. It would only reinforce what he already thought of her father, though God only knew why she should defend such a man.

She clasped her wrist defensively, as if to hide what had been done to it. "It's an old injury," she said finally.

"What sort of injury? How did it happen?"

She laughed nervously. "I'm not your patient."

He absently jingled the change in his pocket, watching her. It occurred to him that she was a stranger. Despite their heated arguments over the past year, they'd never come close to discussing personal matters. Away from the office, they were barely civil to each other. In it, they never discussed anything except business. But he was getting a new picture of her, and not a very reassuring one. This was a woman with a painful past, so painful that it had locked her up inside an antiseptic prison. He wondered if she'd ever had the incentive to fight her way out, or why it should matter to him that she hadn't.

"Can you talk to Drew about it?" he asked suddenly.

She hesitated and then shook her head. Her fingers tightened around her wrist. "It doesn't matter, I tell you."

His hand came out of his pocket and he caught the damaged wrist very gently in his long fingers, prepared for her instinctive jerk. He moved closer, drawing that hand to his chest. He pressed it gently into the thick fabric of his vest.

"There's nothing you can't tell me," he said solemnly. "I don't carry tales, or gossip. Anything you say to me will remain between the two of us. If you want to talk, ever, I'll listen."

She bit her bottom lip. She'd never been able to tell anyone. Her mother knew, but she defended her husband, trying desperately to pretend that Lou had imagined it, that it had never happened. She excused her husband's affairs, his drinking bouts, his drug addiction, his brutality, his sarcasm…everything, in the name of love, while her marriage disintegrated around her and her daughter turned away from her. Obsessive love, one of her friends had called it—blind, obsessive love that refused to acknowledge the least personality flaw in the loved one.

"My mother was emotionally crippled," she said, thinking aloud. "She was so blindly in love with him that he could do no wrong, no wrong at all…" She remembered where she was and looked up at him with the pain still in her eyes.

"Who broke your wrist, Lou?" he asked gently.

She remembered aloud. "He was drinking and I tried to take the bottle away from him, because he'd hit my mother. He hit my wrist with the bottle, and it broke," she added, wincing at the memory of the pain. "And all the while, when they operated to repair the damage, he kept saying that I'd fallen through a glass door, that I'd tripped. Everyone believed him, even my mother. I told her that he did it, and she said that I was lying."

"He? Who did it, Lou?"

She searched his curious eyes. "Why…my father," she said simply.

Chapter Six

Coltrain searched her dark eyes, although the confession didn't really surprise him. He knew too much about her father to be surprised.

"So that was why the whiskey on my breath bothered you Friday night," he remarked quietly.

She averted her head and nodded. "He was a drunkard at the last, and a drug addict. He had to stop operating because he almost killed a patient. They let him retire and act in an advisory capacity because he'd been such a good surgeon. He was, you know," she added. "He might have been a terrible father, but he was a wonderful surgeon. I wanted to be a surgeon, to be like him." She shivered. "I was in my first year of medical school when it happened. I lost a semester and afterward, I knew I'd never be able to operate. I decided to become a general practitioner."

"What a pity," he said. He understood the fire for

surgical work because he had it. He loved what he did for a living.

She smiled sadly. "I'm still practicing medicine. It isn't so bad. Family practice has its place in the scheme of things, and I've enjoyed the time I've spent in Jacobsville."

"So have I," he admitted reluctantly. He smiled at her expression. "Surprised? You've been here long enough to know how a good many people react to me. I'm the original bad boy of the community. If it hadn't been for the scholarship one of my teachers helped me get, I'd probably be in jail by now. I had a hard childhood and I hated authority in any form. I was in constant trouble with the law."

"You?" she asked, aghast.

He nodded. "People aren't always what they seem, are they?" he continued. "I was a wild boy. But I loved medicine and I had an aptitude for it and there were people who were willing to help me. I'm the first of my family to escape poverty, did you know?"

She shook her head. "I don't know anything about your family," she said. "I wouldn't have presumed to ask anyone something so personal about you."

"I've noticed that," he returned. "You avoid sharing your feelings. You'll fight back, but you don't let people close, do you?"

"When people get too close, they can hurt you," she said.

"A lesson your father taught you, no doubt."

She wrapped her arms around her chest. "I'm cold," she said dully. "I want to go home."

He searched her face. "Come home with me."

She hesitated warily.

He made a face. "Shame on you for what you're thinking. You should know better. You're off the endangered list. I'll make chili and Mexican corn bread and strong coffee and we can watch a Christmas special. Do you like opera?"

Her eyes brightened. "Oh, I love it."

His own eyes brightened. "Pavarotti?"

"And Domingo." She looked worried. "But people will talk…"

"They're already talking. Who cares?" he asked. "We're both single adults. What we do together is nobody's business."

"Yes, well, the general consensus of opinion is that we're public property, or didn't you hear what Mr. Bailey said?"

"I heard you scream," he mused.

She cleared her throat. "Well, it was the last straw."

He caught her hand, the undamaged one, and locked her fingers into his, tugging her out the door.

"Dr. Coltrain," she began.

He locked the office door. "You know my name."

She looked wary. "Yes."

He glanced at her. "My friends call me Copper," he said softly, and smiled.

"We're not friends."

"I think we're going to be, though, a year too late." He tugged her toward his car.

"I can drive mine," she protested.

"Mine's more comfortable. I'll drive you home, and give you a lift to work in the morning. Is it locked?"

"Yes, but..."

"Don't argue, Lou. I'm tired. It's been a long day and we've still got to make rounds at the hospital later."

We. He couldn't know the anguish of hearing him link them together when she had less than two weeks left in Jacobsville. He'd said that he'd torn up her resignation, but she was levelheaded enough to know that she had to go. It would be pure torment to be around him all the time and have him treat her as a friend and nothing more. She couldn't have an affair with him, either, so what was left?

He glanced down at her worried face and his fingers contracted. "Stop brooding. I promised not to seduce you."

"I know that!"

"Unless you want me to," he chided, chuckling at her expression. "I'm a doctor," he added in a conspiratorial whisper. "I know how to protect you from any consequences."

"Damn you!"

She jerked away from him, furiously. He laughed at her fighting stance.

"That was wicked," he acknowledged. "But I do love

to watch you lose that hot temper. Are you Irish, by any chance?"

"My grandfather was," she muttered. She dashed a strand of blond hair out of her eyes. "You stop saying things like that to me!"

He unlocked her door, still smiling. "All right. No more jokes."

She slid into the leather seat and inhaled the luxurious scent of the upholstery while he got in beside her and started the car. It was dark. She sat next to him in perfect peace and contentment as they drove out to his ranch, not breaking the silence as they passed by farms and ranches silhouetted against the flat horizon.

"You're very quiet," he remarked when he pulled up in front of the Spanish-style adobe house he called home.

"I'm happy," she said without thinking.

He was quiet, then. He helped her out and they walked a little apart on the flagstone walkway that led to the front porch. It was wide and spacious, with gliders and a porch swing.

"It must be heaven to sit out here in the spring," she remarked absently.

He glanced at her curiously. "I never pictured you as the sort to enjoy a porch swing."

"Or walks in the woods, or horseback riding, or baseball games?" she asked. "Because I like those things, too. Austin does have suburbs, and I had friends who owned ranches. I know how to ride and shoot, too."

He smiled. She'd seemed like such a city girl. He'd made

sure that he never looked too closely at her, of course. Like father, like daughter, he'd always thought. But she was nothing like Fielding Blakely. She was unique.

He unlocked the door and opened it. The interior was full of Spanish pieces and dark furniture with creams and beiges and browns softened by off-white curtains. It had the look of professional decorating, which it probably was.

"I grew up sitting on orange crates and eating on cracked plates," he commented as she touched a bronze sculpture of a bronc rider. "This is much better."

She laughed. "I guess so. But orange crates and cracked plates wouldn't be so bad if the company was pleasant. I hate formal dining rooms and extravagant place settings."

Now he was getting suspicious. They really couldn't have that much in common! His eyebrow jerked. "Full of surprises, aren't you? Or did you just take a look at my curriculum vitae and tell me what I wanted to hear?" he added in a crisp, suspicious tone.

Her surprise was genuine, and he recognized it immediately. She searched his face. "This was a mistake," she said flatly. "I think I'd like to go..."

He caught her arm. "Lou, I'm constantly on the defensive with women," he said. "I never know, you see..." He hesitated.

"Yes, I understand," she replied. "You don't have to say it."

"All that, and you read minds, too," he said with cool sarcasm. "Well, well."

She drew away from him. She seemed to read his mind quite well, she thought, because she usually knew what he was going to say.

That occurred to him, too. "It used to make me mad as hell when you handed me files before I asked for them," he told her.

"It wasn't deliberate," she said without thinking.

"I know." His jaw firmed as he looked at her. "We know too much about each other, don't we, Lou? We know things we shouldn't, without ever saying them."

She looked up, feeling the bite of his inspection all the way to her toes. "We can't say them," she replied. "Not ever."

He only nodded. His eyes searched hers intently. "I don't believe in happily ever after," he said. "I did, once, until your father came along and shattered all my illusions. She wouldn't let me touch her, you see. But she slept with him. She got pregnant by him. The hell of it was that she was going to marry me without telling me anything." He sighed. "I lost my faith in women on the spot, and I hated your father enough to beat him to his knees. When you came here, and I found out who you were…" He shook his head. "I almost decked Drew for not telling me."

"I didn't know, either," she said.

"I realize that." He smiled. "You were an asset, after I got over the shock. You never complained about long hours or hard work, no matter how much I put on you. And I put a lot on you, at first. I thought I could make you quit. But the more I demanded, the more you gave. After a while, it occurred to me that I'd made a good bargain. Not that I liked you," he added sardonically.

"You made that perfectly clear."

"You fought back," he said. "Most people don't. They knuckle under and go home and fume about it, and think up things they wish they'd said. You just jump in with both feet and give it all you've got. You're a hell of an adversary, Lou. I couldn't beat you down."

"I always had to fight for things," she recalled. "My father was like you." Her face contorted and she turned away.

"I don't get drunk as a rule, and I've never hurt a woman!" he snapped.

"I didn't mean that," she said quickly. "It's just that you're forceful. You demand, you push. You don't ever give up or give in. Neither did he. If he thought he was right, he'd fight the whole world to prove it. But he fought the same when he was wrong. And in his later years, he drank to excess. He wouldn't admit he had a problem. Neither would my mother. She was his slave," she added bitterly. "Even her daughter was dispensable if the great man said so."

"Didn't she love you?"

"Who knows? She loved him more. Enough to lie for him. Even to die for him. And she did." She turned, her face hard. "She got into a plane with him, knowing that he was in no condition to fly. Maybe she had a premonition that he would go down and she wanted to go with him. I'm almost sure that she still would have gone with him if she'd known he was going to crash the plane. She loved him that much."

"You sound as if you can't imagine being loved that much."

"I can't," she said flatly, lifting her eyes. "I don't want that kind of obsessive love. I don't want to give it or receive it."

"What do you want?" he persisted. "A lifetime of loneliness?"

"That's what you're settling for, isn't it?" she countered.

He shrugged. "Maybe I am," he said after a minute. His blue eyes slid over her face and then averted. "Can you cook?" he asked on the way into the kitchen. Like the rest of the house, it was spacious and contained every modern device known to man.

"Of course," she said.

He glanced at her with a grin. "How well do you do chili?" he persisted.

"Well…"

"I've won contests with mine," he said smugly. He slid out of his jacket and vest and tie, opened the top buttons of his shirt and turned to the stove. "You can make the coffee."

"Trusting soul, aren't you?" she murmured as he acquainted her with the coffeemaker and the location of filters, coffee and measuring spoons.

"I always give a fellow cook the benefit of the doubt once," he replied. "Besides, you drink coffee all the time, just like I do. That means you must know how to make it."

She laughed. "I like mine strong," she warned.

"So do I. Do your worst."

Minutes later, the food was on the small kitchen table, steaming and delicious. Lou couldn't remember when she'd enjoyed a meal more.

"That's good chili," she had to admit.

He grinned. "It's the two-time winner of the Jacobsville Chili Cookoff."

"I'm not surprised. The corn bread was wonderful, too."

"The secret to good corn bread is to cook it in an iron skillet," he confessed. "That's where the crispness comes from."

"I don't own a single piece of iron cookware. I'll have to get a pan."

He leaned back, balancing his coffee mug in one hand as he studied her through narrow eyes. "It hasn't all been on my side," he remarked suddenly.

Her eyes lifted to his. "What hasn't?"

"All that antagonism," he said. "You've been as prickly as I have."

Her slender shoulders rose and fell. "It's instinctive to recoil from people when we know they don't like us. Isn't it?"

"Maybe so." He checked his watch and finished his coffee. "I'll get these things in the dishwasher, then we'd better get over to the hospital and do rounds before the Christmas concert comes on the educational channel."

"I don't have my car," she said worriedly.

"We'll go together."

"Oh, that will certainly keep gossip down," she said on a sigh.

He smiled at her. "Damn gossip."

"Was that an adjective or a verb?"

"A verb. I'll rinse, you stack."

They loaded the dishes and he started the dishwasher. He slid back into his jacket, buttoned his shirt and fixed his tie. "Come on. We'll get the chores out of the way."

The hospital was crowded, and plenty of people noticed that Drs. Coltrain and Blakely came in together to make rounds. Lou tried not to notice as she went from patient to patient, checking charts and making conversation.

But when she finished, Coltrain was nowhere in sight. She glanced out the window into the parking lot. His car was still there in his designated space. She went to the doctors' lounge looking for him, and turned the corner just in time to see him with a devastating blond woman in a dress that Lou would love to have been able to afford.

Coltrain saw Lou and he looked grim. He turned toward her with his hands in his pockets, and Lou noticed that the woman was clutching one of his arms tightly in both hands.

"This is my partner," he said, without giving her name. "Lou, this is Dana Lester, an old…friend."

"His ex-fiancée." The woman corrected him in a sweet tone. "How nice to meet you! I've just accepted an appointment as nursing director here, so we'll be seeing a lot of each other!"

"You're a nurse?" Lou asked politely, while she caved in inside.

"A graduate nurse," she said, nodding. "I've been working in Houston, but this job came open and was advertised in a local paper. I applied for it, and here I am! How lovely it will be to come home. I was born here, you know."

"Oh, really?" Lou said.

"Darling," she told Copper, "you didn't tell me your partner's name."

"It's Blakely," he said evenly. "Dr. Louise Blakely."

"Blakely?" the woman queried, her blue eyes pensive. "Why does that name sound so familiar…." She suddenly went pale. "No," she said, shaking her head. "No, that would be too coincidental."

"My father," Lou said coolly, "was Dr. Fielding Blakely. I believe you…knew him?" she added pointedly.

Dana's face looked like rice paper. She drew away from Coltrain. "I…I must fly, darling," she said. "Things to do while I get settled! I'll have you over for supper one night soon!"

She didn't speak to Lou again, not that it was expected. Lou watched her go with cold, angry eyes.

"You didn't want to tell her my name," Lou accused softly.

His face gave away nothing. "The past is best left alone."

"Did you know about her job here?"

His jaw clenched. "I knew there was an opening. I didn't know she'd been hired. If Selby Wills hadn't just retired as hospital administrator, she wouldn't have gotten the job."

She probed into the pocket of her lab coat without really seeing it. "She's pretty."

"She's blond, too, isn't that what you're thinking?"

She raised her face. "So," she added, "is Jane Parker."

"Jane Burke, now." He corrected her darkly. "I like blondes."

His tone dared her to make another remark. She lifted a shoulder and turned. "Some men do. Just don't expect me to welcome her with open arms. I'm sure that my mother suffered because of her. At least my father was less careless with women in his later years."

"It was over a long time ago," Copper said quietly. "If I can overlook your father, you can overlook her."

"Do you think so?"

"What happened between them was nothing to do with you," he persisted.

"He betrayed my mother with her, and it's nothing to do with me?" she asked softly.

He rammed his hands into his pockets, his face set and cold. "Are you finished here?"

"Oh, yes, I'm finished here," she agreed fervently. "If you'll drop me off at my car, I'd like to go home now. We'll have to save the TV Special for another time."

He hesitated, but only for a minute. Her expression told

him everything he needed to know, including the futility of having an argument with her right now.

"All right," he agreed, nodding toward the exit. "Let's go."

He stopped at her car in the office parking lot and let her out.

"Thanks for my supper," she said politely.

"You're welcome."

She closed the door and unlocked her own car. He didn't drive away until she was safely inside and heading out toward home.

Dana Lester's arrival in town was met with another spate of gossip, because there were people in Jacobsville who remembered the scandal very well. Lou tried to pay as little attention to it as possible as she weathered the first few days with the new nursing supervisor avoiding her and Coltrain barely speaking to her.

It was, she told herself, a very good thing that she was leaving after the first of January. The situation was strained and getting worse. She couldn't work out if Dana was afraid of her or jealous of her. Gossip about herself and Coltrain had been lost in the new rumors about his ex-fiancée's return, which did at least spare Lou somewhat. She couldn't help but see that Dana spent a fair amount of time following Coltrain around the hospital, and once or twice she phoned him at the office. Lou pretended not to notice and not to mind, but it was cutting her up inside.

The night she'd had supper with her taciturn partner

had been something of a beginning. But Dana's arrival had nipped it all in the bud. He'd turned his back on Lou and now he only spoke to her when it was necessary and about business. If he'd withdrawn, so had she. Poor Brenda and the office receptionist worked in an armed camp, walking around like people on eggshells. Coltrain's temper strained at the bit, and every time he flared up, Lou flared right back.

"We hear that Nickie and Dana almost came to blows the other night about who got to take Dr. Coltrain a file," Brenda remarked a few days later.

"Too bad someone didn't have a hidden camera, isn't it?" Lou remarked. She sipped her coffee.

Brenda frowned. "I thought… Well, it did seem that you and the doctor were getting along better."

"A temporary truce, nothing more," she returned. "I'm still leaving after the first of the year, Brenda. Nothing's really changed except that Coltrain's old flame has returned."

"She was poison," Brenda said. "I heard all about her from some of the older nurses at the hospital. Did you know that at least two threatened to quit when they knew she was taking over as head nurse at the hospital? One of the nurses she worked with in Houston has family here. They said she was about to be fired when she grabbed this job. Her credentials look impressive, but she's not a good administrator, regardless of her college background, and she plays favorites. They'll learn that here, the hard way."

"It's not my problem."

"Isn't it?" Brenda muttered. "Well, they also say that her

real purpose in applying for this job was to see if Copper was willing to take her back and try again. She's looking for a husband and he's number one on her list."

"Lucky him," she said blithely. "She's very pretty."

"She's a blond tarantula," she said hotly. "She'll suck him dry!"

"He's a big boy, Brenda," Lou returned imperturbably. "He can take care of himself."

"No man is immune to a beautiful face and figure and having a woman absolutely worship him. You take my word for it, there's going to be trouble."

"I won't be here to see it," Lou reminded her. And for the first time, she was glad. Nickie and Dana could fight over Coltrain and may the best woman win, she thought miserably. At least she wouldn't have to watch the struggle. She'd always known that Coltrain wasn't for her. She might as well accept defeat with good grace and get out while she could.

She went back to work, all too aware of Coltrain's deep voice in one of the cubicles she passed. She wondered how her life was going to feel when this was all a bad memory, and she wouldn't hear his voice again.

Drew invited her out to eat and she went, gratefully, glad for the diversion. But the restaurant he chose, Jacobsville's best, had two unwelcome diners: Coltrain and his ex-fiancée.

"I'm sorry," Drew said with a smile and a grimace of apology. "I didn't know they'd be here or I'd have chosen another place to take you for supper."

"Oh, I don't mind," she assured him. "I have to see them at the hospital every day, anyway."

"Yes, *see* them being the key word here," he added knowingly. "I understand that they both avoid you."

"God knows why," she agreed. "She's anywhere I'm not when I need to ask her a question, and he only talks to me about patients. I'm glad I'm leaving, Drew. And with all respect to you, I'm sorry I came."

He smiled ruefully. "I'm sorry I got you into this," he said. "Nothing went as I planned."

"What exactly did you plan?" she asked probingly.

He lifted his water glass and took a sip. "Well, I had hoped that Copper would see something in you that he hadn't found anywhere else. You're unique, Lou. So is he, in some respects. You seemed like a match."

She glared at him. "We're chalk and cheese," she said, ignoring the things she and the redheaded doctor did have in common. "And we can't get along for more than five minutes."

"So I see." He looked around and made a face. "Oh, God, more complications!"

She followed his gaze. A determined Nickie, in a skintight dress cut almost to the navel, was dragging an embarrassed intern to a table right beside Coltrain and Dana's.

"That won't do," she remarked, watching Coltrain's blue eyes start to glitter. "He won't like that. And if she thinks he'll forgo a scene, she's very wrong. Any minute now he's going to get up and walk out."

When he did exactly that, leaving an astonished Dana at

one table and a shocked Nickie at the other, Drew whistled through his teeth and gave Lou a pointed stare.

"You know him very well," was all he said, though.

"I know him," Lou said simply. "He says I read his mind. Maybe I do, on some level."

He frowned. "Do you realize how rare a rapport that is?"

She shrugged. "Not really. He seems to read my mind, too. I shouldn't feel sorry for him, but I do. Imagine shuffling two women in one restaurant."

He didn't add that it was really three, and that Copper had been watching Lou surreptitiously ever since she and Drew entered the restaurant. But of the three women, Lou was the only one who wasn't blatantly chasing him.

"He's paying the check," he remarked. "And, yes, there he goes, motioning to Dana. Good thing they'd finished dessert, wasn't it? Poor Nickie. She won't forget this in a while."

"I told her she was pushing too hard," Lou remarked. "Too bad. She's so young. I suppose she hasn't learned that you can chase a man too relentlessly and lose him."

"Some women never chase a man at all," he said.

She looked up and saw the teasing expression on his face. She laughed. "Drew, you are a dear," she said genuinely.

He chuckled. "My wife always said that I was," he agreed. "What are you going to do?"

"Me? What do you mean? What am I going to do about what?"

"About Copper."

"Nothing," she replied. "Right after the holidays, I leave for Austin."

He pursed his lips as he lifted his coffee cup. "You know," he said, "I have a feeling you'll never get out of town."

Chapter Seven

Saturday morning, Lou woke to the sound of someone hammering on her front door. Half-asleep, with a pale pink satin robe whipped around her slender body and her hair disheveled, she made her way to open it.

The sight that met her eyes was shocking. Coltrain was standing there, dressed in jeans and boots and a faded cotton shirt under a fleece-lined jacket, with a weather-beaten gray Stetson in one lean hand.

She blinked. "Are we filming a new series called 'Cowboy Doctor'?"

"Cute," he remarked, but he wasn't smiling. "I have to talk to you."

She opened the door, still drowsy. "Come on in. I'll make coffee," she said, stifling a yawn as she shuffled toward the kitchen. She could have gone immediately to change, but she was more than adequately covered and he was a doctor. Besides, she reminded herself, he had two women chasing him relentlessly anyway.

"I'll make the coffee. How about some toast to go with it?"

"Plain or cinnamon?"

"Suit yourself."

She got out butter and cinnamon and, just as the coffee finished brewing, she had the toast ready—piping hot from the oven.

He watched her moving about the kitchen. He was sitting leaning back in one of her kitchen chairs with one booted foot on the floor and the chair propped against the wall. He looked out of humor and wickedly handsome all at the same time.

In the position he was occupying, his jeans clung closely to every powerful line of his long legs. He was muscular without being exaggerated, and with his faded shirt unbuttoned at the throat and his red hair disheveled from the hat, he looked more relaxed than she'd ever seen him.

It occurred to her that this was the way he usually was, except when he was working. It was like a private look into his secret life, and she was unexpectedly pleased to have been given it before she left town for good.

"Here." She put the toast on the table, handed him a plate, put condiments on the spotless white tablecloth and then poured coffee into two cups.

"The Christmas concert was nice," he remarked.

"Was it?" she replied. "I went to bed."

"I had nothing to do with getting Dana down here," he said flatly. "In case you wondered."

"It's none of my business."

"Yes, I know," he said heavily. He sipped coffee and munched toast, but he was preoccupied. "Nickie and Dana are becoming an embarrassment."

"Leave it to you to be irritated when two lovely women compete for your attention," she remarked dryly.

His eyes narrowed on her face. "Irritation doesn't quite cover it. I feel like the stud of the month," he said disgustedly.

She burst out laughing. "Oh, I'm sorry!" she said when he glared at her. "It was the way you said it."

He was ruffled, and looked it. He sipped more coffee. "I wasn't trying to make a joke."

"I know. It must be difficult, especially when you have to make rounds at the hospital, with both of them working there."

"I understand you're having some problems of your own in that regard."

"You might say that," she agreed. "I can't find Dana or Nickie when I need them. I seem to have the plague."

"You know that it can't continue?"

"Of course I do," she assured him. "And when I leave, things will settle down, I'm sure."

He scowled. "What do you mean, when you leave? How will that help? Anyway, we'd already agreed that you were staying."

"We agreed on nothing," she returned. "I gave you

my resignation. If you tore it up, that's your problem. I consider it binding."

He stared down into his coffee cup, deep in thought. "I had no idea that you meant it."

"Amazing," she mused, watching him. "You have such a convenient memory, Dr. Coltrain. I can't forget a single word you said to Drew about me, and you can't remember?"

His face hardened. "I didn't know you were listening."

"That makes everything all right?" she asked with mock solemnity.

He ran a hand through his already disheveled hair. "Things came to a head," he replied. "I'd just had to diagnose leukemia in a child who should have had years of happiness to look forward to. I'd had a letter from my father asking for money…"

She shifted against the table. "I didn't know that your parents were still alive."

"My mother died ten years ago," he replied. "My father lives in Tucson. He wrangles horses, but he likes to gamble. When he gets in too deep, he always comes to me for a grubstake." He said it with utter contempt.

"Is that all you mean to him? Money?" she asked gently.

"It was all I ever meant to him." He lifted cold blue eyes to hers. He smiled unpleasantly. "Who do you think put me up to breaking and entering when I was a teenager? I was a juvenile, you know. Juveniles don't go to jail. Oh, we didn't do it here," he added. "Not where he lived. We always went to Houston. He cased the houses and sent me in to do the actual work."

Her gasp was audible. "He should have been arrested!"

"He was," he replied. "He served a year and got probation. We haven't spent any time together since I was placed with a foster family when I was thirteen, long before I started medical school. I put all that behind me. Apparently so did he. But now that I'm making a comfortable living, he doesn't really see any good reason not to ask me for help when he needs it."

What sort of family life had *he* grown up in? she wondered. It was, in some ways, like her own upbringing. "What a pity that we can't choose our parents," she remarked.

"Amen." His broad shoulders shifted against the wall. "I was in a temper already, and Drew's phone call was the last straw. It irritated the hell out of me that you liked him, but you jerked away from my slightest touch as if I might contaminate you."

She hadn't thought he'd noticed. He took her reaction as a sign of her distaste for him, when it was a fierce, painful attraction. It was ironic.

She lowered her eyes. "You said when I first came to work with you that we would have a business relationship."

"So I did. But that didn't mean you should treat me like a leper," he remarked. Oddly, he didn't seem to be concerned about it anymore. He smiled, in fact, his blue eyes sparkling. "But I wouldn't have had you overhear what I told Drew for all the world, Lou. It shamed me when you asked to end our partnership."

She toyed with a fingernail. "I thought it would make you happy."

Her choice of words delighted him. He knew exactly what she felt for him. He'd had suspicions for a while now, but he hadn't been certain until he kissed her. He couldn't let her leave until he was sure about what he felt for her. But how was he going to stop her? His blue eyes ran searchingly over her face and a crazy idea popped into his mind. "If you and I were engaged," he mused aloud, "Dana and Nickie would give up."

The words rambled around in her mind like marbles as she stared at him. The sun was out. It was a nice December day. Her Christmas decorations lined the windows and the tinsel on the Christmas tree in the living room caught the sun through the curtains and glittered.

"Did you hear me?" he asked when she didn't react.

Her cheeks burned. "I don't think that's very funny," she remarked, turning away.

He got to his feet with an audible thud and before she could move three feet, he had her by the waist from behind. Steely hands pulled her back against him and when she caught them, she felt their warm strength under her cool fingers. She felt his breath against her hair, felt it as his chest moved at her back.

"Shall we stop dancing around it?" he asked roughly. "You're in love with me. I've pretended not to see it, but we both know it's why you're leaving."

She gasped aloud. Frozen in his arms, she hadn't even a comeback, a face-saving reply. She felt his hands contract under hers, as if he thought she might pull away and run for it.

"Don't panic," he said quietly. "Dodging the issue won't solve it."

"I…didn't realize you could tell," she whispered, her pride in ashes at his feet.

His lean arms contracted, bringing her soft warmth closer to his taut body. "Take it easy. We'll deal with it."

"You don't have to deal with anything," she began huskily. "I'm going to…"

He turned her while she was speaking and his mouth was on hers before she could finish. She fought him for an instant, as he anticipated. But he was slow and very gentle, and she began to melt into him like ice against a flame.

He brought her closer, aware of her instant response when she felt his body harden. He made a rough sound against her mouth and deepened the kiss.

Her fingers caught in the cool flames of his hair, holding on for dear life as his ardor burned high and wild. He kissed her as he'd kissed Nickie at the party, not an inch of space between their bodies, no quarter in the thin lips devouring her open mouth. This time when his tongue penetrated, she didn't pull away. She accepted the intimate contact without a protest, shivering a little as it ignited new fires in her own taut body. The sensation was unlike anything she'd known. She held on tight, moaning, aware somewhere in the back of her mind that his hand was at the base of her spine, rubbing her against him, and that she should say something.

She was incapable of anything except blind response.

She didn't resist even when he eased her back onto her feet and, still kissing her hungrily, slid his hand under her robe against the soft, tight curve of her breast. He felt her heartbeat run away. With a groan, he fought his way under the gown, against the petal-soft warmth of her skin, and cupped her tenderly, dragging his thumb against the small hardness he found. She shivered again. Reeling, he traced the tight nub with his thumb and forefinger, testing its hardness. She sobbed against his mouth. Probably, he thought dizzily, she'd never had such a caress. And he could give her something more; another pleasure that she didn't know yet.

His mouth left hers and found its way down past her collarbone to the softness under his hand. It opened on her body, and he drank in the scented warmth of her while his tongue took the place of his thumb. She gasped and struggled, but he began to suckle her, his arms swallowing her, and she shuddered once and gave in. He felt her body go lax in his arms, so that if he hadn't supported her, she would have fallen. She caressed his nape with trembling hands, gasping a little as he increased the pressure, but clinging, not pushing.

When he thought he might explode from the pleasure it was giving him, he forced his mouth to release her and he stood erect, pulling her up abruptly.

His face was ruddy with high color, his eyes blazing as

they met her half-open, dazed ones. She was oblivious to everything except the taste of him. Her lips were swollen. Even her tongue felt swollen. She couldn't say a word.

He searched over her face and then dropped his eyes to her bodice. He moved it out of the way and looked at the small, firm breast he'd been tasting. She looked like a rosebud there, the nipple red from his mouth.

He traced around it lazily and then looked back up at the shocked pleasure in her dark, dark eyes.

"I could have you on the kitchen table, right now," he said in a deep, quiet tone. "And you think you're leaving in two weeks?"

She blinked. It was all so unreal. He'd all but seduced her. His hand was still on her breast and he'd pulled the robe and gown aside. He was looking at her…!

She gasped, horrified, jerking back from him. Her hands grappled with the unruly fabric before she finally got her body covered. She backed away, blushing, glaring at him accusingly.

He didn't move, except to lean back against the kitchen counter and cross his long legs. That action drew her eyes to something she'd felt earlier, and she blushed scarlet before she managed to look away. What had she done? What had she let him do?

"You look outraged," he mused. "I think I like having you blush when I look at you."

"Would you leave, please?" she asked tightly.

"No, I don't think so," he said pleasantly. "Get dressed. Wear jeans and boots. I'm taking you riding."

"I don't want to go anywhere with you!"

"You want to go to bed with me," he corrected, smiling gently. "I can't think of anything I'd enjoy more, but I saddled the horses and left them in the stable before I came over here."

She huddled in her robe, wincing as it rubbed against her body.

"Breast sore?" he asked softly. "I'm sorry. I lost my head a little."

She flushed more and the robe tightened. "Dr. Coltrain…"

"Copper," he reminded her. "Or you can call me Jeb, if you like." He pursed his lips and his eyes were hot and possessive. "You'd really better get dressed, Lou," he murmured. "I'm still pretty hot, and aroused men are devious."

She moved back. "I have things to do…"

"Horseback riding or…?" He moved toward her.

She turned and ran for the bedroom. She couldn't believe what had just happened, and he'd said something about them becoming engaged. She must be losing her mind. Yes, that was it, she'd worried over leaving so much that she was imagining things. The whole thing had probably been a hallucination.

He'd cleared away the breakfast things by the time she washed, dressed, pulled her hair back into a ponytail with a blue ribbon and came into the kitchen with a rawhide jacket on.

He smiled. "You look like a cowgirl."

She'd felt a bit uneasy about facing him after that torrid interlude, but apparently he wasn't embarrassed. She might as well follow his lead. She managed a smile in return. "Thanks. But I may not quite merit the title. I haven't ridden in a long time."

"You'll be all right. I'll look after you."

He opened the door and let her out, waiting for her to lock it. Then he helped her into the Jaguar and drove her to his ranch.

The woods were lovely, despite their lack of leaves. The slow, easy rhythm of the horses was relaxing, even if the company wasn't. She was all too aware of Coltrain beside her, tall and elegant even on horseback. With the Stetson pulled low over his eyes, he looked so handsome that he made her toes tingle.

"Enjoying yourself?" he asked companionably.

"Oh, yes," she admitted. "I haven't been riding in a long time."

"I do more of it than I like sometimes," he confessed. "This isn't a big ranch, but I run about fifty head of pedigree cattle. I have two married cowhands who help out."

"Why do you keep cattle?" she asked.

"I don't know. It was always a dream of mine, I guess, from the time I was a boy. My grandfather had one old milk cow and I'd try to ride her." He chuckled. "I fell off a lot."

She smiled. "And your grandmother?"

"Oh, she was a cook of excellent proportions," he replied. "She made cakes that were the talk of the county. When my dad went wrong, it broke her heart, and my grandfather's. I think they took it harder because he lured me into it with him." He shook his head. "When a kid goes bad, everyone blames it on the upbringing. But my grandparents were kind, good people. They were just poor. A lot of people were…still are."

She'd noticed that he had a soft spot for his needy patients. He made extra time for them, acting as counselor and even helping them get in touch with the proper government agencies when they needed help. At Christmas, he was the first to pledge a donation to local charities and contribute to parties for children who wouldn't otherwise have presents. He was a good man, and she adored him.

"Do you want children, eventually?" she asked.

"I'd like a family," he said noncommittally. He glanced at her. "How about you?"

She grimaced. "I don't know. It would be hard for me to juggle motherhood and medicine. I know plenty of people do, but it seems like begging from Peter to pay Paul, you know? Children need a lot of care. I think plenty of social problems are caused by parents who can't get enough time off from work to look after their children. And good day care is a terrible financial headache. Why isn't day care free?" she asked abruptly. "It should be. If women are going to have to work, companies should provide access to day care for them. I know of hospitals and some companies that do it for their employees. Why can't every big company?"

"Good question. It would certainly take a burden off working parents."

"All the same, if I had kids, I'd want to be with them while they were young. I don't know if I could give up practice for so long…."

He reined in his horse and caught her bridle, bringing her horse gently around so that they were facing each other at the side. "That's not the reason. Talk to me," he said quietly. "What is it?"

She huddled into her jacket. "I hated being a child," she muttered. "I hated my father and my mother and my life."

His eyebrows lifted. "Do you think a child would hate me?"

She laughed. "Are you kidding? Children love you. Except that you don't do stitches as nicely as I do," she added.

He smiled ruefully. "Thanks for small favors."

"The secret is the chewing gum I give them afterward."

"Ah, I see. Trade a few stitches for a few cavities."

"It's sugarless gum," she said smugly.

He searched her face with warm eyes. "Touché."

He wheeled his horse and led her off down a pasture path to where the big barn was situated several hundred yards away from the house. He explained the setup, and how he'd modernized his small operation.

"I'm not as up-to-date as a lot of ranchers are, and this is peanut scale," he added. "But I've put a lot of work and time into it, and I'm moderately proud of what I've accomplished. I have a herd sire who's mentioned in some of the bigger cattle magazines."

"I'm impressed. Do I get to see him?"

"Do you want to?"

"You sound surprised. I like animals. When I started out, it was a toss-up between being a doctor and being a vet."

"What swayed you?"

"I'm not really sure. But I've never regretted my choice."

He swung out of the saddle and waited for her to dismount. He tied the horses to the corral rail and led the way into the big barn.

It was surprisingly sanitary. The walkway was paved, the stalls were spacious with metal gates and fresh hay. The cows were sleek and well fed, and the bull he'd mentioned was beautiful even by bovine standards.

"Why, he's gorgeous," she enthused as they stood at the gate and looked at him. He was red-coated, huge, streamlined and apparently docile, because he came up to let Coltrain pet his muzzle.

"How are you, old man?" he murmured affectionately. "Had enough corn, have you?"

"He's a Santa Gertrudis, isn't he?" she asked curiously.

His hand stilled on the bull's nose. "How did you know that?" he asked.

"Ted Regan is one of my patients. He had a breeder's

edition of some magazine with him one day, and he left it behind. I got a good idea of coat colors, at least. We have a lot of cattlemen around here," she added. "It never hurts to know a little bit about a good bull."

"Why, Lou," he mused. "I'm impressed."

"That's a first."

He chuckled. His blue eyes twinkled down at her as he propped one big boot on the low rail of the gate. "No, it's not. You impressed me the first week you were here. You've grown on me."

"Good heavens, am I a wart?"

He caught a strand of her hair and wound it around his finger. "You're a wonder," he corrected, searching her eyes. "I didn't realize we had so much in common. Funny, isn't it? We've worked together for a year, but I've found out more about you in the past two weeks than I ever knew."

"That goes for me, too."

She dropped her eyes to his chest, where the faded shirt clung to the hard muscles. She loved the way he stood, the way he walked, the way he looked with that hat tilted rakishly over one eye. She remembered the feel of his warm arms around her and she felt suddenly cold.

Her expressions fascinated him. He watched them change, saw the hunger filter into her face.

She drew a wistful breath and looked up at him with a wan smile.

He frowned. Without understanding why, he held out a lean arm.

She accepted the invitation without question. Her body went against his, pressing close. Her arms went under his and around him, so that her hands could flatten on the muscles of his long back. She closed her eyes and laid her cheek against his chest, and listened to his heart beat.

He was surprised, yet he wasn't. It felt natural to have Lou in his arms. He drew her closer, in a purely nonsexual way, and absently stroked her hair while he watched his bull eat corn out of the trough in his pen.

"Next week is Christmas," he said above her head.

"Yes, I know. What do you do for Christmas? Do you go to friends, or invite people over?"

He laughed gently. "I used to have it with Jane, before she married," he recalled, feeling her stiffen without really thinking much about it. "But last year, since she married, I cooked a TV dinner and watched old movies all day."

She didn't answer for a minute. Despite what she'd heard about Coltrain and Jane Parker in the past year, she hadn't thought that he and Jane had been quite so close. But it seemed that they were. It depressed her more than anything had in recent weeks.

He wasn't thinking about Christmases past. He was thinking about the upcoming one. His hand explored her hair strand by strand. "Where are we going to have Christmas dinner, and who's going to cook it?" he asked matter-of-factly.

That was encouraging, that he wanted to spend Christmas with her. She couldn't refuse, even out of hurt pride. "We could have it at my house," she offered.

"I'll help cook it."

She smiled. "It would be nice to have someone to eat it with," she confessed.

"I'll make sure we're on call Christmas Eve, not Christmas Day," he promised. His arm slid down her back and drew her closer. He was aware of a kind of contentment he'd never experienced before, a belonging that he hadn't known even with Jane. Funny, he thought, until Lou came along, it had never occurred to him that he and Jane couldn't have had a serious relationship even if Todd Burke hadn't married her.

It was a sobering thought. This woman in his arms had come to mean a lot to him, without his realizing it until he'd kissed her for the first time. He laid his cheek against her head with a long sigh. It was like coming home. He'd been searching all his life for something he'd never found. He was closer to it than he'd ever been right now.

Her arms tightened around his lean waist. She could feel the wall of his chest hard against her breasts, the buckle of his belt biting into her. But it still wasn't quite close enough. She moved just a little closer, so that her legs brushed his.

He moved to accommodate her, sliding one boot higher on the fence so that she could fit against him more comfortably. But the movement aroused him and he caught his breath sharply.

"Sorry," she murmured and started to step away.

But his hand stayed her hips. "I can't help that," he said

at her temple, secretly delighted at his headlong physical response to her. "But it isn't a threat."

"I didn't want to make you uncomfortable."

He smiled lazily. "I wouldn't call it that." He brushed a kiss across her forehead. "Relax," he whispered. "It's pretty public here, and I'm sure you know as well as I do that making love in a hay barn is highly unsanitary."

She laughed at his humor. "Oh, but this barn is very clean."

"Not that clean," he murmured dryly. "Besides," he added, "it's been a long, dry spell. When I'm not in the market for a companion, I don't walk around prepared for sweet interludes."

She lifted her face and searched his mocking eyes demurely. "A long, dry spell? With Nickie prancing around half-naked to get your attention?"

He didn't laugh, as she expected him to. He traced her pert nose. "I don't have affairs," he said. "And I'm the soul of discretion in my private life. There was a widow in a city I won't name. She and I were good friends, and we supplied each other with something neither of us was comfortable spreading around. She married year before last. Since then, I've concentrated on my work and my cattle. Period."

She was curious. "Can you…well, do it…without love?"

"I was fond of her," he explained. "She was fond of me. We didn't have to be in love."

She moved restlessly.

"It would have to be love, for you, wouldn't it, Lou?" he asked. "Even desperate desire wouldn't be enough." He traced her soft lips with deliberation. "But you and I are an explosive combination. And you do love me."

She laid her forehead at his collarbone. "Yes," she admitted. "I love you. But not enough to be your mistress."

"I know that."

"Then it's hopeless."

He laughed mirthlessly. "Is it? I thought I mentioned that we could get engaged."

"Engaged isn't married," she began.

He put a finger over her lips, and he looked solemn. "I know that. Will you let me finish? We can be engaged until the first of the year, when I can afford to take a little time off for a honeymoon. We could have a New Year's wedding."

Chapter Eight

"You mean, get married? Us?" she echoed blankly.

He tilted up her chin and searched her dark, troubled eyes. "Sex doesn't trouble you half as much as marriage does, is that it? Marriage means commitment, and to you, that's like imprisonment."

She grimaced. "My parents' marriage was horrible. I don't want to become like my mother."

"So you said." He traced her cheek. "But I'm not like your father. I don't drink. Well," he murmured with a sheepish grin, "maybe just once, and I had justification for that. You were letting Drew hold your hand, when you always jerked back if I touched you at all."

She was surprised. She smiled. "Was *that* why?"

He chuckled. "Yes, that was why."

"Imagine that!"

"Take one day at a time, okay?" he asked. "Let's rock

along for a couple of weeks, and spend Christmas together. Then we'll talk about this again."

"All right."

He bent and kissed her softly. She pressed up against him, but he stepped back.

"None of that," he said smartly. "We're going to get to know each other before we let our glands get in the way."

"Glands!"

"Don't you remember glands, Doctor?" He moved toward her threateningly. "Let me explain them to you."

"I think I've got the picture," she said on a laugh. "Keep away, you lecher!"

He laughed, too. He caught her hand and tangled her fingers with his as they walked back to where the horses were tied. He'd never been quite this interested in marriage, even if he'd once had it in the back of his mind when he'd dated Jane. But when he'd had Lou close in his arms, in the barn, he'd wanted it with a maddening desire. It wasn't purely physical, although she certainly attracted him that way. But despite the way she felt about him, he had a feeling that she'd have to be carefully coaxed down the aisle. She was afraid of everything marriage stood for because of her upbringing. Their marriage wouldn't be anything like her parents', but he was going to have to convince her of that first.

They made rounds together the next morning at the hospital, and as usual, Dana was lying in wait for Coltrain.

But this time, he deliberately linked Lou's hand in his as he smiled at her.

"Good morning," he said politely.

Dana was faintly startled. "Good morning, doctors," she said hesitantly, her eyes on their linked hands.

"Lou and I became engaged yesterday," he said.

Dana's face paled. She drew a stiff breath and managed the semblance of a smile. "Oh, did you? Well, I suppose I should offer my congratulations!" She laughed. "And I had such high hopes that you and I might regain something of the past."

"The past is dead," he said firmly, his blue eyes steady on her face. "I have no inclination whatsoever to revive it."

Dana laughed uncomfortably. "So I see." She glanced at Lou's left hand. "Quite a sudden engagement, was it?" she added slyly. "No ring yet?"

Lou's hand jerked in his, but he steadied it. "When Lou makes up her mind what sort she wants, I'll buy her one," he said lazily. "I'd better get started. Wait for me in the lounge when you finish, sweet," he told Lou and squeezed her fingers before he let them go.

"I will," she promised. She smiled at Dana carelessly and went down the hall to begin her own rounds.

Dana followed her. "Well, I hope you fare better than I did," she muttered. "He's had the hots for Jane Parker for years. He asked me to marry him because he wanted me and I wouldn't give in, but even so, I couldn't compete with dear Jane," she said bitterly. "Your father was willing, so I indulged in a stupid affair, hoping I might make him jealous. That was the lunatic act of the century!"

"So I heard," Lou said stiffly, glaring at the other woman.

"I guess you did," the older woman said with a grimace. "He hated me for it. There's one man who doesn't move with the times, and he never forgets a wrong you do him." Her eyes softened as she looked at Lou's frozen face. "Your poor mother must have hated me. I know your father did. He was livid that I'd been so careless, and of course, I ruined his chances of staying here. But he didn't do so bad in Austin."

Lou had different memories of that. She couldn't lay it all at Dana's door, however. She paused at her first patient's door. "What do you mean about Jane Parker?" she asked solemnly.

"You must have heard by now that she was his first love, his only love, for years. I gave up on him after my fling with your father. I thought it was surely over between them until I came back here. She's married, you know, but she still sees Copper socially." Her eyes glittered. "They say he sits and stares at her like an oil painting when they're anywhere together. You'll find that out for yourself. I should be jealous, but I don't think I am. I feel sorry for you, because you'll always be his second choice, even if he marries you. He may want you, but he'll never stop loving Jane."

She walked away, leaving a depressed, worried Lou behind. Dana's former engagement to Coltrain sounded so much like her own "engagement" with him that it was scary. She knew that he wanted her, but he didn't show any signs of loving her. Did he still love Jane? If he did, she couldn't possibly marry him.

Nickie came up the hall when Lou had finished her rounds and was ready to join Coltrain in the lounge.

"Congratulations," she told Lou with a resigned smile. "I guess I knew I was out of the running when I saw him kiss you in the car park. Good luck. From what I hear, you'll need it." She kept walking.

Lou was dejected. It was in her whole look when she went into the doctors' lounge, where Coltrain had just finished filling out a form at the table near the window. He looked up, frowning.

"What is it?" he asked curtly. "Have Dana and Nickie been giving you a hard time?"

"Not at all," she said. "I'm just a little tired." She touched her back and winced, to convince him. "Horseback riding takes some getting used to, doesn't it?"

He smiled, glad that he'd mistaken soreness for depression. "Yes, it does. We'll have to do more of it." He picked up the folder. "Ready to go?"

"Yes."

He left the form at the nurses' station, absorbing more congratulations from the nurses, and led Lou out to his Jaguar.

"We'll take some time off this afternoon for lunch and shop for a ring," he said.

"But I don't need…"

"Of course you do," he said. "We can't let people think I'm too miserly to buy you an engagement ring!"

"But what if…?"

"Lou, it's my money," he declared.

She grimaced. Well, if he wanted to be stuck with a diamond ring when she left town, that was his business. The engagement, as far as she was concerned, was nothing more than an attempt to get his life back on an even keel and discourage Nickie and Dana from hounding him.

She couldn't forget what had been said about Jane Parker, Jane Burke now, and she was more worried than ever. She knew how entangled he'd been with Jane, all right, because she'd considered her a rival until the day Jane married Todd Burke. Coltrain's manner even when he spoke to the woman was tender, solicitous, almost reverent.

He'd proposed. But even though he knew Lou loved him, he'd never mentioned feeling anything similar for her. He was playing make-believe. But she wondered what would happen if Jane Burke suddenly became a free woman. It would be a nightmare to live with a man who was ever yearning for someone else, someone he'd loved most of his life. Jane was a habit he apparently couldn't break. She was married. But could that fact stop him from loving her?

"You're very quiet," he remarked.

"I was thinking about Mr. Bailey," she hedged. "He really needs to see a specialist about that asthma. What do you think of referring him to Dr. Jones up in Houston?"

He nodded, diverted. "A sound idea. I'll give you the number."

* * *

They worked in harmony until the lunch hour. Then, despite her arguments, they drove to a jewelry shop in downtown Jacobsville. As bad luck would have it, Jane Burke was in there, alone, making a purchase.

She was so beautiful, Lou thought miserably. Blond, blue-eyed, with a slender figure that any man would covet.

"Why hello!" Jane said enthusiastically, and hugged Copper as if he was family.

He held her close and kissed her cheek, his smile tender, his face animated. "You look terrific," he said huskily. "How's the back? Still doing those exercises?"

"Oh, yes," she agreed. She held him by the arms and searched his eyes. "You look terrific yourself." She seemed only then to notice that he wasn't alone. She glanced at Lou. "Dr. Blakely, isn't it?" she asked politely, and altered the smile a little. "Nice to see you again."

"What are you doing here?" Coltrain asked her.

"Buying a present for my stepdaughter for Christmas. I thought she might like a nice strand of pearls. Aren't these lovely?" she asked when the clerk had taken them out of the case to show them. "I'll take them," she added, handing him her credit card.

"Is she staying with you and Todd all the time now?"

She nodded. "Her mother and stepfather and the baby are off to Africa to research his next book," she said with a grin. "We're delighted to have her all to ourselves."

"How's Todd?"

Lou heard the strained note in his voice with miserable certainty that Dana had been telling the truth.

"He's as impossible as ever." Jane chuckled. "But we scratch along, me with my horses and my clothing line and he with his computer business. He's away so much these days that I feel deserted." She lifted her eyes to his and grinned. "I don't guess you'd like to come to supper tonight?"

"Sure I would," he said without thinking. Then he made a sound. "I can't. There's a hospital board meeting."

"Oh, well," she muttered. "Another time, then." She glanced at Lou hesitantly. "Are you two out Christmas shopping—together?" she added as if she didn't think that was the case.

Coltrain stuck his hands deep into his pockets. "We're shopping for an engagement ring," he said tersely.

Her eyes widened. "For whom?"

Lou wanted to sink through the floor. She flushed to the roots of her hair and clung to her shoulder bag as if it were a life jacket.

"For Lou," Coltrain said. "We're engaged."

He spoke reluctantly, which only made Lou feel worse.

Jane's shocked expression unfroze Lou's tongue. "It's just for appearances," she said, forcing a smile. "Dana and Nickie have been hounding him."

"Oh, I see!" Jane's face relaxed, but then she frowned. "Isn't that a little dishonest?"

"It was the only way, and it's just until my contract is

up, the first of the year," Lou forced herself to say. "I'll be leaving then."

Coltrain glared at her. He wasn't certain what he'd expected, but she made the proposal sound like a hoax. He hadn't asked her to marry him to ward off the other women; he'd truly wanted her to be his wife. Had she misunderstood totally?

Jane was as startled as Coltrain was. She knew that Copper wasn't the sort of man to give an engagement ring lightly, although Lou seemed to think he was. Since Dana's horrible betrayal, Copper had been impervious to women. But even Jane had heard about the hospital Christmas party and the infamous kiss. She'd hoped that Copper had finally found someone to love, although it was surprising that it would be the partner with whom he fought with so enthusiastically. Now, looking at them together, she was confused. Lou looked as if she were being tortured. Copper was taciturn and frozen. And they said it was a sham. Lou didn't love him. She couldn't, and be so lighthearted about it. Copper looked worn.

Jane glared at Lou and put a gentle hand on Coltrain's arm. "This is a stupid idea, Copper. You'll be the butt of every joke in town when Lou leaves, don't you realize it? It could even damage your reputation, hurt your practice," she told Copper intently.

His jaw tautened. "I appreciate your concern," he said gently, even as it surprised him that Jane should turn on Lou, who was more an innocent bystander than Coltrain's worst enemy.

That got through to Lou, too. She moved restlessly, averting her gaze from the diamond rings in the display case. "She's right. It *is* stupid. I can't do this," she said suddenly, her eyes full of torment. "Please, excuse me, I have to go!"

She made it out the door before the tears were visible, cutting down an alley and ducking into a department store. She went straight to the women's rest room and burst into tears, shocking a store clerk into leaving.

In the jewelry store, Coltrain stood like a statue, unspeakably shocked at Lou's rash departure and furious at having her back out just when he'd got it all arranged.

"For God's sake, did you have to do that?" Coltrain asked harshly. He rammed his hands into his pockets. "It's taken me days just to get her to agree on any pretext…!"

Jane realized, too late, what she'd done. She winced. "I didn't know," she said miserably. "It's my fault that she's bolted," Jane said quickly. "Copper, I'm sorry!"

"Not your fault," he said stiffly. "I used Dana and Nickie to accomplish this engagement, but she was reluctant from the beginning." He sighed heavily. "I guess she'll go, now, in spite of everything."

"I don't understand what's going on."

He moved a shoulder impatiently. "She's in love with me," he said roughly, and rammed his hands deeper into his pockets.

"Oh, dear." Jane didn't know what to say. She'd lashed out at the poor woman, and probably given Lou a false picture of her relationship with Copper to boot. They were good friends, almost like brother and sister, but there had been rumors around Jacobsville for years that they were secret lovers. Until she married Todd, that was. Now, she wondered how much Lou had heard and if she'd believed it. And Jane had brazenly invited him to supper, ignoring Lou altogether.

She grimaced. "I've done it now, haven't I? I would have included her in my invitation if I'd had any idea. I thought she was just tagging along with you on her lunch hour!"

"I'd better go after her," he said reluctantly.

"It might be best if you didn't," she replied. "She's hurt. She'll want to be alone for a while, I should think."

"I can't strand her in town." He felt worse than he could ever remember feeling. "Maybe you're both right, and this whole thing was a stupid idea."

"If you don't love her, it certainly was," she snapped at him. "What are you up to? Is it really just to protect you from a couple of lovesick women? I'm shocked. A few years ago, you'd have cussed them both to a fare-thee-well and been done with it."

He didn't reply. His face closed up and his blue eyes glittered at her. "My reasons are none of your business," he said, shutting her out.

Obviously Lou had to mean something to him. Jane felt even worse. She made a face. "We were very close once. I thought you could talk to me about anything."

"Anything except Lou," he said shortly.

"Oh." Her eyes were first stunned and then amused.

"You can stop speculating, too," he added irritably, turning away.

"She sounds determined to leave."

"We'll see about that."

Despite Jane's suggestion, he went off toward the department store where Lou had vanished and strode back to the women's rest room. He knew instinctively that she was there. He caught the eye of a female clerk.

"Could you ask Dr. Blakely to come out of there, please?"

"Dr. Blakely?"

"She's so high—" he indicated her height with his hand up to his nose "—blond hair, dark eyes, wearing a beige suit."

"Oh, her! She's a doctor? Really? My goodness, I thought doctors never showed their emotions. She was crying as if her heart would break. Sure, I'll get her for you."

He felt like a dog. He'd made her cry. The thought of Lou, so brave and private a person, with tears in her eyes made him hurt inside. And it had been so unnecessary. If Jane had only kept her pretty mouth shut! She was like family, and she overstepped the bounds sometimes with her comments about how Coltrain should live his life. He'd been more than fond of her once, and he still had a soft spot for her, but it was Lou who was disrupting his whole life.

He leaned against the wall, his legs and arms crossed, and waited. The female clerk reappeared, smiled reassuringly, and went to wait on a customer.

A minute later, a subdued and dignified Lou came out of the small room, her chin up. Her eyes were slightly red, but she didn't look as if she needed anyone's pity.

"I'm ready to go if you are," she said politely.

He searched her face and decided that this wasn't the time for a row. They still had to get lunch and get back to the office.

He turned, leaving her to follow. "I'll stop by one of the hamburger joints and we can get a burger and fries."

"I'll eat mine at the office, if you don't mind," she said wearily. "I'm not in the mood for a crowd."

Neither was he. He didn't argue. He opened the car door and let her in, then he went by the drive-in window of the beef place and they carried lunch back.

Lou went directly into her office and closed the door. She hardly tasted what she was eating. Her heart felt as if it had been burned alive. She knew what Dana meant now. Jane Parker was as much a part of Coltrain's life as his cattle, his practice. No woman, no matter how much she loved him, could ever compete with his love for the former rodeo star.

She'd been living in a fool's paradise, but fortunately there was no harm done. They could say that the so-called "engagement" had been a big joke. Surely Coltrain could get Nickie and Dana out of his hair by simply telling them the truth, that he wasn't interested. God knew, once he got started, he wasn't shy about expressing his feelings any other time, regardless of who was listening. Which brought to mind the question of why he'd asked her to marry him.

He wasn't in love with her. He wanted her. Had that been the reason? Was he getting even with Jane because she'd married and deserted him? She worried the question until she finished eating. Then her patients kept her occupied for the rest of the day, so that she had no time to think.

Jane had wondered if she could help undo the damage she'd already done to Copper's life, and at last she came up with a solution. She decided to give a farewell party for Lou. She called Coltrain a few days later to tell him the news.

"Christmas is next week," he said shortly. "And I doubt if she'd come. She only speaks to me when she has to. I can't get near her anymore."

That depressed Jane even more. "Suppose I phone her?" she asked.

"Oh, I know she won't talk to you." He laughed without humor. "We're both in her bad books."

Jane sighed. "Then who can we have talk to her?"

"Try Drew Morris," he said bitterly. "She likes him."

That note in his voice was disturbing. Surely he knew that Drew was still mourning his late wife. If he and Lou were friends, it was nothing more than that, despite any social outings together.

"You think she'd listen to Drew?" she asked.

"Why not?"

"I'll try, then."

"Don't send out any invitations until she gives you an

answer," he added. "She's been hurt enough, one way or the other."

"Yes, I know," Jane said gently. "I had no idea, Copper. I really meant well."

"I know that. She doesn't."

"I guess she's heard all the old gossip, too."

He hadn't considered that. "What old gossip?"

"About us," she persisted. "That we had something going until I married Todd."

He smoothed his fingers absently over the receiver. "She might have, at that," he said slowly. "But she must know that—" He stopped dead. She'd have heard plenty from Dana, who had always considered Jane, not her affair with Fielding Blakely, the real reason for their broken engagement. Others in the hospital knew those old rumors, too, and Jane had given Lou the wrong impression of their relationship in the jewelry store.

"I'm right, aren't I?" Jane asked.

"You might be."

"What are you going to do?"

"What can I do?" he asked shortly. "She doesn't really want to marry anyone."

"You said she loves you," she reminded him.

"Yes, and she does. It's the only thing I'm sure of. But she doesn't want to marry me. She's so afraid that she'll become like her mother, blindly accepting faults and abuse without question, all in the name of love."

"Poor girl," she said genuinely. "What a life she must have had."

"I expect it was worse than we'll ever know," he agreed. "Well, call Drew and see if he can get through to her."

"If he can, will you come, too?"

"It would look pretty bad if I didn't, wouldn't it?" he asked dryly. "They'd say we were so antagonistic toward each other that we couldn't even get along for a farewell party. And coming on the heels of our 'engagement,' they'd really have food for thought."

"I'd be painted as the scarlet woman who broke it up, wouldn't I?" Jane groaned. "Todd would love that! He's still not used to small-town life."

"Maybe Drew can reach her. If he can't, you'll have to cancel it. We can't embarrass her."

"I wouldn't dream of it."

"I know that. Jane, thanks."

"For what?" she asked. "I'm the idiot who got you into this mess in the first place. The least I owe is to try to make amends for what I said to her. I'll let you know what happens."

"Do that."

He went back to work, uncomfortably aware of Lou's calm demeanor. She didn't even look ruffled after all the turmoil. Of course, he remembered that she'd been crying like a lost child in the department store after Jane's faux pas. But that could have been so much more than a broken heart.

She hadn't denied loving him, but could love survive a year of indifference alternating with vicious antagonism, such as he'd given her? Perhaps loving him was a sort of habit that she'd finally been cured of. After all, he'd given her no reason to love him, even to like him. He'd missed most of his chances there. But if Drew could convince her to come to a farewell party, on neutral ground, Coltrain had one last chance to change her mind about him. That was his one hope; the only one he had.

Chapter Nine

Drew invited Lou to lunch the next day. It was Friday, the week before the office closed for Christmas holidays. Christmas Eve would be on a week from Saturday night, and Jane had changed her mind about dates. She wanted to give the farewell party the following Friday, the day before New Year's Eve. That would, if Lou didn't reconsider her decision, be Lou's last day as Coltrain's partner.

"I'm surprised," Lou told him as they ate quiche at a local restaurant. "You haven't invited me to lunch in a long time. What's on your mind?"

"It could be just on food."

She laughed. "Pull the other one."

"Okay. I'm a delegation of one."

She held her fork poised over the last morsel of quiche on her plate. "From whom?"

"Jane Burke."

She put the fork down, remembering. Her expression hardened. "I have nothing to say to her."

"She knows that. It's why she asked me to talk to you. She got the wrong end of the stick and she's sorry. I'm to make her apologies to you," he added. "But she also wants to do something to make up for what she said to you. She wants to give you a farewell party on the day before New Year's Eve."

She glared at Drew. "I don't want anything to do with any parties given by that woman. I won't go!"

His eyebrows lifted. "Well! You are miffed, aren't you?"

"Accusing me of trying to ruin Jebediah's reputation and destroy his privacy…how dare she! I'm not the one who's being gossiped about in connection with him! And she's married!"

He smiled wickedly. "Lou, you're as red as a beet."

"I'm mad," she said shortly. "That…woman! How dare she!"

"She and Copper are friends. Period. That's all they've ever been. Are you listening?"

"Sure, I'm listening. Now," she added, leaning forward, "tell me he wasn't ever in love with her. Tell me he isn't still in love with her."

He wanted to, but he had no idea of Coltrain's feelings for Jane. He knew that Coltrain had taken her marriage hard, and that he seemed sometimes to talk about her to the exclusion of everyone else. But things had changed in the past few weeks, since the hospital Christmas dance the first week of December.

"You see?" she muttered. "You can't deny it. He may have proposed to me, but it was..."

"Proposed?"

"Didn't you know?" She lifted her coffee cup to her lips and took a sip. "He wanted me to pretend to be engaged to him, just to get Nickie and Dana off his back. Then he decided that we might as well get married for real. He caught me at a weak moment," she added, without details, "and we went to buy an engagement ring. But Jane was there. She was rude to me," she said miserably, "and Jebediah didn't say a word to stop her. In fact, he acted as if I wasn't even there."

"And that was what hurt most, wasn't it?" he queried gently.

"I guess it was. I have no illusions about him, you know," she added with a rueful smile. "He likes kissing me, but he's not in love with me."

"Does he know how you feel?"

She nodded. "I don't hide things well. It would be hard to miss."

He caught her hand and held it gently. "Lou, isn't he worth taking a chance on?" he asked. "You could let Jane throw this party for you, because she badly wants to make amends. Then you could talk to Copper and get him to tell you exactly why he wants to marry you. You might be surprised."

"No, I wouldn't. I know why he wants to marry me,"

she replied. "But I don't want to get married. I'm crazy about him, that's the truth, but I've seen marriage. I don't want it."

"You haven't seen a good marriage," he emphasized. "Lou, I had one. I had twelve years of almost ethereal happiness. Marriage is what you make of it."

"My mother excused every brutal thing my father did," she said shortly.

"That sort of love isn't love," he said quietly. "It's a form of domination. Don't you know the difference? If she'd loved your father, she'd have stood up to him and tried to help him stop drinking, stop using drugs."

She felt as if her eyes had suddenly been opened. She'd never seen her parents' relationship like that. "But he was terrible to her…"

"Codependence," he said to her. "You must have studied basic psychology in college. Don't you remember any of it?"

"Yes, but they were my parents!"

"Your parents, anybody, can be part of a dysfunctional family." He smiled at her surprise. "Didn't you know? You grew up in a dysfunctional family, not a normal one. That's why you have such a hard time accepting the idea of marriage." He smoothed her hand with his fingers and smiled. "Lou, I had a normal upbringing. I had a mother and father who doted on me, who supported me and encouraged me. I was loved. When I married, it was a good, solid, happy marriage. They are possible, if you love someone and have things in common, and are willing to compromise."

She studied the wedding ring on Drew's left hand. He still wore it even after being widowed.

"It's possible to be happily married?" she asked, entertaining that possibility for the first time.

"Of course."

"Coltrain doesn't love me," she said.

"Make him."

She laughed. "That's a joke. He hated me from the beginning. I never knew it was because of my father, until I overheard him talking to you. I was surprised later when he was so cool to Dana, because he'd been bitter about her betrayal. But when I found out how close he was to Jane Burke, I guess I gave up entirely. You can't fight a ghost, Drew." She looked up. "And you know it, because no woman will ever be able to come between you and your memories. How would you feel if you found out some woman was crazily in love with you right now?"

He was stunned by the question. "Well, I don't know. I guess I'd feel sorry for her," he admitted.

"Which is probably how Coltrain feels about me, and might even explain why he offered to be engaged to me," she added. "It makes sense, doesn't it?"

"Lou, you don't propose to people out of pity."

"Coltrain might. Or out of revenge, to get back at Jane for marrying someone else. Or to get even with Dana."

"Coltrain isn't that scatty."

"Men are unpredictable when they're in love, aren't

they?" she mused. "I wish he loved me, Drew. I'd marry him, with all my doubts and misgivings, in a minute if I thought there was half a chance that he did. But he doesn't. I'd know if he did feel that way. Somehow, I'd know."

He dropped his gaze to their clasped hands. "I'm sorry."

"Me, too. I've been invited to join a practice in Houston. I'm going Monday to speak with them, but they've tentatively accepted me." She lifted her sad face. "I understand that Coltrain is meeting some prospects too. So I suppose he's finally taken me at my word that I want to leave."

"Don't you know?"

She shrugged. "We don't speak."

"I see." So it was that bad, he thought. Coltrain and Lou had both withdrawn, afraid to take that final step to commitment. She had good reasons, but what were Copper's? he wondered. Did he really feel pity for Lou and now he was sorry he'd proposed? Or was Lou right, and he was still carrying a torch for Jane?

"Jane is a nice woman," he said. "You don't know her, but she isn't the kind of person who enjoys hurting other people. She feels very unhappy about what she said. She wants to make it up to you. Let her. It will be a nice gesture on your part and on hers."

"Dr. Coltrain will come," she muttered.

"He'd better," he said, "or the gossips will say he's glad to be rid of you."

She shook her head. "You can't win for losing."

"That's what I've been trying to tell you. Let Jane give

the party. Lou, you'd like her if you got to know her. She's had a hard time of it since the wreck that took her father's life. Just being able to walk again at all is a major milestone for her."

"I remember," she said. And she did, because Coltrain had been out at the ranch every waking minute looking after the woman.

"Will you do it?"

She took a long breath and let it out. "All right."

"Great! I'll call Jane the minute I get home and tell her. You won't regret it. Lou, I wish you'd hold off about that spot in Houston."

She shook her head. "No, I won't do that. I have to get away. A fresh start is what I need most. I'm sure I won't be missed. After all, Dr. Coltrain didn't want me in the first place."

He grimaced, because they both knew her present circumstances were Drew's fault. Saying again that he meant well wouldn't do a bit of good.

"Thanks for lunch," she said, remembering her manners.

"That was my pleasure. You know I'll be going to Maryland to have Christmas with my in-laws, as usual. So Merry Christmas, if I don't see you before I leave."

"You, too, Drew," she said with genuine affection.

It wasn't until the next Thursday afternoon that the office closed early for Christmas holidays—if Friday and Monday, added to the weekend, qualified as holidays—that

Coltrain came into Lou's office. Lou had been to Houston and formally applied for a position in the family practitioner group. She'd also been accepted, but she hadn't been able to tell Coltrain until today, because he'd been so tied up with preholiday surgeries and emergencies.

He looked worn-out, she thought. There were new lines in his lean face, and his eyes were bloodshot from lack of sleep. He looked every year of his age.

"You couldn't just tell me, you had to put it in writing?" he asked, holding up the letter she'd written him.

"It's legal this way," she said politely. "I'm very grateful for the start you gave me."

He didn't say anything. He looked at the letter from the Houston medical group. It was written on decal-edge bond, very expensive, and the lettering on the letterhead was embossed.

"I know this group," he said. "They're high-powered city physicians, and they practice supermarket medicine. Do you realize what that means? You'll be expected to spend five minutes or less with every patient. A buzzer will sound to alert you when that time is up. As the most junior partner, you'll get all the dirty jobs, all the odd jobs, and you'll be expected to stay on call on weekends and holidays for the first year. Or until they can get another partner, more junior than you are."

"I know. They told me that." They had. It had depressed her no end.

He folded his arms across his chest and leaned back

against the wall, his stethoscope draped around his neck. "We haven't talked."

"There's nothing to say," she replied, and she smiled kindly. "I notice that Nickie and Dana have become very businesslike, even to me. I'd say you were over the hump."

"I asked you to marry me," he said. "I was under the impression that you'd agreed and that was why we were picking out a ring."

The memory of that afternoon hurt. She lowered her eyes to the clipboard she held against her breasts. "You said it was to get Nickie and Dana off your back."

"You didn't want to get married at all," he reminded her.

"I still don't."

He smiled coldly. "And you're not in love with me?"

She met his gaze levelly. This was no time to back down. "I was infatuated with you," she said bluntly. "Perhaps it was because you were out of reach."

"You wanted me. Explain that."

"I'm human," she told him, blushing a little. "You wanted me, too, so don't look so superior."

"I hear you're coming to Jane's party."

"Drew talked me into it." She smoothed her fingers over the cold clipboard. "You and Jane can't help it," she said. "I understand."

"Damn it! You sound just like her husband!"

She was shocked at the violent whip of his deep voice. He was furious, and it showed.

"Everyone knows you were in love with her," she faltered.

"Yes, I was," he admitted angrily, and for the first time. "But she's married now, Lou."

"I know. I'm sorry," she said gently. "I really am. It must be terrible for you…."

He threw up his hands. "My God!"

"It's not as if you could help it, either of you," she continued sadly.

He just shook his head. "I can't get through to you, can I?" he asked with a bite in his deep voice. "You won't listen."

"There's really nothing to say," she told him. "I hope you've found someone to replace me when I go."

"Yes, I have. He's a recent graduate of Johns Hopkins. He wanted to do some rural practice before he made up his mind where he wanted to settle." He gazed at her wan face. "He starts January 2."

She nodded. "That's when I start, in Houston." She tugged the clipboard closer.

"We could spend Christmas together," he suggested.

She shook her head. She didn't speak. She knew words would choke her.

His shoulders rose and fell. "As you wish," he said quietly. "Have a good Christmas, then."

"Thanks. You, too."

She knew that she sounded choked. She couldn't help herself. She'd burned her bridges. She hadn't meant to. Perhaps she had a death wish. She'd read and studied about people who were basically self-destructive, who destroyed relationships before they could begin, who found ways to sabotage their own success and turn it to failure. Perhaps she'd become such a person, due to her upbringing. Either way, it didn't matter now. She'd given up Coltrain and was leaving Jacobsville. Now all she had to do was survive Jane's little going-away party and get out of town.

Coltrain paused in the doorway, turning his head back toward her. His eyes were narrow, curious, assessing. She didn't look as if the decision she'd made had lifted her spirits any. And the expression on her face wasn't one of triumph or pleasure.

"If Jane hadn't turned up in the jewelry store, would you have gone through with it?" he asked abruptly.

Her hands tightened on the clipboard. "I'll never know."

He leaned against the doorjamb. "You don't want to hear this, but I'm going to say it. Jane and I were briefly more than friends. It was mostly on my side. She loves her husband and wants nothing to do with anyone else. Whatever I felt for her is in the past now."

"I'm glad, for your sake," she said politely.

"Not for yours?" he asked.

She bit her lower lip, worriedly.

He let his blue gaze fall to her mouth. It lingered there so long that her heart began to race, and she couldn't quite breathe properly. His gaze lifted then, to catch hers, and she couldn't break it. Her toes curled inside her sensible shoes, her heart ran wild. She had to fight the urge to go to him, to press close to his lean, fit body and beg him to kiss her blind.

"You think you're over me?" he drawled softly, so that his voice didn't carry. "In a pig's eye, Doctor!"

He pushed away from the door and went on his way, whistling to himself as he went down the corridor to his next patient.

Lou, having given herself away, muttered under her breath and went to read the file on her next patient. But she waited until her hands stopped shaking before she opened the examining room door and went in.

They closed up the office. Coltrain had been called away at the last minute to an emergency at the hospital, which made things easier for Lou. She'd be bound to run into him while she was making her rounds, but that was an occupational hazard, and there would be plenty of other people around. She wouldn't have to worry about being alone with him. Or so she thought.

When she finished her rounds late in the afternoon, she stopped by the nurses' station to make sure they'd been able to contact a new patient's husband, who had been out of town when she was admitted.

"Yes, we found him," the senior nurse said with a smile. "In fact, he's on his way over here right now."

"Thanks," she said.

"No need. It goes with the job," she was assured.

She started back down the hall to find Coltrain coming from the emergency room. He looked like a thundercloud, all bristling bad temper. His red hair flamed under the corridor lights, and his blue eyes were sparking.

He caught Lou's arm, turned and drew her along with him without saying a word. People along the corridor noticed and grinned amusedly.

"What in the world are you doing?" she asked breathlessly.

"I want you to tell a—" he bit off the word he wanted to say "—*gentleman* in the emergency room that I was in the office all morning."

She gaped at him, but he didn't stop or even slow down. He dragged her into a cubicle where a big, angry-looking blond man was sitting on the couch having his hand bandaged.

Coltrain let Lou go and nodded curtly toward the other man. "Well, tell him!" He shot the words at Lou.

She gave him a stunned glance, but after a minute, she turned back to the tall man and said, "Dr. Coltrain was in the office all morning. He couldn't have escaped if he'd wanted to, because we had twice our usual number of patients, anticipating that we'd be out of the office over the holidays."

The blond man relaxed a little, but he was still glaring at Coltrain when there was a small commotion in the corridor and Jane Burke came in the door, harassed and frightened.

"Todd! Cherry said that you'd had an accident and she had to call an ambulance…!" She grabbed the blond man's hand and fought tears. "I thought you were killed!"

"Not hardly," he murmured. He drew her head to his shoulder and held her gently. "Silly woman." He chuckled. "I'm all right. I slammed the car door on my hand. It isn't even broken, just cut and bruised."

Jane looked at Coltrain. "Is that true?"

He nodded, still irritated at Burke.

Jane looked from him to Lou and back to her husband. "Now what's wrong?" she asked heavily.

Todd just glowered. He didn't say anything.

"You and I had been meeting secretly this morning at your house, while he and Cherry were away," Coltrain informed her. "Because the mailman saw a gray Jaguar sitting in your driveway."

"Yes, he did," Jane said shortly. "It belongs to the new divisional manager of the company that makes my signature line of leisure wear. *She* has a gray Jaguar exactly like Copper's."

Burke's hard cheekbones flushed a little.

"That's why you slammed the door on your hand, right?" she muttered. "Because the mailman is our wrangler's sister and he couldn't wait to tell you what your wife was doing behind your back! He'll be lucky if I don't have him for lunch!"

The flush got worse. "Well, I didn't know!" Todd snapped.

Coltrain slammed his clipboard down hard on the examination couch at Burke's hip. "That does it, by God," he began hotly.

He looked threatening and Burke stood up, equally angry.

"Now, Copper," Jane interrupted. "This isn't the place."

Burke didn't agree, but he'd already made a fool of himself once. He wasn't going to try for twice. He glanced at Lou, who looked as miserable as he felt. "They broke up your engagement, I understand," he added. "Pity they didn't just marry each other to begin with!"

Lou studied his glittery eyes for a moment, oblivious to the other two occupants of the cubicle. It was amazing how quickly things fell into place in her mind, and at once. She leaned against the examination couch. "Dr. Coltrain is the most decent man I know," she told Todd Burke. "He isn't the sort to do things in an underhanded way, and he doesn't sneak around. If you trusted your wife, Mr. Burke, you wouldn't listen to old gossip or invented tales. Small towns are hotbeds of rumor, that's normal. But only an idiot believes everything he hears."

Coltrain's eyebrows had arched at the unexpected defense.

"Thanks, Lou," Jane said quietly. "That's more than I deserve from you, but thank you." She turned back to her husband. "She's absolutely right," Jane told her husband. She was mad, too, and it showed. "I married you because I loved you. I still love you, God knows why! You won't even listen when I tell you the truth. You'd rather cling to old gossip about Copper and me."

Lou blushed scarlet, because she could have been accused of the same thing.

She wouldn't look at Coltrain at all.

"Well, here's something to take your mind off your foul suspicions," Jane continued furiously. "I was going to wait to tell you, but you can hear it now. I'm pregnant! And, no, it isn't Copper's!"

Burke gasped. "Jane!" He exploded, his injured hand forgotten as he moved forward to pull her hungrily into his arms. "Jane, is it true?"

"Yes, it's true," she muttered. "Oh, you idiot! You idiot…!"

He was kissing her, so she had to stop talking. Lou, a little embarrassed, edged out of the cubicle and moved away, only to find Coltrain right beside her as she left the emergency room.

"Maybe that will satisfy him," he said impatiently. "Thank you for the fierce defense," he added. "Hell of a pity that you didn't believe a word you were saying!"

She stuck her hands into her slacks pockets. "I believe she loves her husband," she said quietly. "And I believe that there's nothing going on between the two of you."

"Thanks for nothing."

"Your private life is your own business, Dr. Coltrain, none of mine," she said carelessly. "I'm already a memory."

"By your own damn choice."

The sarcasm cut deep. They walked through the parking lot to the area reserved for physicians and surgeons, and she stopped beside her little Ford.

"Drew loved his wife very much," she said. "He never got over losing her. He still spends holidays with his in-laws because he feels close to her that way, even though she's dead. I asked him how he'd feel if he knew that a woman was in love with him. Know what he said? He said that he'd pity her."

"Do you have a point?" he asked.

"Yes." She turned and looked up at him. "You haven't really gotten over Jane Burke yet. You have nothing to offer anyone else until you do. That's why I wouldn't marry you."

His brows drew together while he searched her face. He didn't say a word. He couldn't.

"She's part of your life," she continued. "A big part of it. You can't let go of the past, even if she can. I understand. Maybe someday you'll come to terms with it. Until you do, it's no good trying to be serious about anyone else."

He jiggled the change in his pockets absently. His broad shoulders rose and fell. "She was just starting into rodeo when I came back here as an intern in the hospital. She fell and they brought her to me. We had an instant rapport. I started going to watch her ride, she went out with me when I was free. She was special. Her father and I became friends as well, and when I bought my ranch, he helped me learn the ropes and start my herd. Jane and I have known each other a long, long time."

"I know that." She studied a button on his dark jacket. "She's very pretty, and Drew says she has a kind nature."

"Yes."

Her shoulders rose and fell. "I have to go."

He put out a lean hand and caught her shoulder, preventing her from turning away. "I never told her about my father."

She was surprised. She didn't think he had any secrets from Jane. She lifted her eyes and found him staring at her intently, as if he were trying to work out a puzzle.

"Curious, isn't it?" he mused aloud. "There's another curious thing, but I'm not ready to share that just yet."

He moved closer and she wanted to move away, to stop him… No, she didn't. His head bent and his mouth closed on hers, brushing, lightly probing. She yielded without a protest, her arms sliding naturally around his waist, her mouth opening to the insistence of his lips. He kissed her, leaning his body heavily on hers, so that she could feel the metal of the car at her back and his instant, explosive response to her soft warmth.

She made a sound, and he smiled against her lips.

"What?" He bit off the words against her lips.

"It's…very…public," she breathed.

He lifted his head and looked around. The parking lot was dotted with curious onlookers. So was the emergency room ramp.

"Hell," he said irritably, drawing away from her. "Come home with me," he suggested, still breathing roughly.

She shook her head before her willpower gave out. "I can't."

"Coward," he drawled.

She flushed. "All right, I want to," she said fiercely.

"But I won't, so there. Damn you! It isn't fair to play on people's weaknesses!"

"Sure it is," he said, correcting her. He grinned at her maddeningly. "Come on, be daring. Take a chance! Risk everything on a draw of the cards. You live like a scientist, every move debated, planned. For once in your life, be reckless!"

"I'm not the reckless sort," she said as she fought to get her breath back. "And you shouldn't be, either." She glanced ruefully toward the emergency room exit, where a tall blond man and a pretty blond woman were standing, watching. "Was it for her benefit?" she added, nodding toward them.

He glanced over her shoulder. "I didn't know they were there," he said genuinely.

She laughed. "Sure." She pulled away from him, unlocked her car, got in and drove off. Her legs were wobbly, but they'd stop shaking eventually. Maybe the rest of her would, too. Coltrain was driving her crazy. She was very glad that she'd be leaving town soon.

Chapter Ten

It didn't help that the telephone rang a few minutes after Lou got home.

"Still shaky, are we?" Coltrain drawled.

She fumbled to keep from dropping the receiver. "What do you want?" she faltered.

"An invitation to Christmas dinner, of course," he said. "I don't want to sit in front of the TV all day eating TV dinners."

She was still angry at him for making a public spectacle of them for the second time. The hospital would buzz with the latest bit of gossip for weeks. At least she wouldn't have long to put up with it.

"TV dinners are good for you," she said pointedly.

"Home cooking is better. I'll make the dressing and a fruit salad if you'll do turkey and rolls."

She hesitated. She wanted badly to spend that day with him, but in the long run, it would make things harder.

"Come on," he coaxed in a silky tone. "You know you want to. If you're leaving town after the first, it will be one of the last times we spend together. What have you got to lose?"

My self-respect, my honor, my virtue, my pride, she thought. But aloud, she said, "I suppose it wouldn't hurt."

He chuckled. "No, it wouldn't. I'll see you at eleven on Christmas morning."

He hung up before she could change her mind. "I don't want to," she told the telephone. "This is a terrible mistake, and I'm sure that I'll regret it for the rest of my life."

After a minute, she realized that she was talking to a piece of equipment. She shook her head sadly. Coltrain was driving her out of her mind.

She went to the store early on Christmas Eve and bought a turkey. The girl at the check-out stand was one of her patients. She grinned as she totaled the price of the turkey, the bottle of wine and the other groceries Lou had bought to cook Christmas dinner.

"Expecting company, Doctor?" she teased.

Lou flushed, aware that the woman behind her was one of Coltrain's patients. "No. No. I'm going to cook the turkey and freeze what I don't eat."

"Oh." The girl sounded disappointed.

"Going to drink all that wine alone, too?" the woman behind her asked wickedly. "And you a doctor!"

Lou handed over the amount the cashier asked for. "I'm not on duty on Christmas Day," she said irritably. "Besides, I cook with wine!"

"You won't cook with that," the cashier noted. She held up the bottle and pointed to the bottom of the label. It stated, quite clearly, Nonalcoholic Wine.

Lou had grabbed the bottle from the wrong aisle. But it worked to her advantage. She grinned at the woman behind her, who looked embarrassed.

The clerk packaged up her purchases and Lou pushed them out to her car. At least she'd gotten around that ticky little episode.

Back home, she put the turkey on to bake and made rolls from scratch. Nonalcoholic wine wasn't necessarily a bad thing, she told herself. She could serve it at dinner without having to worry about losing her wits with Coltrain.

The weather was sunny and nice, and the same was predicted for the following day. A white Christmas was out of the question, of course, but she wondered what it would be like to have snow on the ground.

She turned on the television that night, when the cooking was done and everything was put into the refrigerator for the next day. Curled up in her favorite armchair in old jeans, a sweatshirt and in her sock feet, she was relaxing after her housecleaning and cooking when she heard a car drive up.

It was eight o'clock and she wasn't on call. She frowned as she went to the front door. A gray Jaguar was sitting in the driveway and as she looked, a tall, redheaded man in jeans and a sweatshirt and boots got out of the car carrying a big box.

"Open the door," he called as he mounted the steps.

"What's that?" she asked curiously.

"Food and presents."

She was surprised. She hadn't expected him tonight and she fumbled and faltered as she let him in and closed the door again.

He unloaded the box in the kitchen. "Salad." He indicated a covered plastic bowl. "Dressing." He indicated a foil-covered pan. "And a chocolate pound cake. No, I didn't make it," he added when she opened her mouth. "I bought it. I can't bake a cake. Is there room in the fridge for this?"

"You could have called to ask before you brought it," she reminded him.

He grinned. "If I'd phoned, you'd have listened to the answering machine and when you knew it was me, you'd have pretended not to be home."

She flushed. He was right. It was disconcerting to have someone so perceptive second-guessing her every move. "Yes, there's room."

She opened the refrigerator door and helped him fit his food in.

He went back to the big box and pulled out two packages. "One for me to give you—" he held up one "—and one for you to give me."

She glared at him. "I got you a present," she muttered.

His eyebrows shot up. "You did?"

Her lower lip pulled down. "Just because I didn't plan to spend Christmas with you didn't mean I was low enough not to get you something."

"You didn't give it to me at the office party," he recalled.

She flushed. "You didn't give me anything at the office party, either."

He smiled. "I was saving it for tomorrow."

"So was I," she returned.

"Can I put these under the tree?"

She shrugged. "Sure."

Curious, she followed him into the living room. The tree was live and huge; it covered the whole corner and reached almost to the nine-foot ceiling. It was full of lights and decorations and under it a big metal electric train sat on its wide tracks waiting for power to move it.

"I didn't notice that when I was here before," he said, delighted by the train. He stooped to look at it more closely. "This is an American Flyer by Lionel!" he exclaimed. "You've had this for a while, haven't you?"

"It's an antique," she recalled. "My mother got it for me." She smiled. "I love trains. I have two more sets and about a mile of track in a box in the closet, but it seemed sort of pointless to set all those trains up with just me to run them."

He looked up at her with sparkling eyes. "Which closet are they in?" he asked in a conspiratorial tone.

"The hall closet." Her eyes brightened. "You like trains?"

"Do I like trains? I have HO scale, N scale, G scale and three sets of new Lionel O scale trains at home."

She gasped. "Oh, my goodness!"

"That's what I say. Come on!"

He led her to the hall closet, opened it, found the boxes and started handing them out to her.

Like two children, they sat on the floor putting tracks together with switches and accessories for the next two hours. Lou made coffee and they had it on the floor while they made connections and set up the low wooden scale buildings that Lou had bought to go with the sets.

When they finished, she turned on the power. The wooden buildings were lit. So were the engines and the cabooses and several passenger cars.

"I love to sit and watch them run in the dark," she said breathlessly as he turned on the switch box and the trains began to move. "It's like watching over a small village with the people all snug in their houses."

"I know what you mean." He sprawled, chest down, on the floor beside her to watch the trains chug and whistle and run around the various tracks. "God, this is great! I had no idea you liked trains!"

"Same here," she said, chuckling. "I always felt guilty about having them, in a way. Somewhere out there, there must be dozens of little kids who would do anything for just one train and a small track to run it on. And here I've got all this and I never play with it."

"I know how it is. I don't even have a niece or nephew to share mine with."

"When did you get your first train?"

"When I was eight. My granddad bought it for me so he could play with it," he added with a grin. "He couldn't afford a big set, of course, but I didn't care. I never had so much fun." His face hardened at the memories. "When Dad took me to Houston, I missed the train almost as much as I missed my granddad and grandmother. It was a long time before I got back there." He shrugged. "The train still worked by then, though, and it was more fun when the threat of my father was gone."

She rolled onto her side, peering at him in the dim light from the tree and the small village. "You said that you never told Jane about your father."

"I didn't," he replied. "It was something I was deeply ashamed of for a long time."

"Children do what they're told, whether it's right or wrong," she reminded him. "You can't be held responsible for everything."

"I knew it was wrong," he agreed. "But my father was a brutal man, and when I was a young boy, I was afraid of him." His head turned. He smiled at her. "You'd understand that."

"Yes."

He rested his chin on his hands and watched the trains wistfully. "I took my medicine—juvenile hall and years of probation. But people helped me to change. I wanted to pass that on, to give back some of the care that had been given to me. That's why I went into medicine. I saw it as an opportunity to help people."

"And you have," she said. Her eyes traced the length of his fit, hard-muscled body lovingly. He was so different away from the office. She'd never known him like this, and so soon, it would all be over. She'd go away. She wouldn't see him again. Her sad eyes went back to the trains. The sound of them was like a lullaby, comforting, delightful to the ears.

"We need railroad caps and those wooden whistles that sound like old steam engines," he remarked.

She smiled. "And railroad gloves and crossing guards and flashing guard lights."

"If there was a hobby shop nearby, we could go and get them. But everything would be closed up on Christmas Eve, anyway."

"I guess so."

He pursed his lips, without looking at her. "If you stayed, after the New Year, we could pool our layouts and have one big one. We could custom-design our own buildings and bridges, and we could go in together and buy one of those big transformer outfits that runs dozens of accessories."

She was thinking more of spending that kind of time with Coltrain than running model engines, but it sounded delightful all the same. She sighed wistfully. "I would have enjoyed that," she murmured. "But I've signed a new contract. I have to go."

"Contracts can be broken," he said. "There's always an escape clause if you look hard enough."

Her hips shifted on the rug they were lying on. "Too many people are gossiping about us already," she said. "Even at the grocery store, the clerk noticed that I bought a turkey and wine and the lady behind me said I couldn't possibly be going to drink it alone."

"You bought wine?" he mused.

"Nonalcoholic wine," she said, correcting him.

He chuckled. "On purpose?"

"Not really. I picked up the wrong bottle. But it was just as well. The lady behind me was making snide comments about it." She sighed. "It rubbed me the wrong way. She wouldn't have known that my father was an alcoholic."

"How did he manage to keep his job?"

"He had willing young assistants who covered for him. And finally, the hospital board forced him into early retirement. He *had* been a brilliant surgeon," she reminded him. "It isn't easy to destroy a career like that."

"It would have been better than letting him risk other people's lives."

"But he didn't," she replied. "Someone was always there to bail him out."

"Lucky, wasn't he, not to have been hit with a multimillion-dollar malpractice suit."

He reached out and threw the automatic switches to change the trains to another set of tracks. "Nice," he commented.

"Yes, isn't it? I love trains. If I had more leisure time, I'd do this every day. I'm glad we're not on call this weekend. How did you manage it?"

"Threats and bribery," he drawled. "We both worked last Christmas holidays, remember?"

"I guess we did. At each other's throats," she recalled demurely.

"Oh, that was necessary," he returned, rolling lazily onto his side and propping on an elbow. "If I hadn't snapped at you constantly, I'd have been laying you down on examination couches every other day."

"Wh...what?" she stammered.

He reached out and brushed back a long strand of blond hair from her face. "You backed away every time I came close to you," he said quietly. "It was all that saved you. I've wanted you for a long, long time, Dr. Blakely, and I've fought it like a madman."

"You were in love with Jane Parker," she said.

"Not for a long time," he said. He traced her cheek lightly. "The way I felt about her was a habit. It was one I broke when she married Todd Burke. Although, like you, he seems to think Jane and I were an item even after they married. He's taken a lot of convincing. So have you."

She moved uncomfortably. "Everyone talked about you and Jane, not just me."

"I know. Small communities have their good points and their bad points." His finger had reached her mouth. He was exploring it blatantly.

"Could you…not do that, please?" she asked unsteadily.

"Why? You like it. So do I." He moved closer, easing one long, hard-muscled leg over hers to stay her as he shifted so that she lay on her back, looking up at him in the dim light.

"I can feel your heart beating right through your rib cage," he remarked with his mouth poised just above hers. "I can hear your breath fluttering." His hand slid blatantly right down over her breast, pausing there to tease its tip into a hard rise. "Feel that?" he murmured, bending. "Your body likes me."

She opened her mouth, but no words escaped the sudden hard, warm pressure of his lips. She stiffened, but only for a few seconds. It was Christmas Eve and she loved him. There was no defense; none at all.

He seemed to know that, because he wasn't insistent or demanding. He lay, just kissing her, his lips tender as they moved against hers, his hand still gently caressing her body.

"We both know," he whispered, "why your body makes every response it does to the stimuli of my touch. But what no one really understands is why we both enjoy it so much."

"Cause…and effect?" she suggested, gasping when his hand found its way under the sweatshirt and the lacy bra she was wearing to her soft flesh.

He shook his head. "I don't think so. Reach behind you

and unfasten this," he added gently, tugging on the elastic band.

She did as he asked, feeling brazen.

"That's better." He traced over her slowly, his eyes on her face while he explored every inch of her above the waist. "Can you give this up?" he asked seriously.

"Wh...what?"

"Can you give it up?" he replied. "You aren't responsive to other men, or you wouldn't still be in your present pristine state. You allow me liberties that I'm certain you've never permitted any other man." He cupped her blatantly and caressed her. She arched, shivering. "You see?" he asked quietly. "You love my touch. I can give you something that you've appar- ently never experienced. Do you think you can find it with someone else, Lou?"

She felt his mouth cover hers. She didn't have enough breath to answer him, although the answer was certainly in the negative. She couldn't bear the thought of letting someone else be this intimate with her. She looped her arms around his neck and only sighed jerkily when he moved, easing his length against her, his legs between both of hers, so that when his hips pressed down again, she could feel every hardening line of his body.

"Jebediah," she moaned, and she wasn't certain if she was protesting or pleading.

His mouth found her closed eyelids and tasted the helpless tears of pleasure that rained from them. His hips shifted and she jerked at the surge of pleasure.

He felt it, too, like a throbbing ache. "We're good

together," he whispered. "Even like this. Can you imagine how it would feel to lie naked under me like this?"

She cried out, burying her face in his neck.

His lips traced her eyelashes, his tongue tasted them. But his body lay very still over hers, not moving, not insisting. Her nails dug into his shoulders as she felt her control slipping away.

But he still had his own control. He soothed her, every soft kiss undemanding and tender. But he didn't move away.

"A year," he whispered. "And we knew nothing about each other, nothing at all." He nibbled her lips, smiling when they trembled. "Trains and old movies, opera and cooking and horseback riding. We have more in common than I ever dreamed."

She had to force her body to lie still. She wanted to wrap her legs tight around him and kiss him until she stopped aching.

He seemed to know it, because his hips moved in a sensual caress that made her hands clench at his shoulders. "No fear of the unknown?" he whispered wickedly. "No virginal terror?"

"I'm a doctor." She choked out the words.

"So am I."

"I mean, I know…what to expect."

He chuckled. "No, you don't. You only know the mechanics of it. You don't know that you're going to crave almost more than I can give you, or that at the last minute you're going to sob like a hurt child."

She was too far gone to be embarrassed. "I don't have anything," she said miserably.

"Anything…?" He probed gently.

"To use."

"Oh. That." He chuckled and kissed her again, so tenderly that she felt cherished. "You won't need it tonight. I don't think babies should be born out of wedlock. Do you?"

She wasn't thinking. "Well, no. What does that have to do…with this?"

"Lou!"

She felt her cheeks burn. "Oh! You mean…!"

He laughed outrageously. "You've really gone off the deep end, haven't you?" he teased. "When people make love, the woman might get pregnant," he explained in a whisper. "Didn't you listen to the biology lectures?"

She hit him. "Of course I did! I wasn't thinking… Jeb!"

He was closer than he'd ever been and she was shivering, lost, helpless as she felt him in a burning, aching intimacy that only made it all worse.

He pressed her close and then rolled away, while he could. "God, we're explosive!" he said huskily, lying very still on his belly. "You're going to have to marry me soon, Lou. Very soon."

She was sitting up, holding her knees to her chest, trying to breathe. It had never been that bad. She said so, without realizing that she'd spoken aloud.

"It will get worse, too," he said heavily. "I want you. I've never wanted you so much."

"But, Jane…"

He was laughing, very softly. He wasn't angry anymore. He rolled over and sat up beside her. He turned her face up to his. "I broke it off with Jane," he said gently. "Do you want to know why, now?"

"You…you did?"

He nodded.

"You never said that you ended it."

"There was no reason to. You wouldn't let me close enough to find out if we had anything going for us, and it didn't seem to matter what I said, you wanted to believe that I was out of my mind over Jane."

"Everyone said you were," she muttered.

He lifted an eyebrow. "I'm not everyone."

"I know." She reached out hesitantly and touched him. It was earthshaking, that simple act. She touched his hair and his face and then his lean, hard mouth. A funny smile drew up her lips.

"Don't stop there," he murmured, drawing her free hand down to his sweatshirt.

Her heart jumped. She looked at him uncertainly.

"I won't let you seduce me," he mused. "Does that make you feel more confident?"

"It was pretty bad a few minutes ago," she said seriously. "I don't want… Well, to hurt you."

"This won't," he said. "Trust me."

"I suppose I must," she admitted. "Or I'd have left months ago for another job."

"That makes sense."

He guided her hand under the thick, white fabric and drew it up until her fingers settled in the thick, curling hair that covered his chest. But it wasn't enough. She wanted to look…

There was just enough light so that he could see what she wanted in her expression. With a faint smile, he pulled the sweatshirt off and tossed it to one side.

She stared. He was beautiful like that, she thought dizzily, with broad shoulders and muscular arms. His chest was covered by a thick, wide wedge of reddish-gold hair that ran down to the buckle of his belt.

He reached for her, lifting her over him so that they were sitting face-to-face, joined where their bodies forked. She shivered at the stark intimacy, because she could feel every muscle, almost every cell of him.

"It gets better," he said softly. He reached down and found the hem of her own sweatshirt. Seconds later, that and her bra joined his sweatshirt on the floor. He looked down at her, savoring the hard peaks that rose like rubies from the whiteness of her breasts. Then he drew her to him and enveloped her against him, so that they were skin against skin. And he shivered, too, this time.

Her hands smoothed over his back, savoring his warm muscles. She searched for his mouth and for the first time, she kissed him. But even though it was sensual, and she could feel him wanting her, there was tenderness between them, not lust.

He groaned as his body surged against her, and then he laughed at the sudden heat of it.

"Jeb?" she whispered at his lips.

"It's all right," he said. "We won't go all the way. Kiss me again."

She did, clinging, and the world rocked around them.

"I love you," she murmured brokenly. "So much!"

His mouth bit into hers hungrily, his arms contracted. For a few seconds, it was as if electricity fused them together. Finally he was able to lift his lips, and his hands caught her hips to keep them still.

"Sorry," she said demurely.

"Oh, I like it," he replied ruefully. "But we're getting in a bit over our heads."

He lifted her away and stood up, pulling her with him. They looked at each other for a long moment before he handed her things to her and pulled his sweatshirt back on.

He watched the trains go around while she replaced her disheveled clothing. Then, with his hands in his pockets, he glanced down at her.

"That's why I broke up with Jane," he said matter-of-factly.

She was jealous, angry. "Because she wouldn't go all the way with you?"

He chuckled. "No. Because I didn't want her sexually."

She watched the trains and counted the times they crossed the joined tracks. Her mind must not be working. "What did you say?" she asked politely, turning to him.

"I said I was never able to want Jane sexually," he said simply. "To put it simply, she couldn't arouse me."

Chapter Eleven

"A woman can arouse any man if she tries hard enough," she said pointedly.

"Maybe so," he said, smiling, "but Jane just never interested me like that. It was too big a part of marriage to take a chance on, so I gradually stopped seeing her. Burke came along, and before any of us knew it, she was married. But I was her security blanket after the accident, and it was hard for her to let go. You remember how she depended on me."

She nodded. Even at the time, it had hurt.

"But apparently she and her husband have more than a platonic relationship, if their forthcoming happy event is any indication," he said, chuckling. "And I'm delighted for them."

"I never dreamed that it was like that for you, with her," she said, dazed. "I mean, you and I…!"

"Yes, indeed, you and I," he agreed, nodding. "I touch you and it's like a shot of lightning in my veins. I get drunk on you."

"So do I, on you," she confessed. "But there's a difference, isn't there? I mean, you just want me."

"Do I?" he asked gently. "Do I really just want you? Could lust be as tender as this? Could simple desire explain the way we are together?"

"I love you," she said slowly.

"Yes," he said, his eyes glittering at her. "And I love you, Lou," he added quietly.

Dreams came true. She hadn't known. Her eyes were full of wonder as she looked at him and saw them in his own eyes. It was Christmas, a time of miracles, and here was one.

He didn't speak. He just looked at her. After a minute, he picked up the two parcels he'd put under the tree and handed them to her.

"But it's not Christmas," she protested.

"Yes, it is. Open them."

She only hesitated for a minute, because the curiosity was too great. She opened the smallest one and inside was a gray jeweler's box. With a quick glance at him, she opened it, to find half a key chain inside. She felt her heart race like a watch. It was half of a heart, in pure gold.

"Now the other one," he said, taking the key chain while she fumbled the paper off the second present.

Inside that box was the other half of the heart.

"Now put them together," he instructed.

She did, her eyes magnetized to the inscription. It was in French: *plus que hier, moins que demain.*

"Can you read it?" he asked softly.

"It says—" she had to stop and clear her throat "—more than yesterday, less than tomorrow."

"Which is how much I love you," he said. "I meant to ask you again tomorrow morning to marry me," he said. "But this is as good a time as any for you to say yes. I know you're afraid of marriage. But I love you and you love me. We've got enough in common to keep us together even after all the passion burns out, if it ever does. We'll work out something about your job and children. I'm not your father and you're not your mother. Take a chance, Lou. Believe me, there's very little risk that we won't make it together."

She hadn't spoken. She had both halves of the key chain in her hands and she was looking at them, amazed that he would have picked something so sentimental and romantic for a Christmas gift. He hadn't known if he could get her to stay or not, but he would have shown her his heart all the same. It touched her as a more expensive present wouldn't have.

"When did you get them?" she asked through a dry throat.

"After you left the jeweler's," he said surprisingly. "I believe in miracles," he added gently. "I see incredible things every day. I'm hoping for another one, right now."

She raised her eyes. Even in the dim light, he could see

the sparkle of tears, the hope, the pleasure, the disbelief in her face.

"Yes?" he asked softly.

She couldn't manage the word. She nodded, and the next instant, she was in his arms, against him, close and safe and warm while his mouth ravished her lips.

It was a long time before he had enough to satisfy him, even momentarily. He wrapped her up tightly and rocked her in his arms, barely aware of the train chugging along at their feet. His arms were faintly unsteady and his voice, when he laughed, was husky and deep.

"My God, I thought I was going to lose you." He ground out the words. "I didn't know what to do, what to say, to keep you here."

"All you ever had to say was that you loved me," she whispered. "I would have taken any risk for it."

His arms tightened. "Didn't you know, you blind bat?"

"No, I didn't! I don't read minds, and you never said—!"

His mouth covered hers again, stopping the words. He laughed against her breath, anticipating arguments over the years that would be dealt with in exactly this way, as she gave in to him generously, headlong in her response, clinging as if she might die without his mouth on hers.

"No long engagement," he groaned against her mouth. "I can't stand it!"

"Neither can I," she admitted. "Next week?"

"Next week!" He kissed her again. "And I'm not going home tonight."

She laid her cheek against his chest, worried.

He smoothed her hair. "We won't make love," he assured her. "But you'll sleep in my arms. I can't bear to be parted from you again."

"Oh, Jeb," she whispered huskily. "That's the sweetest thing to say!"

"Don't you feel it, too?" he asked knowingly.

"Yes. I don't want to leave you, either."

He chuckled with the newness of belonging to someone. It was going to be, he decided, the best marriage of all time. He looked down into her eyes and saw years and years of happiness ahead of them. He said so. She didn't answer him. She reached up, and her lips said it for her.

The going-away party that Jane Burke threw for Lou became a congratulatory party, because it fell on the day after Coltrain and Lou were married.

They almost stayed at home, so wrapped up in the ecstasy of their first lovemaking that they wouldn't even get out of bed the next morning.

That morning, he lay looking at his new bride with wonder and unbounded delight. There were tears in her eyes, because it had been painful for her at first. But the love in them made him smile.

"It won't be like that again," he assured her.

"I know." She looked at him blatantly, with pride in

his fit, muscular body, in his manhood. She lifted her eyes back up. "I was afraid…"

He traced her mouth, his eyes solemn. "It will be easier the next time," he said tenderly. "It will get better every time we love each other."

"I know. I'm not afraid anymore." She touched his hard mouth and smiled. "You were apprehensive, too, weren't you?"

"At first," he had to admit.

"I thought you were never going to start," she said on a sigh. "I know why you took so long, so that I'd be ready when it happened, but I wondered if you were planning on a night of torture."

He chuckled. "You weren't the only one who suffered." He kissed her tenderly. "It hurt me, to have to hurt you, did you know? I wanted to stop, but it was too late. I was in over my head before I knew it. I couldn't even slow down."

"Oh, I never noticed," she told him, delighted. "You made me crazy."

"That goes double for me."

"I thought I knew everything," she mused. "I'm a doctor, after all. But theory and practice are very different."

"Yes. Later, when you're in fine form again, I'll show you some more ways to put theory into practice," he drawled.

She laughed and pummeled him.

They were early for Jane's get-together, and the way they clung to each other would have been more than enough to prove that they were in love, without the matching Victorian wedding bands they'd chosen.

"You look like two halves of a whole," Jane said, looking from Lou's radiant face to Copper's.

"We know," he said ruefully. "They rode us high at the hospital when we made rounds earlier."

"Rounds!" Todd exclaimed. "On your honeymoon?"

"We're doctors," Lou reminded him, grinning. "It goes with the job description. I'll probably be trying to examine patients on the way into the delivery room eventually."

Jane clung to her husband's hand and sighed. "I can't wait for that to happen. Cherry's over the moon, too. She'll be such a good older sister. She works so hard at school. She's studying to be a surgeon, you know," she added.

"I wouldn't know," Copper muttered, "having already had four letters from her begging for an hour of my time to go over what she needs to study most during her last few years in school."

Jane chuckled. "That's my fault. I encouraged her to talk to you."

"It's all right," he said, cuddling Lou closer. "I'll make time for her."

"I see that everything finally worked out for you two," Todd said a little sheepishly. "Sorry about the last time we met."

"Oh, you weren't the only wild-eyed lunatic around, Mr. Burke," Lou said reminiscently. "I did my share of conclusion jumping and very nearly ruined my life because of it." She looked up at Coltrain adoringly. "I'm glad doctors are persistent."

"Yes." Coltrain chuckled. "So am I. There were times when I despaired. But Lionel saved us."

They frowned. "What?"

"Electric trains," Coltrain replied. "Don't you people know anything?"

"Not about trains. Those are kids' toys, for God's sake," Burke said.

"No, they are not," Lou said. "They're adult toys. People buy them for their children so they'll have an excuse to play with them. Not having children, we have no excuses."

"That's why we want to start a family right away," Coltrain said with a wicked glance at Lou. "So that we have excuses. You should see her layout," he added admiringly. "My God, it's bigger than mine!"

Todd and Jane tried not to look at each other, failed and burst into outrageous laughter.

Coltrain glared at them. "Obviously," he told his new wife, "some people have no class, no breeding and no respect for the institution of marriage."

"What are you two laughing at?" Drew asked curiously, having returned to town just in time for the party, if not the wedding.

Jane bit her lower lip before she spoke. "Hers is bigger than his." She choked.

"Oh, for God's sake, come and dance!" Coltrain told Lou, shaking his head as he dragged her away. The others, behind them, were still howling.

Coltrain pulled Lou close and smiled against her hair as they moved to the slow beat of the music. There was a live band. Jane had pulled out all the stops, even if it wasn't going to be a goodbye party.

"Nice band," Dana remarked from beside them. "Congratulations, by the way," she added.

"Thanks," they echoed.

"Nickie didn't come," she added, tongue-in-cheek. "I believe she's just accepted a job in a Victoria hospital as a nurse trainee."

"Good for her," Coltrain said.

Dana chuckled. "Sure. See you."

She wandered away toward one of the hospital staff.

"She's a good loser, at least," Lou said drowsily.

"I wouldn't have been," he mused.

"You've got a new partner coming," she remembered suddenly, having overlooked it in the frantic pace of the past few days.

"Actually," he replied, "I don't know any doctors from Johns Hopkins who would want to come to Jacobsville to practice in a small partnership. The minute I do, of course, I'll hire him on the…oof!"

She'd stepped on his toe, hard.

"Well, I had to say something," he replied, wincing as he stood on his foot. "You were holding all the aces. A man has his pride."

"You could have said you loved me," she said pointedly.

"I did. I do." He smiled slowly. "In a few hours, I'll take you home and prove it and prove it and prove it."

She flushed and pressed closer into his arms. "What a delicious idea."

"I thought so, too. Dance. At least while we're dancing I can hold you in public."

"So you can!"

Drew waltzed by with a partner. "Why don't you two go home?" he asked.

They laughed. "Time enough for private celebrations."

"I hope you have enough champagne," Drew said dryly, and danced on.

As it happened, they had a magnum of champagne between them before Coltrain coaxed his wife back into bed and made up for her first time in ways that left her gasping and trembling in the aftermath.

"That," she gasped, "wasn't in any medical book I ever read!"

"Darlin', you've been reading the wrong books," he whispered, biting her lower lip softly. "And don't go to sleep. I haven't finished yet."

"What?"

He laughed at her expression. "Did you think that was *all?*"

Her eyes widened as he moved over her and slid between her long legs. "But, it hasn't been five minutes, you can't, you *can't…!*"

He not only could. He did.

* * *

Two months later, on Valentine Day, Copper Coltrain gave his bride of six weeks a ruby necklace in the shape of a heart. She gave him the results of the test she'd had the day before. He told her later that the "valentine" she'd given him was the best one he'd ever had.

Nine months later, Lou's little valentine was delivered in Jacobsville's hospital; and he was christened Joshua Jebediah Coltrain.

* * * * *

0910_NEW VOICES

New Voices

Do you dream of being a romance writer?

Mills & Boon are looking for fresh writing talent in our biggest ever search!

And this time…our readers have a say in who wins!

For information on how to enter or get involved go to

www.romanceisnotdead.com

BL_224_IP

There's nothing these rugged heroes won't do for love!

Featuring three linked stories, available for the first time in one volume:

Mercenary's Woman
The Winter Soldier
The Last Mercenary

These three tall, tanned Texans are determined to protect the women they love.

www.millsandboon.co.uk

M&B™

BL_202_H

The only woman he wanted – and the one he couldn't have…

When a moment of unbridled passion results in a kiss, wealthy ranch owner Jason realises that he's falling for Gracie. But Gracie harbours a shameful secret that makes her deeply afraid to love. Stung by her rejection, Jason leaves, ready to put the past – and the one woman he can't have – behind him.

But when danger threatens, Jason will have her heart forever!

www.millsandboon.co.uk

M&B™

1010/24/MB308

All the magic you'll need this Christmas...

When **Daniel** is left with his brother's kids, only one person can help. But it'll take more than mistletoe before **Stella** helps him...

Patrick hadn't advertised for a housekeeper. But when **Hayley** appears, she's the gift he didn't even realise he needed.

Alfie and his little sister know a lot about the magic of Christmas – and they're about to teach the grown-ups a much-needed lesson!

Available 1st October 2010

M&B™

www.millsandboon.co.uk

1010/26/MB307

Spend Christmas with NORA ROBERTS

Daniel MacGregor is the clan patriarch. He's powerful, rich – and determined to see his three career-minded granddaughters married. So he chooses three unsuspecting men he considers worthy and sets his plans in motion!

As Christmas approaches, will his independent granddaughters escape his schemes? Or can the magic of the season melt their hearts – and allow Daniel's plans to succeed?

Available 1st October 2010

www.millsandboon.co.uk

WEB/M&B/RTL3

Discover Pure Reading Pleasure with

MILLS & BOON®

Visit the Mills & Boon website for all the latest in romance

- **Buy** all the latest releases, backlist and eBooks
- **Join** our community and chat to authors and other readers
- **Win** with our fantastic online competitions
- **Tell us** what you think by signing up to our reader panel
- **Find out** more about our authors and their books
- **Free** online reads from your favourite authors
- **Sign** up for our free monthly eNewsletter
- **Rate** and review books with our star system

www.millsandboon.co.uk

Follow us at twitter.com/millsandboonuk

Become a fan at facebook.com/romancehq